DEATH IN VANCOUVER

June 23, 2009
To Lorraine

with love,

Lorrie(e)

DEATH
IN
VANCOUVER

Garry Thomas Morse

Talonbooks

Talonbooks
P.O. Box 2076, Vancouver, British Columbia, Canada V6B 3S3
www.talonbooks.com

Typeset in Adobe Garamond and printed and bound in Canada.
Printed on 100% post-consumer recycled paper.

First Printing: 2009

The publisher gratefully acknowledges the financial support of the Canada Council
for the Arts; the Government of Canada through the Book Publishing Industry
Development Program; and the Province of British Columbia through the British
Columbia Arts Council and the Book Publishing Tax Credit for our publishing
activities.

LIBRARY AND ARCHIVES CANADA CATALOGUING IN PUBLICATION

Morse, Garry Thomas
    Death in Vancouver / Garry Thomas Morse.

ISBN 978-0-88922-607-4

    I. Title.

PS8626.O774D42 2009   C813'.6   C2008-906195-0

I am an ephemeral and not too malcontent citizen of a metropolis believed to be modern …

—Arthur Rimbaud

Contents

One Helen

"Why?"
"Because otherwise I could not see you."

—James Joyce

Ignatius Murphy took a seat in the semicircle made of fake black leather. His pint of Red crashed down on the table, a honeycombed hive of thick glass. He looked up at the little white clock furtively. Near four. With each swig of beer, he felt his spring fever heighten into a sinal knot of tightening pressure, then unvise open again. At this time of afternoon, the largest arc of sunlight was likely to stumble over dilapidated cornices & through a translucent window behind his back. The chiaroscuro arc widened, touching his right temple. Ignatius winced gently. More pressure. Still near four. Turning away, he looked leftward over one of the booth's rather indolent arms. He was waiting rather pathetically, eh? Waiting, that is, for a very tall woman to pass. Relatively speaking, she was not all that tall, only taller than the other women about her. By her own idiom, she was too tall to drop forks on a warm Friday. Ignatius squinted through a small window in one of the double doors in front, trying to catch a glimpse of her shape or shadow in passage. A darkskinned fellow near Ignatius burst out laughing.

"It don't say nowhere in Da Bible, 'Thou shalt not drink!'"

His Persian companion nodded, gesticulating authoritatively with a sweeping palm, punctuating each murmur which sounded like part of a sermon.

"Imbibe."

Ignatius squeezed the soft place between his thick eyebrows, thinking of devils on the shoulders of Abraham & this hint of magic inherent in the dark chap's accent. Barbados? Some place where a snapshot's considered stealing. The soul. Ignatius cursed his ignorance, listening to the man's melodic voice, losing any meaning to his words, following only the pleasing thrum of his working throat. Any minute now you'll be laughing & joking with 'em. Past four. She still had not passed. Unless he had missed her. Waiting for beauty to pass, you may as well make up your own. The sun sank lower. The place was starting to darken. I mean Christ & the devil having a wee chat, that's all. Ignatius pinched harder, sniffing away even more pathetically, in recollection of that crazy old bag in McDonald's who had chased a black customer to a corner of the establishment with her agitated chant.

"He's a devil he's a devil he's a devil … "

He had changed seats & turned away towards his modified chips & pink shake. A few others had followed his example. Nothing to do with me. She was a martyr. She did favours for people. Penance, that's what they call it.

"He's a devil he's a devil look at that devil!"

Ignatius rubbed his eyes. They were beginning to water. Not good. Still no sign of her. It was this time of day he found the most alluring, when the light was best. He would feel the drag of every other place, an atmosphere thick as cheesecloth, dragging him downtown to this fading hour. She must have existed before. But she never became real to me until that quiet day, walking along Cordova, in those drab black clothes she loved to wear. Theatrical, even. She had only troubled about a mauve shawl, which lent her height a subtle charm. Unseen, Ignatius had watched her funny shadow move ahead of him, past the protruding backstreet likeness of Baudelaire, with knees self-consciously bent beneath an invisible ceiling & her slender body cast against three-storey buildings already bloated full of sunlight. She had paused to shield her eyes & peer upward at the demolished department store parking lot under reconstruction, where the long arm of

10

a crane swung over her tight brunette plaits, raising a cylindrical vat of concrete above a maroon truck that read LAVA PUMPING LTD. Thinking of her tall dark figure, enshrouded beneath the glare of a lingering predusk like those exotic mourners he had read about in secondhand poche-livres, Ignatius longed to commit her stance to memory, to make it physical, even in a sinuous dark streak of oil, awkwardly reverent before that long tube of maroon. Regrettably, he had given his easel & paints away to a local preschool. For a year at least, those kids would learn the unpredictable pleasure of oil upon paper. Their teacher had reassured him, showing him some books chockerblock with Monet & Degas, not to mention some ages three & up packed with startlingly graphic anatomy. Ignatius had looked away from her own startling anatomy, turning aubergine in spite of himself. No, Ignatius could not draw, not in the slightest, & words seemed to elude him even more. They were too slippery for his tastes. He never felt he could quite trust them. Ignatius tapped his fingers up & down playfully upon the table, waiting. For what, man? Maybe the moment that had so easily passed & would never return, that's what.

"Yes," agreed the man from Barbados, revealing very white teeth. "I wish I'd met Angelique first, dat's all. But this one had bigger boobs."

He put the photograph back in his wallet & began to laugh, until his friend joined in. Ignatius looked down. His glass was empty. The little white clock read a quarter past.

"Hey, leakyglass, yawannannutha?"

He grinned weakly, with a touch of puckering.

"No. That's fine."

What's the matter with me. Why can't I paint this fucking feeling? Cats & monkeys can paint faces & shades & I fucking can't. Ignatius kept his eyes peeled for sable hints of her approaching shadow, along with lucky pennies lost to the gutter. It had not been long since he had seen her on the street. Nonetheless, Ignatius began to look for her apparition more fastidiously. I have a fever. He dabbed his forehead with a stray serviette from his coat pocket. I have a fever. If she did appear, that would mean she existed after all. More than that! He would set to work at once to decide upon the correct medium through which her beauty would be best expressed. Maybe over a lovely pint & she would have her own views on the matter. Ah, where are you, love? Was Ignatius in love? No, he was just coming down with something, under the weather, etc. He wanted very much to capture these moments in life, these beautiful moments simply begging for some medium to express their essence, flitting away from the corners of eyes, virtually unnoticed.

"Barbeque."

"That'll be one loon."

As Ignatius rose to leave the dark interior, he heard a sound like a pistol shot near his ear. He started & looked around wildly before stopping to grip the spot at the bridge of his nose as he felt a rush of sinal pressure. He turned to see a man in a fedora with sunglasses & greasy long hair, holding out his open bag of potato chips. Happy that he had got some reaction out of Ignatius, he suddenly fell back against the bar & held his side as if he had just been shot.

"Ahhooowww, I'm hit. I'm hit … "

Ignatius shrugged.

"A ripoff you know. They get them next door. It's a markup from three for a buck."

He walked out into the remainder of sunlight, hearing bellows of laughter behind him. Was Ignatius in love? Not quite. Ignatius was in debt. Sure, it was hard enough to be a college student in this city. However, his persistent notion of finding a new medium for beauty had browbeaten him into purchasing a used grand piano. Just to learn, he had pleaded with himself. Time, time, time. One day there will be time. Ignatius sat at his piano every day, pondering the way a variation of Bach, or a sliver in F-sharp from *The Well-Tempered Clavier*, as performed by his inept fingers, would begin to manufacture a low-budget sonata, plunking each key clumsily down in tandem with many a whim of light being grudgingly indulged by his grimy yellow drapes. Ignatius wished to express such thoughts or sensations very much. He felt less desire to express himself, although he sometimes had a fancy about speaking notes, about breathing birdsong & stammering the twisted notes of Stravinsky in lieu of those words he found so slippery upon his tongue. Of course, that would never happen. All the same, this idea struck Ignatius as rather appealing. He plodded along, snailing out another chromatic chunk of Sebastian, finding some comfort in the work of a depressed compadre. How he must have hated Handel! No, not like I do. All those singing eunuchs & wretched countertenors! The light continued in its steady decline & the music came to a stop for Ignatius. Beauty, eh? It was more than that. She had her little habits too. O here we go! Keep moving, lad. The way she walked, as if afraid of looking statuesque, as she did. The way she leapt about with peculiar jolts of enthusiasm. From what? Ignatius fondly recalled how she had talked so vividly about buying a fresh set of sheets at Army & Navy. He could remember eating his first *everything included* at the Old Spaghetti Factory in a former railway car & going with his family to be weighed afterward on the second floor of Army & Navy. That old scale of theirs. Ignatius guessed that the life of someone who so often occupied his thoughts had the potential to appear to run parallel to his own existence, as if every moment of the day had some type of overlap with hers, as if every private moment were a touchstone or a word between them. As for her delight in buying things, by her own account, that she did not need, he found such hints at the mystery of her domesticity quite charming. Amid such minutiae, he felt the presence that he found invested in great paintings, that brief & sudden look into the personal affairs of another soul, invited or dismissed by each visible belonging within their possession. Imagine if we were lovers. Whupps. Where did that come from? At least it was trendy to talk about Vermeer again, to buy a coffee table book about the insinuations made by his everyday objects, like those white porcelain jugs scholars insisted had been brimming over with wine for a married woman smiling in the company of two rogues. A basket of apples or an open window.

13

Unpainted cherubim behind the canvas. They can tell with X-rays. *Tall Woman Buying Sheets*. That's what they'd call it. The orange logo, the label detector, the darting eyes of Army & Navy guard, the flat blue folds peeking out of a plastic bag in her hand. He only needed to look at the bricked alleyways about Cordova to be reminded of Vermeer's own rendition of *The Little Street* across from the public house in which he used to live & paint. Within this picture, he could make out Helen, one of those diligent figures at work, nearly faceless & completely absorbed within her own sphere of unfinished things to do. Yes, he could definitely see Helen in that painting. Hmm ... what a fever! A grizzled dog made his way across the crossing's white lines, fighting arthritis, while his shaggy owner moved slower behind the lead, out of sympathy. Another man with a dingy cap & a red beard muttered something in a neat diagonal across the curbs, looking flustered. Another grungy fellow brandished a universal salute.

"You're playin' me, man!"

At that remark, Redbeard's eyes flared up into merciless little coals. He raged across the street as if wading through swampy water, ignoring the red signal & the honking of screeching cars.

"Fuck you crackhead!"

Ignatius stopped. Redbeard seemed to expand like an inflatable raft, looking stronger than a second ago, his face flushed with blood, making him all one colour. After releasing the tympany of his fists, it was surprising to see him fall underneath the pummelling of his much slimmer contact. A grim series of utility vehicles passed the street corner & began to honk harder. Ignatius tried to peep through the grove of traffic to no avail. Mesmerized by the noise & percussion of punches, Ignatius felt a voice inside him urging him away from the spectacle of violence. Keep moving, Iggy, keep moving. He back-tracked for a few blocks, partly to walk off the derelict buzz of his beer & partly to air his thoughts. Down an alleyway, he could hear a choral doremifaso ... Sirens. The ambulance. A man passed, dragging a clanking bouquet of black plastic skunk cabbage, or so it looked as he did, up toward the altos & a lone soprano, chiming in with his erratic clunks of shifting aluminum & glass. Ignatius walked on, examining a navy blue dumpster. Is this my can, behind the old fabric shop? Used to smash the dead fluorescents here so they'd fit properly & stand on the piles of collapsed cardboard & flatten 'em when the blue prop slipped & the lid crashed down on my skull, heavy as hell. A bump. How long did I lay there inside that navy blue mystery with that sound still echoing in my aching noggin THUNKERRUNCK THUNKERRUNCK? This headache has nothing on that. Did she exist before that afternoon of the shadowy walk, or for that matter before this throbbing in my head? Ignatius found an empty bench in Victory Square & sat down. He watched a series of kids board down the incline in front of him. Peace, there's no peace to sit & think anywhere. My head throbbing. Another explosion of noise. Ignatius slowly craned his neck upward to admire the full majesty of the Dominion Building, with candied reds & golds that made him think of gingerbread roofs or melting walls of warm toffee. Some fable I have forgotten. The ironwork about the top & back were especially interesting to him. Whenever he saw that ornate railing, he thought of the Z-pattern of the fire escape on the other side & felt a shock run through his body, as if the architect's fingers were his, loosening their grip on that flimsy bit of biscuit or red wafflecone & leaving him to plummet all those stories. Even in dreams & even from where he sat in the square, Ignatius was terrified of heights. Even more of that sensation of falling through air & time & space, falling all those stories. Did he know? Did he jump? Whenever he passed the juncture at Cambie & Cordova where he had first seen Helen, Ignatius would look up at the fire escape & think of that nameless architect, clinging desperately to his creation. In grotesque parody of a gargoyle. Ignatius lowered his gaze & noticed a series of letters engraved on the memorial obelisk. ALL YE THAT PASSETH BY. No, I've got it wrong. That was not the first time I saw her. Ignatius recalled that he had been invited to a private bash by a gang of writers at his university, due to various drunken outbursts & visible fits which he believed had convinced them he was some kind of artist. In fact, he had almost come to believe it himself, in vague & unexpected moments of boldness, such as now, still listening to that lingering buzz of beer. Here in the alley, he could remember those wafting scents of Irish Stout & Scotch & the Whisk(e)y so transparently translated in so many global languages, while one of the professors scoffed at the very old red bricks, questioning their authenticity with a frown.

"Is this a good time?" he posited.

Ignatius assured him that at the very least, it was *an excellent simulation*. Raucous laughter. Merry & intoxicated, the laughter became warm wadding about us between the very old red bricks, holding the entire universe together. He had first noticed her behind the makeshift bar, illuminated by those strange lights intended to enhance the magic of those orderly bottles, which as a side effect, left the pallor of a white fireside flashlight upon the tender's face. The owner strove to make conversation & memorize the inventory of our names for the sake of a scroll of damages that were inevitable at the end of the night. She would hand signal for various concoctions & the tall woman would, like a good lieutenant, set about the arcane creation of innumerable mindrobbers. Ignatius, as conversation drifted toward citations & the proper names of theorists, found himself drifting as well, floating higher & higher roofward like one of Chagall's lovers while a blue rooster watched him greet the ceiling & as his eyeballs began to spiral. Playing with his half-empty glass, he found it immeasurably pleasurable to watch the tall woman staring back, blank as a sentinel with her narrow elongated face, which appeared more than porcelain in that spectral light. He drank in her tense poise through his enigmatic glass. She was live, she was game. It was the green eyes that got you. If that wasn't enough, there was a green amulet around her neck, maybe jade. Ignatius had read of Baudelaire's *guignon*, that evil eye, that third eye between her breasts which only magnified her charm. She stared back impassively, looking through the very old red bricks, beyond. Ignatius felt his Celtic blood rise. How much? I'm a mutt, a Heinz 57. Why green? She continued to look through him, less animate than her amulet. Your name. I need your name. Helen? Is that what they had called her? No, she was too tall to be a Helen. Ignatius kept walking. He followed his feet. He knew they were aching to circle the last round of cobblestones & pass her immediately. Then he veered off in the opposite direction. Ignatius rose to go as a cold breeze passed through his slim bones. Spring & I feel hollow. He thought of the odd nagging regret & swallowed. To sing, to play, to paint, to write. What? A proper jack of all trades, Iggy, that's what you are. He walked past the underground washrooms & recalled the time they sent him packing out of Starbucks. Yes, I am going to buy a coffee just let me go first. Please. Sorry chief, we can't do that. Store policy. Smoke. Ignatius studied the rich purpling of tile that led down into the Men's & inhaled a thin layer of smoke as it arose from those mysterious depths. Probably quite nice. All the same ... Wonder what the tourists do. You'd think with the boats & trains & express ride to the airport, the guards would leave off brandishing that sign in the station, all those Americans asking goshdarn where the heck is it in that drawl of theirs & always someone fresh off a train with a Traveller lid hopping about underneath that painted banner of Banff, wanting to go before they catch their plane home. Not like the real train station near Main. Ignatius plodded along, thinking of a newspaper clipping from 1944, the front page no less, his grandfather sharing the same crooked smile as himself & carrying his British wife over the station threshold, standing with her in his arms in front of the double doors. WAR BRIDES' BABIES REFUSE BANANAS—Elongated Fruit Never Seen Before By New Overseas Arrivals. Ignatius had chuckled over that second headline in bold letters. I could look at that picture for hours, staring harder & harder at those little dots & still never know the man. A man like me? No. Different. A stranger. I can only remember that visit to the island as a kid & noticing as he was talking that he had no thumb. No thumb? Grandpa has no thumb. Impossible. This is some kind of magic trick. So I thought. Ignatius stopped, allowing cars to pass ahead of his crossing. He remembered that last visit to his grandfather, turning it over & over in his mind, wondering at his multiple sorrows. In the war, he had lost his thumb. Shrapnel in his side. But it was during manoeuvres when he had thrown a live grenade into the wind. This cold breeze of early Spring. The wind. They had told him it was not

17

live. Why was it live? A young man had died that day. For what? Why? When his grandfather had returned, he had knocked on the door of the young man's parents, & in their narrow flat, he had explained about the wind. But now, he could not even remember *that*. Now he could not remember anything. Ignatius thought of his last visit, when he had watched his grandfather emerging from his room in Nanaimo Village, rising for his latest visit from a family he could not remember. Why? For the sake of that smell, maybe. For the sake of that cigar that he loved, locked safe & sound in the cupboard by his keepers. No, it wasn't healthy, not when your mind has departed, to have a single cigar every day, no, absolutely not. Is memory what makes us? For the life of me, I have no memory. Only the way he used to light his pipe or the smell of that cigar or the smoked salmon he would make for us. I remember a toy squad car he once sent me. Now there's only the smell of that cigar being lit for him on the patio of Nanaimo Village. Only that smell in the wind. Ignatius paused on Water Street in front of the terracotta faces of Verlaine & Baudelaire to stare at the crowds of people having their picture taken in front of the steam clock & other people taking pictures of them, being captured by other people taking pictures of them & so on … *ad perpetuum*. His crooked smile on the front page. Don't take too many tea breaks, he would tell the auto parts dealer or watchmaker if he thought they were trying to pull the wool over his eyes. A hard man to reckon with. But now, to lose all of those cares & anxieties, to let go of all that why he looks like an angel. He no longer remembered his heap of sorrows, the bottles of Scotch or waving his policeman's special around in a dinghy. So calm & completely relaxed, so beautific & carefree & to have lost his home & mind like Lear, what is that?

"Spare change spare change for swill hey I'm workin' on a hard dollar I'll beat my box for a buck buddy, no? Spare change spare change … "

Ignatius continued to shake his head, eyes cast down towards his leaky shoes with the frayed laces & loose stitching. A minute later, his eyes darted up to take in a standing façade. Heritage. Light glinted through those holes, hiding that hidden pit of emptiness, already spoken for. SOLD read the sign. Arghh, the buzz was wearing off & his feet were leading to Helen, that one Helen without a name. Past the architectural elbow & the emerald statue of a man standing upon a whiskey barrel, stumbling a little over the stones, Ignatius managed to evade the film crew & a bank of rain machines. There was a large round woman sitting at their feet amid a variety of tripods. She glared up at Ignatius.

"Could you buy me a cawfee?"

He shook his head nervously. Then he squeezed the handle of a green door & shoved it forward. "Lights, camera ... "

The door crashed shut behind him. THUNKERRUNCK!!!

"Allo Iggy! Smith'icks, is it?"

Ignatius nodded & sat at a lone table, right in the front, touching two fingers to his temples. Sit tight. Relax. This way I'll see her, at least. The pint arrived & Ignatius sipped thoughtfully, taking in various shards of colour in reflections & shadows skewing with jutting rooftops as he sipped a little faster. It's all math, really. He gloomily surveyed the pub's quietude, a state which seemed to agitate the servers more than him. Clustering together, chatting & laughing. Ignatius didn't get a word. Where was she? Mechanically, he lifted the pint glass to his dry lips, to the painting of a surreal crowd he knew was over his head. For Helen's sake, there is still a bleedin' war on, out there. He pointed at nothing in particular. No one paid him any mind. The boxbeater passed, singing ginsoakedly & looking in enviously.

"I've lost my soul ... to a cleft in the road."

I've sat here before. Regularly on Mondays, day of the moon & diurnal urges, on the slowest afternoon, when dot-comers & Hollywood northerners drop in for casual meetings on sunny days. Ignatius could hear cell phones ringing right & left. He began to rub his snivelling nostrils with his knuckles.

"Then I wrote a play ... "

She had revealed herself to the man in denim shorts upon a stool. Ignatius had stolen glances at her excited green orbs, animated by her talk.

"I'd really like to work in radio. I didn't think I'd end up like this."

"Whaaa?"

"Tending bar, here. But anything creative, well, the money's far better tending bar."

Ignatius had tried to catch her eye, furrowing his brow in utter futility at her bent head & the tight knots raised like shortwave antennae or even the pricked ears of a listening bitch. Ignatius had lowered his eyes as quickly as he had raised them.

"Yeah, I'm thinking of moving back to Winnipeg."

Ignatius felt his heart sink to hear that phrase of hers in his head, clinking like one of those lost pennies into the gutter. A dead wish. How many nights in the past month had it been like this, with his fever raging, his mustard or custard sheets damp with expectorating toxins & sweat induced by the excellent lava of some Szechuan hot & sour soup, tossing & turning, wrestling with her slim tall shadow, watching her sharp lips release round after round of profanity intermingled with the compassionate *Dear* she had mastered the enunciation of. Lately, he just wanted a smile, even that. Too sharp for me. With eyes watering & throat itching over a minute ball of phlegm, Ignatius tried to get his act together. In movies, the expression of emotion was polished, was timely, was proximate, was perfect. If someone coughed, you knew they wouldn't last to the end of the film. You knew by the cough they were terminal. I would just like to say goodbye properly. She had been tending at the time, rather than standing under the clock as usual. Ignatius liked to watch her standing under the clock, staring up at the painting over his head with her eyes raised like a perverse Botticelli, since he had an excuse to study the time, to be that busy, to be late for some date or appointment, to have that ball of curiosity in his court. Then she would go silly & say she was giddy, too giddy, too tall to drop forks on a warm Friday!

"I'm a jack of all trades," she offered denim shorts. "I just don't want to grow old in an apartment. That's partly why I'm moving back to Winnipeg."

Many of his friends had already left, or were just passing through. Ignatius beheld innumerable visions of his heart being dashed to the smooth floor & being tenderized by her gleaming teeth before being served up with a masala mix of spices. The afternoon light was nearly gone. Ignatius looked down at the lingering ring at the bottom of his pint glass.

"Another, Iggy?"

Another, Iggy? The front door burst open in a flash of green. Helen came through, bending her knees in smart black boots less than usual. A new handbag to boot.

"I made it!"

She reddened for a second with exuberance.

"No," answered Ignatius.

He drained his pint & stood up. Passing the tall woman on her way in & needing to pee all the same, his eyes felt like mud puddles swallowing those stark but courteous flashes of green recognition in rather confused response as he focused on the white mole or wart or beauty mark upon her left cheek.

"Wasswithyou?"

"I just have an *aversion* to someone who comes in every day," she mumbled. "He's young."

Behind his back, he felt her eyes persist into early evening, cold as rolling cat's eyes, rolling to a close with the hinges of that large green door. THUNKERRUNCK!!! Inside, the pint glass was tipped off the very edge of the table & fell to smooth floor, shattering utterly. But this time, as the large clock hand struck five, there was neither laughter nor applause.

21

Nailed

And he said unto her,
Give me, I pray thee,
a little water to drink;
for I am thirsty.

—Judges 4:19

The door of the Fog & Flagon closed, muting a rainy whoosh of passing cars. Gerald looked up, blinking & shaking the wonky spokes of his black umbrella. Stupid wind. A shape appeared, shedding yellow through the inner dim. Nothing. A young woman turned her back, receding back into dishclattery gloam. Gerald took a seat, elbows upon table. Each green door supported nine window panes & they were united by cobwebs of rain. A figure in a yellow slicker rushed past, arms swinging. Hate those so & sos with their long pointies take an eye out, them, right through the head, swinging & swinging. Debbie returned, swaggering out from behind the ebony bar, disturbing his sphere of quietude, then softening the deliberate friction of her slouch.

"How are you?"

Her soft voice rolled down the visible terrain of tight wool. A beer landed upon the table, albeit heavily, as she about-faced & walked away from his faltering gratitude. He took a sip from the inner gold, eyes following long navy skirt over the musical rim, clammy in hand. Cars continued to slug along grey street. Whoooosh. Past his station as neighbourhood fixture, her feet began to creak again across hardwood lines. Soft relief to look at it that way. Strength of body, self-building, a project, that. Grace? Honest effort, this faux coziness. Fake

22

clock, always ten past six, imitation leather, jumbleshop lamps, etc. He blinked, heavylidded. That's my eyelash. Gerald blew upon it gently & the lash flew off, falling somewhere to floor. Debbie passed again, half siren & half sentinel, giving him an impatient look.

"Making a wish," he tried, uneasily.

She nodded without a word & began to rotate her wrists, making cracking noises, turning them all about. Bad circulation, bad blood. With all that exercise? Takes its toll on ankles the first to go. She stopped & looked at him again, almost thoughtfully. His pallid face began to flush into an impulsive laughish shape, becoming merry & rubicund, the colour creeping about the corners of his lips. Huh, that was a bit of alright. She sashayed by once more, her hair patted flat & combed to one side like a listening sunflower. Well at least Van Gogh listened to them. Traffic began to speed up amid evaporating rain. Ah, the flux of things, the slow persistence of this artificial bouquet ...

"Hey Debbie!"

"Yeah?"

"Could I have a glass of water?"

"Sure."

Flatlined. A look that read why don't you go home & wank off or something. The door burst open & two sexagenarians entered in a flurry of damp points. The taller fellow with the radio announcer voice looked around through the wiry rims of his glasses, his eyes small & crustaceanlike, for his favourite chair. Can hear him in every room. His portly companion took his usual seat on the couch beside him. Debbie hurried beyond all slouching to the lager pump & began pumping out two glasses of the alchemic gold on special.

"She's got quite the *right* body type," whispered Portly.

"I still think you're making Mohammeds out of mountains," warned Radiovoice.

"Well, I don't see you bringing Maria here," exclaimed Portly.

"Hey, your glasses are getting all steamed up," rejoined Radiovoice.

The glasses were plunked down before their claps & hurrahs.

"Good afternoon, Debbie," they grinned in tandem. "If we could settle up now … "

"$6.25, that's the damage," she broadcast.

"Ooh, that's gone up a loon," worried Portly. "Three dollars, I really wonder," he added, lost in consideration.

"That's fine, Debbie," assured Radiovoice.

The water crashed down upon the table in a swish of clinking ice.

"Hey Debbie!"

"Yeah?"

"Wanna go out some night, I mean if you're not too busy?"

Her eyeballs widened & began to planet larger, first gyrating out of orbit, then once again becoming agog with her usual look when visibly juggling figures in her head. Accounts reckoned, she nodded firmly. A sound came out, inaudible to Gerald, before pragmatism asked for a second audit.

"Where would we go?"

"There's that new Greek, or Thai, or sushi? All you can eat?"

She smiled out of weirdness & he beheld a magnificent banner revealing a veritable smorgasbord of specials.

"I'm off tomorrow," she stated. "Here's my number."

Whisper & glide, no slouch this time.

"I just cannot believe how the price of pickles has gone up," mourned Portly. "What next?"

Radiovoice nodded ignoringly.

"Have you ever noticed that you *can* get into a real pickle, a fix I mean, but you can *never* get into a gherkin?"

"Not even a little one," agreed Portly after a lengthy pause. "Anyway, they give me cankers."

The appointed day was very warm. Gerald fiddled with a pre-knotted tied for thirty-three seconds, then out of frustration loosened it & stuffed it into his pocket. I hate ties, the way they tighten about your neck so hard to breathe. Watches too, the way they close about your wrists. Debbie appeared beside him in front of Clytemnestra's, nudging closer.

"Hi."

He looked down, eyes tracing the lines of the purplish dress that clung tightly to her shapely body. "Heeello."

He raised his index finger, disrupting the preparations of a brand new staff still noising about the kitchen.

"Yes, señor?"

Accent. A blast of bouzouki burst to life out of a suspended loudspeaker.

"Two for dinner & a wine list, please."

The little man smiled at Debbie & moved lithely toward the table.

"My name is Tuna & I will be serving you this evening. But for wine, let me say, we have our Shiraz on special this very night."

"A bottle of that," waved Gerald with what he imagined to be a gesture of flamboyance.

"Certainly."

Debbie straightened up in her chair, fiddling casually with the crosshatch of mauve & chartreuse straps across her back. Pop.

"Will mademoiselle taste?"

Tuna laughed, taking in the pair of them with a touch of intrigue. Debbie watched him pour slowly before lifting the glass to her lips. Purply smile.

"Mmm."

Tuna poured a second glass & delicately centred the bottle before vanishing.

"How's it going?"

"Hmm. I duhno."

She stretched her arms fastidiously.

"I'm pretty tired from yesterday."

"Works you to the bone, eh?"

"Well, she's my aunt."

"O."

"That's okay. She does work me to the bone."

Debbie lounged a little, smiling even more purply.

"Free lunches. No such thing. What about you?"

"Me, nothing special. Another suit, that's all. After being in the office all day, with the airlessness & freezing air-conditioning, I love to get free early & see you, that's all ... "

He trailed off, confused but satisfied.

"Are you ready to order?"

Tuna leaned forward with a hint of menace.

"I'm fond of lamb."

"Ladies first, señor."

Debbie grinned.

"Calamari," she said, with winesoaked syllables falling out of her purply mouth.

"I'll have the lamb special," added Gerald.

"Right!"

Tuna floated off, leaving Debbie & her dress frankly purpling & flowing open with understanding.

"You sure love them specials."

"Hehhmmm."

Gerald felt his blood reaching for her. The wine, it's the wine.

"Debbie," he ventured. "I sure like the look o' you tonight."

Gold & teeth.

"Shucks. That's nice of you to say."

Across, upon, hands clasping into first touches. His mind screamed with desire.

"Calamari, for the hombre ... "

Gerald frowned.

"I had the lamb."

Tuna smiled, his voice lightly coated yet heating up upon a well-honed skewer of audible smarm.

"Sí, señor, you are the liddle lamb!"

He switched plates with a minimum of effort & after another glance at Debbie, scurried off.

"Mmmm" she purpled.

The TKCLINK of their glasses. Gerald watched her while his tongue worked anxiously to free a long strand of the gamey meat between his teeth. Enamel, hope that filling doesn't go. Should get that looked at.

"Yahmmmm," he suggested.

He could feel her foot brushing his. Under. Blue eyes gleaming. Glugging back all purply. Debbie tore apart her squid & downed full forkfuls until the plate was crumbless.

"What's next?"

Gerald grinned.

"You're a speedy eater."

He probably shouldn't have said that.

"Thirty-two times that's me, a stickler for chewing, hmm."

Debbie smiled & sat back in post-calamari bliss.

"Always?"

He could hear Tuna bursting out of the kitchen & yelling back in excited Español. Then ferociously, he clapped his hands together. The dishes were removed.

She pressed the pedal harder. He watched her thighs. Not while driving.

"Come over," the thighs murmured.

Come over & come on in. Debbie smiled at him, the night blurring by behind her.

"You wanna come in?"

He slammed the passenger door.

"'kay."

He closed her apartment door & looked overhead at the overhanging muh ... She helped him turn the deadbolt closed & there was a satisfying THWUNK.

"That was my grandmother's."

He nodded sagely, since his green shirt was beginning to unbutton. They pressed together in the dimly lit corridor.

"Come in, come in."

Gerald felt her hand tugging him down the corridor.

"Watch your head."

A lamp was opened & a stained glass dragonfly was illuminated. He recalled past summers, sitting about Beaver Lake & reading snatches of Hesiod, listening to the red-winged blackbirds & watching the dragonflies, fluttering reds, angrylooking things mating midair how do they with oranges? That outraged blue one intervening.

"C'est un péché," the French-Canadian visitors had pointed out. "Un péché."

Or were they just talking about fishing? Laughter, ancient laughter, ancient summers, the heat about my legs & stomach, keeping eyes peeled for the promise of Aphrodite's enchanted girdle. He puzzled over an old candelabra on her mantle, covered with dust. She spread out a light comforter on the living room floor, tossing a pair of yellow shams on top.

"Funny how in movies, people come home in the afternoon to houses full of burning candles ... Not just one, but twenty or thirty.

You think they'd put them out before going to work. A hazard, you know ... "

He rambled on nervously. Debbie stood barefoot on the comforter, her back to him.

"Sometimes I think about you like *this.*"

She began to play with her short hem, talking to the wall. Flesh. Hint of flesh. Higher.

"You ever think about *me* like this?"

"Yes," he answered in a hush.

"Ahmmm."

Surges of power, electricity.

"Maybe I want you for tonight. Maybe I want you a lot."

She pulled at the flimsy straps & rolled them down her firm biceps. Then she stretched like a cat, stepping carefully out of her dress. He touched her abdomen from behind, enjoying its small abundance of flesh, thinking of those cicadas he had read about that sang for mates through their middles KUAN KUAN while caressing her tiny paunch. Suddenly impatient, he clawed at her black panties, raking them down her thighs. I am unused to such a pretty one. Gerald did not want to displease her, no sir, not one iota. But he stripped to the anticipatory sound of discarded zipper teeth & she let him so warm & wet against him she let him. Ooooh it felt so good how many so many men. She knew so well how to.

"You got protection," she barked.

Sheepishly, he reached for the inverted heap of pants, drawing out a turquoise square. Losing time. She let him, exciting him with her naked body, writhing about him & touching him playfully. However, she suddenly seized the light bluegreen wrapper & tore it open.

"I'll help you."

He nodded & shut his eyes, concentrating on her rough pinches. Then she was on the comforter, full of fury & encouragement. Tightly, she let him. Gold by yellow. Dirty blonde. Dragonflies

29

fucking red & orange & blue. She let him. He pulled at her black-blonde streaks, gently to test angry then angry how long? He felt the heat overwhelm him & his mind was buzzing & he saw nothing.

"Little bitch," he heard himself say.

She turned her head slightly & he saw a flash of silver in her feral smile.

"That's right."

He grew angrier. He could feel the curve of his palms about her white throat. Monosyllables began to shudder out of her mouth & with that growling *fuh fuh fuh* she let him.

"Uggnngh."

Sweet release. Sweating, he fell over her & they curled up together, sweating & breathing heavily, beginning to drowse. I am slippery. She.

A week later, Gerald sat anxiously on the Alma, tapping the passenger bar with vigorous tap taps, flitting eyes upward at a Canada Council poem from time to time. She says they take up advertising space, but I don't see the harm. *At the mouth, where river runs under, in, to the immanence of things.* Number Nine, number nine the lovely Muse is mine is mine tap tap. The brown was warm with his fingertips.

"Push the door! Push it!"

There you go, that's right. Once you get the hang of it, easy as falling off a bike. He got off the bus at least two stops early, looking around with a hand over his eyes & getting his bearings. The double doors attempted closure behind his back. O well. The antennae swayed from side to side as the bus stuttered forward again. Ah, the smell of all this green & the sound of *Carpodacus purpureus*, otherwise known as the purple finch, like a sparrow dipped in raspberry sauce, keeping aloof & elusive amid the trembling of light & appley hangings. Pik pik pik pik pik. They have different calls for different things, funny that. A single note then a spherical sort of warbling for some other purpose, what? Whatever. Gerald smiled to himself as he walked down West Broadway towards the end of Alma while heart pumped to head heart pumped to head & soon he would see her. Soon. Pik pik pik.

When he squeezed the door handle, happily thumbing the sunlit faux bronze & yanking it out of the humidity, he was greeted with a cold gust of air-conditioning. The first thing he saw was the blue anvil he knew well enough by now, high on the right buttock of Debbie, peeking over a sarongish cotton skirt the colour of most hotel towels. Hers & His. He felt a pang of lust, watching the anvil disappear into the back, then stopped, noticing that the owner was planted there, with a child's toy eyepatch to match her red kerchief.

"I'm playing the pirate."

She cackled softly. He heard a volley of laughter in the adjacent division of room, followed by resonant guffaws. Taking off the eyepatch, the little pirate woman got up & scrambled over to him in a hushed voice (although she always had the appearance of being about to share some clandestine tidbit of information). Gerald expected her at any moment to pull out a map of Spanish Banks & mark a large X on it with a butterknife.

"We're just on the tail end of a wake," she apologized. "Where would you like to … "

She cradled a menu & looked around for an empty place, waiting for his lead.

"It's one thing to ssselerate a death, rememering & so on but I dinna even know 'er!" Gerald took a seat on the far side of the bar, right beneath the giant mirror that read GUINNESS.

"Just one more just ONE more," they laughed, hilarious. Still, an honest notion, to make light of it. What can mourning do for the dead anyway? To think of them must be what matters, tears or not. More than they got in life maybe, who knows? What would they have done for me, sit shiva behind black drapes behind black everything

31

because I knocked up the wrong shiksah while I was alive? & if I did the honourable thing? Even Debbie, who must be part, at least, non-practising. You are dead to me you are dead to me. Here's to white veal & another helping thank you very much, half the holy city prefers to bring the bacon home. The front door opened, then closed slightly, then opened again. It was Radiovoice & his sidekick Portly. They walked a number of paces, then staggered about a little, bewildered by the wake party, whose members were restless & had decided to usurp their usual chairs. Finally, after scouting around, they chose a corner booth of fake leather, where they began to settle in with sour looks of discomfort.

"Change *is* good," Radiovoice laughed weakly.

When Debbie resumed her revolution from the other side of the kitchen from where she had disappeared, Gerald lay in wait until she moved to pass him. He got up quickly & quietly, creaking only gently & wrapped his hands about her exposed abdomen in a guesswho fashion.

"Hi."

Debbie looked over her shoulder with a toothy grimace.

"Not now."

Gerald let go with surprise. Over her shoulder, the owner also had a grimace of disapproval on her little pirate face.

"That's not a good sign," decided Portly, struggling to be heard over the wake party.

Radiovoice offered some allusion to Maria that Gerald couldn't quite hear.

"She was just like that."

Portly stirred in his shorts excitedly as the discount lager took effect & he began to relax.

"You just come here to oggle!"

"The word is *oygle*," corrected Radiovoice.

A pint came crashing down in front of Gerald.

"Here."

"But Debbie!?"

"Later. We'll talk *later*, after."

As she bantered with Radiovoice & Portly, Gerald scanned her face for the visible edges of a mask behind that fixed smile, for that now hidden flicker of a grimace. Maybe such moments show the real person, however rare, behind all that smiling. Nah. There are a hundred complications affecting you, thousands, including digestion, with the power to distort a sweet face into one of utter despair. Perhaps a touch of gas. Probably nothing.

Later did not arrive for Gerald, or at least not for a few days. He had left one or two or three messages on her answering machine & had received only one in return of a vague & distant nature.

"Hi, I am not home right now," repeated the voice chirpily.

Silence. Pick up pick up.

"You know the drill."

Brrrrrrrrr ... Silence. Four. That flash in the dark, number four. Where the hell is she? As a mere formality, Gerald had considered writing her a letter. He hated this uncertainty more than anything. However, the thought of another visit like the last gave him the willies. Time to show up naked at her work. Now where did he pick up that piece of advice? At length, after much scratching of bed-headedness & much biting of nails & far too much pacing about his bedroom, to the extent that the violent sound of a broom handle ejaculated beneath his thudding feet, he decided to confront her one last time, & in a calm & gentle manner to briefly tell her where to go & so on & so forth. In any case, he had to re-evaluate the situation & whether there was one to take stock of. Pik pik pik! Yeah yeah, shut up already, I'm going, no need to kvetch! Rather than hop on the express bus & savour that feeling of a runaway troika, today he decided to walk from his apartment down to the old bricks of Alberta Street, even slowing his steps & meandering up & down quiet avenues tucked neatly behind the main thoroughfare. He slipped aside to avoid the open door of a truck whose sideboards read GARDEN SCULPTURE & found himself listening to a nest of ribald New-foundland woodpeckers. There, a cyclist stopped to watch a hawk stealing the brood of a pair of crows in hot pursuit, or so he indicated to Gerald before pedalling off. & there was the most beautiful house in Vancouver, some massive green entity with a sign in front of it. Gerald took in each spectacle in stride. He felt his endorphins increasing, although this release of energy only felt like it was feeding the resilience of his mild heartsickness, that dull pounding dogging his steps. However, to walk beneath the rows of trees, those emerald awnings, felt cooling to his skin & quite serene. Indeed, even the space-devouring gabling on some of the older houses caught his eye, the pièce de résistance among those comely blues & indiscreet violets. There, another purple attic seeming to be turning inward, toward its own interior. Never do that these days, not anymore. Maximize space, they do. Gerald continued onward, past the curbed outskirt of City Hall, stumbling here & there upon small patches of greenspace, some-times vacant, sometimes crowded with young waders in bonnetish headgear & barking progenitors & unleashed groups of dogs, con-tent to gambol about the block of green, oblivious to the warning signs about their cousins across the North Shore who swim across on hungry quests. I guess there's that glimmer in all of us. That bearing of teeth. O come with me to the little park off 14th & Pine. That sounds like a poem. That's how they start, I suppose, with a single line & grow from there. Gerald stopped to cover his eyes with his hand & studied the elevated heritage houses that appeared to be danc-ing on stilts over an empty construction pit. He turned away & no-ticed a tall woman with green eyes necking passionately with a young man who incessantly stopped in order to rub the spot beneath his nose with his index finger. She watched him, mimicking him a little & rubbing the moist spot beneath her lower lip. They laughed & con-tinued to enjoy themselves. O hell. Too hot to be in all that black on a day like today. Leaning on a Folkswagon like that in public. Lousy Eurotrash. Get a room already.

A few small parks later, Gerald reached the neighbourhood surrounding the Fog & Flagon. He deked down another short avenue, staying close to a row of applegreen hedges, & passed a flapping poster, purpling more fiercely in the bit of breeze which was refreshing each block of tidy flora. DJ GATSBY'S LAST STAND the sign purpled. Gerald paused. He recognized the name. Of course he did. He had gone to school with a James Gatsby, who was known by everyone as Jay. Apparently, his mother had been very fond of the American novel & the idea of the title character & she was a Robert Redford fan to boot. Not kosher enough for my tastes. Yet, he had grown up with that similarly ephemeral quality that perhaps only fair-haired blue-eyed creatures can possess. Gerald could even remember another Jay from his urchinhood who had so affectionately run to meet his bus, even in the rain, a child who had glowed throughout his effulgent episodes of hyperactivity, when not gobbing upon his coat or someone's coffee table. No, not a character in an American novel. A fair-haired hero, a Beowulf, a Siegfried. In this way, Jay was beautiful. In this way, Jay was blessed. In contrast, Gerald had always felt gnomish, more like a dark frowsyhaired troll, an alien visitor, a mere Nibelung most ungraciously begging to borrow a bar of coal tar soap from the world for his awaiting shower in some godforsaken barrow of his own. So the pair of them, once inseparable, were now like any two friends who abide one another throughout the earnestness of childhood & even the excitement of adolescence, but grow apart in adulthood, having chosen diverse roads to live along, though they be less than a mile apart. & feeling very much like the rather functional Mr. Carraway, an impoverished interloper, an observer very aware yet excluded from his old friend's new life. Gerald did not think of Jay often, but from time to time he would hear the odd word about him, that he was dating so & so or appearing in X city at Club Y on the arm of Z. He would be reminded of his old friend by a listing in a local paper or by a sign like the one he had just passed. This was a source of secret pleasure for Gerald, who enjoyed divining the existence of this whole other person by reading telephone poles. He, on the other hand, not content to be a mere character, had striven to be a Fitzgerald. He wished he had been able to get the drinking down, for starters. With the writing part, he was even less successful. One day I'll show them all. Ahh, pour me another, why doncha, sport? Now that's a bit too strong, isn't it? & how much for that? *Ov gevalt!* What kind of operation you running? On rare occasions, he would meet a woman he could declare to be a Zelda in the making. She would become his complete joy, his reason for being, all while he drank excessively in her presence & hinted at several new levels of ruination & debauchery he was about to sink to. But he never did. Instead, every day, he took the bus to a pale room with such an excessive amount of air-conditioning beating down on his neck & back that he rarely went home at the end of the day without feeling nauseous. But one day I'll meet my Zelda & she will drive me absolutely mad. She will inspire me to tuck my first masterpiece under my belt & we'll live together off the proceeds. & that will only be the first notch, you understand! Others will follow, O yes. Meanwhile, Zelda had not yet arrived. What about Debbie? Could it be her? She was certainly starting to drive him crazy. Perhaps it was time to break the news to her, to fill her in about his masterplan for a literary existence which would bind both of their lives together. Yes, there would be suffering & countless hardships to endure. But they would have each other. Gerald could already imagine himself revealing his best of intentions & making an ardent plea for literature, for which Debbie could do little but recognize the passion in his face & voice, however much she would appreciate the subtlety, practicality, & overwhelming sagacity of his words. Yes, she would be totally bowled over.

"What are you writing," she had asked him once, goaded on by the little pirate woman.

"I'm not a critic," he had answered, attempting to allay the owner's suspicions.

Otherwise, he had stammered out a few replies at once.

"I dunno beats me nothin' really I dunno … "

But now was the time! Time to disclose his divine plan to his waiting Zelda! Even her name appealed to him, when she was just plain Debbie & not Zelda. A biblical name for a start. What was her story? Make a mental note. Fitz would have looked that up for sure. Whenever he heard her name, Gerald was reminded of his great-great-grandmother & her last ditch efforts to flee Poland & its encroaching pogroms. A close shave alright. Even so, at immigration, the officers, searching for a spot of fun to relieve the monotony, decided to play a little trick on the poor woman. Her original name was inscrutable & since there was no time for accuracy, only time for the amusement of the officers, they decided to name her. They created her, those unknown officers, those strapping chaps! Heroes!

"It is like when you *doff* your hat, yes? Like doff."

The man persisted, his lips curling into a smile.

"Quite close enough," another officer chimed in, also smirking.

"Then you are Debbie Doff," declared the first officer, filling in a few blanks on her papers before stamping them madly & ushering her along.

"After all, we don't have all day here."

It became a selfish delight for Gerald, since this imagined memory of the officers was instantly evoked whenever he heard Debbie's name. In fact, his mental faculties had forged an unbreakable chain between these two Debbies, although they were separated by more than merely one generational gap. The more his imagination went to work to define his great-great-grandmother & her encounter with the officers at immigration, the more he felt like a *real* writer. In this way, Debbie was not actually Debbie to Gerald, but a figment which embodied all his literary aspirations. & when he looked into the pretty but profoundly Teutonic face of this newfound Zelda, he could trace her lineage to a particular set of fleeing Jewish Poles. All from a name. Thus were Gerald's thoughts occupied as he approached the main boulevard again, sidling up to the music shop on the corner. Above a posted sign offering free lessons, he could hear a dwindling horn, which bumbled a few abrupt sounds out of the upstairs window, before sputtering back into silence. The Rite of Spring. They always have that sound when someone's losing their mind. Or sometimes Strauss. Remember Electra. Pik pik pik. Instead of walking right up to the front door, Gerald chose to skulk in lowly fashion along the adjacent wall until he reached the last frosted window of the Fog & Flagon. Then he peeped through the clear glass outlines of merry jiggers, drummers & fiddlers. The pair of dark brown eyes went unnoticed by the two people standing inside. His eyes began to widen with a strange watery gleam until they were brighter than the clovers & shamrocks upon the window panes. Debbie (his Zelda!) was standing very close to a man with blond hair & one might say not at all like they were strangers. & what is more, this Nordic creature, this Übermensch, this Visigoth, had the audacity to plant a light kiss upon her one could not say withdrawing cheek, a kiss which lingered & what is more, made her blush all over, even through her peroxide locks. The blond man made a motion to leave & Gerald did a rapid about-face to the time of uncertain drums practising at no expense to their inexperienced owners, but before he could reach the corner, he had a ghastly premonition that he was a dark object already being recognized, a stumbling crow about to take flight.

"Hey Gerald!"

Shit. Nailed. Turning around, O yes why not, it was his old friend.

"O hello, Jay."

It was certainly not a matter of brightness. Gerald could remember them both being chosen for special classes, even when they had poorer marks & were more unruly than the other students, those ones who excelled to perfection when faced with any problem or challenge they put their minds to. You know, losers like that. But if it was not a matter of brightness, it might be a matter of how the pair expressed themselves. Some bloom outward & others experience an internal form of fecundity. Some seem not to bloom at all. The blond child, like his fictional namesake, had appeared to thrive in the presence of others like a plant that needed to be surrounded on all sides by sunlight. The darker fellow had accepted his nature, cultivating his instinctive distaste for the company of others & the general spectacle that society is. For him, loneliness was a food he strove to store up & learn to prepare, so that at any time he could search for this state of being & apply it to his idea of art. Gregariousness would kill that nurtured love of loneliness, just as loneliness would murder that desperate gregariousness his friend exhibited so well. Some people are afraid to be alone. Perhaps that was why Jay had always flourished among other people, whereas Gerald was alone in the crowd. Wherever he went, he felt rebuffed, irritated, annoyed, vexed, most perturbed, even going so far as to anticipate rejection where it was not, inventing it if absolutely necessary. So his friend, this tall shining *tournesol*, had made a career out of his brightness, travelling into a perpetual night in innumerable cities. Gerald had nurtured his own inner light on home soil. & what was he for that? A bit of skunk cabbage among a few stray weeds, a cumbersome heliotrope near squashing, the deceptive toll of angel's trumpet, the bitter taste of nightshade, or maybe even a smattering of purple loosestrife. & what good were all these ideas that occurred to him if he hardly ever took the time to write them down? Now, if he could only get down to business. Fuck Debbie. Fuck Zelda. & here he was again, just like in grade three, having to reckon with his old counterpart. His old friend. What had he to do with *his* Zelda, anyway?

"Hey, whatcha doin' up here, boyyy?"

Jay crossed his arms in rapperly greeting.

"Umm ... bookstore, used books, I came over this way to pick up a book."

"O yeah, a book, that's slick, man."

"Maybe a Fitzgerald."

Jay winced, dropping his arms.

"O no, not that one. Maybe the one with Dick Diver & the saucy starlet, I mean."

Jay Gatsby slackened his posture & grinned with an affectation of nonchalance which melted warmly into his sunglasses & cap turned backwards.

"Well, I just dropped in to see my girl Debbie. She's a cool chickie."

"O there," blurted Gerald. "I think I know who you mean, I umm … might know who you mean."

"Well, I gotta haul ass. I gotta gig, if you can read tha sign. Stop by, man."

Gerald nodded stupidly, covering his eyes from the leftover sunlight, watching his old friend slink off in feline fashion. Suddenly, Jay stopped in midstep of sneaker & turned around, pulling his shades down, revealing his very blue eyes with red rims.

"Hey man, if you're in the mood for something, some real kinky shit, you might wanna look into this. Heh heh, it'll fucking blow your mind!"

Gerald took the stiff rectangle of mauve cardboard from him without looking at it.

"Yeah, thanks man."

"No prob," replied the reapplied shades. "You're a pal."

Then he slouched off again down the sunlit boulevard. Gerald looked down at the neat & slender characters in a sans serif typeface, at last permitting himself to feel sick.

***

The man stood with his hands over his head, fastened together & tied to a large cylindrical pipe, another ornament of the *dungeon*. His feet just barely touched the floor & he shifted continually to become more comfortable & found that he could not. He was wearing a mask out of the Italian theatre & he resembled Gianni Schicchi caught in an awkward part of the opera. His mask was the contorted face of tragedy. He was wearing nothing else but a tight leather belt & corresponding black loincloth which the loose flesh of his large paunch hung over messily. His pudgy nipples gleamed now & again & Gerald could make out a tiny gold piercing in each one. It was at that moment Gerald noticed a female figure sitting in the shadows, slightly to the right of the hanging man. The camera was positioned on an angle & appeared to centre on the woman rather than on the man. As if on cue, she broke the stillness & stood up in the darkness. She moved towards the dangling lightbulb & revealed a mask that was counterpart to the man's, the mask for comedy. Gerald felt disconcerted, staring through the glass into those dark eyeholes of perpetual levity, suspended over a congealed grin. She was wearing a black leather girdle with holes cut into the stiff material to strategically accentuate the curves of her flesh as she walked. She looked quizzically into the camera for a second, offering her cleavage through the roughly cut peephole of her outfit & illuminating that sickle of a grin. She wore ridiculously high leather boots with unforgiving heels that dotted the oilstained floor like semiquavers, a sound for which the hanging man stirred, attempting to lower his head & prick up his ears. She turned her head toward the man & then looked at the camera again, as if disclosing the secret of his predicament. She held a neatly gloved finger to fixed smile & reached with her other glove for the ample girth of him, for the emphasized expanse of his *love handles*. As he felt the coarse material brush his belly, he shifted from foot to foot with that attached face of agony, tightening both wrists about decorative pipe & belt about excessive gut. He let out a low moan, yet loud enough with its current of enthusiasm for Gerald to imagine his smile underneath that tortured mask. The loincloth seemed to soften for the hanging man as his growing excitement became visible. She walked slowly over to the farthest wall, allowing the hanging man & Gerald to hear each bewitching step, before taking down a coiled object which had the appearance of a small bullwhip. She walked over to the hanging man, standing mask to mask, yet maintaining choreography for the camera's pleasure. Gerald blinked, focusing through the gloom & observing her shiny white back & her blonde hair tied back behind the mask into a short knot. Her head cocked to one side & the gloves went out. Gerald could see one of them lifting the loincloth & holding it up in a tight fist, but her body obscured the rest. He could feel his temperature rising. She was leaning forward just enough to whisper over the hanging man's shoulder. Gerald heard only murmurs. The man twitched while listening. Then the gloves shot out & seized his bare shoulders. He groaned as the loincloth flapped down again. The gloves insinuated their will & the hanging man let himself be turned in the opposite direction. Gerald & the camera lent their field of vision to his thinning grey hair & raw pimply buttocks. The three tassels attached to the small whip were offered intermittently to each red cheek, tickling the man. She moved closer & filled his ear with nothings for a full minute, while he shook (as much as he could) like a broken marionette, breathing heavily over her inaudible words. Having prodded him into this state of bound excitement, she stood back matter-of-factly & with a sudden flick of her wrist let the whip fly. The lash was instantaneous. A slim neat mark appeared on his exposed bottom.

"No," he answered. "No."

The wrist flicked again. Then again.

"No, I won't do it again."

She backed up a few paces, studying his miserable hanging body, before putting her whole arm into the attack. The whip flew at him & formed a sizeable cut on his lower back. He began to howl.

"Forgive me, you have to forgive me!"

In response, she turned her head back towards the camera, flashing that plastic grin, before whipping his body again. The motion of her body caused more laughter in her clothing. A hundred laughs opened in her girdle like a jigsaw puzzle of flesh for the imagination to finish. High on her left buttock cheek, a small tattoo made its debut for the camera, then vanished beneath the strain of leather like a nearby star suddenly enshrouded by a brusque & ponderous cloud. Gerald leaned forward to catch another glimpse of the navy blue mark, but the woman wheeled around, turning the man like a large slab of meat by pulling his loincloth in her direction. She bent her knees, arching her back in feline fashion & stretching her arms towards the camera. The mask continued to cackle absurdly. She eased her body backward in slow movements until the hanging man could feel the curves of her rear through the leather. Then she stretched forward again, catching her hands on a lowhanging pipe the size of a gymnast's apparatus. Balancing like so, she raised her left leg behind her like a startled mare & placed the heel of her boot against the man's groin, applying pressure measured by his increasing groans.

"Ooooh yaaa."

She turned him sidewise so that his mask became a half-grimace. She sidled up against him, a half-grin at his baggy flesh & the bumpy loincloth beneath her begloved hands. She lifted the coiled whip up to his chest, letting the three tassels tickle his body hair & letting the coils catch upon his gold piercings while she whispered other things into his right ear. The hanging man began to squirm.

"No. No. I don't know, maybe."

With that, a wicked weakthroated laugh flew into his ear. The woman stood back, her mask grinning into the camera for a prolonged spot of visible ecstasy. Then she lifted the whip & began to lash the man severely, taking no care this time to find a target. Weeping could be heard, coming from under his tormented mask. Also groans. His body began to tear & break into smiles, until it looked like a grotesque parody of her tattered girdle.

"Noooouhh!"

She whipped him again. The hanging man shuddered for a few seconds & then his head fell limp. Feeling queasy, Gerald reached through the semi-darkness for the doorknob. The last thing he saw was the woman's mask smiling into the camera on a slight angle. Then behind his back, accompanied by a series of cackles, he heard a lone word.

"¡Bañera!"

Gerald did not return to the Fog & Flagon anymore. That is not to say he was not interested in this riddle. That is not to say he didn't make time to be & remain quite interested. That is not to say he didn't hide in the surrounding bushes outside the same establishment whenever he could, watching. However, after a few days, the situation seemed hopeless. He had failed to catch his Zelda coming in or out, or for that matter to run across her drinking Black Velvet out of a slipper, or even passionately entwined with a new lover. He was musing this way before opening time, when he saw a bike whizz by & stop in the alley. Gerald peered around the corner. It was Mr. Gatsby. Jay dropped his bike in the gravelly lane with a crash, as he would have done when they were kids. Then he knocked three times on the rusty back door of the Fog & Flagon. The door swung open & a manila envelope was thrust outward, flapping into Jay's arms. He paused for a moment to lift the orangishyellow object up & to tilt out its contents. Small dark rectangles darted out into his hands. Photographs? Jay examined each one, laughing to himself, before slipping the contents back in & lending his tongue to the adhesive strip with a playful rakish look. In response, the back door slammed shut & he giggled again. Lifting his bike out of the dusty lane, he tucked the envelope under his arm & started pedalling around the corner & up a slight incline. Gerald struggled to follow at a distance, finding he had to run at some lengths of street in order to keep Jay's mauve toque in sight. Then the bike came to a halt. Gerald came to a halt as well, huffing & puffing. Jay had stopped in front of a nondescript creamcoloured house. His bike lay upon the lawn & he had disappeared behind a hedge. Gerald crept up to the topiary as quickly & quietly as he could, craning his head around its body yet failing to discern what kind of animal it was supposed to be. Jay had put his sunglasses back on. The door opened.

"¿Sí?"

Jay muttered a name.

"Please to wait."

A heavyset man appeared upon the threshold & Jay launched the envelope at him. Gerald could not quite see the man's face through one of the quadruped's green legs, but something was familiar about him, all the same. There was no time either. As the cherry sneaker turned on itself, Gerald sprinted along the other side of the hedge towards the alley. He heard a dog bark & for a moment thought that the topiary had come to life & was nipping at his heels in flight as he fumbled with a small wire gate, afraid to stop & look over his shoulder. In fact, he ran for nine blocks until he felt he was safely out of sight, then collapsed upon the manicured grass of a neighbourhood lawn. Why had he run? & what was all that about?

Gerald did not return to the Fog & Flagon anymore. Nor did he dwell on the riddle of its existence. He was quite content to let the whole matter rest. In the evenings, he began to walk the seawall around Vanier Park, admiring the eclectic collection of mutts along Dog Beach & finding he was not entirely indifferent to the remainder of nubile bodies leaping across the seascape & bunting volleyballs over nets with their wrists & tightly clenched fists. It was only when he saw a shapely blonde woman in the distance that he felt a small pang of regret gently stirring in his slacks. She sat down on a bench & as he drew closer, he could see her ultrawhite teeth gleaming in the mysterious orange glow of sunset, undoubtedly the result of increasing pollution. Beautiful. She was just a smile underneath her open novel & Gerald read the title. CONFIDENTIALITY. He took in the richly embossed illustration of doctor & degowned patient in a torrid embrace (so torrid in fact that the doctor was about to drop a very peculiar instrument). Gerald guessed that the woman probably took ten to twenty of these out of the library at a time & read them ravenously. Ahh, Zelda, why read such plot-driven pulp? One excellent book is enough. A masterpiece is perhaps enough for a lifetime. So Gerald mused as he walked & it occurred to him that he was not at all like the protagonist in the formulaic drivel of most pulp mysteries. It was not that he was not curious. However, as with most people, curiosity gave way to the pleasures of idleness & to further energy expended in order to combat a general sense of lethargy which accumulated the more he fed his habits. So he walked the beach. He admired other dogs & observed other women, all with a sense of new-found delight, until a few days later, when he became completely bored with scene & sunset. On that day, he came straight home from work & noticed that his white semicircle of an answering machine was flashing its red alarm. PLAY.

"Two messages," soothed the metallic female voice.

Debbie. On the first message, she said more than usual, although she hardly threatened to fill up the machine's digital memory. Gerald turned away disinterestedly, only catching some part about needing to talk. No thanks. FORWARD. The second was from Mr. Gatsby. It was short & sweet & about old times & about getting together & so on & so forth. O, an invitation to Gemini. Gerald did not sleep very well that evening & when he awoke, he had almost no fingernails to speak of. The next morning, the mezzuzah looked down at him like a raised eyebrow.

"Gerald Moss."

He gave his name to the burly dude in front of Gemini as if he knew what he was talking about & what's more, as if he would be *known*. Burly dude responded by raising two fingers in front of Gerald's face & subsequently jabbed him in the ribs. Gerald doubled over, more hurt than surprised.

"Hey Gerry, hey man, I'm sorry bud, I didn't mean to total you. Don't know my own strength. What a way to wail on an old pal. Hey mannnn ... just fuckin' witcha!"

Gerald righted himself, recognizing the voice.

"Gerry, don't you 'member your homeboy? It's Francis. Francis Mailloux."

Gerald held his ribs, trying to smooth out his dignity.

46

"I should have known a Frog Jew was behind this," he attempted.

"Ahhahhah, dat's me, mon frère!"

Gerald was instantly reminded of a time when Frank had mercilessly teased a friend's cat all afternoon, before seizing Gerald's bare arm & submitting it for the feline's exactive measures.

"Scratches, stop that," the owner had said.

Gerald also remembered that Francis had a twin sister whose fair hair was lighter than his & that as kids she had pointed to his small & dark figure crouching awkwardly by the pool.

"I can see your wee wee," she had tittered.

Neither of these memories helped to restore Gerald's wounded confidence. Francis rolled back against the door in beerkeg fashion, once more becoming bouncerly in stance.

"Why don't you come on in?"

The velvety double doors closed behind them.

Gemini was empty, expect for a striking girl with bright scarlet hair, spiked upward into a mocking sort of cockscomb. Her eyes were cobalt blue & very cool to look upon. A tiny microphone was pinned to her left lapel. She stopped. Moved. Stopped. Moved again, very mechanically. Her cold eyes remained distant, lifeless. Meanwhile, the brief wiry movements of her small body beneath the charcoal pinstripe suit gave the impression that an automaton or marionette was being manipulated by some powerful remote. Her head swerved suddenly, to completely face Gerald & he started backward.

And the raven quoth, nevermore, nevermore, my darling O my darling Clementine ... "

Not at all suddenly, Gerald felt very weary. Her red lips had not moved & at the same time, he was certain he had heard a voice. He studied her beautiful blue eyes & the minute lines underneath them, hoping for a hint of movement to betray the smoothness of her pale skin. They were so very cold to look upon, like a pair of sapphires caught in the tight clench of their hollow coffers. Let go let go sit back sigh & release. But where did that voice come from? As if in answer, her head tilted back & one of her robotic hands made a perfect arc upward, lifting a piece of paper in front of her face, as if touching a new groove to automatic needle.

"There is a clacking chain of tender logic / thought, friends, we shall come to know in our time. Now. Fierce. Feral. Now."

The voice seemed to be coming from the very back of the club. Frank nodded approvingly in her direction.

"Yeah, she's dis poetess, so she says, eh. But helluva ventriloquist! That adds a little spice, hey? But man, I found her pretty freaky at first."

Frank slipped casually behind the bar, while the voice droned on & on behind a nervously bestooled Gerald.

"Wanna drink, pal?"

Frank poured out something the colour of Windex Extra Shine into a shot glass most expertly & pushed it forward.

"O no Clementine, the utter horror of the forest!"

Gerald hesitated. Think of Fitz. Bottoms up. Down the fucking hatch.

"What a dark wood we weave / when we first practice to receive … "

The stuff went right to Gerald's head. Quite the kick.

"Yo boyyy you never come round / Why no, stuff replied / here, never-more nevermore / silly it tolls for thee / not to talk outta my ass / but I've given you all / & now I'm nuthin' / O yer friends are alz ya gotz / whistlin' under them floorboards / a gleam in the eye / so luminous … "

Frank looked at him blankly.

"Hey buddy, you okay?"

No, Gerald did not feel well at all. The darkness was starting to spiral about him. The bar itself seemed like a winding stairwell or a glistening sheet.

"Tired, feel tired & sleepygrogambitomuthhh … "

With bouncerly finesse, Frank forklifted his arms under Gerald's & plucked him off his stool, dragging him towards the back & the source of that incessant voice.

"Time to see da boss man."

The scarlet plumage veered back towards Gerald in a brief display of animation. At least he thought so, until the head spun around a hundred & eighty degrees from the velvety double doors & the automaton's small body.

"My darling Clementine O my darling darling ... "

"Hey, you didn't see fuckall," shouted Frank.

The head snapped back into its original position.

"Ow," managed Gerald.

Sitting at the very back of the spinning labyrinth of stairways & tunnels & linoleum was his old friend Jay Gatsby, sporting sunglasses with his satin knees splayed.

"Evenin' hoss. O' should I say our little informant?"

One of the words rang through Gerald's skull, dragging a lowing cowbell after it, although he still could not tell which word it was.

"Whuh?"

"Yo boy, cut tha crap. Why you tailin' me? See any shit worth writin' 'bout, you little rat?"

Gerald reached up to hold his floating head in his hands, because it felt like that would solve all of his problems, but rather numbly, he felt they were pinned behind his back. Then, they faded out of focus & the jerky motions of the scarlet-plumed girl in the pinstripe suit occurred to him once again. Where had he seen them, exactly? Physically, he felt he was being moved. No, not floating. The catacombs appeared to have grown & his good friends were not quite people. Taking great care with wheeling red eyes of fire, to watch their ramshorns & flicking tails, they lifted him up & dropped him in another cubbysection of the subterranean maze, one much smaller & darker. Slippery. Wet. There was a thud & a splash. Then laughter.

Slippery sound. Wet. Body, his. Even in the dark, even in this deeper nocturnal nocte of mille noche, Gerald recognized that sense of wrinkled fingerprints rubbing against porcelain & that skid of tub be careful it's slippery yeah that's it. Almost relaxed, so near sleep at that point, the rest of his nightmares became much simpler & innumerable as violently tugged shower curtain hooks from old movie rip-offs. Each seemed to be striking his body, yes the utterly drenched body of he, while a glassy circle loomed over him & as he tried to see who was behind that impersonal eye, he felt a sharp blow to his chest, then weight & pressure. Here to save me, yes? Breath stopped, then began again. Splash of a plash. Glugggg ... Watery the skylight & glassy stare this time of century to break this abrupt downpour of faces. The age of interruption & economic downturns. Gerald smiled. In this eternal moment, he felt a kinship with the mechanical girl, that his voice was somehow external to himself, above & beyond all this sogginess of existence or this overwhelming mood of submergence. In spite of the small glass of clarity he now remembered & this newfound possibility of being shanghaied & freshly delivered to the promised land *if thou wilt go with me then I will go but if thou wilt not go with me then I will not go* or at least some paradisal garden, he thought he could see a gilthaired woman in the background, pacing back & forth behind the other shadowy devils, & by no means clear to the naked eye, but instead bathed in soft focus lighting, the beautiful queen of some neighbouring Myopia. Whispers. A phone perhaps, cradled against gold head with soft hand. Gerald strained to look more closely through the translucent veil, to see the gold & purple figure through the sharplyhooked celestial webbing that had descended about his head & flesh, but then that pressure sank his chest again. Blub-blubbb ...

"No no no, meeester. Goils, duhdaduhdaduhda all I really want is goils duhduhdaduhda ... "

Something colder than the water pressed against his temple. Gerald turned & laughed, because he had seen enough home improvement reality shows to identify the object touching his left temple. He closed his eyes, wondering how they stick up those flowers in the shower &

earthy twigs on the wall & cardboard wallpaper & pinecones at Christmas & if you can actually clean around them on a daily basis & how long all that rubbish lasts … A sound erupted right in the middle of his speculations & the slam poetry session upstairs & the dingy splashing & the dinghy plashing & the delicate murmur of recycled rap lyrics before everything went absolutely & unequivocally black. Pik pik pik.

"As I lifted up her petticoat …"

Whispers, rising above a snatch of old song.

"You know I don't know why she gave me the bird like that. Well, not really, but you know what I mean, she may as well have done."

La La glared with folded arms, her large dancer's legs prominently annoyed.

"Yeah," concurred Debbie.

"Since she's dolled herself up, at one of those treatment centres I bet, she's too good for us."

Debbie nodded, noncommittally. La La was leaving for Europe.

"& you should ask for that hour," she decided. "I mean, it is your time."

Debbie propped open the front door & put out the dark green chalkboard with the $2.99 special written on it in large purple letters. Then she went into an adjacent alcove to have a quick smoke & to read another couple pages of MELTDOWN, a popular & most definitely topical spy thriller about a secret thermo-nuclear reactor in the middle of an unnamed desert. Then she looked up & saw two figures approaching along the boulevard, one tall & wiry, & the other shorter & more portly. O hell. She extinguished her cigarette & came back inside, while La La looked on.

"Ahh Jesus Murphy, I forgot the ***** in the car. You go in & order what you will."

Portly smiled.

"What I know you will," Radiovoice added hastily, resonating down the street. "I'll be right along."

Before Portly could even reach his favourite seat near the artificial clock, Debbie had already plunked down two glasses of dim yellow lager.

"How are you & thank you for the pickmeup," ogled Portly.

"Good," answered Debbie with a rapid display of teeth.

"The sun's going … I hate it when it gets dark earlier & earlier," offered Portly to her back as she slouched away into the shadows. Radiovoice also made his ebullient greeting to her smooth back.

"I think it's stuck in the groove," advised La La, with one eye on the television screen behind the bar.

"*… to see what I could find … *"

Radiovoice sat down across from Portly in his usual paisley chair as if it were his by Royal appointment & began to scratch his white moustache thoughtfully.

"Copper for your thoughts," said Portly.

"Hmm," answered Radiovoice, dreamily.

"I said, a penny for your thoughts. You seem to be hatching something."

Radiovoice hesitated.

"I need a gun," he said at last, adjusting his glasses.

"What!?!"

Portly sat up in his seat, incredulous.

"Well, the problem with tasers is that you have to get real close to the little buggers. If only there were a way to create the same electrical current & something that looks like a nut they would go after … "

Radiovoice stopped in the manner of a controversial talk show host introducing some scandalous premise to his already overstimulated audience.

"*O what a bonny lass … *"

Portly relaxed back into the comfort of his seat, feeling the folds of himself sinking deeper into the cushions & virtually becoming one.

"O, you mean for your squirrel problem?"

Radiovoice nodded with a touch of condescension creeping into his wry grin & the amplification of his ideas.

"Well, we have to do something. We can't have bears waltzing into people's backyards. There is no reason we should be at the mercy of these wild animals which have gotten out of control. Some years ago, I remember looking at a BB gun at Army & Navy, for goshsake. Now, well that's my question, where does one go?"

"She didn't seem to mind ... "

La La & Debbie inched farther into the back.

Portly eyed his friend seriously.

"Well, I used to know this Iranian chap downtown. But I don't know where the devil he got to. But what about this taser idea? Can't you just get on the Internet & download the appropriate instructions?"

Portly sounded out every syllable, thereby underlining their importance in the cosmopolitan sense.

"Or can't you ask your friend with the police?"

Radiovoice played with moustache & glasses for a moment, his eyes like those of an elderly crustacean, crinkling & twinkling in the escapement of sunlight from shifting overcastness.

"I think we should just be able to put the furry little suckers out of their misery. A pellet gun would be much better. Exterminate the brutes."

He came to this conclusion cheerily & with his glass raised to his anticipant lips.

"What about Targét," tried Portly, rather warily.

"O, the store. You mean Target," corrected Radiovoice, smugly rubbing some steam from his glass with his pointing finger.

"But in Canada, we prefer to pronounce it as *Tarjay*," rejoined Portly with his own brand of smugness.

A diminutive shadow crossed both of their faces.

"Afternoon, gentlemen."

"Why, good afternoon, Roachin," chortled Portly.

"Sorry about our sluggishness today. We're just on the butt end of a wake."

Radiovoice rubbed his hands together.

"Just in time, Roachin. How about a glass of water for old time's sake?"

The little pirate woman smiled cautiously.

"Yeah okay. But you know, water's for plants."

Salt Chip Boy

"Umsglubgug ..."

—Robert Anton Wilson

ling ling

Logos RJ-45 lolled out a lone verbal of graveyard. No. There was other. K arose, now aroused but still minimum agrog.

"Ling ling!"

K refreshed. Whazük?

"LING LING!"

"Lang," he leisurely deviced.

"Salutations y mucho recriminations! Cumple on, Citizen K! This hour clicks your inception! Many felicitous returns!"

Vox was shadowed by a blaring toccata.

"Zük," he boomboxed back, drumming it down. "I'm online nanos ago."

Then K muted. Lost in neurot, he projected CLEANSE n so it was. He even allocated another Marsec to reverb before he genied out, smooth n sleek to rovings. Not long after first click of graveyard. He clovedly ungnarled alpha limb n tactiled his. Skin. Uhgn. Tray Sesh. Logos, *n verbal was made life.* So his chip chirpily sloganed. So it was.

K genied out of dome n counterclocked across circuits of jumpstarted nox. Apparitioned longer each diurnal, longer n longer. Niet! Redundancy RD-69ME droned on, recycling stray neurots. K muted this small muse n janned into levy. Woo woo woo woo!

"Salve ... Señor K. Tangentially, mucho recriminations!"

Doubles parted n he penetrated Pent Cloud-99, physical.

"Salve, Señor K!"

Vox. Ubikay? A minute figure aped out of Bureatia. Corridor, slash n burn Arcade. Spoor! That novel Friday.

"Salve ... my bad. Oblivioned your handle."

"O. Input Delphi 7.0 Meridian Stellar Nova the Twenty-third. Locals interface me D. Premater dinged the crooner. Shuttled to Plutonimoanium Nine to spectate him special. Short consume. She was maximum dwarf in those petulant x/60s."

K attained PAUSE. He sussed high level of hubris in this upstart internal. Prognostication: long diurnal imminent.

metropolis

Rosea. K sank via levy n hovered out heavily. Finite skytrams zeeped by. Finale, K hooked one. He beeped, while skytram line YLLALRT-3FT salvaged n junked his buffer. Hardlucks were initiating spamjack postamscray.

"Vandime? Surplus vandime to supplement? Got transience? Rendayvoo. A quirk zük. Vandime a ride, Bucky."

Access n transfer. K was en route. Skytram feelers cubbied him quirkly. Solaris rayed each rider n each was bronzed n lovely to scope n all were scanning a chain of mountains. Mountains. K glossed that word. They apparitioned steeper n plus jagged. Maximum high. He prepared himself, ere projecting UNVISOR. Mountains eroded. Solaris faded. Grey smog snogged in. Zow. K projected RETINAL MASSAGE n attained minute relief. His lids flicked with vitez. He wanted. Affirm *wanted.* He wanted to scan grey about whizzing girders. Additive others, cubbied, however mountaineering. He wanted to hardcopy ... unvisored.

"Confirm affirm?"

Pressure clamped his temples.

"No," cast K, projecting VISOR. Déjà, bronzed n lovely denizens returned. Mountains menaced.

"Proximate Metropolis."

Skytram zeeped to stop. Feelers unfurled his ball of flesh n unhooked him. K floated out over volumed platform.

"Velkommen Metropolis. You are here."

K janned inside n conveyered by stream of floaters. Delay later, triangulator handshaked his chip, intensifying low level span. Metropolis was realized n so it was, affiliating with Logos RJ-45. He visualized other metrovermin. Absorbed by last minute images, bending n flexing n blanking their nanobanks. Some minimum scanned their pathways. Metropolis lefted them. Autotons gested behind gallery fields. Queried with multiferous devices.

Kuh. Kuh. Spoor. K projected UNVISOR. He scanned lumpish denzien in dim corner. She zippity vipped her silver form to pallid neck, manholing accountable scars. Then her visor clamped shut. Realtime, K was bizt. Kuh! Kuh!

"Ack contact?" K acked request.

"Andro, we gotta be technocrossed. Syntoxic. Handle?"

"Affirm," rebounded K. "Input Kardio."

She uploaded happiness.

"Savoury, Kardio. My clone name is Kamute. Contrary handle me Kathleen. Dayold affirmative."

"No," rebounded K. "Fresh piping. Inciter down."

"Negative. Vidoed this ere realtime. Permits abrogation if accompany? If perform compatibles. Mind?"

K uploaded accordance.

"Pleasure. Option me in."

Xstasia

The railing was thick & strange underneath his fingertips. Everything cried out in a tongue of its own, cried out a name. *Wood,* the railing clanged. *Railing,* the wood creaked. All in their own way, each beneath his fingertips. It was pleasant to walk in this body upon a short pathway towards a tall gate. He stopped to examine the blades of grass that he passed, wondering at them as much as the nameless weeds in the alleyway cracks. He felt his mind subside & each translation became clearer. Soon, I will be totally immersed. I must try to forget what each word means, or what it meant. His feet felt sore in his sneakers. Sore! *Sore* as they walked upon the concrete. Here, everything felt wonderfully incomprehensible.

There was a patch of rust along the grates of the gate. He touched it slowly, allowing it to colour & scratch his fingernails & the palm of his hand. He started, hearing a foreign noise. He turned around to watch a shiny vroom drive by, slowly manoeuvring over the uneven terrain of the alleyway. He was astonished by its clunky motion, wondering what kind it was. Clunky. An old clunker. He liked the sound of that. Then he heard another. He noticed that he was standing near a courtyard behind the gate & that a door had opened. A woman stepped out, pulling the door closed & turning her key in the lock. She walked a few paces towards the gate. Then she stopped, turned back & tested the doorknob. Yes. It was locked. He smiled to himself. Yes, that was a nice touch alright. He eased back behind a wall covered with green overgrowth. She did not see him. He waited a moment, before peering around the wall. She was heading in the direction of a nearby copse. She walked at a brisk pace through a pair of cedars. He started to walk behind her, keeping at a distance on the same trail. He was very conscious of the movements of her body, as well as his own. It was a summery day & his blood was on fire & his heart was pumping as he kept sight of her along the path of gravel & wooden shavings. Everything smelled wonderful & his body felt strong & whole. Before long, she had arrived at her destination. She was wearing these thin fabrics he had never seen before. At least not in his monitored life. He tried not to think of that. As she sat on a scorched log, he was distracted by the scattering of ants & then something else & then the mild ripples of water. Water. He licked his dry lips & watched those hypnotic undulations, illuminated by intense sunlight. Then he turned his eyes back to the woman, who was standing up in the light which brightened her dark hair. Without hesitation, she removed her top & then her shorts. He saw the way they softly crumpled upon a dry stump in the sunlight. He also saw the full shape of her naked body slowly wading into the water, splashing her reflection about until the water rose to her throat. She turned around in the water & looked right at him, knowing all.

"Hello," she called out. "What's your name?"

"You know my name," he said.

"Yes," she wailed. "But don't be a spoilsport. Any name will do."

"Then Karl."

They studied one another hungrily.

"I'm Kathleen," she said at last. "I'm rather old-fashioned, you'll find. I love the woods & water. I feel so alive here, so near to nature. Why don't you try it? Come into the water. I know you want to. Why don't you come into the water?"

Karl watched her watching him. He could feel everything in this magnificent body. Everything was beckoning. But he reached for his temples first, wondering what the chip would think. Kathleen made a face.

"Don't worry about *that*. It won't hurt anything. It feels so good. Come into the water, Karl. Come into the water with me."

In response, Karl meekly stripped & started to wade into the water. She watched him, keeping silent. Her hazel eyes seemed to glint green in the sunlight. The water was cool to his warm skin. He took time to enjoy this sensation before swimming out towards her. As soon as he reached her, their hands became busy searching & exploring one another, fondling elbows & squeezing shoulder blades & caressing buttocks in a writhing mass of robust limbs. Their lips touched & they meticulously tasted each other. This was almost too much for Karl & he suddenly felt the need to option out. Kathleen sensed this & held his body fast, kissing him harder. Then he felt his limbs relax & desire supplanting his panic.

They sat in her living room. Kathleen had invited him in to take a quick shower. Karl looked up at a large frame on the mantel.

"He doesn't get me," she said quickly.

She looked at the wall, looking through the picture.

"I'm always getting left on my own. I get lonely sometimes."

She eyed him hopefully.

"Hmm," said Karl.

She walked into the bedroom. Karl followed.

"We better be quick," she said, untying her robe. "Sometimes he comes home early."

Karl felt hot all over. He felt his blood burning with jealousy & maybe rage. But it felt good to hate. To hate a stranger, no less. It felt good to feel this fury that was anything but emptiness. He opened his robe & looked down at his virtual erection, surprised by this manifest sensation. Karl always felt surprised. It was strange to have a body like this. Kathleen smiled & offered a series of expletives that made

Karl laugh. However, they also made him hot & confused & angry & hard.

"It's been so long. Give it to me, Karl. Right now! Or how about this? Is this what you like? I would *never* do this for him. Never never." Karl moaned, stroking her dark hair with both of his hands. He could feel the flesh of her shoulders & breasts being pinched beneath his fingertips. So tactile. He was surrendering to each of these sensations, particularly the thrill of overheating within the waves of her warm aural system. He stopped for a moment, his senses reeling. What had led to this biological turn of luck? He glitched the lumpish shape waiting outside in a dim corner of Xstasia. He reached down, fingering his organ tentatively, questioning its seemingly independent pleasure. Why did she want to go vintage like this?

"Hurry up," she said curtly. "Jim'll be back & he won't like it."

Closing her eyes at the thought of that, she placed her palm between her raised thighs.

"Want me to tell him you couldn't? Is that it? Wanna watch instead?"

Karl lost his temper & lunged at her. However, instead of landing upon her body or the bedspread, he hovered several inches over her.

"O yeah. A floater, hey? Jim hasn't been able to float for months."

She reached up & gripped him with her right fist, dragging him to & fro until he began to feel like one of the parade inflatables he had scanned in past archives. Satisfied with the small puddle on the ceiling, she pulled him off minimalist headboard & drew him closer. He felt her heat against his. In the archives, this action of bodies & moving buttocks always looked rather ludicrous. Yet in Xstasia, you quickly became lost in some similar activity. A sullen look had crept over Kathleen's sweating face.

"Zük me, Karl! AX / BX me, you züking trog!"

Karl obliged. Classic. They were interfacing at accelerated pace when suddenly Karl recognized the clunky wheezing sound of a vroom parking outside. A door opened & then slammed shut. Karl instantly started to float off but Kathleen's fingernails dug into his shoulders.

"No no go. Not yet … "

They both turned to see a large figure in the doorframe.

Sensorium blackened. K proffed himself unvisored. Illumined protubes iggled over grey matter. A dim noid egged his tissue from behind. Yip!

"Üte Magnus, cram to scam Xstasis? No if me, Magnus?"

Noid clinched his rivelled whelps. Yip yip!

"Omnigood? Good yearn, you vert?"

K turned to starched form of noid n ghastly big buttons.

"Arc," he flattened.

Mixer descended from synthex. Glove unvirted from Xtensions of K.

"Backword," snarled noid. "Rewind n recriminations."

Noid reverbed Xtensions n clinched female … Kamute?

"Pause. Ubikay amscray?"

Kamute salivered. Noid monstered.

"*Si fas est.* Kamute offend yonder glove. Lottery you Arc. Fifty millifigures. Contrary, she all out of keno."

Noid scruffed minute perpvert, tazing her mucho.

"O Arc! Zük me zük me you largo Arc! Alarum, ixnay assistant from züking invalids."

"Invalid," K refreshed blankly.

"Si, she invalid for double blog n smurf, negative transmit sparking."

Aftermath, they flashlighted off in a giant clamp of spoke.

K unvisored nanoly n scanned giraffe of levy n shreeling saucer of workspace. Other hist to reform. Omnigood think. He scanned holograph letters before janning into levy. A-R-C—V-A-N. Member. Mine. Instanter, D finned out n podded K, who floundered midfloat. "Üte Señor, audioed techdiff @ Metropolis." D scanned his scanner, projecting PAUSE. "Minute errance. Demarginal. Wrong handle." "Si? Üte, Arcs all get Xstassed, mucho on sojourn." "No equit," stressed K. "Wrong handle. Omnipresent, hik primary n finite Infomat."

"Hok. Si," clicked D, uberonline.

K doubledimmed.

"Esty histographx. Access feed hunk. Then app censor ... "

"[Sic] censor," glowed D.

"Hmm," nurfed K.

He notioned n images n microtxt were inkblotted n substituted. D overshouldered heppedly as noids n firstbloods were blackboarded out n digiswapped with authorizers or plainspeak nil. Handle *Red River* was rebaptized Siltwash Straight n googleyed firstblood was percentiled n cleansed.

"Propodata inputs hunk. Hunk is netted n apped, solike."

"Ganda," boomboxed D, maximum unplugged.

"Sweatshop."

D radiated accord. K highthreaded n projected D into glibstream, mucho felicitated to sever connect. Neurots flooded his inputs. He barred thru blits n microtxt. But query bugged n glitched. Ubikay she amskray? East DT probstat 93.5% Non neurot ample 6.5%. If blogger or smurfer, she busted n vamoosed East DownTime, substratum in Zero Occupancy Zone. K spazzed. He never unlevied down to ZOZ. Contra, he audioed random feed in WestVille, proximate peripheria of VanCom. Ratio upside. Non denominator. ZOZ teemed with UnOrgs, circa broadband contention with Norms. UnOrgs inked Wordloss in exilio. Such K audioed. ZOZ was mega gateway for Hepstance n other materia to fix for bitblitters. Spacialwise, ZOZ ran maintenance for cells of bloggers n smurfers negative transmit sparkers n blank accounts.

Arcboot. K linked partition via partition. Sector nunc. Blit of Stalemate Sq. Visualize. Precipitation factor 15.6%. Rain taboo section x9883 sub 73 incompatible interface for logos.

"Selfanalparalysis," admonished chip.

Unnormal obelisk. K gambitted addon n scanned blit ere query refuse bin.

"Nonprod percentile 99.8%."

K zeroed censor dump access xx1231237. Ebb Marsecs. Chip sterned up. K flacked xcess blits. Acknow rush blood shift slash nerve fit. Vittoria! Vittoria! Koral shant in jollitum. Victory equivalency percentile casualty. Victory squared. Victory glossed. The dead. Visor dimmed. Wipers on. Chip reverbed. Resume neural garden. Recon path. Reboot cogsense.

gigagig island

Flex. K roved about rapidum. Nonhabitual data break. Subito K nerved volition for contact visa inuit intuit. Sole font for interface was inuit Istomene Glowering. What he voxed *old vhs*. Temporal misindexed his torqued lexicon. Inuits qualified for extrapolar extirpation within nanos of lithium loss. *Eskimo* was antique gloss to unplug elders n portage total data into white noise. Istomene roosted iridose condome with standard law Shelley. K scraped up mucho vigilant of grats. *Gigagig Island of the Mind* transferred marquee from mean x/70's. Antique teeth. Bloated grat pterapped by. Deficate but no wirebite. Isto[his handle trunked] divined *gulls* n *rats* pastwise n random. Access process of *natural evolution*. Oldentime Isto triangled Island in *superb* hoist. Grats be scours of joisters. Bite wires like articles. Nosh you up 50/50 percentile you stay online. Nosh vitals of carp you ask. Affirm *those glutty spointy rabirds*.

"Heeeeey!" Isto warmed ante fanned.

"K! Machininator. Oot. Ticker und hip half licked."

K readjusted. Scope *rusty*. Isto downtowned *strange* ling. K queried chip executive sum.

"Spare parts!"

Shelley materialed.

"Rationale for lift," she handshaked in cityspeak.

"Info re:oldentime." Isto chartled.

"Quoi I reaccess acronyms! Fudge n beer recollect Shell? Antonym you deny. Jongleurs n dramaspeak ante speakword. Then murders of grats gulleted them. We etched über them Manuals … "

Shelley tapped his repo flat.

"Newbie! Upstream demand spamless."

Isto spindled then machinated.

"Affirm."

"Victory Sq," pressed K.

Isto klacked then throttled.

"Urmmm not channelled Victory in untallied threads n slices."

"Not to vortex … ere Gigagig Island conflict ubied. Freeloves interfaced in Victory Sq. Hardlucks donkeyed on *grass* n *nettles*. Boarders traversed surface. Happyheads toked n unplugged not like these blitbitters omnipresent … "

Isto snaked round.

"Like grats ideas in things shift hey non optimal outcome. Allusional hesterna singledawn Sextus traipsed nostos in oblivion. Tickwise they bitblitted beyond obliviot stream grinding balks of fishbone n elementals."

"Victory Sq renaited Stalemate Sq via fibreneural," conjoined Shelley.

"I is forgettable. They stoned in drew out megawords in metatype. Then contention. Tendrils retissed out n omni left was charcoaled jaws. Remain refrain of demolished brokenword. *Is it nothing to you.* Boots me antique tech to reaccess that!"

K refreshed at alien monolog n attained cogsense nonewise.

obelisk

Steep. Even grats n crag doves elevate over film likewise. K spasmed in Stalemate Sq. Obelisk was fraktled n laurel of UnOrgs. Kristalice-capmemjack. Bitblitters n Intprops trassled K.

"Yen gig just a gig spare drive get gigalitzed! Katablogs get nil interface esta! Commod fresh liquid transact!"

K bypassed debrits n accounted blanks. *Stone woman* n *green dome* in uptimal lapse. He hummeled in grate n by dims of alloyrinth. Slash arrays of zubber n teel. Datacheck. Mega automort high percentile fume bind. Classify *drive* verbal usage. Scour lex. Ionic n Doric awning. Obsidian cornice n ash arabesque. Glass disavowed under pain of. Sub canvas. Scan infernal engines n roar of nutterblits. Ack neurochem input. Environ estimate toxicologic. Stimuli scan eternal pinball lightup of metaframe re: *the soul* fuel inflect n just additional blit pre inforoad.

Neon awning. Hulks. Soft focus bullet of dive. Lobefeed redux of *colourless green apple sleep furious.* Swilling blades. Seahorse n ovaltine infect buddha jollity. Gardens haunted. UnOrgs swamping. Circuit Scouts n Headwipers plugged into retro Skullspace hunting beam.

"Dig levy? Base salary 8K pyramids of inventory. 38K prism. Wreq: digitson intangible."

K unvisored primal. Feral narine. Transjects. Grey faces all glowed up by mimeogaffes. Total hardware. Slimline n swarty prime musist sensored over.

"Honour they handle me Ackmod."

Searches tag pneumatic n antique music. Scourge of Westville. Engage presently. Ackmod wiretapped K. Excrutiate.

"Baroque device. Antonio avec *Summer.* Or mayhap monsir desire in atonal manifest. Audio este. Manta quaint."

K wafted off extratemporal.

"O," skulked Ackmod. "Was toff in transit?"

K hivered. Ackmod was blitnab. Chip diluted into signalmasses. K tremored bluescreen. Arc swap rilled both. Visor of Ackmod hazed. Case of image famine. Ackmod oblonged edge of unspawned dessicant awry from chip. Shant of antilog n logrhythms.

"Tempo K. Groove in with we. Zük factory spazz. Finger E flat n F sharp minor a minute gift from Johnny S Bach."

K audioed *praeludium drops of lost rain pellucid n echoes of empty.* Kromatic levy then tonic return. K inverted. *Woman like stone* frag free to plash. F sharp progress in pulmones. Meditatio. Crooness divas self. Digits autoplunk *soft.* Her. She rerun.

"Subject creeps F sharp to C sharp inexorable sink. Doubleclock two notes countersing. Climax then reiterate. Sublime mellow West-Villager."

"F," adhocked K. "F n Subdwells?"

Transjects n hulks radared handle. Ackmod rizzled.

"F sharp on account she finger it sublime nay subliminal. Token upload consensual portage." Transject set interrupt.

"Advert that wire hortiscan? Bluebox that blank n handle tiff-taff?"

Ackmod clustered n blinged him sober mega mimeogaffe. "Prick up, gif. Treat this arc stylewise. Or access minor Shönberg on cottoncandy wideload! Or twisted rib sonata? Strikes temporal for Ludwig. Megaripe. Seven. Allegretto ... "

K projected QUIETUS otherlimb hooked n threaded into Meccavox of Ackmod. Chords twizzled cells n vox subsistered.

"Amicus uncover pit proximate. F sharp key n signature validate rebate while quantitude lingers."

gastroboar

Spectral grey spire fire n autoziggurat mirage of Gastroboar gleaned for unsubscribed. Gloated nairy hardlucks anted about Crag Dove Park. Bitblitters roached n klacked mutual. K sensored mescalinos across visor n siecle heartstarts in audiomit. Then K visualized antilogos: *word GREEN* ere entrance. Brick n wood. Schmattered potscram. Figure flicked. Minor marquee. F Sharp buttoned Erebus.

"Darkly they went through dark dark."

Charm. Unflawed simcast. She. F Sharp. Tall silverwhite skin. Utensilish stare unglittered. Minute mimeogaffe on cheek. K examed ixnay of organic flux. Denied.

"Nunc is inception."

F grizzed.

"O cumple on! Thimble gratis."

Chip restablish process. Logos was unrelayed. Tarded. Dark materia. Glass. K scanned sulfuric eyes. She weirded at him. *Jettatura.* Then he siphoned oblique.

"Zük chip," he sacrilevered.

Fleshshimmer at thresh hallugen blit degraded green green *stairs* furious. Peasoup liminal crosspatch. K paused. Forwarded. Adjust to reiterate blit. Chip prohibit field of reals. Eyes. Coldhot absinthe comfort fodder. Acid rain blig. Project past into past. Dark dark. F Sharp was undertown referent. K aspired übik. Greyscape. Silvergreen n bluethrob vein. Smart black dark black eke silverblue. Quantum non ego sum. Hook hat hung up. Fix credo. Dreck logo. Soma data departation. For figurehead hellish swap. Inc dec. Begin end. Fantasm plus plus. Ling abandon hinc. Greywhit print. Drawn up. Green green antilogos green *stairs* n *railing.* Brick. ConneX then unconneX. Vox. Mystic n etheric. Scan astrocrab. Vox. K crumped nilward. ID: replica of tarned *bed.* Brass. Cubby over. Touch. Horritable horns wonderlust touch. Vocabulate!!! Additional additional additive. F Sharp plunked onto splintered bench n keyed fatal progress. Undertownsavvy. Roadwise, Ackmod schizzled.

"Affirm you perceive glastnost. Mean as neckbolt twitch. Tetchy n spannerish likewise."

She progressed. Hammered each mute. K regressed n rolled fetal. Silver pedalled grey. Flesh manufractured flesh. Antilog … Key torted. Score autovandalled. K scrunted beastish. F F F sharp. She sank unto CX then DX. K grinced like oldentime lock. He unvisored n unfolded member by member. Vox stressed. Gignon jettatura jinx green whiteblue silverwhite flish. Log on leg over omnipresent. Telessence resonance n static. Seudochagrin wirewise. Attenuate inkflesh. Rabbit silverwhite signal marked down instanter. Logo imprint. Passage. Tag online. Motion from pulp to phat reportage. K lipped bed of dark sheets. Antique. Chipsputterrrr. Wordflow up ankle n wristline. Vox. She husked into eargrass green on porperous wet conch. Sea. Si si si. She crooned minute n sirenish. K frazzled for heart n lung. Chip no

69

kaput inputwise. F Sharp strapped on input n swift withdrewloaded.
Banks n blits sflopped on bed. Vox. Withdrew data. Wildsalmoned
WestVillewise. Vox. Folders of Arc spewed unto musicologic nautea.
Unload. Breathe n release. Si si si O si. Laaaaaaaaaaaaaaaa. *O to green-
space to meet at the little park on 14th & Pine.* Ecolog line infused. K
sensored grey flesh marked fragile. Si non si. Feral savage uncaged.
Gone allegorical after inum nanos. K uprighted. Drained. Chip down.
Solo antilogos. Negative. Solo logos. A *word.* F Sharp sardonized him.
Her word. K thumbled physical n lilypadded out. Green ta ta. Grey-
elbowed n bluekneed harsh cogglestone.

ohmward

Hic word dataflooded circuits. Hoc vox. Installation of *long.* I long?
K was on minimal react. Chip was demisputtered. K relogged her
guidance relays. He chagalled by natches of UnOrgs with obliterates.

"Nostos twonk Villager!"

Stelps n scurdles. Nostos. Ubikay? Vox. Worded about lobes.
Fauna. He subrouted her diexis. Canem bark. Kamute had expired.
He synced her oblizt. But F Sharp had achieved neural wipe n
inrooted new lexicon. Chromastutter. He registered optimal flush.
Blank accounts had amskrayed to ripe verdance. She savvied fact n
bartered a low rez upc. Once chip was stilted user could wack into
slushield n update access. F Sharp n Subdwells sang of Artivice n
greenworld n word beyond logos. Mythologic. A greenspace of Ohms.
They dwelled in Fauna via calumnia. Ohms. Tall n silverwhite n
potent. Oogle them. Venn them. F Sharp had sussed his grey
shoulderflesh. Look froward. No more rewind.

"Ling ling!"

"Citizen K."

"Passcode?"

"Green green 1984."

"I cannot do that K cannot suss why why why green green green green 1984."

"Arc Citizen K. Today is my inception."

Interface channeled antidata strain n adverted clearance.

"Salutations y mucho recriminations! Cumple on ... "

Then local manifest of Logos RJ-45 lolled out a lone verbal of graveyard n warrantied outward in mega divide by nil syntax errance.

salt

K proferred upc n auralled yeasty click. Autonon. K leaned feebrile on antique *revolver* n ultimate resultant truffed it free. Thhhhhhhunkkkkk!!! Glass joisted him down on grass. Ahhhhhrrrrhowoooooooooo. K sensored lungs inflatus. Oxidation. Nostrilled skank. Spool. Witnessed in blits. Subito uninterfaced beast pterapped over him on black sign. Scan *Comox Street*. K autocoveted under bush in mortal. Chip jammed. Some type of avian? Avian rapped up to tall blum. Mucho avians beaked voluminous. Grand avians bent blums. In mega nidos immature avians divided rodentia. K spindled away sans feedback. *Water. Sea.*

F Sharp had mercanted dark unction of dissonance. K fell on grass. Debilitate. Ubikay she plunked keys. *This one is for Salt Chip Boy.* K levied unction n bouleversed gross mead. Skald. Fire. Elemental. Words gracked livid. F Sharp was fantasma dream vocab. She glushed through the veins of K. *Logos is dead. The chip of your inception is nothing anymore. The dessicant is about to expire. I am your radio now, so listen to me Kardio & listen well. You must be very weak this tick. Come into the water. You must come into the water. There is water everywhere for you to drink. You must drink it & live. I know I must sound ugly but this is the old way they sticktalked, all epic with overlong utterances. Drink the mead. You will forget the city & even the floating*

71

world & Fauna will become your home. The chip that fed your body with salt is dead. You must come into the water. I will even sing to you. Only you must come into the water. The Ohms will soon find you. They will help you. & take care. Watch out for pterons!

Kardio felt the phrases electrifying his mentality. Words were springing out of untapped regions. His head hurt. The chip had limited with its intelligent design. It had tried to ixnay his possible evolution, what the dream of Kathleen & F Sharp had shown him. He limped toward the water, falling upon the shore. Sand. This is sand. Exhausted & feeling near death, he still marvelled at the feeling of it against his grey flesh. He rolled over & lay prone where the water lapped toward him. His visor was now shattered & broke open easily from his bleeding skin. Light. Sand. Blood. Glass. Fire. I am on fire. Light tried to access his eyes. Water. In spite of his exhaustion, Kardio felt invigorated by the rush of oxygen into his lungs. He could hear F Sharp in a distant diminuendo & he knew he was not alone. It was as if he could hear her pulse in his ears. & her mesmerizing voice. *Mar, mare, mère.* He was being reborn into this language. Then Logos was dead. He needed only this baptism of salt & water. Hence, he cupped the sea in his palm & drank. Kardio heaved himself off the shore & felt his frail grey body submerged in the water. He panicked at first & paddled frantically about with aching joints. Then he found himself floating with some difficulty, lapping at the saltwater all the while. Alive. It was not long before the stillness of that ancient place was disturbed by a single word upon the lips of a man set adrift upon the silvergrey waves of a mild afternoon. Utterly jubilant, his voice gurgled to life through a mouthful of saltwater.

"DEAD!!!"

Two Scoops

Benway steps back and holds up the chocolate.
The man drops to his knees, throws back his head and barks.

—William S. Burroughs

Beneath a dense collection of cherry blossoms, Candice Coton knocked on the dry panel of wood. She glanced up at a rubric of faded spray paint the colour of spent charcoal. DE/BUNKER, the sign might have screamed in its heyday, but now only buzzed faintly like a faded newspaper headline. Candice (Candy to her friends) turned her attention back to the cherryosity of her immaculate nails & the formal placement of her babysitter/schoolgirl/spirited cheerleader skirt, arranging a sufficient flounce of plaid. Above, a tree of red & black sneakers dangled from the telephone wires & the blowing blare of noon was no reminder that the sun was overhead & rather warm. Her crisp white blouse opened to a proportionally represented bronze, or depthless brown & she was happy at the honks & catcalls speeding past & standing at 5'8" she was perfectly able to take in her perfect stature & the way a single button was perfectly holding together a snug & letterless scarlet cardigan that accentuated her arresting 36–25–35 figure in the side panels & tinted glass of the obsidian vehicle. As two fingered whistles persisted, a nuclear Chinese family passed, the parents with their two children, a boy & a girl of about five years each.

"SUV," the boy shouted with excitement.

The father smiled with pride, nodding politely at Candy as his wife gave him a severe look.

"Son, do you know what SUV stands for?"

But Candy had no time to hear the end of *that* informative lecture. She had work to do. She returned her attention to the dry panel & gave it the shove of any truly intrepid reporter or neighbourhood busybody. A satisfying creak.

"Hello?"

She whispered since you could always say O I shouted hello I shouted & shouted & nobody could hear me. She peered though the open panel, which appeared to be a hingeless door into a garage or basement suite. She adjusted her dark thick frames. The bunker, as she had determined this place to be, was a tornado of paper, a confused vision of books, schematics, diagrams, reports, photocopies, journals, old clippings, & a number of unidentifiable objects. Inching deeper into this sterile whirlwind of grey & white, she observed a number of circuitboards & mysterious wires that disappeared behind panoplies of paper. A few of the books were completely unreadable, looking like Michelin tire tracks of type had run over every page in all directions. Other inkblottered pages lay in virtual shreds.

"Hello?"

She tapped one of her long cherryred nails upon an open text, accidentally knocking a roll of Indubitable-Tape to the floor.

> Because of communication asynchrony and unreliability, a controlling agent could never have complete and up-to-date information on the state of the systems. In such sense the system is *decentralized.*

Candy perused several of the open tomes, readily cramming her mind with unprocessed phrases & inaccessible vocabularies, since the forgetfulness of facts involved simply a gradual decay in weights measured as W_{ij} when given the connection between neurons N_i & N_j when given the alteration of the signal strength as inconstant, variable or the diagrams showcasing image thresholding, the process of low-level vision which involved the convolution theorem (but of course!) & nine numbers in a 3x3 square but what the heck was a Sobel mask sounds pretty kinky to me & that is pretty.

In the first step, the crossover operation that recombines the bits (**genes**) of each two selected strings (**chromosomes**) is executed.

10101 1001 10011
10101 1110 10011

The second step in the genetic manipulating process is termed **mutation**.

"Far out," thought Candy out loud, tracing the pretty arrows.

Composite molecules in which foreign DNA has been inserted into a vector molecule are sometimes called DNA *chimaeras* because of their analogy with the Chimaera of mythology—a creature with the head of a lion, body of a goat and the tail of a serpent. The construction of such composite or *artificial recombinant* molecules has also been termed *genetic engineering* or *gene manipulation* because of the potential for creating novel genetic combinations by biochemical means. The process has also been termed *molecular cloning* or *gene cloning* because a line of genetically identical organisms, all of which contain the composite molecule, can be propagated and grown in bulk, hence *amplifying* the composite molecule and *any gene product whose synthesis it directs.*

Candy felt her mind reeling with these strange expressions in tiny italics, like *cloning vehicles,* like *foreign or passenger DNA,* like *plasmids,* like *vectors,* or like *bacteriophages* ew gross like gag me. Of course she had heard of *syntax,* at least of a syntax error, or of *semantics.* Didn't she use that word all the time? Hadn't she posed that question before on separate occasions with varying success to respective professionals & political leaders? She remembered lovingly reviewing tapes of past interviews.

"But isn't that just a matter of *semantics*?"

Then she would peer over her dark frames & lean forward slightly & the interviewee would be relatively floored.

"That's all well & good but we're not talking *semantics* now."

That was another good one. But what was all this stuff about *fuzzy reasoning* or *fuzzy Petri nets*? A self-referential knowledge base? Candy stifled a yawn with her bright fingers. She blinked at the textbook on her lap, trying to fathom the meaning of the sentences which were part of extensive analysis.

"The milkman lays packets full of milk in the corridor."
[MILKMAN] lays [PACKETS] full of [MILK] in the [CORRIDOR]

In addition to the indecipherable information regarding each word, Candy noticed that someone had written the word SOY in red ink directly above the word milk. I guess that is better for you.

"I see you are getting acquainted with my friends, Minsky & Chomsky. Unless you are, I mean, already familiar with those great names?"

Breath. Golden well-coifed hairs stood fuzzily & uncooperatively upon the bronzed nape of Candy's neck.

"I trust you are Dr. Juan de Fuca Cuiller de Kanada."

Broad smile. Very very white.

"Call me Dr. F, or just F. Evrrrrybudddy does!"

Smoothing vivacious mane behind her ears for effect, she offered her palm.

"I'm Candy Coton, from channel EFM. We spoke on the phone."

"Ah yes, I'm rather absent-minded sometimes. I almost completely forgot about the interview. Forgive me. Lovely to make your acquaintance, Miss Coton, & how I hope it is Miss Coton!"

"O Doctor, stop!"

"So you've come to spy on me?"

An enormous chortle issued from the depths of F, who was rather debonair for a diminutive greasy man with a touch of liverspotting. He picked up the roll of Indubitable-Tape from the floor & examined it thoughtfully.

"This stuff holds cars together."

Candy smoothed hair & skirt again. I will not chew the end of my pen, she smoothed, with a broad smile. She cleared her throat, talking around the half-life of a decaying mint & narrowing her gaze over those intelligent black frames.

"Chiefly, I am interested in the nature of your scientific work. Word is, you have received a large grant from Indian Affairs in order to continue your research. I am sure the question on taxpayer's minds is how your research project will affect their lives, daily or in the future, & whether there's the validity for such a huge allocation of public funds. What about healthcare & education, for instance? Or the economy?"

F stroked his greasy black & grey beard with interest, saying nothing.

"In addition, there are pressing concerns on a startling number of reservations, where there is an alarming mortality rate, due chiefly to drug & alcohol consumption. I guess the question is, in the face of public funds being directed to your project & perhaps being diverted from these other vital cultural centres, will your project address these concerns, or merely leave those people in the cold?"

F rubbed his hairy hands together & smiled through his beard.

"O but you shall see firsthand, Miss Coton!"

"Call me Candy, please."

"Candy," he repeated with a slight lisp & tip of tongue in corner of smile. She took the taupe chair he offered her in front of a large ebony box with electrical hazard signs all over it.

"Word is, F," she prodded cheekily, "your work is worth millions."

She crossed her legs with determination & looked over her black frames at the doctor, expectantly.

"Well, Candy," purred F, stroking his greasy goatee, "it is quite simple. Funny how we say things like that. Nothing is ever simple. All my work & research involves the intersection where technology & the human mind come together. The way in which we talk & learn is known as our cognitive process & of course there are well established models of such behaviour. There have been different models … "

He trailed off, rubbing mouth & beard.

"With engineered human cells becoming more & more the norm, it is only a matter of time before we develop a computational model which can consistently interact with our own, um, god-given models. & may I say yours is very fine, Candy."

He stroked his greasy beard a little harder. She smiled, flirting back, a tad disoriented.

"Now, these models of cognitive amelioration, as we like to call them, have been in the works for decades."

F pointed to a rainbow diagram that was loosely pinned to the wall. CYBERNETIC COGNITION CYCLE swirled its psychedelic letters in front of her.

"The mind works rather like a laundry wash cycle. There are these two settings, if you like, one for supervised learning & another for unsupervised learning. As you can see in the diagram, the open road to unsupervised learning is quite simply raw perception. Perhaps you are unfamiliar, but there has been a plethora of generously funded research completed on the theorem of convolution. Honestly, our most open-handed contributors have been, um, advertisers. You've heard about such cases as the ice cubes that spell S-E-X, haven't you?"

"No, forgive me," answered Candy, feeling thirsty.

"Well, that is the most accessible methodology for reaching the status quo, just as your broadcasts reach a number of people who appreciate your personality & image. You are a *trusted* personality. I mean, the most accessible method is to reach the majority of people via some visceral image. Technology enters the picture here, since we have a number of subroutines to thresh the image (determining the ratio of frequency to intensity of its form). After that the psychoanalysts & phenomenologists get to play with that data & work together to hammer out new formulas which will aid our research, testing them on fresh pop samples. It has always been suspected, at least since Freud, that the parental *fuckbuddy* trigger is paramount, especially when combined with the stimuli of strangely coloured vegetables. The threshed image already has a source surface, chosen for its immediate level of visceral stimulation. Yet it retains a certain *je ne sais quoi* of pixelate patterns beneath the surface which enter the retina & form minute impulses within the brain of the sharpest & dullest subjects alike. Philosophically, this technique embodies the antithesis of your average work of art that also seeks to stimulate action in the viewer. On the contrary, the advert is designed to pacify the viewer for an indeterminate amount of time & quell any residual instincts to waste energy in what we deem to be unprofitable activity. The advert instills the volition in the viewer for a specific form of action, thus creating a latent desire that directly relates to an arbitrary object, say the product in question. This very act of purchasing power is a form of subduing the Action & Planning stages of the brain's cognition cycle & instead promoting the Acquisition cycle to take the position of the Action stage. Now here you see a cognitive map of facts, where the +/- signs are indicative of how increasing & decreasing facts relate to one another in the human brain ... "

He was nearly whispering now, pointing greasily at another open tome.

"Whoa," thought Candy out loud, tracing out the cognitive map for Middle East Peace with her bright nail, which she would remember in precisely the following arrangement:

$$(-) A (+)$$

B <-   -> F

(-)

$$(+) -> C <----- E <- (+)$$
$$(-) -> D <- (-)$$

A   Islamic Fundamentalism

B   Soviet Imperialism

C   Syrian Control of Lebanon

D   Strength of Lebanese Government

E   PLO Terrorism

F   Arab Radicalism

(-) Decreasing Effect

(+) Growing Effect

"If we refer back to the convolution theorem, we can estimate how complex a series of signals actually is for our senses to receive them & communicate them & develop into perceptions, which are based on all the relations they share among themselves, whether it be as primitive a sensation as pain or merely a *feeling* one develops about a situation based on the information one has obtained. You see, Candy, when you *get an idea*, or *solve a problem*, or have a *memorable experience*, you create something we shall call for lack of a better word, a K-line. This K-line gets connected to those *mental agencies* that were recently active, ie. which were involved in the memorable mental event. This same K-line is later *activated* by the appropriate stimulus, thus creating a partial mental state that resembles the original state of mind. Sadly, the problems we ran into with our earlier experiments always involved a lack of communicability. The forerunner of our current research was known as Project Wonderland, because we required our subjects to ingest our latest batches & our motto was DRINK ME. You may have seen one of our taste test challenges on a streetcorner near you."

Candy licked her lips & nodded with enthusiasm.

"Well, we had a number of methods & as I said, the advertisers are very interested in obtaining such information. In any case, to overcome this hurdle in our research, this is what we have come up with!"

He swept his hand in a large arc about the room, pointing at nothing in particular.

"I don't see anything," Candy confessed.

F's eyes began to gleam & he fondled his beard with increasing vigour.

"That's just it, empty space! What you do not see is in fact an airborne particle, a floating neuron which acts with the properties of something you might call H_2O."

"O," interjected Candy. "I did take biology, Doctor."

"Of course you did," he soothed as she smoothed.

His eyes were clearly enjoying her perplexed 36–25–35 figure & his tongue was evidently glued to mouth corner.

"Of course you did. But with Project Looking Glass, there is no need for the subject to ingest the particle. The subject will in all probability be affected if she comes even remotely close to the particle, within a few metres of it. You will not be surprised to know that our motto for this project is not DRINK ME, but THINK ME! Our trademark name is *The Gap Gene*, since it eases its way into that crowd of confusion in the human brain & um, well provides some direction, if you will. In fact, we have distilled it into spray form & are currently testing its efficacy via the application of its customized coating to certain products."

Candy blinked.

"Let me show you what I mean. Look at this picture & if you can manage, let your mind go blank as you look at it." F held up an old copy of *Vague* in front of her eyes for only one or two seconds. Then he pulled it away with the motion of a conjurer performing his final trick. O that was the look then I remember it well.

"What gives, Doc?"

F scowled, a tad disapprovingly.

"Quick, Candy, what do you feel like?"

Candy shrugged & looked around the room while running her fingernails along the imitation leather strap bandoliered across her chest & reaching into that supple bag for her compact & a fresh stick of Indelible. Peach, to be precise. F nodded with a wealth of understanding in his eyes, appearing for all the world like a concerned father, studying her every movement & stroking his small greasy beard.

"You see, you hesitated. That split-second of hesitation is the interval necessary for activation of & what is more, the impetus, the driving motivation for the invention of *The Gap Gene.*"

Candy nodded abstractly, reapplying peach to her full lips.

"Look at the magazine more closely. Don't worry. I won't take it away this time."

Candy felt a sense of relief when he said that & returned her gaze to the glossy albeit much-abused cover.

"Although this cover is already composed of millions of colours, more than are discernible to the naked eye, we have … "

F paused to lick the corner of his mouth & rub his hands together gleefully.

"We have come up with something quite special, I think you'll find. Instead of the airbrushed & typically doctored pixels you are used to bypassing when you see a magazine cover, we have replaced them with a series of voluminous pixels. But these are no mere voxels. They would result in a barely noticeable raised edge, which would only cry havoc with the blind. & in case you are wondering, my querisome friend, we are already working on tactile & aural & even intestinal editions for the sensually challenged. But first things first. In order to initiate stimulation of the viewer, it was necessary to create a focal point within the layout of the magazine cover that would remain virtually invisible, yet retain the viewer's attention."

F stopped & smiled, shaking his head from side to side.

"Sad, isn't it, how people never pay attention anymore."

"What," said Candy.

"With this magazine cover, I know, I know, it's only a prototype, but with this cover, we decided to concentrate on the mole. This may look to you & me like an ordinary, & might I add rather famous, mole on a human face. Yet if we were to make that assumption, we would both be making a rather naive supposition."

Candy blinked & stifled a yawn.

"BECAUSE," roared F with wild eyes, "THE MOLE IS NOT A REAL MOLE AT ALL!"

"Okay, Doc, I believe you. Just chill, okay."

F smiled at her & mopped his forehead, which had broken out in a sweating throbbing thing.

"My sincere apologies, Miss Coton. I must admit, I love my work! But to get back to what I was saying, the mole is in fact not a mole at all. It is a faux mole. We have used the latest developments in nanotechnology to develop voluminous pixels with powerful microscopic properties that can impress themselves upon the human brain invisibly & without an ounce of physical contact. This mole is in fact a means of transmission, a booming broadcast to the majority of young women in your respective age group. To reiterate, this mole is not a mole at all!"

Candy resisted an impulse to roll her eyes ceilingward.

"Sure, Dr. F. I realize that you have learned to fake a mole. But scientific jargon aside, what does that mean for the average Jed or Joline in the street?"

"Why not take a look for yourself?"

He held out a second copy of the same magazine in front of her face. In no time at all, the glossy cover appeared to disperse into floating dots that grew smaller & smaller. Then in its place, she could clearly see the image of the featured supermodel opening a refrigerator full of nothing but rows & rows of yoghurt & as the silver flash of the yoghurt containers gleamed, Candy felt that she could taste their sour lightweight content, that the images of peaches & cherries were coming alive in her mouth. Although she felt slightly lightheaded, it was also kind of a buzz & everything was light & ethereal in that soft focus & her head full of colourful fruit & light & good & it was good because it was light. Candy Coton sat back in her chair & took a moment to catch her breath. She had given up smoking years ago & suddenly she felt an intense craving for one just one to relax. Of course, also to keep those pesky pounds off.

"Wow, that was awesome! That was some trip, Doc! Um … I mean F."

"Indeed. The art of suggestion in advertising all began with language. Of course, language itself is suggestive, chockerblock full of meaning, without us monkeying about with it. We just want to slim it down a little. Perhaps for only nanoseconds, until the Planning stage of cognition is utterly inhibited."

F continued in that melodic voice of his while massaging Candy's shoulders.

"There is a slight delay in mental reception that occurs for the subject's active faculties. During that delay, a small cluster of neurons form a rather baboonish coalition, if for the sake of argument, we compare the brain's instinctive impulse to think with a male baboon's rutting instinct to mate, & hold those thoughts off until the correct choice is made. & then baby, we see some real fireworks!"

Candy made a mental note to buy groceries on the way home. Just a few light items. No, not heavy, not heavy at all. Light. That's right. F studied her furrowed brow carefully.

"You might be experiencing a smidgen of resistance. Perfectly natural. Perfectly."

He clucked softly to himself.

"About one out of ten subjects will experience a classic rejection of the suggestion embedded in the mole or wherever. However, one way we have of measuring our resultant & overweening success is through the club purchase program available at superstores or supermarket chains."

F winked, massaging more intensely.

"We strategically place our revised product in selected stores. Then we purchase all the consumer data for a given period. All of our *sensitive* items are flagged, you see. We have done a crosscheck with each run of data against our product development model & in each case, our projections have paled in comparison with the actual increase in sales of each *sensitive* item."

F held up a floppy chart.

"Here is the tangent of the rising curve. Once a marketing trend is set for a given product, we can saturate it with newer & more potent suggestions. You might say they are buying a real can of words. Speaking of which, you can certainly see the possibilities for alphabet soup."

Candy held her fingernails to her temples.

"No, don't fight it, there's a good girl. That will only make it worse. In addition, we came to learn that after a given number of years, in some cases less than others, the Action stage cycles down into one of utter redundancy."

F's eyes glowed with causism.

"Imagine, Candy, that you never had to worry your pretty little head about anything ever again. No more useless & unfulfilled & bitter passions! No more futile actions & aggressive outbursts! Why, it might even put an end to war. Not only that, but no more rubbish, no more perfume samples & flyers & you may have already won letters & cereal boxtops!"

At the mention of the word *cereal*, Candy could see the supermodel once again, this time sitting down to a light & nutritious & very light bowl of cereal & the flakes seemed to dance in the light & the milk seemed to shine with celestial brightness.

"Yes, that's better. Just sit back & relax & look at the picture. Look at the picture, Candy."

She raised her head & found herself facing a dogeared copy of *Pop*. There was the picture of a very familiar man cocking his groomed head to one side & playing with a cleft in his chin. THE SEXIEST MAN ALIVE stared at Candy & she stared right back into that cleft & felt the sheen & shimmer of his designer suit & the sting of his cufflinks against her smooth & now reddening cheek. OmygodOmygod. Part of her struggled. Part of her knew she was still staring at a pack of soupedup pixels. But whether it was the light yoghurt or the very healthy cereal or the way the letters were stirring in that bowl of consommé as dark & deep as those comehither eyes, she could feel the heat & blew upon it as the cindery light enveloped her entire body. Glossy. Luminous fingers all over her clothes, touching the material of the clothes she had chosen while listening to some of her most often downloaded tunes. Yes, touch my material, touch it. Yes, those eyes dark as fields full of ethanol or the cooling tar of parking lots at dusk. She could feel the exhilaration of her every living encounter. Smooth & then neatly stubbled & then smooth again shaving exquisitely in antigravity outer space the best he can get & she gleaned that he had just freshly spiffered the floor so shiny & smooth & the date would be at the beginning of febreezey. The wedding would be televised, of course. But before that, the talk shows with audience members screaming & swooning & even exploding with envy. His nails were neatly pared & his hands felt good under her blouse, squeezing her more than accentuated breasts. Breath on her neck. The snap of elastic. Fragrant. For him. For her. For everybody. Then huffing & puffing & sweating & throbbing. The cover was so glossy & slippery but the magazine was nice & stiff & sooooo controversial. Yet it was hard for Candy to fathom exactly what happened next. She knew they were still in the early days. No breakups or settlements or live streaming upskirts or tubed reparations yet. However, she could hear a metallic ringing, a series of beeps & bops which sounded like one of her favourite songs, but it was very faint. & although she had no recording device with her, she would have sworn that the chocolate tiles were zooming in, coming closer & closer. It was very light & very bright & a voice was telling her to relax just relax. & it was very difficult to resist. You only had to look at those letters.

"Hello? Gee whiz. They must have hung up."

Candy Coton folded her phone closed & slipped it back into her koala bag. How long had she been conducting this interview?

" ... that's where the fuzzy reasoning comes in. What we use are known as Petri nets to catch the grammatical logic. It's all relational ... "

Candy shifted in her chair. Kinda damp down there. How long have I been interviewing this guy? I must have dozed off. Great. Just great. & now a backache to boot. Nice one, Candice. Real nice.

" ... we call those subverts, since they interrupt the process. You know how it is when you are watching your favourite programs & they are peppered with advertisments ... "

"I hate that."

When would he get to the point already! She had groceries to buy. She twirled her ankle about slowly & pointed her toe at the blithering interviewee, an old reporter's trick of hers to return to the topic at hand.

"Indeed, Dr. F, but I am sure the question that is on everyone's mind is how these experiments are to benefit First Nations reservations."

F burst into laughter.

"They say forgetfulness is a gradual decay in weight between neurons. Why, there's a formula ... Err, to get back to your question, our methodology is part of a comprehensive program to improve, um ... initiate a process of self-amelioration for our ancient friends. We have a well-measured & extremely well-controlled way to harness the wisdom of these gentle & beautiful people & to encourage their application for empowerment, in other words to encourage their successful integration into the *civilization* you & I consider to be our own. Merely to get some citizens out of the stone age, you understand. A damned stubborn lot, when it comes down to it, but also so mystical & gentle & beautiful. We would like nothing better than to welcome our First Nations friends & family into a vast sweeping *global* family. The world *is* changing & this process is a vital step toward their survival as a diverse nation."

Candy grinned her lopsided goodbye grin.

"Well, thank you Dr. Juan de Fuca. It's been quite an education. I sure have a lot to write about & already it's getting late. I must confess, I have to run & do some shopping on my way home."

F smiled politely in response.

"Of course you do."

Candy found herself outside the nearest Emerald City on 4th Avenue, anxious to shop. A tremor of anticipation passed through her entire body. She hesitated, looking down at a bedraggled man sitting on a flattened cardboard box that was as wet as the sidewalk. Must have rained. The man craned his neck to peer into that verdant world of produce & promises of longevity as the shuttering doors were automatically cued open & closed by each pair of legs that briskly passed him. She looked down at the man's whitefaced solidbodied but slightly fleabitten lab who stared up at her affectionately with wet olives for eyes. Human interest story. Make a note for the last five minutes on my way out. Candy entered quickly, in perfect time with the chartreuse lips of those swooshing doors that closed behind her, shushing the incoherent murmurs of the man on the sidewalk, as well as the soft whimpers of his lab. She spared a single look back at the gleaming coins in his overturned cap before returning her attention to that collardcoloured world of organic experiences, as a rather elfish cashier with a nose ring gave her a smile of greeting. Then without looking, she opened her marsupial bag & searched through a heap of cosmetics for the tiny scroll of paper she had written. Funny, I don't remember when I wrote the damn thing. O way to go, Candice. She unrolled the list in front of the glutinous nongelatinous & extensively tested smiles of the greenuniformed family of baggers. A single sentence caught her endearing eyes that read FILL IN THE GAP. She stared at the white space underneath the emerald lettering & felt belittled by a skill-testing question she could not solve without pen & paper. Underneath that blank, she felt especially mesmerized by a block of slender black strips overlaid upon a white background. The sensation reminded her of the drop-in meditation course she had taken last summer. Repeat your mantra & empty your mind & think of nothing your mind is a blank empty your mind that's what the instructor said. A fine thing to say when *your* hands are full. Candy reached for a very green basket. She flounced over to the heads of lettuce & other assorted greens & felt her wrist getting soaked in the path of a timed spray. She selected some Swiss chard & a pretty bundle of iridescent kale before moving on absentmindedly through each spurt of wet. Moving along, she stopped in front of the white chickens & asked a nearby clerk about the *happy chickens*.

"They'll make you happy alright," he said with a sly wink.

She went through several aisles, picking out only the most essential six packs of vitamins. Why, it must have been in *Pop* she had read that psychology & chemical imbalances were moot if you only exercised properly & took many vitamins. Her favourite actor had stressed this was so & it probably was. She stopped in front of a woman who was holding out a tiny purple spoon.

"Would you like to try a sample, Ma'am? It's our organic low-fat nutty crunch frozen yoghurt. It's quite scrummy."

Candy reached for the spoon & their fingers brushed. She let it melt on her tongue as she watched the moving pink lips of the frozen yoghurt woman.

"Mmm ... good."

The frozen yoghurt woman took the spoon back & grinned pinkly.

"I knew you'd like it. Now buy some."

Candy smiled in reply & responded in action now words by pinking up two two-dozen cases & dropping them into her tisket a tasket her very green basket. O so very good. A few dried herbs & multicoloured powders later, she was dragging her Emerald City basket towards the cashiers when she remembered that she still needed milk. Fuck. She walked up to a large man in a very green apron & tapped him on his very broad bicep.

"Excuse me, I think you are out of *milk*. The kind I like, anyway."

He turned around, smiling squarejawedly in such a way that made his leathery brown skin shine in the bright lighting. Candy heard a distant sound like a flute & felt a doe-eyed tremor as she stood in front of his dark eyes.

"What kind of *milk*?" he asked.

"Non-homogenized."

"O I see. You are in the market for some *non-homo milk*."

The letters on his apron melted into a greenish haze. A mystical wind arose from one of the aisles & blew his long black hair about with a certain urgency.

"There might be some in the back."

His large hand closed about hers & in his eyes she could see a primordial land of bucolic mud rifts on a deliciously warm afternoon. She touched her finger to her lips, incidentally moist with anticipation for the magical journey that was most certainly about to begin. Indeed, she felt infinitely spiritual & one with nature & all things green & massy as he seized her by the wrist & pulled her through a pair of doors with a great double flap. Green I want you green. He produced a couple of Purty's health drinks & tabbed them open.

"Drink this. My name's William Big Horse Longhouse. But everybody calls me Horse ... for short."

"Candice Coton," she replied between creamy sips. "Mmmmmm."

The more she swallowed, the more the store muzak seemed to speed up. *Kanetaunekuin hey hey hey hey.*

"Is that Green Day," she murmured dreamily.

"No, it's Kashtin," he answered, giving her a gentle squeeze.

She stepped back & drank in the grey sterility of the back room as Horse untied his green apron & revealed his eyecatching navy blue painter's pants ($29.95).

"Or do you want me with the apron on, eh?"

Candy could not believe she was quite herself, pouting & pursing her lips at this stranger. The health drink had gone right to her head. She struggled to collect her thoughts & from sheer habit, recalled an old interview she had done.

"Are you making a veiled allusion to *redress?*"

Candy suddenly wished that she had her quizzing glasses on.

"Or maybe I am telling you to *undress*. A much faster process."

Candy knelt upon the cold grey floor & the music sped up faster & faster. She was impatient for the überhealthy homeopathic deity to unbuckle his raven belt & to unzip his reduced navy blues & reveal his long & sturdy cedar beam. She glared up at the static eye of the security camera in a corner of the ceiling.

"Do it, Horse. Give it to me, you big bad Indian!"

Horse looked down at her, his brown hands full of her wild curls.

"Technically, I prefer the term *First Nations.*"

—   —

Grant Smith clicked MUTE, allowing the grainy onscreen activity to continue for a full minute in the dry field of his vision. He reached for a small green bottle & applied the dropper to both of his eyes. He stared at the ceiling for a few seconds while his colleagues continued to gape glassily at the mutual gallop of Candy & Horse.

"Well gang, what's the verdict this time?"

Janet Buckshaw folded her sweatered arms, shivering slightly.

"I need a cigarette."

Dennis Dennis lifted his hands out from under the table & clasped them on top.

"There's uhm … no obvious sign of physical abuse. She's not one of the ones gone missing, eh?"

Sally Ann Hunter turned to him & nodded slowly, dabbing her eyes with a pink tissue.

"It's really a beautiful story in so many ways. The crosscultural narrative involving Miss Coton & Mr. Longhouse is rather touching & I dare say, even a touch racy."

Grant looked at her for a long time, cocking his head to one side, which was his way of saying to a speaker *look at me & see how I am listening.*

"Unhuh. Yes, I must say that I agree with your sentiments, Sally."

Sally beamed. Dennis looked restless but not pensive. Grant raised his eyes for a moment, stifling a yawn. The elfish cashier with an emerald tongue ring was peeping through the double doors of the back room, openmouthed with astonished eyes. The happy chicken salesman was standing behind her & smiling broadly with an excited rooster in his arms.

"Also, I like the Canadian content in this one. Of course, I would have preferred Ontario."

Everybody laughed. Dennis gesticulated with enthusiasm.

"It's better than the one in Montreal, what was it called?"

"Smoked Meat," answered Sally with a faraway sigh.

"So, do you guys think we are ready to give this one a rating?"

The others made several noises of affirmation.

"Soon as I have my smoke," added Janet.

Grant tapped MUTE, releasing a series of moans & screams & repetitive cries of *white buffalo* & *studhorseman.*

"Cockadoodledooooohh."

Then he turned back to Janet, staring at her glassily for a long time.

"You can have one of mine."

The Book

He watched, and felt on top of the world. But suddenly ...
You often come across this 'But suddenly ... ' in short stories.
And authors are right: life is so full of surprises!

—Anton Chekhov

These early morning hours are very lucid. I choose them & they are very special, since you reside within them & additionally become them. They are a window in your hectic schedule through which I am stark raving ... You are no doubt aware of the trouble you have caused me over the past seven years, you who have scrunched yourself into more forms than those who occupy this lone curdle in the lumpy grey mush of my brain which has gone so wrong. It must have been those last conversations we had when you coyly suggested to me, rubbing my leg under the table with your stockinged foot, that it would be nonsense to think you were more than a figment. Of what, I wanted to know. In answer, you raised your Lapsang to your lips & sipped, very slowly & yes, I think you were smiling behind that saucer, yes. You knew I was in the mood for a serious conversation & sensing my mounting impatience, you made up your mind right then & there to aggravate me further. Vancouver, cut it out. I'm not in the mood. You're trouble, do you know that, Vancouver? I am no fool. I know this is our little game. I keep saying, Vancouver, not now, this is most inconvenient, & that only excites you. I say these things & then the more I give you the brush off, the more you rub my leg with your stockinged foot. Yes, they are very nice. Yes, they are new, yes? Vancouver, I am asking you a question here. It's the crumbs of time you feed me that make me craziest. Quiet afternoons, before supper.

You arrange them in advance, you leave notes in my shoes & I have no idea how they got there. Vancouver, you know I unfold each note with shaking hands, hoping it will say a few words I want to hear from you, even once. Vancouver, you know an appointment with you will rob me of sleep, that I can't think of anything else, not my work, not my health, not the woman in my bed. I am most angry after midnight when I most know I am going mad from terrible creakings & a sound like turning pages. I lie there & stare at the dim ceiling with all its little white continents. On the contrary, she is a heavy sleeper beside me. I mean literally, she turns to lead, while I lie there, arms folded, running over phrases in my head & thinking how to answer your latest note. This always makes you laugh, that I have this embryonic book inside of me, a filthy stowaway you don't believe is there because you never find him. That's right, Vancouver, you never find him! You won't, not ever! I'm very upset then, to listen to a broken tap trickling away. I am cruel then, Vancouver. I start to yell at you with such a thick silence that it buzzes in my head like flies about a deserted skull, through the coffers of my eyes & so on. It is something I have never done, something I would never do, but I want to slap you all the same. Around two, I can't stand it any more. Her elbow is often on top of me, just a little bit, but it feels like a crane moving a slab of concrete over a mausoleum just to get that elbow off me. She is used to me. Mostly, she rolls over & mumbles nothings. Other times, she sits up & looks worried, because there is this hunger I have & where will I go & so on. Nothing is so simple. You can't just go & pay a woman for that. Even you, Vancouver, when you forget yourself & get tired of talking. But answer me, Vancouver! You just want me around because you are getting ideas. You smile & rub me with your foot & you write down my sayings in your purple book with the broad lines. You are too frivolous to understand I have work to do & how these hours make me unwell. I tell myself you are balm for my condition. I stumble out into the night & feel the stars are razors for my bristles. You laugh. Vancouver, I want to rest my whiskers against your cheek & whisper the rest of my mania into your ear. Even you admit you're a real bitch. So, you take me for a fool, do you? It is well past two & I am walking under the scaffolding of the hotel's deteriorated face & the water is black & your voice is more biting than the air & you are a different breath than mine, visible, soft as fading vodka, complaining in your kitchen much earlier, saying O by the way that scribbler was here today yes you missed him again no, not handsome, no, not at all & quite quite stupid. But all the same, a man who feels with feeling. You drop that, you crafty minx, to flatter yourself with the idea of a man you toss out with the trash. You also know that poets provide their blood so the world may sip wine. This is when I know I am crazy to still be speaking with you & I want to slap you all the same. Forgive me, Vancouver, forgive me. You are not wrong that some nights I am tired of talking. I have tried most things but even since my young years, nothing has affected me more than this prolonged loss of sleep which only snowballs into more lost sleep. I walk the streets—I noctambulate & try to fix my head on the problem of you but your average bush is a ferocious topiary. I mean, things move. They leave strange scratches all over my body, not that I see them, exactly. Ach, how I worry that woman! Be patient, Vancouver. I know what you're thinking, I know how your mind works. You say he is not there—he is out telling tales to lonely women until it's time to fall off a stool. You are right about a place ... a man needs to hang his hat somewhere, no? Night after night, I sit, writing. On account of my dark overcoat, they nicknamed me Anton, but I far prefer Seattle. I will be sorry when it wears out, although I imagine going first. It is the only thing my father ever gave me besides his disappointment & a terrible wallop to match. So, night after night, I sit & have a word with Alberta, who is something of a flirt. It is quite funny, since she is quite tall & always tipping over plates & utensils. I take my regular seat in the corner & begin to write & before I look up, I hear her percussive approach & give her a good evening. On dead nights, she will sit down & ask her Seattle what he is writing. A poem, I will say, for a lady too tall to drop forks. Then she will blush in a tired sort of way, or lean her elbow upon the table & manufacture a little sigh. Alberta wants to be a writer, or so she tells me. She strikes me as one of those who imagine a time when all their work will be completed, when all their responsibilities will be cast aside, & when all their hours will be so perfect (for instance during their retirement) they will finally be free to achieve a brief masterpiece, capping a full & virtuous life. Vancouver, I should talk! So I shout at her for a good few minutes, spewing out the bitter seeds nurtured by a man who understands that loneliness is very necessary to his trade & desires that others should paradoxically join him inside of it. The poor dear, hearing the passion in my voice, decides I am in some mystical place & therefore better off. She lights up. Now this man is a writer, she thinks, returning to a noisy table of young men masturbating the table with their fists & shouting her name, Alberta, Alberta & so on. Thank goodness I have you, Vancouver, to tell me what I'm really worth, to tell me I'm a no-good-for-nothing. It's true! Now it's my turn to sigh. I'm a hundred times worse than Alberta, believe you me, since I think there's a masterpiece inside of me at all times. Sphinxlike, I sit, writing, waiting for some stranger to approach me with the correct riddle or phrase & paff paff paff, out it comes, all over for everyone to see, plain as their noses. Proof of that secret cure-all is already dormant in the lines I occasionally constipate out. It is so clear to me they are the clincher in some epic, sitting like a heap of blank forms, waiting to be filled in. Even on these dead nights when Alberta slips into the wooden booth beside me, there is something missing in our chatter & in her discreet squeezes. Her eyes seem to narrow to a speck on the horizon of her future, where her masterpiece is already gathering dust & a few grey hairs. Her hand is clammy with beer as it falls into mine & I think of the pincers of lobsters & snapping turtles emerging from a frothy head of lager. & my eyes are already outside, searching every street & alley for my own masterpiece. Are you hiding under those heaps of refuse? Vancouver, sitting like that, I know we are waking in completely different hemispheres. I've slept through your duties, your dates, your dailies. So there she holds me on a vacant night in the realm of beings who rise to watch the sun set & close their eyes before dawn. This is the best time to talk with a person, in these precious hours before blue leaks through blind. There is the illusion you are the only two people in the room & that the whole city is your living room. Pay me a visit? No. Cruel one, extend your invitation to me in your one window of frivolity, after the office has squared your thoughts nicely, before he gets home, late as usual, in order to plane their opposite edges. Yes, Vancouver, you rouse me out of bed with your sudden call to *high tea*, at the time of day you know I am weakest, like an ascetic beast you march through town on an invisible leash—that is the madman walking up & down in front of the pretty shops, muttering to himself, with an empty stomach to boot. You see, Vancouver, like those prolonged patches of sleeplessness, a fast is holy rite, to fast is part of the masterpiece. Lunch is the cardinal sin. Coffee is far better, with a bit of milk. All that food slows the brain, you see. The masterpiece has no patience for you to sit there digesting & developing your rump (along with numerous carbuncles). The brain needs that blood & here you are, sacrificing it for a sad repast of oil & starch. Don't worry! *Chef d'oeuvre* gets a kick out of faking it. *Chef d'oeuvre* merely pretends to feed you. On top of everything, my stomach is still burgeoning with that book-to-be. What to name it?! I'm a starving artist because I'm eating for two! There it is! Vancouver, now you know I'm having a book. I feel bloated. I wake up sick. This being in the literary way takes all of my energy. I feel very vague when asked about passages of time. Buddy, you have the time, strangers menace. I don't know. No, I'm not sure what day it is. My watch strap is broken. A present from my mother—snapped! I'll replace it. I put it off. A man gave me his watch ... but that's another story! Still, what is time to the book, which is perfect to begin with, no question. Go ahead, Vancouver, I see you, asleep beneath the weight of his body, my delicious book abandoned to an indifferent lamp chain on your night-stand. How many orphans are born like that? Ach, you must think this scribbler is full of it! You have no idea that during the grace period of your engagement, when I felt this most impossible hope, the book was only a scrap of scaffolding, a few sentences like stray planks, or a ladder leaning unluckily against a dilapidated wall. You, Vancouver, will be worried about the peculiarities of the wall & where it goes. As I am speaking that ladder is growing longer, reaching into the bodies of vagabond clouds. Aren't you glad I've come to you in this vital stage of the gestation process? Happy, Vancouver? As for the book, its hunger outweighs my own. I have a fever, a headache. My hands are shaking, although they feel a surge of blood to be active, to be the sacred profane instruments of a mind making such unusual propositions. I walk about aimlessly with rings under my half-open eyes, with my face averted to all familiars, as if they were large stereos tossed into the tepid bathtub of a bathing book, their hairy legs & forearms sloshing aside the tiniest bubble of profundity. Yes, Vancouver, the world's to blame! My body twists in this frigid wind like a filthy towel. Am I so old? I feel arthritic, rheumatic, in short, everything. Remember when a stiff drink used to help? Instead, I pivot, I dervish into myself, a face full of late apologies. Strangers, they let their eyes float over me, a nervous man hunched over narrow lines of scrawl, dishevelled, ill-shaven, smelly, shivering, trollish, walking about with my head down, muttering under my breath like the troupe of penitents in *Tannhäuser*. But when I do look up, I imagine my glint of concentration is the image of roadside ditches, enpuddled mud rifts stricken by a ray of light, strange messengers forecasting Spring too soon. I rub my hands together over elemental letters I am forging. I sit back with delusionary confidence, lit up like a zealot with a thousand relics to sell after an initial knock has brought you to the door. You see, Vancouver, I knock first. I am knocking now. I stoke every character, turning them over & over in my head, which feels like a can of crap on fire. Faces blur before me. I sneeze upon those virgin sheets of paper. You see what you do to me! Passersby appear to go mad with momentary curiosity, with a flicker behind their eyes, abruptly snuffed underneath the agitated fluorescents of a nearby mall or chain—the giant linoleum whale that swallows them alive. I am a much kinder cannibal (or so the rumours go). I chew them over, performing a feat of mastication whereby I begin to breathe words as if I were picking out choice strings of beef from between my crooked teeth. You must understand that I am content with a bowl of soup. The book unfolds itself as if to ingest the world. Still, you are quite wrong to think this feeding is to stave off loneliness, which is on the contrary, a pleasant necessity for my métier.

What is far more tiresome is any interruption to that blessed state which severs even the most remote umbilical link to the book, so beautifully formed already, which comes out wrongly, feet first, covered in unspeakable lesions. A pretty face may as well approach & shake me out of such a trance, but it has the same effect as if the person in question just sat on my hat or spat on my shoes. Even so, how wonderful to stretch one's legs, to escape the confines of a chilly room with its few wiry sticks of assembled furniture, along with its particular sounds—thuds, murmurs, hummings, creaks, elevator drones & so on. Vancouver, this loneliness is like the nectar of your left breast. I can't say how—see how you make me! What is more tedious is this compulsion to make a fuss, to hem & haw & yell your head off about the benefits of loneliness in order to remain aloof about what is so shamelessly advertised. I don't mean that your body & hand holding & so on wouldn't suffice. They seem quite nice to a man like me. The deficiency is not yours, Vancouver, but that of humanity. There the people are, brushing by without a thought, crowding & jostling & in the end, if there's some accident, cutting off its last gasps of air, merely out of a heady mix of curiosity & morbidity. But there they are, prostrate before the book that speaks to them in their own language, only mysteriously out of their reach, or the author's, for that matter. The diary of a man remains tightly locked & the contents are tossed (key & all) back into the sea of tongues. What a find! Ach, this book in my belly. Have I the heart to tell you it's yours? Vancouver, you say your memory is poor. Were our leavings bitter? Was there some falling out? How you sway your great head from side to side, lowing a series of confirmations under your breath. No, I don't want to remember. Do you still talk of beautiful moments? I sit & stink in this prison of observation. Through its walls of enigmatic glass, I listen to the world. The beautiful moments, they barely have the time of day to hock spit at me now. I eavesdrop. I rifle through the world's pockets & steal what I can. There's my pedigree & papers for you! But I tell you, Vancouver, this fantastic book of ours bears a parental likeness all right. Any fool who knew could tell. Those lines in its perfect little face—they are the expressions missing from yours, the memories you've lost, the atavistic creases of laughter so familiar to your ancestors. I jot them down. The paper tears. Other vixen barge inside. They turn ferocious if I even begin to bring up my obsession. I continue to follow the soft claws of your comedy, along with the shape of your nose, before & after surgery, even the way it marks the change in your voice as a battlefield turned into a memorial park where lovers go for walks on weekends & holidays. At least I go mad thinking of your lovers, those you never fail to remind me of, imprinting the finest places with some sordid deed, if not the possibility of an omnipresent rendezvous. They live there, awaiting that immediate kiss in the profile of your nose. Ah, your sense of smell … your visceral pangs! Vancouver, I watch you succumb to the vainglorious crowd—their heat sweeps through you, leaving your face terribly flushed. I want to people myself with that crowd, to reveal their voices & bodies at an awkward hour & watch your skin turn that unique shade of crimson. Naturally, I don't blame you for drawing me closer, any more than a moth on summer evenings blames a precariously dangling light fixture for becoming the immediate source of all hopes & dreams. On the contrary, Vancouver, like our friend the moth, I blame the wretched window with its deceptively transparent panes which strip body & wings of that mating light. In that way, Vancouver, I blame the doorman without even calling him yours. What gleams in his eyes & what curmudgeonly suspicions written into his young face! Handsome, I admit, but very forgettable, aside from the fact that he escorted me back outside with such gleeful diligence. Why talk of this, you ask. Well, neither of us remember the way you stormed out, shouting at me, your voice tinged with rage & embarrassment at a second goodbye, as if slapping the sentry's broad shoulders with multiple epaulettes, installing a touch of heroism in the crack of his forgettable ass. But now, as if in a courtroom, the subject being introduced in a moment of emotion now irreversible, you will wholeheartedly agree with me & subsequently talk of nothing else. The most forgettable man will become memorable. You will go out of your way to make conversation, to exchange names, to flirt with him, to date him if possible, merely because I have lent him interest. Then you will sit me down & offer me tea & rub my leg under the table with your black stocking & offhandedly bring up the subject of his immemorial ass. No, Vancouver, I won't give you that satisfaction! Let us instead, like senile codgers in the park feeding pigeons, practise the art of forgetting. This jealousy is a giant fishhook breaking the ice between us. I want to stand back. I know where those thoughts lead. No, instead, I bow to you & you to me & me to you & so on. Ach! I can't even blame the doorman. He is young & after all, only doing his job. What unpleasantness. Vancouver, you know I couldn't possibly blame you. However, it is entirely possible to find a culprit, if not a conspirator, in the door that sent me packing. So you see, Vancouver, I lay all my blame with the spinning bottom of your complex, that is, with the revolving door. There are nights I lay awake & curse the name of Theophilus von Kannel for inventing the damned contraption that would become such an obstruction to my happiness. There he was, the forgettable man rushing through that glass monster as if I had not just stepped out through it, with peasant superstitions & old wives' tales getting the better of him, as if there were a double of me in those spinning panes, aching to break loose in a sudden flash of daylight. Yes, there was your knight of the twenty-four storey aspect, sticking his foot into business that wasn't his, I repeat, business that was frankly beyond him. As if there weren't enough problems already. It wasn't the first time you had shouted at me through a spinning door or turnstile, O no. There was that time I forgot my books under the table in Brooklyn & you barked at me through a subway turnstile like a real hellhound. You were fresh from fighting with your mamma but that was alright. To me, you were spicier than the vodka penne. You were ferocious. I was overcome. I wanted to have you against that little brick wall. Or there were nights when I would roll around noisily, listening to your strange breathing noises & my body would ache for you while my brain would collapse into an embryonic ball, rolling around in order to comprehend your peculiar vows that made my passion feel so filthy. But to leave you on such a sour note, that was not my idea of igniting any passion. I could not speak the entire cab ride to Kennedy. In the airport, I began to write. Perhaps it was then, as the lightning was tickling the dark runway, that this idea of a universal book came to me. It was more difficult than I will admit. There was a man working on a laptop nearby, who was arguing with some unfaithful other. He hung up & continued to work for about five minutes. Then just as suddenly, he burst into tears. In truth, I felt like that. I wanted to express my sorrow & rage in such a way, but I couldn't. Already, the book was beginning to take hold of me, covering my heart with its white clutches. I turned away & continued to write this correspondence of cold eternals. Ah, these early hours. It is too hot. The covers are too heavy, tucked in too tight, & so on. Even in the dark before dawn, birds start chirping. I stare into the gloom & pretend I'm holding vigil for your letter, posing as your insomniac hero. Remember how your letters would always come on a Sunday? I would sit & worship their flourishes as my spires & their spiked characters as my Norman arches, through which your pauses let in a little light. The slightest phrase would become liturgical & like an ancient frieze of roadweary donkeys, they would seem to bray their complaints & snort parables between the lines. Well, it's Sunday. There's a touch of rain. Vancouver, where is your letter? In the outstretched grey frieze of Sundays & corresponding *chain letters*, the worst, I must say, would have to be the one that announced your engagement. However delicate your choice of words, those donkeys looked very tired. They were in a bit of pain that day. The church bells were tinny, yet malevolent, with the echo of an old superstition or much worse, a suspicion that has already been uttered so many times, that in the realization of the fear it was warding off, it only has the strength left to softly warble before falling dumb as a stone kicked back into the dust. I hear you in the gloom, raising your eyebrows & giving not even a half-smile. The man is mad. He is messing up his punctuation on account of seeing churches & temples & friezes all falling into dust upon the page at a bit of news which displeases him, since there is no satisfaction this once that his worst fears were spot on. He is broody. A whiner. He wears your excellent news like a thorny garland. Your laugh is hot. I want to slap you but I let you do your worst. Vancouver, the writer is no more than a parasite, a leech, a sucker of blood. You find my fangs this morning, decked out to the nines, ever so gently envenomed & you fail to recognize they are a token of affection. The walls begin to bend. Haven't you ever mumbled in your sleep, nearly awake, in another language if not a newly improvised one, about some nasty piece of work like me, a thing with hands & tongues, covered in the ink of a lampless room. Whether this is true or not, the writer believes it on many a night. These are the terms of a symbiotic contract offered to the highest bidder. When deprived of one or two sources of energy, the writer instinctively attaches itself to the nearest host (in this case hostess). You wake up suddenly. You stop yourself from screaming. They are just the jitters, only a few doubts. But for a second, they were tendrils tossed over your wall, something touching your thighs. There was a burst of pollen, the sizzle of a light bulb burning out. You saw sunflowers. In fact, you could hear them humming. In this strange process of cross-fertilization, these are the lovers, clinging to your dewy body in the dark like barely visible aphids. But what about the book? That's my own personal parasite, a relocation of all my emotions. A change of venue then! You want out, drop by drop, rolling across the exquisite pages of such an erroneous transcript. You frown. You scratch. You are not there. You never said such & such. You can't remember the rest. Even today, I am an invalid, wounded by the thought of your news. Another fever! I need air. An accordion of hours without sleep flexes its outer hands. I hear knuckles crack. They are twisting into the pleasant eccentricities of city streets. Some early gloves are sprinkling the sidewalks with salt. There are tiny imperceptible wounds in the snow. I want hibernative sleep. I want to migrate far away from your happy news. I want the soft thaw of our bodies. No, I want to be too heavy to care, ready to digest this fantastic scrap of news for another year. Why not take away your foot, Vancouver? We are to be good friends, no? I rush outside. Clusters of family members are starting to form like congealed snowflakes. I am caught behind every slow unanimous herd. Hurry up, I am very hungry! I snap at the air with my teeth like a dog hunting for bugs in the early morning hours. Vancouver, they are cluttering the boulevards with their bouquets of poisonous shopping bags, their bodies wafting alien fragrances. They are starting to flood the streets of my metaphorical city. What's to be done? Nothing. Sundays are not much better than Mondays. This tyranny of work cycles makes me want to tear my hair out. I would like to have a word with Alberta. Ach! She's not there yet. Another woman, short & very stout, bellows across the room at me out of sheer recognition. Ah, hullo Leah. She shouts out whether I want a drink. I slink into a dimly-lit booth, avoiding the accusative glare of any sunlight. No Leah, I am hungry. Just some soup. So no drink she clarifies with such a gnashing of teeth that it chills my spine in collusion with the sleet that has crept down the back of my collar. No, Leah, no drink for now, no drink, thank you. She rotates slowly on her thick ankles & launches into a snubbing gesture which makes her look a few inches taller. I grin in spite of my chill. It's not as if I've not sat in here before, eating supper, even while in the adjacent courtyard, heroin addicts have stared at their shoes for hours, or on worse occasions, have let their bad trip spill across the old world macadam & into the establishment while everyone pretends to go on drinking, stuffing faces with bangers & mash & heaps of curious cheese, until the ambulance eventually arrives, often accompanied by a few officers & a fireman. Nevertheless, my failure to order a drink immediately earns me scurrilous looks from everybody which only ally with Leah's bullhorned indiscretion. Yes, I see what you're thinking, Vancouver. You think I am the kind of man who skulks down to places like this & looks for passing action in the shadows where the occasional scandal can't be seen. Bah! I just want to be left alone for a bit, to get my head together, especially after so little sleep. But the book sustains me. The book pumps oxygen into my lungs & dizzy blood. The book comforts & the book reassures, even if Alberta is not here & you, beautiful monster, are engaged. The book is alert. The book is preserving their annoyed & mortified looks for posterity. A new frieze is growing out of their marbled stares. A song is playing. It doesn't matter which. I won't dare insult the book with such a common riff. The words are simple. The melody is soft. The instruments are also quite arbitrary. The combination of such accidentals in the history of sound, from the most primitive throat-clearings made to the scalars that mark the footprints of a particular tune, has the effect of charming me, of lulling my senses into a calmer state, of carrying away my mind to some other place. No matter how deeply I try to dissect the piece of music, as simple as the mingling rhythms of the street—an automatic cleaner, a can shaking with a couple of coins inside for lonely shills, or a woman late for her next interview, clomping along the pavement in ridiculously high heels— these noises merge into the melody of a frustrated busker or a droning selection of shopping centre muzak & achieve the same effect as a composition in progress by the finest maestro. Do you know, Vancouver (of course you do) that French families, peasants & nobility alike, would be very grateful for the opportunity to work for generations on the smallest & most remote blocks of an unbuilt cathedral? It would only be after centuries that the reality of their family name could be realized by the individual bricks they had set their hands to. Not like these places today we would love to make a killing on & then watch them bow, leak & crumble in lieu of some other shack in the same lifetime. The very last opportunity, Vancouver! Get in on the ground floor! What am I getting at? This is how the book can seduce & flatter a loitering parasite like myself. It promises me the future in a voice, barely even a whisper, & I believe it. Then a blank page. A blank page in your little notebook. How charming. Literally, it's nothing & that nothing is a literal terror, Vancouver! Unless it takes some shape we can appreciate. Genius (I hear) is something very similar, although at the moment the author with a name not so different from mine is far more distracted by this blank page which precedes or follows whatever you are currently reading. Of course, dear reader, you may never bear witness to that naked page. For all I know, it might as well die in a cluttered drawer stuffed with bills & bank statements & kindergarten drawings & god-knows, if not in some quiet corner, smothered by dustbunnies. The blank page. What a perfect candidate for the book, Vancouver! Why bring it up? You may have noticed I refer to a dear reader who is no doubt dear but when it comes down to it, I'm not above a little bootlicking or browntongueing. So lick lick! You might imagine I'm writing to you like an exhibitionist in a downtown store display. Whose eyes are those, reading our letters? I only know that the blank page is staring & staring up at me. I look back nervously. I want to smear its recycled off-white body with peculiar cuneiforms, to dirty its body with nonsensical poetry & therefore poetry, warpainting its wan face. That's when the terror steps in. Ahhh Vancouver, neither you, me, nor our delightful editor, have the luxury of looking into the hidden face of that untouched body. No, it's not enough that the blank page coils into our cold spines with a touch of fright. There is also a certain conspiracy. I mean, a certain set of circumstances which do so little for living souls & yet work on the sly to forecast the outcome of a single book. These are forces I have deemed in the past as spiritual, or as cruel attributes of FATE, since they ferment in a bottled moment that waits in the cellar of our lives to be uncorked & then releases such spirits which can only play havoc with the imagined order of those lives. That's how it is with you, Vancouver, you & your stockinged foot. Or for that matter, a woman like Alberta, who may inspire the composition of a letter full of fury & passion in one instance, even based upon our level of toxicity at the time, which only dissipates into a long dead letter, the next. Then, to be found out by those serendipitous forces capable of erecting or demolishing our happiness. Terrible! I feel subjugated to this FATE, chained to this fountain pen of my own creation. FATE, everywhere around us, in the street, in the hovels, in the knots in Alberta's hair! This is merely restaurant etiquette. Still, I flatter myself more often than I should. I say to myself she is binding her raven hair into braids for me. Such are the names of knots we have forgotten, knots we used to know by name, now tightening their grip about one name in the dark we do know! Let me see, I do know that name when I hear it, yes! It's when your name falls too easily upon the lips of strangers, indirectly even, & your smallest habits & whims become more predictable than weather patterns, that you start to feel a creature at their mercy, like a thing in their power to be auctioned off at the sudden wave of a lady's hand. Vancouver, then this system of friendly knots becomes intolerable & you feel networked to death. On the other hand, any character who can decode these patterns, as well as signs & smells, is at an incalculable advantage to the rest of us. This talent is not unlike that of neighbourhood hounds who noseread recent history from ghostly trails of spoor left beneath city streetlamps. For instance, there is a man downtown who looks like a Chagall sketch of Plyuskin, whether scavenging under bridges, going through his inventory of dead souls, or quite simply pouring a drink for his guests. This man's tongue is in constant motion. He hovers in black garb. He buzzes about temporary peers until they cease to lose their significance to his empty pockets. He moves in & out of a company of figures imagined to be nefarious, suspicious, wanted & so on. He has never been caught, to anyone's knowledge. Upon questioning, he never fails to produce at least three or four alibis which coincide, rather than conflict with one another. Whenever his one hundred eyes catch sight of any action remotely touristy in nature, he halts in midsentence & abandons his unsavoury clan, diverting the flow of his conversation by an abridged particle of speech to this new dialogue, leaving only the residue of what he was just saying far behind him. This elegant movement of Plyuskin, not to mention each animated gesticulation, is overwhelmingly musical. It involves no less training than ballet choreography, or if it does, it is cheaper to get front seats to this fellow who exudes the rapture of a young upstart uniting with the principle for a single fleeting scene. So where you boys headed? Looking for a place to drink some beer & smoke some weed? He spoke readily & gallantly, with a honeytongued lyricism. He oozed amiability. His sneakered steps never lost their exact time with mine, or those of my friend. But it didn't take long for him to stop, confident as piranha in the same deep puddle as a cow's hindleg, that he had succeeded in slowing my friend down, along with my own impassivity, through the power of his moving teeth. Are you from Egypt? He began to chat with my companion, testing him with touches of fluent Arabic. This latest demonstration of talent was a revelation to me & I wondered, not for the first time, how many other cards he had hidden up his sleeve. I had heard innumerable other stories, one about a work injury, another about his show of artistic integrity & his subsequent black-listing, yet another about a departed daughter, god rest her soul! Vancouver, these stories are too many to tell right now. Save them! That's what the book is telling me. I understood nothing of what he was saying but like a novice at the opera, I could read the surtitle of what he was about to sing, his usual aria regarding some kind of donation, really anything we could spare. My friend turned out his pockets & gave him what he had. In true Chagall fashion, his purpose served, he floated off merrily down Carrall Street. Vancouver, you may find that fact sad or funny or astonishing, but I must draw your attention back to the book, for there is no beggar more subtle, nor con artist more conniving, than the accursed book, although I tremble to speak ill of it. My knees shake. I hope no one notices. I want to sleep very much. The world goes on working with its wacky cogs, here & there, but the book is tireless & often argumentative with me. I do need sleep, Vancouver. You taunt me with your stockinged leg, yes? You dare me to dive into your open lap & teach you a thing or two about pleasure, no? But just as much, sometimes, I want to fall asleep with your hands stroking my hair. To forget about the book & to fall asleep like that. So often, I have to beg the book for a spare moment to think! I follow the world then. I stalk its parade of potential pages. In this state of mind, things, people, places—they merge into conspiracies I have merely whispered of. A simple case of the shivers. They continue to creep through me. They penetrate. My left arm aches. But there is still pleasure, some kind of sensation, a terrible pleasure, a terrible tingling … Then comes the coaxing. You surrender to that. The book is in on it. It browbeats. It cajoles. Give in already. Even as readers, we have to give way a little. Some hours of liberty, at least. That's part of the coaxing too. Let's spend the afternoon together. What are you doing tomorrow evening? O, come to bed already! There's a real snare to the promise of pleasure, since you expect to do everything right, in order, like the others. Then comes the accident of a passing face, or some jogger struck down by a wheat germ truck. It makes no difference. You're dying, that's all, minute by minute. This realization is ghastly, no matter whether you discuss it flatly or not at all. There's no going back, Vancouver. Not exactly. The question of it coaxes. So I am dying? The whys persist & stick in your throat. At the apex of despair, a detrimental little joke is played upon us. Irony is abundant, proving that nature has a sense of humour. What are you writing, about me? Of course. Cheers. Who am I talking to, Vancouver? Is it still you, two-dimensional & slightly tilting, straddling the wooden wall? Cheers. You're alright, man? Yup, sure, who wouldn't write about you? There is the touch, one of those touches to the shoulder that communicate so much or nothing at all. No, seriously, what are you writing? A very long letter, I think. Hey, this dude is writing a nah nah nah. Her teeth are gnashing. O Vancouver, why now? You're awesome, the man screams, banging his shaven head with approval in my direction. She squeezes me harder. I just got off this floating university. Here's my name in Japanese. I don't get these characters. I don't get it. I am writing toward a magnificent book, a thing revealed to me alone. *Alone*, I repeat. But you may witness its first inklings tonight, right here in this pub. O yeah, I'm like a poet. She presses closer & shouts into my ear over the jangled rockabilly. CHOMSKY! There's this CHOMSKY NAH NAH NAH! A motorcycle purrs angrily outside. Likewise, her voice carries on & on … I nod with the calm of a veteran reporter onto a hot exclusive. Hmm, poet, hmmm, floating … She leans in, much closer. I'm pretty far gone. Her scent is thick & welcome. I can't think like this. Her faux fur trails over my legs. Vancouver? Where is your stockinged leg now? She writes her name in English. Ott … no, it must be Vancouver after all. One of your little games, eh, Vancouver? You know there used to be a woman in St. Petersburg who dragged around a box wherever she went, fastened by a short length of rope. Inside the box was her husband's decapitated head, or so they say. She would drag the box behind her & then drop the rope into the snow outside of some shop & deal with all her affairs. Would you believe that not one person ever tried to open the box to verify whether the story was true or not? She went on dragging it from shop to shop, unmolested. It may be thought that people are too squeamish to do that sort of thing, but I think their fear was that if the box were ever opened, there would be nothing left to talk about. I think they needed her. Without that closed box, she would fade from the city's imagination—she would cease to exist. This is what it is like to drag the book about, pounding in your brain & beating in your heart. It hurts your nerves. It makes you wary. Were someone to touch it or dare try to open it ... ? These are no longer my hands on her brown faux fur. She is floating away, flushed with red & yellow hues. The men are tugging her home. You're awesome, the bald pate repeats, shimmering with an unearthly light. The pain is not loneliness nor any type of isolation. The pain is this proximity, this sudden human touch that prostrates & bewilders. I almost forgot the book, waiting in the dark with a white & wicked grin. What to say when I see you, after muttering your name to myself for so many nights. Names. They have an inherent power to unlock misplaced memories from a locked drawer of past sensations. I mutter your name as prayer against that lull in the day, against that ebb & drag of a city congesting into dust & fumes. Such are the random pressures that squeeze a stream of people together to a point where eventually, a familiar face is pressed out like a lone pip. First, the name emerges, a sweet nectar to repeat upon your tongue, withdrawn from that thick haze of pulp & membrane the city is. Ah yes, it happened, Vancouver! At the moment I was most resigned to that state of urbanality & my own postmodern malaise, resigned to my dreary knowledge of every bump upon the circuitous route once known as Robsonstrasse, my eyes resigned to large signs for sushi & gelato & indigo lingerie, my mind already certain of the stuttering vehicle stretching its insectile antennae about a particular corner & beginning its slow journey all over again, a familiar name lolled out of a stranger's mouth, magnified by a German accent. She sat down & only her silhouette entered the outer reaches of my senses. I saw her shape perhaps, through the corner of my eye. I half-heard her name repeated upon the stranger's lips. Without looking up (I did the opposite) I knew she was there, Vancouver. Her name swam through my soupy brain. The capillaries in my face felt about to burst. Yes, she was near, but her name alone created this change in me. I looked out the window. Alien faces smiled & grimaced back. I

111

reddened for no reason, inexplicably, unbearably. For no reason, Vancouver! Well, there was a memory. Reduced to an interior of resuscitated sensations, I saw hands tightly clasped in a darkened establishment & then embraces beneath a light rain. She passed before my eyes. I could not see her. I blinked. I blushed, Vancouver. I decidedly shrank against the window, safe behind a thick & stubbly head. I had no desire to be seen. Not out of the usual awkwardness, or a fear of twangled talk. No, not this time, Vancouver! I very much wanted to preserve this burlesque pleasure, dizzying as the colour in my cheeks. Premeditation may instill a thirst in us, a raw anticipation of what is to come, but its rival is immediacy, assaulting & seducing our senses more quickly & by virtue of this initial shock to our nervous system, leaving a far more resilient impression. These times of surprise become precious to us, since they work to oxidate the thick torpor of city life, to rip apart the rigid squares which dominate us, from menus to calendars to itineraries to warning signs to digital readout in an unclean corner. There arises an exquisite longing to be alone in the crowd & lost among those strange faces. The passengers pressed closer, some smiling bemusedly & others cursing under their breath. There was such confusion & I was so distracted that for a good few stops, I thought she was still aboard, kept resident by the garrulous German of her friends. When they rose, a quiet glee crept over me until I realized she had vanished as if by magic from her empty seat. Vancouver, it has occurred to me that the writer tries to brick out the world with words at one extreme & learns to listen to its natural rhythms at another, which gives him flashes of omniscience, or at least some validation of his imagination in the real world. Vancouver, by this power alone, I knew she was on the bus directly behind mine & that she was on her way home to a sticky situation. There seemed no other alternative. I yanked the cord twice. The bus shuddered to a halt & I leapt off the back steps, elated. I could feel the sheen on my cheeks, the afterglow of this recent state of flustration. I smirked into a sinking horizon through glass buildings & their jutting affectations of mountains & streams. Whether or not she had seen me, I was piqued by this explosion in my step & this surge in my bloodstream, triggered by these random scraps of life we tend to shortchange before some stony idea of FATE, in reality as fragile & indifferent as an untugged bus cord ... Vancouver, with a name like that, how can you want to move? No! I refuse to believe it. Don't quantum mechanics show us our doubles & triples in some universe directly next to ours, passing in parallax? Hell if I know. I would rather report that I went to sleep right there on the sidewalk. I would rather report there was no chase, but Vancouver, it was so ludicrously cinematic, that even in its happenstance, I was very aware of its tragicomical proportions. Who runs without reason in this city, spontaneously, unmechanically, not as part of any program & unaccompanied by a sweaty team of office moppies. I crossed with care from the rear. The bus lurched forward. False alarm. It shuddered to a stop once more, its advertised flanks trembling like a great bull about to mate. She was the woman seated behind a grimy window. I recognized her slouch right away, since this was the definitive melody our bodies had shared in the background of dreary childhood, when our respective parents were performing a choral recitative of 'sit up straight' which resonated through an uncanny combination of calcium & phosphorous in our bones, now irrevocably curled in similar directions, due to those sketchy impressions of habit & heredity. For a second, she sat looking straight ahead, examining the balding crown of the next passenger, who was vigorously rubbing his nose rhubarb. Then, like a loose table leg providing only the most sparse instructions in Swedish, her neck cranked to the right in a most satisfying manner. A sidelong glance. I was prepared. I placed one hand over my heart, almost smiling, as if to say, see how I am still alive & so vibrant & smiling although my heart is somewhat sore at the moment, if you really care to know, but of course you don't, so I will go on grinning like an imbecile, only it's no trouble really & thanks for asking & so on. She smiled back in mock surprise, not bitterly enough for my liking, in the manner of Albinoni's adagio, the way strings answer a mournful organ of pallbearing keys, a piece of music no more complete than this standing façade of a department store in the style of a past century. I watch her face & read her formal

113

yes these are beautiful moments aren't they, but it is unwise to expect more than this, you adorable fool, since you must know it's quite out of the question, so let's do away with these nonsensical charades. The bus jerked forward again without warning & to everyone's genuine surprise began to make good time up Granville, trailing its electrical antennae like the feelers of an insectile lover. How my heart sang! How I prayed for one, just one of those miraculous trolley sparks. My feet started after her. My eyes became imaginary blotches of colour in a photograph, gallant mudpuddles beneath her suspended foot. In their reflection, her face, looking back through another unwashed window. She saw me in flight. Bad show. The moon may be a pale eraser nub, but she can't rub away such shows of desperation, especially tonight, when it is so clear my life is a fugue. Yes, Vancouver, a fugue! *Mein Herz singt!* My head lolled back impatiently, then took a rest, like a wealthy old miser waiting for a distant niece he intends to give nothing, pressing economical pincers together, lightly kicking his tray of medicinals with faded loafers & tapping a long mahogany table with gnarled arthritic digits, impatient, yes, yet so stingy & reticent to open up to her imminent apparition & admit the orchestral tumult she creates within his organs & the electricity she supplies his nerves, that there is nothing for him to do but lean back in a leather chair & rest, or spend another hour calculating the riches of his dark imagination, accounting for her dizzy steps away from him in the double-entry system hypocrisy is. O, what a fool I am to believe it, Vancouver! The book takes in all these faces & many others for my lintel & frieze. Yes, a fellow needs a place to hang his hat & another to get him there, even to an imaginary place down the road, some lighthouse around the corner. In the end, even beyond the limits of my vision & the horizon of a hundred years, my name will allude to their petrified faces so immediate to my slight irritation. But Vancouver, what am I saying? This is not the place for their faces. One must save something for the honeymoon, eh Vancouver? What I mean to say is that the charm of such music, even the recycled loop of this song, is like your choice of Sunday to answer a letter. Through repetition alone, this habit of yours leaves an indelible impression upon me, since many of your others are too erratic & impulsive to leave any. Forgive me, Vancouver. There is a charm in having a regular schedule for such chaos. Ah yes, Sunday. A letter from Vancouver. I could pass it off with a certain nonchalance, but that is only from practice, as if inoculating myself from a most fatal disease by treating myself steadily to its most common symptom. The book is jealous, of course. Jealous as I was about the doorman or your fiancé, although less so of him, since in that photograph you sent, he had the presence of a cardboard cutout or a male display mannequin in a bridal store. Congratulations. He is glossycoated & whitetoothed as a morning newscaster. I am not jealous, no. I am sure you will be very happy with your display demo. Your face is already becoming a caricature of his. Vancouver, it is natural that people who spend a number of years together (as immediately they start to share the same living habits) start to share the same facial features & posture, or at least the cumulative sum of parts that is left behind by the choreography of their bodies, which out of necessity learn how to exist in the same space. Gradually, the lines that make up the profile of their faces are rubbed out by an invisible eraser nub with the speed of any cliff subject to erosion by a lapping ocean, making this phenomenon impossible to observe until suddenly those years of morphing have passed & the couple are nearly indistinguishable from one another. The book tells me that with you, the choreography would be a regime that involved a lot of browbeating & irrational wailing, one I could never stomach. Just as the perfect soldier never questions his cause & a religious devout never questions his faith, I carry a number of trusty pens in my left pants pocket & reams of paper, along with a slim note-book in the inner pocket of my faded coat. Monkish, I do away with the dreaded distraction of colour. I want only black in my closet. I wake up afraid. I live in fear of some bright sweater leaving biased flecks in my eyes, distorting everything else I see. Vesperly, I mutter to myself. This could be all wrong. That sweater, like a hot bath, could be exactly what I need to get the blood circulating again, to finish the book—that finicky masterpiece! But as I've meant to say, habit makes us slaves. It puts our noses out of shape. It realigns the sculptural line of our bodies with the peculiar functions they pursue. They bend us to their ways, rather than the other way round. Some people like to be reassured. Everything will be alright. You'll land on your feet. It's probably nothing. The writer thrives upon the uncanny ability to invent that voice of reassurance, even striving to modulate the ways in which it sings. Here is the altar of such a scribe, this dirty table beyond description, still covered with crumbs. Leah! This pew, still damp with small puddles of melted snow. Ugh. Vancouver, I barely have the heart to say you are the most beautiful figment I have ever imagined. I sit back, stubborn with worship. Even Alberta would stare at me sometimes & wonder what I was seeing or thinking about. Seattle, what is that in your eyes? Ah, Alberta, whatever it is will be written in the great book I have mentioned so many times. This trust is the necessary factor, a quality not unlike love. I need to relieve myself. I'll leave my things here under the same guise of unearthly protection. The book needs me. The book is the essence so clearly obscured by the veils of life. The book arranges innumerable aspects of life in order to exist. More than that, like a fine wine, it may learn to BREATHE. Sometimes the book stumbles home, drunk on its own unscribbled potency. I continue to sit here with my own salt-covered sacraments, with my own waters of ablution, with my own rites, each as simple as drawing a pen from my left pants pocket & filling the inky chiexas of that cursed blessèd book, capable of adjusting the most stringent rules of life to get along with its mysterious doctrine, also unwritten. Vancouver, that's the damn trouble. Here, you make my eyes & thoughts wander. There are psalms & precepts to write & there again I feel your stockinged leg under this filthy table. Listen to Dvorak's *Largo* for a second, to the unextinguished vacillations of this candle, to shadows it casts across my elongated face. You rub harder. The friction is maddening. I want to rake your stockings with my trembling hands. The book is furious. I am lost. I give myself up to familiar strangers & their washing cycle of whims, to the randomness of a room budding with intoxicated love. The room is spinning. Vancouver, the world is just a waiting room for the masterwork. Please wait until your name is called. Yes, like that. A couple of hours, a light sleep. This is a hunter's sleep. Footfalls in the night. Our animal instinct, feral, alert. Someone is creeping up on me in order to cut my throat. Ach, it's only the unwritten book, rousing me into semi-darkness & transposing a concerto of nocturnal sounds. A foghorn sounds, then lingers like the first chords of fate when Brünnhilde's enchanted slumber is disturbed by an anxiety-ridden Siegfried. But a woman continues to snore beside me. It is not Alberta. Nor is she some creature made from the restless movement of my ribs in the night. A lone skateboarder rolls down the street, happy to have that moist stretch of twilight to himself. The birdsong outside wavers between two sharp notes & then one retarded by the foghorn's sweep of resonant melancholy. Outside, there is a sudden tumult, a mysterious rattle. Then it rests. We are a city of the dead & snoring when the neoluddite hunters are out & about, careening down narrow lanes & over bumpy streets, leaning upon cages of rattling metal, often tilting to the side with one wobbly wheel, before being drawn back to the course of their next destination, since with long sticks they are fishing for glass & aluminum stars. Mostly bearded for winter, they move on to the next receptacle of success, often with an old grizzled dog that follows with grim loyalty & love, wearing the heavy matted coat of his ancestors. On civic holidays, they are busiest, collecting the discarded spirits of other people's parties, along with the electric martyrs of their freshly replaced appliances & brand new devices. I get up in the dark, skittish as an antelope so terrified by the clamour & cacophony of mating leopards that it leaps right into their lair & provides their dinner. So I want to go out there toward the unknown sounds, my arms full of bottles & used goods for some phantom of my imagination. Hours spin about me. They lose their shape & meaning without the teabag brown texture of habit to reinforce their authority. I will drop off later, for a little bit, for a few winks. It seems to me now that an afternoon has passed. I am stiff. My joints ache. Did I work all night? Did I help you at all, you nagging masterpiece? Or did I just roll over & let the heating element slowly lull me into itchythroated sleep? One thing's for sure—these thick little slugs of congestion. One can always count on them. Then I must go out. The room is stale, is disarranged as the pieces of my mind! Vancouver, I must go out. These four walls, this box, it's not right. No time for a shave or hairwash. I should go right now. The sky leaves a spatter of rain upon my pounding head. I can still hear the elevator droning from my ride down. It's invigorating, the rain. I have an umbrella but I hate the things. They always bend in the wind & then where are you? I fear an encounter. I always imagine slights or take a look wrongly & then the glare grows in my head, larger & larger, into a forest of dismayed stares & then I get pretty tetchy. I shout & squeal. I point & mutter. Mostly, I try to avoid. That would be *not nice*. Ill-shaven, with my boots covered in yellow mud from some construction site. As they would say in some novel, Anton Antonovitch, I have not seen you in so long! Then those awkward hugs that are hardly sincere. Vancouver, you know I do not like to be touched! How are things? Ah well, they are alright I suppose, yes yes, how are things with you? Yes, marvelous. Yes, that's wonderful. Good for so & so & so on. How much of life is this meaningless drivel & ceremonial pomp? At least once this gloomy afternoon, I want to say no, I am not well at all, please excuse me & kindly go to hell. Would they even hear me? Yes, I'll try to make it. Yes, thank you, thank you. I see the blankness in their eyes. No, leave me alone! I'm working on a book, can't you see that? Is it that book you're always working on, Seattle? I press my lips tighter. How can I trust them? Don't betray me! Sometimes in the demidark, near closing time, I whisper about the flutter of its pages when I am leaning my forehead against Alberta's tired neck. Poor fool, she thinks I'm some kind of genius! She laughs softly, so as not to stop the spittled flow of information becoming ginsoak prophecy after a few drinks. Then she knocks back another whiskey & soon enough bursts into tears, then stops herself as quickly as she started. Seattle, I'm very tired. All I do is work! I want to comfort her, to do something for her, to cheer her up, except she's for the most part pathetic & I have my own share of troubles to keep me occupied. Drink up, babushka! She adjusts the red kerchief tied about her dark hair marked by a touch of grey. Drink up. Then she laughs a little & rubs away the wet triangles on her face with a bit of tissue, although they are starting to hang permanently like small stalactites underneath her weary, cavernish eyes. Drink up, babushka, that's right. I so have a case of the *blahs*, don't you ever get them? Yes, I suppose everybody gets them. But pointing to an unswept corner in oracular fashion, I murmur feebly about the book keeping me busy, certainly too busy to think about these *blahs* of hers. Ah yes, the book. Tell me more about your book, she decides, leaning happily against my body, full of minor aches. Ach, Alberta! Leave me alone for a while. I need to write. These books don't write themselves, you know! There is an instant where words you've just released seem to hesitate & your breath seems to hang midair. Apprehension. What will happen? Anything. But as expected, Alberta smooths out the words on her smock & stands up, as if she had been standing that way for hours. I'll let you get back to it then, she sniffs. Come to think of it, the statue says, I might just answer your letter. She was referring to a letter I'd written her on a particularly busy night. There are such moments when we are inspired to perform an absurd action, even cruelly, just as the desire arose in Baudelaire to chuck the glass-seller & his wares down several flights of stairs. All great art is subject to this transition, to the instantaneous leap from the verboten to the commonplace. I am not sure why I wrote the letter. Perhaps to have some fun with Alberta. Whether I let it slip under the seat or left it on the table is difficult to know the next day. Perhaps I went to sleep that night, feeling satisfied. I have no idea now about the letter's contents. I think Alberta knows I don't remember a word & this is a sore point with me. Whenever she's miffed with me, she gives me a wink or a half-smile & threatens to answer this famous letter. This letter has become a running gag of ours, like my joke about her being too tall to drop forks. Vancouver, do you remember the time you wanted to buy me a tuque? It was blue. You know I can't wear blue. For one thing, I might wake up & forget all about the magnificent book in my bloodstream, simply because that flash of woolknit blue overstimulated my senses & then where would I be? If only it had been black! Black like every other item, or even charcoal! I am sitting by the window tonight. The last candle in the establishment is almost finished its shift. I make a screen out of the drinks menu for that stubborn candle. I am afraid of setting the place on fire, along with these pages, not to mention those of the book yet to be birthed. Remember that night the old woman said the trees along the boulevard were like Irish lyres. Of course you don't. The water is calm & black. Any minute, Alberta will come back with a complimentary bowl of figments. Ach, I have a temperature. My joints ache. I think I caught a chill. When? My temples are throbbing. I want to get warm. Meanwhile, you keep rubbing me with your stockinged foot. What's the use? I just want to sit back & enjoy a hot cup of tea. I want to get warm. You look tired, Seattle. You have a fever. Bushes don't move like that, not like beasts in a horrible forest, that's for sure. Seattle, why don't you lie down? But look. There are gators floating over adjacent marshland. My legs are not working. There's a puddle on the grass. The book is a many-headed beast. It writhes in my loins, scratching with razorsharp serifs. The grass is so slick & safe to roll in. Now is the time for agreements with God. Don't let them catch me! They must live in the black water. Don't you see them, snapping their jaws? No, of course you don't. Hey, guy, are you alright? Yes, yes, leave me here to freeze, to snap in two in their greasy jaws. I have said, Vancouver, that I don't blame you in the slightest, rather humanity. I understand how my letter was put aside by your significant other. I understand these little tricks of nature which we can only give the pathetic name of fate, when they are just a different outcome than we imagined. There it is in the darkness, hanging between his stubby fingers, with his other hand stroking his chin, musing away. I see it was to his advantage to lose it for a whole year or longer. No, I'm not bitter. Here I am in this neighbourhood swamp, about to be devoured by listless fauna underneath a dull orange streetlamp. Feet pass frequently. Would one of you be gallant enough to extend even a fingerless glove? Bad show, gentleman. The gators tear into my nerves. They are swimming gaily in the river of my blood, blowing bubbles & so on. No, those feet are clearly preoccupied with another terror close at hand. Run home to your heater & hot baths, to your abundant fridges without a withered lemon to speak of, to your five dollar coffees & your daily newspapers—ALL LIES!

Tomorrow's edition clacks down on me. I am giftwrapped in it. Already the orange cart is rolling across the cement—THUNK THUNK THUNK! LOCAL GOON GOBBLED UP BY GATORS. On such & such, a quiet winter night was no Swiss picnic & so on. Meanwhile, he is putting that ugly rock on your finger, while I am rolling through a local swamp. No, I'm not bitter! Vancouver, you are merciless with that stocking. It's moving like spiders up my leg. Or those giant fire-ants who only bother with the very very lonely. Mad propositions dance before my eyes. They are so blurry. Just try to stand, mister. But the city is full of rumours. These nefarious exchanges, these clandestine brew-ha-has, these illicit encounters. A bigass tabloid. Look, Vancouver, there I am on page three. Who's that crazy guy walking up & down? I admit, I used to snigger a little myself. Now who is laughing, Vancouver? But neighbour, is that not Anton or Seattle the poet? Is he not at work, thinking up great things? Happy as a pig in you know what, making it up as he goes! No, the swine are not thinking that. They whisper loutishly, indecipherably, smiling those alligator smiles. Go ahead & bite me already! Do they know about the book? Maybe they want to touch it roughly, to use it as a coaster or what's worse, to sign their own names in the gutter. I am lost. I must hide. Alberta, she might be able to help me, at least for tonight. She has a soft spot for me, without a doubt. Vancouver, just look at her drowsing upon the counter beside that damp cloth. Rubbing her eyes. Her voice is cold, cloudy, & perhaps a little gatorish. Vancouver, I feel the ring on your finger where you touch me. You are laughing & scratching the mirror. At least, that is what Alberta sounds like tonight. Ah, it's you, Seattle. Did you forget something? You, tall lady. I forgot you. Even through her fatigue, she beams. I feel foggy. Why am I here, Vancouver? Ah yes, the book! I nearly forgot. Book, I see you in these walls closing around us. Book, you are muttering in the wainscotting. Sweetie, won't you see me home? She offers, matter-of-factly. There is no mention of the letter this time. No joke. Alright. She shrugs gently, with a tilt of her eyebrow & a tiny half-smile & finishes wiping the counter. Something is gleaming in it. Alberta slips into a little change room & tugs on a chain, illuminating her silhouette through the familiar closet door that is slightly ajar. She loses the uniform & resumes her state of daily mystery, reappearing in black jeans & a taupe blouse. Let's go, then. Ah, Vancouver, the city is beautiful at this lonely hour. You are silent. I feel you rubbing harder. My body is a roadmap of tensions. You are coaxing me to sit back, relax, sigh & release. I am a chatterbox. What am I saying? Alberta is comfortable to lean against. I am very wobbly. I want another drink. She shakes her head & looks away into the distance. Vancouver, you are getting aggressive. You are getting excited? Need I remind you of your habit of not existing when I most require your services! It is near dawn & the blue sliver of light is killing me. There is a poet who says he watched her face collapse into a thousand years. I certainly can't put that in the incomparable book, can I? How I have followed you, Vancouver! How I have stalked you in the worst hovels, hoping to supply you with a perfect view of finery & all the furniture I imagine & must negotiate past, moving it here & there in corners & lanes. *Es muss sein?* No, it's not like that at all with Alberta. I'm thinking more of the Allegretto from the *7th Symphony*. You are fading out, I can feel it! Her little hand squeezes mine. I can feel her pulse. We are moving faster now. She eyes me quizzically. Seattle, I live here. The building is very old. Boxes within boxes. Going home from one box & climbing into another. *Qu'on me loue enfin ce tombeau!* No boxes for me, no thank you. Cast me into the chuck. Let's walk some more. I feel better out here. Alberta nods. Vancouver, you are merely a figment & here she is, this still life of a voluptuous creature, come to life. We are cold, both of us. We huddle together like two statues. Yes, we are two children in the garden & all that jazz. Vancouver, I know you expect some sort of apology. The geese honk. Black widow black widow. That is not here. That is some echo from downtown. Alberta moves like a bobbing merganser to put her keys back in her bag. The gravel creates a delicious static beneath our slow march. Look at those maples. See how the English Ivy is strangling them. What, no. They expectorate. The leaves & berries clear congestion, no? Then an idea occurs to me, Vancouver. No, it is too ludicrous. Is it? Maybe. Vancouver, what if I offered this woman to the book? I can sense you are smiling behind those sips of tea. You withdraw your leg & say very little. I bite her earlobe softly. Alberta, I want you. She looks back at me with a mixture of sleepy mischief & tired consent. There is a white stone in the park. The Natives won't go within a mile. Do you want to see it? She smiles from weary surprise. We walk along the winding path. For some minutes (or hours?) I have been pawing her. She takes my hand in hers & guides my caresses. In a pale clearing, she encircles my neck with her arms & presses closer. I can barely feel you there, Vancouver. I feel numb. But her lips are moist & her tongue is welcome. My hands fumble all over. There is a striped necktie in my pocket from the lost & found. I seem to have brought it with me. When? When she was undressing in the little room? It is a hideous accessory to behold, looking like the vertical hold gone wrong on some broken television set. Now hanging from my hands in front of her. Do you want to play a game? Her eyes shrink into small flecks of obsidian. She is motionless, a statue. She is made out of flint. The book is already intruding, blotting out her lovely vision with heavy sheets. She turns to look at the white stone to the left. What is it? Do you believe in magic? I hold the green & blue necktie taut in front of her dark eyes. She gasps. I tie a loose knot about her head. It is much easier to look at her smiling trembling lips. Seattle, I think this is quite kinky. I help her off with her coat & lay mine beside it upon the earth. A cobalt light plays about her grinning lips. Vancouver, I wonder what she is thinking about. No, I wonder who she is thinking of. I press down on her shoulders & she nearly trips, dropping her bag. Shoot. Then she sees. Mmm Alberta, I want you. I help to guide her hands. She touches me through the fabric of my charcoal pants. Who is she thinking of? Vancouver, I can barely feel you there. My head is clearing. I remember how you said you loved to perform this act for fresh victims, to feel them surrender to you, to feel that power over them. I can hear the tricky teeth of my zipper. Yes, her little hands are small but powerful. She is tentative at first, finding her fingering along this small sad oboe, nervous to begin some ancient serenade. My body reacts automatically, even through the chill of this dawn but I feel numb to every sensation. It is farcical in fact, a very human tragicomedy, how the thrusting of buttocks or the touch of a muscle can induce such illusions of shared nobility. Literature on the subject, for the most part, fails to mention how bodies sag & wither beneath the clothes that keep them, or how strange veins crop up & spoil the imagined moment. However, the most dominant factor in lovemaking is the suspension of disbelief, the withholding of laughter in critical instants when an amusing thought takes us by surprise, or when the instinctive motion of our bodies is reduced to soda jerk philosophy. We laugh. Our partner, if the slightest bit prudish, will convulse in spasms of paranoia, or retract their most recent state of passion. A cosmic joke at best. But for the moment, Alberta is not laughing. It is very warm to be enveloped by her mouth, to imagine her veiled eyes through the makeshift blindfold, her body bobbing in the cool breeze like a statue of Dike. Both hands are squeezing now, large & powerful. She is playing dithyrambic on my body in what might have been called a bacchanalian mystery in the past. Then there was the white stone, wanting some inscription of our respective insanity for its tablet, perhaps older than the fall of an overtly decadent Rome & all its remaining poetasters. Vancouver, I am not laughing either. In lieu of those pristine pages turning to stone, I see this disgusting state of affairs. These are the rites & this is wretched life, throbbing in a throat, muddying that soft white stone & the book, Vancouver! The book! It would take one motion, almost nothing for Pygmalion to smash his festival idoless. She threatens him with life. Life, Vancouver! Ach, it takes one motion for the necktie to slip down her parrot's nose, past her smacking lips, & down around her white throat. Ah, poor swan! The knot automatically tightens. There is a great flapping of wings, of her open blouse & exposed breasts, but little resistance. I am sorry, Vancouver. So terribly sorry. You must accept this token of my love. Her eyes bulge. She turns colour. Carefully laid in the dirt with her long legs outstretched & her head leaning against the white stone, she appears to possess a Pre-Raphaelite sheen, just like one of those painted beauties of past centuries. I bequeath her to the book in your name, Vancouver. That throbbing in my head has stopped. My fever has broken into a mild sweat. Blue light is creeping merrily through the trees. Ahhhh these lucid hours, they belong to you & me alone, Vancouver. It is so clear. Let me stay awhile. Let your foot rest in my lap. *Rimani, rimani ancora un poco.* There's a line from somewhere. I see you are still flipping through the pages of a fantastic book. Is there anything in there about me? Vancouver, what are you reading? Vancouver? You nod & sip your Lapsang in silence. Well then, don't say a word.

—— Epilogue (director's cut) ——

Seattle, you can't end things like this. For one thing, the postmoderns won't like it one bit, you leaving that lady in the muck like some fin-de-siècle basketcase. Also, where are the phylums of cultural characters, interacting in some interstitial manner that teaches them all some profound lesson, ultimately that people have very different flavours & are very different kinds of nutbars? Even metaphorically, to kill a lonely metaphor is hardly chilling. The enlightened neo-Marxist neo-luddite neo-liberals might appreciate your sense of the cycles of production & the way society manufactures consent in a cheap & tawdry manner. But what exactly does this would-be writer work at? He never says. Personally, I think you ripped off a bunch of stuff from the Russian & French writers & just pastiched it together in some namby-pamby manner. Then to make it overlong with this epilogue, no less! Over-elaboration is so last week! That said, your ending was how shall I say, not very nice. Weren't they going to settle down & get married? Where is the scene where a dishevelled Seattle flies back to New York & takes an amusing & speedy cab ride to the nearest cathedral, bursting in at the last moment, just when Vancouver is about to agree to marry the American, whatever his name is. Walt Whipplewhite? If that's too cliché, how about a satisfying mad scene at the wedding, something so outlandish & over the top, we can no longer doubt Vancouver's hidden love for Seattle!

Ah well, Seattle, you may have just nodded off. A few winks never hurt anyone. & there's Alberta, still wiping the counter & turning over empty chairs as usual. Winking slyly & wagging her finger. One day I'll answer your letter. Yes, of course you will, Alberta. There, you see, much better. & there you are in the mirror. You look like shit! What'd you eat for breakfast, a leftover cereal square? Your life is shit! No time for anything. Best go home & shave. A man is buying me another drink, on the house. An act of caritas. Why? A good day on the market? No, a terrible day. A funeral? Better, a wake! What leads these stray men like mongrels to this counter? I should talk. I am somewhat offended. Just because I look like shit! I have pride, you know. I don't need your help, thank you very much! I drink it down & thank him warmly. He doesn't want to talk. Good. Fuck you too. I'm busy here. A shoe lands on the floor, thrown from somewhere. Alberta comes running. It's nothing. What an image before me. I think I see Queen Mab! Just look at me. My coat is splitting in the shoulders. I feel heavy with books. My pockets are full of paper & spare pens. The place is very busy. A phantasmagoria of faces comes to life, the whole place breaking out into Sweet Caroline, shattering my last illusion of this being a Russian short story by one of the masters & along with any hope of truly being alone. It is harder to be lonely than you think, lonely in the crowd. At this moment, I can see how belting out an old song can be more satisfying than these scribblings in an epic never to be written. There might still be time to catch that morning flight. O don't start all that again! I guess I'll head home for another sleepless night, crawling uselessly into bed with that woman, Alberta or Vancouver, or whoever she is after a given moment of satiated appetites. In order to truly possess you, dear reader, I would have to know your real name. You can call me Seattle.

Dry Gray

'Geoffrey, I'm so thirsty, why don't we stop and have a drink?'
'Geoffrey, let's be reckless this once and get tight together before
breakfast!'
Yvonne said neither of these things.

—Malcolm Lowry

On day twenty-two, according to the black felt X, Gray searched for
a place upon the bricked pavement, trying not to follow the progression of each curve. Finding one, he pulled out a brown iron chair
with a bottomrest of inlaid wooden slats. The chair scraped against red
brick. Do do do do ... Quarter to five. A series of flashes. Crowds of
people stood on diagonal corners, pointing & snapping silver buttons.
Some panoraming in a steady sweep of palms. Some phoning &
touching their perspectives around the world. Different voices were
bubbling about him. The smell of smoke. Behind his back, the
comforting chug of locomotives. Voices, bubbling about him,
Spanish, German ... unknown, *alien*. Gray. Why the sky is sunny not
gray. That is not even how I spell grey. That is not even my name. A
lanky man in a toffeecoloured denim ensemble & rainbow sneakers
lifted one brown ashtray after another, searching for an extravagance
of halfsmoked butts. At last, he pocketed a handful before moving
on. No, I was so hungry, there was nothing for it. I went straight to
Fatburger. He had announced this course of action to himself like a
threat. He definitely remembered that. Her voice as well. A steady
stream of relaxedly Californicated Cantonese. At least those intona-
tions beneath the Consumer English. There had been a delay of

course. Then they had emerged as a kind of music. Brief messages. She had cycled through every possible option, leaving him in quite the state, struggling to reply in time, so as not to appear odd or ill at ease. O anything but that!

"Your name, sir?"

He thought he had said it loud enough in time yes that is certainly what he had thought at the time. Four clacks & a slam later, she had lifted the lolling receipt from its jagged mouth & had handed it to him with a number on a red stand. After finding a free table for his fizzing pop, he had examined the bold letters. GRAY. So be it. For today if not tomorrow, I will be Gray. Five. Steam fluted out of the clock. There was another more intensive series of flashes & sweeping palms. A pale man appeared, wearing a black cap with florid yellow writing on it. He approached a table where five Latinos were seated.

"Jurgen."

They shook hands with the man earnestly & nervously before accompanying him down Water Street. *Esta es mi amigo* Jurgen. It is a chemical in my brain. Or lack of one. Glue, glut, glutamate? Yes, that was it. Easy to imagine. The quake of a superstore basket & the tremble of a wobbly supermarket cart, all of them waggling & veering about a dozen aisles with identical displays. Spanking proud they by no means contain glutamate. Aisles & aisles of faceless No-G products. Minute after minute. I can almost hear the ticking now. No, that's silly. This clock makes no sound. It simply creeps. But what about the one inside? A voice. One of the ones bubbling about him? Maybe. People said the strangest things. Minute after minute. The sunlight had shifted, moving into the middle of the street. The coffee burned his throat, pouring too fast through the pinhole on top of the lid. Gray quickly dried his pantknee with his palm. A group of clock-watchers were watching. Then, a screech of tires. Gray held his right temple with one moist hand as a motorcycle patiently & agonizingly followed a far milder stream of noise. No recycled napkin. Shit. The sound died down & instantly little brown birds returned to generous crumbs of biscotti & banana loaf upon the red bricks. Arrrgh. So much noise. Two burly men in black with tattoos & high-pitched voices approached, talking over the sound of fresh scrapings. Shortly after, a blonde woman joined them with some trepidation, intending to negotiate the pell-mell assortment of tables & at the same time to maintain the perfect balance of her caffeinated sundae creation. She adjusted her frizzy mane & leopard print skirt before clogging friskily towards them. Scrape. Gray held his head & looked down at the brown table, even as his ears involuntarily pricked up for her indecipherable greeting. The air contorted & curved over the bricks as they talked at one another. Laughter. Is that English? He reached down to straighten his bunched up socks, finding solace in this activity. Esperanto? He got up with a loud scrape, momentarily disoriented by a flutter of yellow nails. Yes, I am *irritable*. That is the lack of that glutamate stuff. I know, I know. I read an article. But I cannot erase the thought of that blackboard or the sound of that terrible scrape. Yellow on black. Snaps of steaming leopards. Scalding. Terribly painful to see & hear. Gray touched his earlobes as another chair scraped towards him, this time almost snarling. Nonetheless, a girl with glasses & very fine brown hair sat within its tender jaws, minding the wooden teeth & brown scales, immediately becoming absorbed in a shiny new novel. Gray stopped, craning his neck to catch the title. Stop moving. No, he couldn't. All he could see in a lower corner of the black cover was a puddle of blood. One of the men said something & made either an amicable or obscene gesture at him. Gray nodded at the suggestion, before flipdropping his cup into the nearest receptacle & leaving this dismal retinue of growling zoo animals behind. He stood back on the cobblestones as a red double decker swept past, full of waving creatures, with some of the windows reflecting flashes. Live. Underground. In Gastown. A theatrical adventure. That must be that new place.

I would rather go to the theatre than to a museum.

He walked across Water, still rather bemused. He stopped, noticing a couple sitting down to an early dinner. They were looking at a wine list. NO SMOKING NO LOITERING. Gray read the plaque attached to a jutting chunk of grey office building & promptly moved on.

I usually notice car number plates or similar strings of information.

He waited for the light to change on the corner of Cambie & Cordova. Across the street, the party had already started. Outside, behind the dark girder, an assortment of souls were sitting & tittering & raising full pints of light lagers & dark ales. Gray squinted in the sunlight, licking his lips. A rottweiler was tugging at its leash & howling at the loose knot in the bars. Smoke rose into the sky. The light had not changed. Gray looked at the raised outline of a red hand & then back to the laughter & rising smoke. Above the grinning teeth & lips, he could see cartoonish words emerging & bubbling merrily about him. C'MON. JUST ONE. Finally, he was signalled to walk & he felt very much like the skeletal outline he was moving toward. Empty. He averted his face from the toothy satisfaction of two men in dusty work clothes coming out of the corner Money Mart. He turned his back & faced his escape. They were talking about him. They were. Yes. The light changed & he was walking quickly away. This narrow artery of Cordova had never seemed so narrow before, so close & suffocating. If only I weren't so thirsty. If only I could just turn back & … Shut up. Today you are Gray. Shut up. Gray is going to stay dry today. He saw a cluster of people waiting for the Main Street bus & it took an eternity to navigate past their floating bodies. He was still fuming to himself when a tall woman walking stiffly & briskly down Homer nearly collided with him. He looked up at her greygreen eyes. Both annoyed & neither budging. Stalemate. They each stepped aside & continued moving without a word. Gray stole a look back at her crisp white blouse & smart black skirt. No impropriety there. Worth a giggle, if you ask me. All the same, not even my type. He was halfway up the block before he remembered he was thirsty. Stay out of trouble, Gray. Best to look for books. He pushed the door of a corner store open, only to knock over a pile of books. Someone groaned. A pair of purple hornrimmed glasses approached him. He bent over to pick up the books & reheap them. Jesus Murphy. So much dust.

"Sir, we are closing up."

The purple horns were talking to him.

"My name is Gray."

They steamed up, absolutely furious.

"Mr. Gray, we are closing now. Come back tomorrow."

The door slammed & locked in his face. The purple horns disappeared. Like I need another anthology. There had been an article a year ago about this very bookstore. Yes, it was Blanche who showed it to me. A place to meet eccentrics & weirdos. They took my photograph, unawares. She had laughed & laughed, flapping it in my face. Kneeling in the dust. Is this the right street? Yup. He walked further up Richards. Here is the other shop. He stood in the open doorway, peering in tentatively.

"Hello. Are you still open?"

"For a few more minutes."

Gray entered the dark store. She was dark & smallish. Not mysterious. Means nothing to me. She was looking out toward the sunlit street with a faraway look in her eyes. Another aspiring writer. I will get out I will get out. How many times have I heard that one? No, nothing mysterious there. A sweating man in a mauve overcoat rushed in while Gray inched away down one of the aisles. He's got a bomb he's got a bomb under there.

"You know where I can get some good gelato round here?"

"Uhhmmmnotreally. There's a lot of places to drink around here."

The man left in a huff. Gray stormed out of the back, holding three books. Today I am Gray & today is for W & the W was for Why had she said that to the sweating man without a bomb? That didn't take long. Two Ethel Wilson. One Sheila Watson.

"One more."

"Huh?"

"If you buy one more, you get a twenty percent discount. The price of a book, maybe."

There isn't time. No, there isn't time. Not when I am so goddamned thirsty.

131

"Sorry, I couldn't find anything else."

She looked down at the three slim books, slightly Sapphic, according to her critics, but not at all mysteriously.

"I think you must live in my neighbourhood. I see you, sometimes."

"Wha? O, uhuh. Could I have a bag, please?"

Paper or plastic. Yes, she was small & dark & omniscient. She was in the fastest checkout lineup behind a copy of *People* or the *Enquirer* or *Amazing Tales*. Her inquisitiveness knew no bounds. She lived in sparse bushes & tree nooks, feeding upon grubs & roots. She bored into papyric trunks & withdrew the wild sap teeming with life. She moved cautiously with that local family of raccoons. Her dark eyes shot out of the night. They were everywhere. In my neighbourhood. She dropped Gray's books into a beautiful blue bag & doublewrapped them in the plastic like a gift for that extraspecialsomeone.

"Well, see you around."

"Yeah, bye."

I enjoy social chitchat.

Ask her. No, then you will give the whole thing away how you love to look & listen. Scribe & scribbler, small & dark & darting lashes, locking up behind him. The article spoke of irritability. But not the jingling of her ring of keys or that twisting jangle. Nor the intense frustration on a summer's day. Cool pints pouring into one another, mingling with dark interiors & the intrusion of light. Doors heaved open & sighing shut. No, anything but that. The other. Turning down the lane, no more stupid words. A touch. Under her furry truncated blazer, her fleshy blouse. Button after button. Then a warm touch for Gray against the crooked bricks, so hotmouthed & dry. Even the words couldn't tell where. That's not even my name. The blue bag crinkled in his sweaty palm. He rubbed his forehead & eyebrows with the back of his hand. The others at the bus stop were grim & steelyeyed. A pair of ladies managed to look appalled.

I often notice small sounds when others do not.

Another question from that Internet test. Learn your AQ in under one hour. They had made him even more confused than ever. But he wanted to give it a go, to strive for normal. Mostly for Blanche. He turned towards the ladies, who returned to their bunting match of social gossip & workplace complaints.

"Then I had to clean out his cubicle his jogging things & everything!"

"No!"

A touch of sympathy, hand laid across hand. Removed.

"Well, last week I caught him watching a DVD. Y'know, I think he wants to get fired. Sometimes over the hum of my computer & my typing, I can hear this small sound in the background. So I stand up to look & find out that it's Cecil. He's face down on the other side & snoring away! He can't get fired. They would just bump him if worst came to worst & he's pull the same shit somewhere else."

Gray turned away, blue & crinkly & wanting to plug his ears with his fingers. No. Hang on. We were on the second floor of Sears. Blanche was looking for a matching bra in yellow for the one she already had. In pink? Blue? I was staring through the glass on the second floor. The blonde woman came up the escalator in a red suit. The brunette woman in black. Kiss kiss.

I find it difficult to work out people's intentions.

That voice. I remember that voice. She started in right away about her failed streaks. That voice & the clip of their heels their manicured claws moving through cotton & silk & synthetics on the rack. "Can I help you sir?"

"No, I am waiting for someone."

No, I am watching those two women among your most frivolous undergarments. I am watching their superficial kisses & unhooking of belaboured camisoles. I am already reaching for my ringing phone to hook up with them in some local seraglio of late night viewing pleasure. At last, Blanche. Thank god she bought something sensible. I have forgotten this was ever an opera house, although for a moment

I slipped into the dark balcony & lingered there, watching the wine gown spillage of agitated divas. Hah! I don't care if I'm never a divo!

When I'm reading a story, I find it difficult to work out the characters' intentions.

The light changed. Gray stood back as the bus swerved to avoid striking his skull with its silvery mirror. Much obliged. He received his transfer & rushed to his favourite one-seater. He could see the small dark woman up the street. Just locked up. The light is red. No chance. She won't make it. His view was suddenly obscured by two new passengers, slightly out of breath. It was the leopard. She moved down the aisle with a glint in her eye & sat opposite Gray. A hyenalike creature with bold tattoos made a garbled remark & sat down beside her. Gray sat, quietly crinkling as the bus stuttered to life. Maybe she can still catch it. No. She got on the one behind. It would be so easy to go right now & ask. The next stop, even. Pull the cord, Gray. Across the aisle, the inhuman gibberish reached a feverish pitch. The hyena snickered & howled. She adjusted her leopard. Gray felt queasy, lost in the sunlight & spots floating before his eyes. Each burst of laughter threw him off balance. Let me be! Leave me alone, all of you. If only there were time & a quick slice of quiet!

I like to collect information about categories of things (eg. types of cars, birds, trains, plants).

No, nothing. Haven't had a drink in ages. A mild touch of autism. Took the test, read the article. Kisses & heels clipping across the broad tiles. I did not stop to count them, no that I did not do. I heard every word after word after word. Just a quick one. Just a filter for these infinite grounds. Just a firewall of Napoleon brandy. Just a quick nip of sanity. The leopard & hyena began to make beastly love on the sticky seats & it was Gray's turn to appear appalled. He reached for his dusty bowler but was disappointed to discover he no longer had one, if ever. Over the deafening roars & groans & scutter of passengers listening through pint glasses, he listened for the distant pulse of the used bookstore girl on the sister bus, steadily sniffing the behind of Gray's trudging chariot.

I would rather go to a library than to a party.

For she has learned to breathe life among dust & ruins. O Gray that is so romantic. After the rain, the sidewalk strewn with white blossoms. Pungent under our squeaking shoes. Frail & wet, she sticks me behind her flapping ear in the movement of her dark hair. A wizened man with trembling hands put down his opera binoculars. Post-coitus, the successful circus team shared a mediumsized cigar. The driver sneezed but said nothing. Passengers began to cough. Two of them collapsed at the sprouting tips of her mottled wings. But in spite of the cigar, the pair were starting to look sullen & spent.

"Let's get off & get a drink babe."

Animal laughter. The hyena winked at Gray as the leopard sized him up. On the bus behind, the small dark woman was holding her breath & turning blue. She was immune. Immortal. No pandemic or plot device involving a new form of tuberculosis could touch her. Not even that inevitable dust.

Day twenty-three was Friday god forbid & Gray was still dry. He flipped the calendar page & marked the first square with quaky black felt. The first of July had beckoned an innumerable number of nuclear families to spend quality time together in one place. Gray felt a splash of remorse at not being able to appreciate this wonderful happening, but he needed the ocean just now. Not a seat or booth to be had at Fatburger.

It does not upset me if my daily routine is disturbed.

No, the screaming of ferocious perambulators & the licking of green & lavender gelato spirals had nothing to do with his own spectrum quotient. Of course not. Nor the hawthorn bush of male faces peering inquisitively out of yet another coffee establishment. Arm in arm & interlocked, no one seemed to be interested in his condition or his real name. Eyes followed a stream of young men draped in Maple Leaf capes. In that brief spectacle lay all their indulgence & envy. He walked along the seawall, suspended in a perfectly slow gait behind a wall of family. Behind him, two men were admiring an approaching woman in a low-cut tank top.

I notice patterns in things all the time.

"Did you see that?"

O yes, we are all on parade. As for him, they clearly thought he was some kind of rock star on such a sunny day. Gray Rock, that's me, here for a benefit. Maybe I should carry my coat. Gray rubbed his forehead gently, feeling irritable once again. He veered off onto a stretch of sand beside the Burrard Street Bridge, escaping the disconcerting fried egg on the seawall sandwich of flesh. At last. The water lapped at his soles.

Night twenty-four turned into day twenty-five. It was a sultry night & Gray could not sleep. Blanche's eyes were already moving rapidly. Gray got up as quietly as he could & went into the kitchen & turned on the element. *True "teas" are made from the dried leaves of the Camellia sinensis, the tea plant, which was first cultivated in China and found growing wild in India.* Last bag. He sat in the dark living room & listened for the unwatched pot. At last, the water started to simmer. Careful of his bare body, Gray poured out a single cup of the last thing he wanted. *A gentle, contemplative drink that brews up golden in the cup, with a slightly sweet flavour. Sip it plain.* O shut up. He could hear the cries of partygoers & lovers through the walls & upstairs & outside. He pressed the bag against the inside of the mug until the water turned light green. Gray sat & stared blankly at the chipped mug with three red birds & an open book on the side. He sipped carefully, trying not to listen to the clip of inebriated heels amid throbbing vehicles in the street. His pulse raced & his body felt the thrum of the cosmos & the slightest movement of these shuffling organisms in low-rise scraps of clothing. & where was the secondhand girl from the secondhand shop? Somewhere out there, watchful & darkeyed. Gray couldn't stand it any longer. He finished his tea & got dressed. I want to go home. I want to walk through the warm air. I want to see some stars. He reached for his felt before unfastening the chain & letting himself out. Gray turned the corner & took his usual route up Nelson. The catalpa trees stood in columns & formed a great cupola over the street, through which he could see a few stars only partially obscured by shifting wisps of cloud. A family of four raccoons babooned by. He stepped gingerly over white blossoms upon the concrete, keeping his eyes lowered from passing couples. He walked around a roaring foursome in front of a six storey. Gray raised his eyes to see a grey stone that was large enough to sit on. He was turning to get a look at the four people laughing when a shoulder appeared from behind the stone & shouldered him. The impact hurt less than it shifted Gray from his path. He felt like a meteor burning up in some planet's unfriendly atmosphere. He looked up to see a tall figure in a hooded jacket & some loose unstructured pantaloons. Gray could only make out the darkness of a pair of eyes glaring at him. The figure was moving away, but hesitated, seeing that Gray had stopped to stare.

"What's that sucka? Whatcha gonna do? Yeah. Whatcha gonna do?"

The hooded man lifted a long stick of wood & started twirling it like a baton. Must be ninja night at the …

"Whatcha gonna do, fool? C'mon."

Gray just stared at him. He wanted to leave, but he felt some animal sensation awaken within him. He stared simply at the man, saying nothing. There was something familiar about all of this. Where had he seen him before? The foursome had gone inside. He tried to make out the features under the hood but the man did not step into the cast of the streetlight. Gray wanted to be angry, but instead he felt that overwhelming buzz of irritability filling his mind. It was like a minor oblivion that opened in the street between them. In the face of that sight & sound, Gray & the stranger seemed infinitely small & far away. Hell, it would devour them all. But the hooded man, seemingly satisfied with Gray's inaction, moved away into the middle of the road, muttering audibly to himself.

"That's right. Fucking _____ & ____. Coward."

Gray watched him walk away, waiting for the light to change for the sake of a single oncoming cab.

Day twenty-six. I hate Mondays. Maybe the worst day of the week. Most certainly the best day to re-establish familiar joys & drown foreign sorrows. Gray's memory of the sleepy weekend was slippery at best. On the other hand, it had seemed to take forever to pass. He appeared in the liminal of the used bookstore. Nobody. There. He halfsmiled at her & started down one of the narrow aisles.

I am a good diplomat.

"Hey, you know you live you live right across the street from me. You live at the Diplomat. I live at the _____."

"Huh."

"The Wedding Cake?"

"O, they painted that one."

"They painted all of those buildings. It's like a Wedding Cake. I live in the Wedding Cake."

I find it easy to 'read between the lines' when someone is talking to me.

"No. I just stay there sometimes."

Did I actually say that? What a dolt. Shouting down the aisle like that. Bad form. All wrong somehow. The small dark woman resumed her conversation with a young man in orange & pink.

"I write. I mean, not yet. I am making steps. I am going to write."

Gray perused the wall of books for changes, listening, always listening, unable to help listening. He picked up a black spine & flipped through the first few pages.

I go downstairs, startled and terrified, my clothes in disorder, my hair all wild; people turn round and laugh when they see me, and think I'm a

young rake who has spent the night in the tavern or elsewhere. I am
certainly drunk, though I haven't had a drink, and I even have the
drunkard's uncertain step, sometimes slow and sometimes fast.

"Are you in the film industry?"
    Here we go.
"What's this?"
"That's like that bar mitzvah they did in Duddy. Have you seen
that? They made it with whatshisname."
    Fingernails, snapping at dusty air.
"Dreyfus. I'm a movie buff, you know, a cinephile. Well, I'm
Jewish. Are you Jewish?"
"No."
"You look Jewish."

I go from street to street like a dog which has lost its master, seeking
everywhere, very anxious, very alert, turning round at the slightest sound,
slipping into every group of people, oblivious of the rebuffs of those I jostle,
and looking everywhere with a clarity of vision which at other times I do
not possess. Then, suddenly, it is clear to me that I am mistaken, that it
certainly isn't there, that I must go further on, to the other end of the
town, perhaps beyond.

"No. Mostly anything to do with like music & stuff like that."
    Flash of nails. Turquoise. Orange & pink starting to shuffle. Gray
emerged at the top of the three stairs with a towering headache.
Orange & pink looked up at him & stepped to the right, however
lingering about the brown counter. She took the Gautier book from
him & tapped her candied nails upon an oversized calculator that
regurgitated the barely visible numbers upon a small slip of paper.

"Three forty-four. You two make a nice couple."

Gray fought against the sudden flood of glutamate & frustrated longings to remain composed. He handed over the money as a series of visions flashed before his eyes, accompanied by a small strings section in the corner of the store. This small dark creature lived not just in arbutus crooks & oaken nooks, not even exclusively in pouty looks. She was part of that quorum across the way. Yes, she was one of those figures, lifting fork to face & so neatly cutting into plate, yes, with all of their eyes peering across at he & Blanche at the very height of their repast. Now the cellos ... There's the longing. There's the pain. He studied her, understanding indubitably that she knew their brunching ways & the very depth of their vast salad bowls. All this time, her dark eyes were peeping away & rollicking about the window pane, feasting upon their most private moments & intimate exchanges. She stared out darkly at night & watched their most ardent interplay of shadows.

"I never see you. Yet, you seem to know all about my life."

Gray appended a nervous laugh in order to softly punctuate his violent reaction. Orange & pink grinned fearfully. The small dark woman looked downward, appearing hurt, before releasing a mock sniff. Must be Garbo week at Cinémathèque.

"I only meant you guys make a cute couple, that's all."

"Do you write, then?"

"I mean, that's all I meant by it."

"Are you a writer?"

She stared widely through her contact lenses in the light, catching the gold shade of her sweater. "Yes. Do you want a bag?"

It is nothing. Soft now. It is just a chemical in my brain. Iron sulfide.

"Thanks."

"Thanks."

Day twenty-seven. The first bird. Gray turned over, awake. He was in quite the state. He watched the small dark woman take shape. A few of her delicate semitic features took form, at least in the semi-darkness. Already, a hint of morning was in the sky, following the insistence of a single bird. Shadows rippled & merged, taking shape. Nothing he could quite see or comprehend, only a gathering of lines or a single contour that his blood seemed to scream out for. They say we don't drink. A small bottle revealed itself in the darkness. A flask of dead memories. The passing waft of a woman. Esther, in the arms of her uncle. The bottle had no need & not even the desire to speak. It merely tapped at a tiny cupboard open under the kitchen sink. There was a real genie inside, aching to get out. He only needed to reach behind its yawning mouth & at last he could relax. The other birds joined in with that first song of the bottle. Robins & chickadees & her dark beauty. With song & light, these images sank to the floor. Gray watched them depart & wondered if they had untucked the sheets. Blanche rolled over, snoring heavily. Well, may as well get up. He flicked on the light switch & waited the essential seconds for it to come on. One, two ... Must be the steam. Then there was light & he saw a giant silverfish through a crack in the cover for the stubborn fluorescents. Gray considered pulling the cover off, even as it scurried away underneath its translucence, a massive thing the size of a shiny beetle, but decided against it. Didn't know they grow that big. Damp places, that's what they like. Bay leaves keep them at bay. Drip drip drip. Damn faucet. Blanche always lets it run all night. The bath too. He lathered up his face & splashed & towelled it clear. Opening the medicine cabinet, he drew out a razor & a can of shaving foam. *Peau sensible*. He rubbed the blue gel about his cheeks & chin & began to draw the triple blades across his bristles. Ouch. He watched the agitated bob of his Adam's apple as he ran the razor upward & chinward. Once finished, he turned on the tap & watched the stream of water wash the tiny dark hairs down the drain. All of them dead. The giant silverfish returned to the crack & twitched inquisitively. Can they see, those little clerics? No, I rather think they are secular by nature. By no means like the thumping mantis who sat in the corner of the bathtub

141

& pleaded with him to change his selfish & unsavoury ways. Would you look at what you're doing to yourself? Gray flushed in response & both creatures were lost in an apocalyptic vortex of water swirling them counter-clockwise into the sea. Nicked but relatively smooth, Gray began to dress. He moved towards the Venetian blinds & quietly lifted one of the lowered slats. No, that was a crazy notion of his. She was not with the diners who watched him eating half-naked. That was some mad fancy of his. He looked across at a window with burgundy drapes. This window was always dark & always the same, with those burgundy drapes flapping in the occasional gust of bay wind. Gray watched the drapes dreamily, stroking his freshly smooth face. They poured out into the postdawn breeze & began to fill the bleak grey goblet of sky. He could almost taste the drapes on his lips. No, that was tart. Water. My name is not Gray & I am dry for another day. It had started to rain. He reached for his black super mini & took the elevator down. Cats & dogs. An excellent day to film, I should think. He moved briskly along Nelson, turning at Denman & walked into the propped open door of Starbucks. A number of people were anxiously waiting for a customer to finish reciting his inventory of instructions for a particular drink to his liking.

"A double tall non-fat no-whip Diabetto … "

Something about the exact temperature. Gray felt his own temperature rise. No, I will not be irritable, no. Quite the cocktail. Imagine going around with that in your head all day.

"A tazo chai banana split sandwich & side of hash browns with extra syrup … "

Another man elbowed past him with a carton tray of cups & hurried to his car.

"'Scuse me I'm in a hurry."

A woman in front of Gray, apparently older & less anxious, turned around to face him, visibly poopooing the very notion of a lineup.

"O you go ahead. Don't mind me. Just getting a wedding present for the niece. She's getting married! & I'm buying her a present at Starbucks."

"Umhuhm."

"Can I help you? Hello, sir!"

Gray stood there for a few seconds, struggling to squeeze out the essential information so simple yet so elusive while warding off another glutamate assault. This was difficult, since the staff was frighteningly enthusiastic at this particular location & the more so the earlier it was. Can't read the pink chalk.

"Short Komodo Dragon."

"Mind if we put it in a Fretti cup?"

"Yes ... I mean no."

It seemed to Gray that he was speaking to four people in green smocks at once. They kept circling one another before his eyes like a troupe of performing monkeys. One reached for a brown sleeve & holstered the cup. Another asked additional questions. Another rang the amount in & took the money. Another manoeuvred around the others & proferred fresh greetings & questions & transparent pastry selections. Gray accepted the cup knuckled toward him by a hairy fist & made for the nearest heap of lids. Phew. He felt an uncontrollable burst of osmotic monkey energy. He remembered to draw out a new recycled serviette. *Extirpe les secrets de mon esprit.*

"HEY!"

A slightly greying man in a mauve comfy chair looked up sublimely.

"Do you know what extirp means, or umm extirpation?"

The man closed his eyes for a moment & appeared to consider the question in all sincerity. Eyes open.

"Well, why no, I don't believe I've had the pleasure. But hey."

He pointed his index finger at Gray. Wait a minute. The man reached deeply into his bag on the floor & calmly felt around. At last, he pulled out a small blue gadget that began to glitter for his gentle caress. Gray had expected candy or an offering of trail mix.

"Let me just punch that up."

The man lifted a pointless pen & started to tap at the surface of the small device. There was something strange & simian about the man's movements, although he was managing with relative ease to manipulate that small slender pen without a point. After several more tentative taps of the nub, he lit up. Gray had a vision of the first man discovering fire as he offered him the glowing list of results.

extirpate:

1. *Make disappear completely (unroot, destroy)*
2. *Tear up by the roots until it cannot grow back*
3. *To remove radically -> extract -> Remove a tumour*
4. *To make (person, thing) leave with difficulty.*

So you see, they are going to completely uproot & eradicate the secrets of my soul. The greying man palmed his device & stared back sleepily. Gray pointed to the dark writ on the brown serviette. "See, that's what the napkin says."

Pleased to have found a confidant, he even threw in a word or two about their flagrant use of leopards & hyenas. Only the slightest outline of the aforemused activity. But at that very moment, a garden gnome battling with obesity squeezed between Gray & his greying consort & swiped one of the comfy chairs. The gnome stroked his coarse beard with a hint of wisdom. He glared at Gray thoughtfully, before extending a plasticky paw.

"Here. Strictly hush hush if you get my drift."

Gray understood at once. He closed his hand around the proffered item, fingering it for only the briefest of seconds (he dare not risk another nano …) before safely pocketing it. As the gnome stole away through a side door into the alley, Gray noticed that the greying man was reaching deep into his bag, no doubt for his pointless pen that in all probability wasn't pointless at all. Leave quietly. "Well, see ya."

But Gray had already bolted.

Rain was pelting the streets, trickling through his hair & saturating his clothes. Gray took no notice. He was waving his unopened umbrella around like a valiant sword. He moved with confidence past each cluster of shivering summer folk. Ha! Ahah. Ha! Now the thong is on the other foot, or rather, cheek. Gray abandoned the idiom, basking in this newfound feeling of empowerment. Of course, he had been a loyal subject for a respectable period of time. As for his previous demeanours, they had earned him only a slap on the wrist at best. They were history. Long ago buried. Dried husks. & why not? I am dry. Even my brain feels nice & dry, crisp as a side of spring rolls. My flesh is wet, yet impermeable. A fat drop fell from a candy-caned awning & plunked his forehead, making him laugh as he tasted another drop. See how thy grail is in season! Yes, it all followed that his good behaviour had been observed & taken note of, jotted down on the back of a napkin perhaps. For this reason & this reason alone, an emissary had been dispatched on his behalf. The gnome had only spoken with a generous helping of body language but that was unquestionably an intricate form of communication. Within the gnome's discreet jiggling of girth, Gray had fathomed a complex system of encoding that left no doubt as to the nature of his assignment or the authority that the card bestowed upon him in every jurisdiction & in several constellations as an agent of jiggle-jiggle-giggle-slap-tickle-jiggle-snap.

Contact. He walked into the secondhand bookshop, dripping. The door was propped open, although he heard a distant tinkling as he entered. Empty. No. She was stretching on her toes, far behind the counter. Gray watched the small dark woman in her black turtleneck as she gathered dust in a crawlspace behind a shelf. She was oblivious to the sopping apparition of Gray standing near the doorway. He waited a full minute, watching. She was reaching behind the shelf for something. Gray surmised that maybe after all, she longed to be nothing more than a doorstop or missing book, like one of the parts of *Orlando Furioso*, never to be found with its other half among the dust, no matter how hard you searched. Perhaps it was hidden behind the shelf. Or maybe that's where she keeps her nestegg, among the dust & cobwebs, only for rainy days like today. Gray started backward. Books were starting to creep about her well shod feet. A few of them shot binding threads towards the back of her dark slacks & started to shinny up her pant legs. Gray stood motionless, bewildered by their exoskeletons of raised & ridged words. She was their lifegiver goddess & they were going to devour her, piece by piece, page by page.

"Hi."

Barely a sound. She turned around. A pile of books fell to the floor. She beamed.

"O hi!"

"What's your name, by the way?"

"Rosalie."

"Uhm … Gray. Uh, I wanted to apologize for yesterday. I felt bad about being so standoffish."

She made affirmative noises of bemused agreement, appearing very pleased. Taking this as a good sign, along with the retreat of the climbing booknids, he held out a small card with some printing on it. Then he asked her.

Day twenty-eight & Gray was elated. The mere thought of any kind of assignation, even for such a noble cause, might be enough to keep anyone from sleeping. But this was vital, even topical, of cosmic significance. He stared from wall to windows & back to clock & then back to ceiling. It seemed a terrible pity to sleep. He touched his lips & bit one thumbnail. He even had to remind himself that he had been dry for close to thirty days. A single moon. I made it mine. I don't even feel like a drink. My nerves are nice & prickly. Fantastic sex nettles. Let's get lost together among the turgid weeds. He looked over at Blanche's rapidly moving eyes. She was not one for the water. Let's wade through weed & brine when the tide is out. He could envision all of the global ramifications now. His excited breath. Her small dark frame wading through a vast network of tangled kelp, gathering slime about her forbidden ankleflesh & smiling at the diving exercises of green-eyed monsters. *Dipso* they say he said. & so it was, that every lifeform became uberaware of impending evolution. Life had just been sped up. Perhaps it was something in the milk or mystical circles of beef. Bottles & chutes. Gray would take her hand on this, their name-day, & together as one they would cast off all disdainful manner of smoke & dust & pestilence & rape & violence & especially all of that overcast grey. Clicking pens & swinging keys & tapping fingers & ticking things would come to a complete standstill. They would learn to master the use of their freshly developed gills & unite beneath the great & wobbly & undulant drink beckoning them onward. The time had come.

Almost five. If he hurried, he would get the first cup of the day. Gray turned the corner & took his usual route up Nelson. The catalpa trees stood in columns & formed a great cupola over the street, through which he could see a few stars only partially obscured by shifting wisps of cloud. A family of three raccoons. He stepped gingerly over wet blossoms upon the concrete, keeping his eyes lowered from no one in sight. Maybe they would take the card, although he was reluctant to use it for such a trifle. He walked past a six storey. Maybe a pastry today. Gray raised his eyes to see a grey stone that was large enough to sit on. Threeberry. There was a grey mare of an idea nagging at him. He had forgotten something.

I frequently get so strongly absorbed in one thing that I lose sight of other things.

Gray turned to see a long object, raised by the hands of a hooded figure.

"_____!"

Everything went black.

Another Helen

Yes: a brief syllable. A brief laugh.
A brief beat of the eyelids.

—James Joyce

O my word whatdhe make he was dying for I dont like to see it with
a bit of beard left on thats swarthy then ya can see it always that look
of sad pathetic death in the eyes & scraps of poetry gloaming about
his throat & all that shite & so very tragic cock&bullstory I cant bear
it anymore my new do & everything to go with these new stockings
& what the hell do I care what do I care hes not so fine looking not
so foine as the Sowthern woman on the number three lisping under
her breath elp me elp me up with that & so I did she nearly lost her
wheely cart in the street yer a foine foine gurl tank ya green eyes tank
ya O here you go having the nerve to ask for a glass of water every
time as if I dont have enuff to do flashing rings for his lowered eyes
to what end I wonder if he can tell by the way that ones pointing old
gypsy trick to catch the eye at least in the pictures heavy that cart
especially right after work & green eyes did she call me blessherheart
that dear wanker didnt notice not really not one iota no no no the
trouble we go to & for what their snivelling away & sadsack sayings
all over a fresh pair sometimes they like to tear them not on my watch
go & buy me some new ones no they dont do that do they &
surprised the git with im didnt point & laugh they usually do he didnt
blurt it outright this man has a poem in his pants for you he does Id
bet his liver on it but I love a cider far nicer not that swilling into
oblivion every minute then finishing up on the steps Ive seen it before
& hate to see it that old joke about the two Irishmen who walk out

of a bar & the terrible answer impossible as if it were some kind of riddle & I hate to see it but even Menzi likes a nip now & again O the man changes I dont like how he changes it just goes to show that men cant be trusted to their own company he bringing in that look like he was dying & nowhere to shove it & whatever does he write in those hideous notebooks flipping & staring & underlining & scratching so absorbed all for a single bloody word I reckon like he cant get it all out & I wonder if hes quite right upstairs a loose shingle in the roof if you know what I mean with a look like nobodys business & nose in a book so infuriating to see why not stay home & do what one likes rather than inflicting this spectacle upon others this reading & writing well I suppose the Bard was like that dont you little creep in the corner scribbling down everybodys thots & dreams they couldnt themselves but he had the live theatre the little people the peons the hoitytoities roaring all right put the bums in seats for four hours of poetry you cant pull the leg like that today of course theres the net to click click licketysplit & find anything almost any question & who needs a teevee along with that just make a mental sticky to find out the name of the Bards dog & click on search & another reminder to get the blast away from here & the likes of im not that he ever made a scene or fallingdown commotion save that look like death lightly sauteed & warmed over gives me the willies not a spot of bother those mangy mongrels come to lay at yer feet can I use your phone missy can I use the loo can I borrow a loon can I can I always lookin for someone then they show up in the kitchen creeping about maybe harmless for all I know but the cooks hate that dont they especially that brown fellah who slips round the corner to have a good pick & thinks I dont know O let me use the loo O let me use the loo Im burstin & customers only there are public washrooms just up the street beside Victory Square lest we forget we will remember forever that great big thing like a henge in the Hebrides sorry but you have to be firm about such matters when you run a business its enuff to mind your own but that big bird lying at the bottom of Gassy Jacks barrel green as the gills of that statue with her childs voice begging will someone buy me an ice cream will someone buy me an ice cream its

150

enuff to break the heart to see someone in that state of affairs will someone buy me a coffee or sandwich & on & on until the downtown security not that I blame em makes her get up & move along but is that really worse than a lone bagpiper busking right outside yer premises is that worse than the addicts studying their feet as if about to cram for some heroin exam floating off into the old bricks & then coming down at the foot of the old jail & that reminds me Id love to check out that Storyeum place but its quite steep isnt it over twenty-five loons the price of history I suppose with actors to boot & I wouldnt mind a stint there but how do they even break even you begin to wonder about places in this city those empty shops & highrises those faceless owners who are they when theyre home but blimey it was a treat real romanticlike when Menzi & me went up the Grouse Grinder offering that old crone a place to sit on the way up & her refusing what I thot was polite enuff no apparently not she said you can get out of the way I guess she does this everyday well sorry I said to her & she said sorrys not good enuff just like that O I was so mad at the time Menzi had to calm me down but not when Im in a temper but later on you just look back at these things & laugh & laugh donchya but we had to come back for our first date date & after the price of the lift thingee you dont want to pay the same to eat at the top but going Dutch it was relatively inexpensive or normal prices for this city & how romantic to look out at the mountains you can see as far as our neighbours holding hands over a plate for a fair bit of bob or even more thinking yes I will yes I will sincerely think about it supernatural British ascendent peaks & all manner of odds & sods & a glass of unpronounceable to boot just one & why not a bit of tipsy to add to the bargain sitting hand in hand its been over a year now & happy thats a funny question always asking but arent I now I cant complain but why not ask that git with all his gilt words about the hundred year celebration extravaganza O I wouldnt be caught dead on such a lovely summer evening no no Id nip right home & walk Spanners ahhh my sweet wiener dog I would & then that note in the lift a blanket blew onto my balcony wednesday june sixteen if you can describe it you can have it back O keep yer smellyoldblanket but funny how words have a way with them at times a life of their own reminds me of the time I won that beach towel at Army & Navy & dont it just pay off to fill out yer name everywhere well no not that time first they ring you out of yer warm bed & then all this rigamorale to see Tessa in Playtex & have my picture snapped its free advertising thats what that were & they have some nerve to put you smiling in their window with only a towel to show for it & if you can describe it you can have it back funny how people are with im asking in his weakkneed way about the sign on those bricks for june sixteen with housemaids knee more like it & who needs weak ankles up to ere standing on yer feet all day O quite the life let me tell you & always clammerin over overtips a fine line my young buck between gratuity & foolhardiness & the forest echoed fool I read that in schkoool ehh & the bleddy nerve of that tart in the hoodie looking for Ford girls I near shat myself in the middle of Metropolis as if Id fall for that again once yer past the mediumsized three O you wonder where the time all got to true you got talent kid but I imagined Id be out of ere by now yes nows the time to roll up yer sleeves & line up all yer duckies in a row & settle well why settle why not make a proper ninetofiver out of the lot & keep the lions share no more of this jackofalltrades-masterofnone approach to life but that face Spanish maybe sometimes he says gratzy well he didnt say shine or shitola that last time & I dont see the stupendous draw as if she were reading out of her own book they show it on the nightstand in that hotel ad the chap fast asleep & snoring away thats the right idea but they say it all appens on a single day in the life O go on & say nothing why bother to wear my hair long & why bother to flash that smile of mine keep looking till yer eyes ache you wont find a split end a ladys crown that what our mum our Sylvie calls it & only once did I dye it red & crop it close like Annie Lennox & she wanted to murder me a right family crisis a ladys crown cut to shreds & I heard im telling his little friend she passed & smiled at him near the zoo incidentally where its all happening in Central Park as if there were nothing finer to smile at hes got some chip on his shoulder that one but ever since Ive kept my hair neat O she could have killed me on the dime & boy have you changed yer tune & I cannot believe I said that but he creeps you out a thing a wind would wither sniffing & snivelling away but then those eyes looking right into your life thru the window you always know when hes coming I turned my back & in the glass I could see the glint of im a shadow just a dark blobby thing in the glass & its off to the races ducking under the bar & ready with the whatsyerpleasure monsieur a Snakebite well he never did that before & I remember I was happy that my letter about Eeeraq getting on Endoubleyew that maybe if people drove less Essyewvees full of gas up to the nines the economic pressures would be a sight different & then of all things I hear Bruno has enlisted with his dual citizenship & all & I said if I got my hands on im Id kill him first & that got a laugh but he had a right hardon with something to prove all men are the same that way I suppose you cant half trust em turn yer back & another hallmark tomfoppery has gone down before you could have a tiny word but how would we get up to Banff I wonder its beautiful this time of year I still remember that summer I sold ice cream & it was the sameoldstory some bloke I dont know from Adam ha ha comes in & asks for the usual & looks about to freaking weep as Im dishing out two scoops of strawberry & then before I can blink a busload of Japs & not a word of a lie every one of them wants the same flavour forming an orderly queue & one after another going VANIL VANIL but very polite all the same & I thot wed run out long before we did they were right pleased but an invite on the radio cant hurt everyone always saying put those voice acting skills to use more often & write more plays & put them on the radio & they should talk wouldnt that be the life as if I didnt have a living to earn as if I were the spoiled young gentleman with his stupendous amazing pen & ink all over his fingers the way he gets up my nostrils sometimes but you have to keep plugging away I suppose plodding away more like it some days I feel like that old woman on the bus wheeling her cart behind her & I have done my share of Canimation but wheres the up front & centre tho I loved that program Pond Life or nothing better than to tape Corrie on Seebeesee & put yer feet up at the end of the day & sit with the dog & see what hijinkers Blanche or Leanne are up to this week or that dippy bird whos been on the show for donkeys years tho her hearings shot these days but she still understands the odd command you have to train them early with hand signals & what was Jacqui going on about when he said if I were to cry out among the angels who would answer or the like & what did she say O something about angels being deaf I could have strangled her on the spot one minute hes a complete loser & the next hes kindofcute but she has her moments she always says my ladyscrown looks like Princess Leia when I bun up & I overhear her saying to customers on more than one occasion thats Helens word or thats what Helen said & between you & me I hope hockey is gone for good theyve never been so popular with all those movies even if theyre a mite daffy preempting right & left but isnt that just like anything governmentrun you go to one office & they give you the runaround & send you to another where they send you back to the first place & all the while nobody is in its Im not here right now please press one press two press three to sod off I mean I watched the final game just to see what Menzi was on about its after years of growing up back home with nothing else only grainy hockey games & paintdrying games of curling & endless airings of Repulsion the one where you see everything thru her eyes that Frog bird actress whatsit & on the brighter side the old Jubilee a banjo on my knee strumming away in the blood & snow & its funny the things you miss da tings you miss tank ya tank ya thats what she sounded like but I suppose shes a gentle soul really a bit goofy at times but there you have the Irish those flighty souls not nearly so grounded like us Scots & for all the world like a kid sister in her way always looking up to me quietly & never taking the rise & saying that is Helens word for it in her pink pancho they were having a sale on Hastings all the rage werent they are you going to see Ramón the Jambón the Hambone I wanted to say but he must have come in with those writer chaps at that gettogether & O I tell a lie he was going off at the gob about John A the man on the money & how he thot his tribe was the most uncivilized the worst I guess they leave that bit out at Storyeum all Indians & Prime Minister singing with Chinese miners I suppose before they play the canary for one of the Dunsmuirs all the same what a lot of lovely things they

154

built in those days not like now so I suppose hes not Spanish then but what in the blazes is that Greek writing glowcopees thats what that fellow in the restaurant told me & wasnt he a bit fresh a right helping of muck & a touch full of imself but the bit about the Sun Tower gave me the shivers comparing me to one of those grey what do you call them carryahtiddies in their birthday suits will you the sound of the old newsies clacking away & my eyes like oxidized copper what a strange thot its a beautiful building to stroll about come to think & I remember that day I was sweating & sweating & decided to take a bath & youd think he heard the water running drop by drop to read it not that Id fancy im half baked mind you they dont make em like that nowadays & theres nothing for it measures must be taken as dad used to say or else Its time to show up naked at his work at least thats what Im always telling Beryl & she was in stitches over my impressions the other day Im in my verkskirt I said in my Frau voice not that Im not flattered but call me conservative theres no way a girl wants to be taken out for a spot of fun by the likes of im on yer bike miladdy sling yer hook as if I had nothing better to do I like being on my ownsome with my dog what more does a woman need in the long run I know I keep saying to Bill not to give ideas mind that I might meet someone but in my salad days I was more experimental I admit but now Im fed up with the old doublecross theyre so loyal even if they cant hear you just wave & they come running so feral & primal & lovely Id much rather sit at home & set to work on my website & feel her moving about my feet they dont give you even half the troubles I know like that Yid I went out with & his mother who looked like punch staring down her nose at me & the way their neighbours kept asking are you going to marry a Scotch girl & the way they said it I could have given them a proper black eye with my ring finger these days they put their names on the sides of buildings & nobody knows they went all day without eating even Darlene & when you asked the mother said they had brekkie or lunch & the daughter no no thats a bloody lie & the way theyd come in to use your phone to move a property & make out they were skint every second wanting to go halfsies on a head of lettuce or a bunch of carrots & now they name

155

those halls & theatres after them & the brightest & best young whip-
persnappers mill on by none the wiser to the names of the dead &
what they were in their lives & what about the other one appotroppey
that waiter chap grinning & whats he smiling about & hiding his face
when you turn away a liddle bit & I said sounds like a dogs breakfast
to me & he laughed & laughed & how they waltz in here & go on &
on about the bus well its too warm you want to dip your toe in the
ocean just for a minute & these blokes who need a right hosing down
stretch their fuzzy edges their white sleevelesses plastered to their
chests & not a word of a lie a fat line of dirt about their shoulders &
neck what they need is a proper winter like back home to freeze the
germs to death thats what Im always saying if theyre so allergic to
lather a soap for the things they say if the driver refuses to stop & a
roachmotel soap leftover for behind the ears O try the Mainline
sometime its like they shoot it right into your arm that wacky ride &
something always goes down like I end up sitting behind some fellow
with a boil in the back of his neck the size of an overripe mango &
couldnt bear to look another minute I always move if something is
funny even that witch with her fortune telling duck or that old bag
with her fresh eel in plastic & what about the day that dark chap was
jawing on & on about the posh situations hes turned down a number
of smart hotels & the like because he couldnt run his own kitchen the
way he wanted & his friend nodding & saying his faretheewells &
then that other bloke getting on outside the seeennenn & darting all
about sitting down one minute & leapfrogging up the next a right
jackrabbit I kept my eyes peeled for him the whole time & only this
Chinese girl holding the pole was between me & im when all of a
sudden the cook jumps up & hes twice the size of the other chap &
he grabs his wrist like hes caught a fly between his fingers & gives it
a twist to free up a yellow bus pass for the start of April & it turns out
to be the girls from her back pocket he lifted it without her feeling a
thing you cant trust anybody these days & shes thanking the cook &
hes not listening handing it back to her & trying to eject the other
bodily shouting to the driver to STOP & everybody groans as if some
brolley is stuck in the doors & then this dollybird nonetooswift might

I add turns around & starts giving a long lecture a real penny for yer
thots about how to get on & off the bus & the cooks trying to talk
over her saying what if it was your purse honey & thru the rearview
the other bloke is waving his fist & cursing while the cook is smiling
to the other passengers & saying hes a slippery little bastard O I got
right up & passed those souls picking things out of their hair & flicking them to the floor & the rest of the stickie Johnnies & tranceing
bounders & past the gentleman caller by the stepdown its Kismet in
an undershirt of dirt turned insideout you half except to say excuse me
& watch him blow away down Main Street like dandelion danders
growing in the pavement not that you wont see some homeowner
with tanks strapped to his back & a gas mask bent on poisoning two
or three dandelions in the eventide to get the perfect lawn but there
among the laughter & the confetti like a bad game of darts lightning
strike me dead if I tell a lie a syringe comes sailing thru this open window & whizzes past O it would have been curtains & it just goes to
show that had the bus not rolled back it would have been curtains
the end of yours truly & the death of a real diva only the next day
back to water balloons full of godknows like those pages of writing he
leaves open for the whole world to see not that I ever took so much
as a peek who could read that black scrawl like cobwebs all the same
but Helen you look a touch down in the mouth & I stood right up
& denied there was anything as if I would care about some cafe-
haunter or neerdoweller & then Jacqui blathers on & on about my
using that word with a French or German U so I had to look it up a
lovely thing you can look up anything on the Internet & they call it
diareesees very like a painful case of the runs if you ask me & they are
all thieves I guess picking words like fleas off the back of a stray mutt
I am sure I remembered to feed Spanners tonight yes I did yes its the
way they look up at you that gets you O sure if you have a house they
have the run of it but not in the city you have to give up your job to
tire out a border collie they just stare & stare until you get up & go
out just the way they hypnotize cattle but working dogs are like that
but not at these prices Id sure like to go back home this winter meet
the folks & take Menzi tobogganing & even see if Repulsion is still

on even if he is the last man in the modern era I might add who has
never boarded a plane in his life hes a shark come to think buying &
selling peoples hopes & dreams & profiteering off it hardly an
honestdayswork that mortgage is a funny word as if it were the rate
of mortality I mean take a risk for once in yer life still I have no idea
what those funny Greek words really mean but I could just look at the
swans & triangles & sums that strange lettering all day not like my
own handwriting gone to the dogs & the red & yellow cover of that
book about gay Paree he got on sale that got me talking about my old
photographs of dog owners & he opened it & showed me that carnival
of black & white animals & then for whatever reason that cheeky
slapper sitting on the stoop outside that House of Pleasure in my boots
& you cant help but get a bit put off when they spoil it like that no to
learn it by ear thats my way & if you dont fancy that you can bugger
right off & thats what I wanted to tell that Tessa she pulled out some
brodingnagian thing it would cost at least two loons to have that
washed & gaudy as hell it says B A N A N A B O A T in big letters &
there he is again a shadow skulking about town & slinking into the
Limbo without a second look like he owns the place thats bad news
just like one of those little Hondurans always loitering about in shorts
& dark hoods on a summers day & there I am buying something else
I dont need & haggling over a banawna towel & it must have been
im who wrote that letter who else with the nerve not to sign it just a
single initial I & addressed to H just to leave me guessing & no hed
never admit a thing the silent type he is no no not with thumbscrews
or tacks or cat o ninetails would you draw a word from the mouth of
that drinking horse like those pictures of half men in my books as a
nipper or when Lucy went thru the wardrobe & met Mr Tumnus
beneath the streetlamp in the snow & then im being so mannerly &
eyesdown about that short changing business & I had forgotten it
completely O he wishes & he gets right up my nose asking how I am
one minute & winking & smiling the next with that bit of beard the
more tight he gets & then at last that sadness that look like hes dying
of it O they are so full of tricks & japes sometimes you dont half see
them coming I like all the facts up front a firm handshake O they

would all say his name but I wouldnt if you payed me even if I heard it day & night he was a nobody I would have a laugh to myself & say hello YOU until at last they made me say it after one or two years was it & he said something snarky about being promoted & I turned bright red the nerve of some people as if you owed them your whole life no I like all the hearts face up on the green but who can wear the same old pants for eternity everyone cutting down their carbs to fit into a size zero when I was a kid we had the four basic food groups & that coloured chart I was telling the new cook that not all bloodtypes are the same low carb this & low carb that some people not a word of a lie have dropped dead of Atkins tho that chap in France lived to a hundred & three on a few slices of meat & a hunk of white bread every night with a moderate helping of wine to wash it down & when it came time to celebrate his longlivedness they made ready a great feast & there he is toes up on his hundred & third birthday speaking of mine Jacqui was just saying how many Cancers there are in this place & its im again complaining about the new menu & the lack of chicken soup for the soul the lack of comfort food thats it & something about his copper grandfather & the smell of smoked salmon but that cook seems a randy sort when hes not playing with his chives & cilantro with all that talk about polygamy & his beliefs but call me oldfashioned or conservative or what word you like theres still something about loyalty or whats the point of shacking up in the first place or maybe those years are behind me Im not one to preach but its a bit flowerchildish isnt it you make yer bed & now you have to lie in it you have to make a choice in the end yay or nay no I prefer a cider myself not a boatload of that dark stuff & a mild Sunday morning when its nice to have a bit of peace & time to oneself if I could only have time to think sometimes to lay my hands on my keyboard when Im not in a temper a proper good mood & write another quick riff because you cant trust the words or make use of my Flash classes well Im no expert but its amazing what you can do with very little like that dragon of mine download it now but Menzi is always saying dont tap the flat screen & I find myself pointing with my nails tap tap tap it drives Menzi crazy & it must have been Mr Ubiquitous

who started it what with Erin asking the entire bar hey who coined
Pandemonium & he doesnt answer right away no he waits for it until
nobody knows & then with those long tapping fingers makes a fist &
slams the table & shouts Milton & waxes on about his threehourexam
O the poor dear & Erin laughs & starts another whipround about
that old sweet song with the ether & sawdust in it & I knew but kept
it under my hat & all the while the music is turning & turning like
right out of some demented carnival & the faces in that surreal
painting behind his back starts to reflect down on all of em drinking
& thinking & crawling off down the road & wouldnt it be lovely to
get some leave & take a trip back to the old country the little markets
at Petticoat Lane & still the memories of those mad pullers O darling
come in come in have I got just the frock coat scarf or shawl for you
come in come in & a smashing pair of knickers on your way out right
out of Dickens & whirling about Picadilly in that compact car I
thought the double deckers would squash us like silverfish all the time
Gran going on & on about the way they used to trim the selvage the
excess fringe inside the lining & a stroll from Ten Downing thru
Profumos where they filmed that picture & what his wife must have
thought the one from Kind Hearts & Coronets & thru onto the cool
green promenade of Regents Park but it must have been Hyde gran
was telling us when the bombs started falling she was born in
twentythree yes letmesee yes thats right younger than I am now &
they were having a lovely stroll her & Harrywhatsit & she used to
sing that old tune Im just wild about Harry but her mother called im
the Bulletshead Oy Maggie Arry the Bulletsheads ere but I suppose he
was welltodo after all & he was elbowing her with a wink & propos-
ing right when the air raid sounded & you couldnt get a piece of fruit
or take a proper bath all ersatz & rationbooks with the bombs falling
every bleedin minute all those beautiful narrow bricked flats in ruins
but the question barely uncorked let alone popped he grabs her arm
& starts to drag her all cromagnonlike toward the shelter & thats just
typical no she wanted to walk some more to think over things & he
screams well Im leaving & hightails it towards the nearest shelter like
it was Chariots of Fire so that was the end of it just another of her

sagas I imagine but she was always taken aback that Annie Goldberg didnt miss a trick saying if you dont want Harry can I have him O yes be my guest but that didnt pan out in the end for her & some things are just not in the cards & hes a selfmedicator if you ask me the way he downs em one after another & gives that look like hes dying some days his face so tired & his nerves clothespinned to the line & swaying in the breeze I suppose we are all entitled to our own brand of sadness but the things he says & does some days what is he a split personality a drunk what is he in love with me but you never can tell with men after game seven Menzi was so plastered he was a proper potted plant Im sure but that was a special occasion but what got me was when he didnt have a pen & I said he could write on the table & as Im walking away he mutters something about his epitaph & thats a wonderful howdeyedo & I dont think O theres the sound of that first bird alone in the dark & its not even four yet strange how its just one bird & then that weird silence & he thinks he can charm em off the trees but for im I suppose they sing in Greek like in that book of poems Kalli gave me on Burns Day a few lines cant do any harm for a change I mean yes I want to tell him yes to touch him yes it was the sweetest thing I mean never before quite like well maybe Ill sort it in the morning gawd its that now after all it was such a lovely letter I am flattered of course its asking for a proper tank ya tank ya a single tar sung in Greek in the alley & from the rooftops that would be a laugh but I mean it thank you O do you hear that Spanners darling dogsbody its started to rain in the summer theres sometimes a down-pour colder this year than most & then it just stops altogether I hope its nice later today then you & I will go walkies O but it has started to come down that robin will be appy at least when the worms start to wriggle out at first light I love it like a symphony when they go hunting in the grass catching em with their little beaks but I wont forget that day cats & dogs it was coming down in buckets funny how life comes down to a few moments that change everything forever all ye that pass by but he should not have winked no no I felt so queer & it was chilly & damp so I turned up the heat & he was sniffling away like a total wanker a few hearts short of a deck & saying

all the while no its nice its fine & smiling with those dark eyes & I
think he could overhear me saying to the cook what is he an alcoholic
is he in love with me & then he winked & I gathered my things & got
right out of there as soon as the clock struck five & after they told me
he never even finished just paid the bad news & ran off out the back
door into the night over the stones out into the rain & I was right hes
a complete loonybinner a complete nutbar with a complimentary bowl
of figments tossed in that made me so mad I wanted to take im by the
scruff of the neck & chuck im in the tank by the loo with the ghost
like they did in the olden days but then his letter & poems the sweetest thing its enuff to make one jealous I remember telling Menzi on the
phone I was doing my big nude scene on L Word with another woman
to dead silence on the other end what is one to say not that I dont
have my share of admirers maybe not beating the door down but sniffing about all the same right Spanners you cant even ear em coming &
the rain drops upon pellucid roof & all his peculiar talk of snow &
music pellucid thats a funny word why not just plainspeak O my dear
my faraway darling always talking in riddles but cometothink you can
almost hear it that bit in eflat going drip drop plopplopplop drip drop
plunking away the rain a few centuries back on the dirty roof covered
with leaves a smatter of light creeping thru but he left that back door
open & I can even see the wet cobblestones that night I can hear the
rain against my pane & you are dreaming arent you Spanners sniffing
the air I can see you & on the Internet there was that piece by that
painter he was going on about the woman with her lute being handed
a letter & both of them giving it the eye O that sounds like the wheelybump wheelybump of the paperchap I dont envy them having to
wheelybump on nights like this in the rain & to hear it I can almost
see his dripping orange cart banging along with his grey canvas bag I
hope he has a yellow slicker in case there I was right Spanners I can hear
the drone of the lift that sound from the future funny how everything
is like a song in its own way that woman built like a linebacker downtown accosting everyone with her spare quarter spare quarter its a weird
kind of music shes been here forever thats what everybody says & I
hear she knocks back the bottles with all the loot she takes in & Love

what old landmark would you revamp if you had enuff loons not bad
that must have been that day I was shooting off about the things I
would rebuild if I had enuff in the kitty so to speak & he turned his
back to leave & he stood in the doorway waiting & waiting for me to
finish my sentence as if I had to tell im everything that popped into me
ead no you can sling your hook mister but mindstealing herony I dont
mind they are so strange the bluegrey way they wait & wait when they
fish along the water now theres the thunk thunk against the door its
just as well you didnt hear Spanners sleep sweet princess sleep & once
I hear the lift start up again Ill pop out to grab the latest but you know
that old hotel always captured my fancy a little bit of history from the
first moment I got here the sign flashing red as a fireengine in the darkness & those creeping vines about the sides & that oldfashioned chalky
sign like some lovely old airplane writing D I N E I N T H E S K Y on the
side yes there it goes yes hes off to the races I bet I can get my paper
faster than he can get back to his orange cart you are on Helen sorry
Spanners & there we are the chain back in place & the perfect crime
you can still smell the ink in the dark those whopping headlines of
halibut wrap theres not even much of a moon something about a local
man tragedy O how they love to use that word terrible terrible tragedy
today if not a calamitous calamity no Ill have a gander later over tea &
a biscuit after I do my jumble & theres the orange cart clanking off
into the night & that bird has gone dead quiet but its early theres still
time to catch another forty before sunup you & me both Spanners &
I guess he means well even with that O so tragic look like hes dying
that memorial for the dead in the square WHAT IT IS TO YOV a funny
way of putting things & maybe thats all that matters a slant of light &
a sliver of hope if I could just get my songs wrapped up then maybe I
could release my seedee & get out of this place & start over on a fresh
page yes that would be lovely yes Helen yes yer such a jellyfish sometimes & perhaps at last I know what to write back what to reply yes
thru the double doors of the train station & rushing past the statue
THEIR NAMES BE NOT FORGOTTEN yes that day I saw him face to
face what to say yes to that look like hes dying of it yes I will have a
word yes

Death in Vancouver

A hotel is like a theatre, with its life in the wings on the one hand, and life in the auditorium on the other.

—Georges Simenon

I

Maxwell Wittman the Third, with the free spirit name Padam, flounced past the handkerchief tree along Giltford Street, admiring its expanse of gentleman's pleasures, a plethora of flowering breast pockets & burgeoning frills. Quite Carnaby Street, to be exact, a well knit troupe of hoofers all round, wearing those same favourites, those splendid ties of mine, wrought by my impoverished but happy, & I admit, much younger hands. Lovely to see this kind of tree! He came to the bench right outside his own window, where an elderly woman with a thick Ukrainian accent was holding court, as she loved to do on a daily basis. Nearly time to change the guard, I shouldn't wonder. Today, a man with an equally thick accent was sitting beside her, gingerly maintaining a large & tentative space between his faded brogues & the orangepekoe stockings so tantalizingly rolled down her ankles.

"Do you vatch *Six Foot Under?*"

"No."

"Vy don't you go home & vatch dis program den come back tomorrow & ve can talk about it."

"Da, yes yes, I will, yes."

"Alright."

They began to face in opposite directions, listening to the sustained longing of a red-shafted flicker perched somewhere up the street.

"Evening, Marfa," chirped Padam.

"Yes, hi."

"I see you have a friend."

"Vell," she mumbled.

Her turnipcoloured skin was turning aubergine. I'll leave them to it. Padam smiled mischievously & bounded off again, thus demonstrating he was still in excellent shape, even well past his dancing days. What poise, what grace! One of his favourite questions to himself that he, Padam, would leap at the bar to answer, was "What does tomorrow bring," the reply having been on various occasions of his history quite scandalous. However, these were tamer times & the answer would often be one of the following options: "Tomorrow, I am training some adults for the post-Olympic figure skating trials, or tomorrow I am advising a young woman how to point her toes & lift in relation to the bar in my studio or else notwithstanding, I am adding the finishing touches to my latest masterpiece ... " For it was no secret in the neighbourhood that Padam was an all-round artist & that whenever he was sitting still, he would lend his hands to some manner of visual or physical art with a display of talent that only the gods can bestow upon their most flexible mortals. His raw ability, coupled with the sensibility by which his mind was able to visualize the primitive shapes that struggled to arc & ease their way out of marble & clay & even terracotta, provided him with an immediate appreciation of the Istoria. From the first moment he saw the walls of that grand landmark, overwhelmed by thick climbings of Virginia Creeper, he was enamoured of their tenacity to live & what is more, their capacity for freeform dance. Padam peered upward through his thick lenses at the wild undulations of tangled green & mentally transfigured their curvature into concrete forms, puzzling over the potential hint of intrigue within their erratic interweavings & how it would be best represented in marble, clay, terracotta, or even fragments of glass. Such were the workings of his mind, he being none other than Maxwell Wittman the Third, known to all his friends as the absolutely fantabulous Padam. He shook his head, passing under the lintel of the main entrance only to encounter his sexagenarian countenance in the mirror as he leapt up the stairs. None too shabby. Then he made an elegant right & jaunted into the hotel parlour (in other words, the bar). A lithe Irish & Chinese server materialized before Maxwell Wittman the Third, immaculate & neatly musical in his crisp white shirt & well pressed black pants. Grant appeared relatively ageless in spite of his decades working in the hotel (he was nicknamed by Padam, who adored petnames, *The Immortal*). Ah yes, he was what we used to call *smart*. Padam & a few of the other regulars were aware that *The Immortal* was in possession of a degree in sociology, which only made them curious as to the extent that this training increased his general ease & rapport with customers, a distant yet cozy brand of charm, the kind that readily came & went with the crisp turnovers in this medium-sized yet transient *city*. Not that statistical curves would produce anything other than a verbose propagandist, save for the fact that this education had nurtured his unique faculty of memory & now he applied this aptitude to his years of labour & to the innumerable lives of seasonal visitors, as if he were a living attachment to the history of the hotel. But with Padam, one of the *chosen*, he would relax his waiterly gait & let his white shirt puff out a little about the waist, dropping the poker face that masked his dry sense of the human comedy. In other words, one could say that he *knew* Padam. Not like the usual riff-raff & fly-by-nights or even those regulars who got into the habit of stretching their credit or begging you down a pint or two. Then let the good times roll, they would come streaming in & blow a wad on booze all round, based on some longshot, waving about a ridiculously crumpled wad of cash & barking orders & you couldn't say nada until the end of the night when you brought out the chalkboard tally, the written history of their previous misdemeanours, & then their lips would fall silent, stuck in a withered pucker of surprise. Then you would hear some wallets crinkling & some purses creaking open & not a word of a lie, a family of speckled moths would flutter out & everyone would applaud in a flurry of drunk & raucous cries.

"Hey, Padman, how's it hanging?"

In the years that Padam had been coming to the Istoria, he had made several attempts to correct Grant on the matter of correctly pronouncing his free spirit name. Grant would nod with complete understanding, & yet, as if to counteract the degree of affability he owed to the universe of tourists & visitors who happened to stumble through the hotel, he would persist with almost a sadistic merriment in shouting out the artist's name wrongly, much to the consternation of he, Maxwell Wittman the Third, who would murmur a continuous mantra of *well I never*.

"Padman," Grant repeated, tapping the table with glee, "how's it hangin'?"

"All in the right places, the last time I checked," replied Padam.

Then he chuckled at his own joke with his customary Cheshire grin.

"Pint o' the pale ale, is it sir," asked Grant, feigning a Cockney waif in a Dickensian workhouse.

Padam nodded.

"Anything for you, my liege."

Settling into his seat, Padam looked around the interior, spotting the usual collection of hotel guests & passing tourists, as well as a number of neighbourhood residents, the regulars that Padam referred to as the *Irregulars*. There was the old woman, who had come to the hotel in her youth for her high school graduation, who now frequented the bar, entertaining the other visitors with her liverspotted wit while giving out handfuls of Werther's Originals, for the most part appearing quite merry, but other times quite lonely, staring down into her beer & presumably thinking of her very successful children who had all absconded to other provinces for the sake of better opportunities. There was also the university professor, just on the verge of retirement & for the most part presumably thinking of his pension & *la vita nuova*, the new life that was to make its appearance directly afterwards. What might he do? Where should he go? He could always write that epic work of fiction he had been musing over for ages. Yes, that was a pleasing thought. Perhaps a trip to the Norwegian fjords to finish that translation of the *Elder Edda*. Or even to Salt Spring. In this manner, he would stretch out his legs & toy with his police constable (or some might say toilet brush) moustache, dreaming up such projects. There was also a burly bearish man past middle age who felt he was plagued by a toxic combination of increasing lethargy & poor decision-making skills, suspecting he had frittered away his one chance at a life he imagined suitable for himself. So it often is, that we live the life that is most suitable for us, while continuing to insist to ourselves that a series of misfortunes have kept us from a quite different existence, although if we were to actually live that life, it would be intolerable. How often it is that a person lives within their means for most of their young & even middle years, only to find complete & total ruination in old age, due to some sudden inheritance or a set of lottery numbers that finally pay off. We live most easily out of habit, & the shock to our system from the fantastical trans-formation we have been seeking is just enough to kill us. Habit is our sole master, even so much that the habit of complaining about another life we are in fact incapable of living is its own comfort, even if it is a habit of making ourselves unhappy, since that habit contains a kernel of happiness, because it is familiar as an old friend & provides the same kind of warped pleasure we find in shivering outside a build-ing to return to a half-smoked cigarette, or returning to a badly poured pint in a local watering hole, because we have learned what to expect. There was also the woman in the middle of the road of her life, sitting by the window with a glass of Gewürztraminer, watching the sun continue its slow descent until her tiny cobwebbed writing was no longer illuminated by the natural lighting, only by the candles Grant was bringing to every table, casting an eerie glow across her stern countenance. What was she writing anyway? No one knew. This secret was a source of much curiosity & consternation for the *Irregulars*. Slightly removed from her, yet studying her intensely, was a small & stout red-haired man with thick bushy sideburns. As he watched her, the inclination of his head made him look like an ageing satyr just having chanced upon a tired dryad who, to be honest, had been around the woodblock in her time. The more intently he looked at her, the more his bloodshot eyes appeared like those of a passing snapper or rock cod, gleaming with interest, as if doused in a spicy citrus sauce & then slightly overcooked. But beyond the movement of Grant's delicate hands & the gold & liquorice embers of ale glowing beside the deposited flicker, Padam noticed a fresh object coming into focus.

"We have five senses."

He repeated this maxim to himself, allowing the new shape to enter his field of vision & filter through his buzzing brain & then trickle down into his relaxed nerves. Already, he sensed something wonderful was happening to him. Shadows, only a shadow at first. He continued to sip from his glass, tickling his grey whiskers & meanwhile peeping at a figure in the darkest corner of the establishment. It was a young man in his mid-twenties, clothed entirely in black. Like the cassock of a monk. No wonder I didn't notice at first. The simple dignity of his *habit*, the dark falling lines & a sense of complete dimensionlessness, were contrasting sharply with a tinge of red in his black hair & a feral look in his roving eyes. The young man was also writing something. After downing most of his pint, he began to write more feverishly, as if possessed. Then every so often, he would look up at the woman by the window before returning to his mad scrawl. Padam sat in awe, watching the young man's full & curved lips, muttering softly to the notebook in front of him. Immediately, Maxwell Wittman the Third began to form a replica of the young man's face in his mind, just as he had done with the ivy climbing up the hotel wall, except with far more interest. The eyes were dark & they moved about the establishment restlessly, catching each flicker of light. Padam was reminded of an exquisite sculpture of Orpheus he had seen in a European gallery, a figure trembling in the clutches of the disgruntled Maenads, trying to look over his shoulder at a melting Eurydice. Then upon the stage of his memory, where he was forever in the spotlight of past performances, the sculpture of Orpheus came to life. We were doing that wonderful number to the music of Glück & I, Padam, was right beside that delicious principal. *Dance of the Serene Spirits*, I think that's the one. Orphée had been a naughty boy & now he wanted his girlfriend back. That beautiful boy began to play & all the trees & rocks & souls in the underworld were moved to hear him play upon his lonely reed. & who could resist that sound? No one, not even I, Maxwell Wittman the Third. Then, while that beautifully hollow sound echoed throughout the theatre, the principal began to move his body & in every step, there was the increasing sorrow of another ebbing note. Orphée will lose his great love & die, no matter what he does. Long story short, the women still tear him into tiny pieces. O never mind about them. *I* will save you, Orphy.

Padam woke up the next day with a sore throat, or rather, a slight irritation. He was grateful that he had no students. Hmm ... must have slept in. Best to go for a walk, Babushka, best to walk it right off. He showered & scrubbed his throat & his delicates & the slight glow about his cheeks before throwing on a green windbreaker & a most flattering pair of jogging pants. Time for a brisk walk, old friend. But Maxwell Wittman the Third had not gotten far before he saw the young man leaning against an aquamarine railing above the beach bathhouses, lovingly cradling a green & yellow book. Padam stood upon the pavement for a moment, gently massaging his throat through a striped scarf. A vapour, that's what I need. Some sort of vapour rub.

"Good news," Padam began, his eyes probing Grant's face.

Grant did not miss a beat in reverting back to his servitor demeanour, unsheathing a suitable response from his hidden arsenal of quips & wisecracks.

"Language of love, Padman. Me no speak."

Padam laughed with a note of apprehension in his voice.

170

"What's his name this time?"

Grant prodded Maxwell Wittman the Third playfully with his white-sleeved elbow. Padam struggled to maintain the Cheshire smile that was expected of him, the one he had flashed for adoring masses in the dance halls & opera houses of the world.

"Hey, well keep me posted, Padman, of any future developments. Now, a pint of the usual poison?"

"Sure, sure."

Maxwell Wittman the Third sat by himself in a corner, watching diligently as the young man flipped back to previous pages of his notebook in order to verify or correct some beautiful phrase, then flip forward again, at times apprehensive to continue writing on a fresh page. Padam noted that the young man had a nervous habit of looking up suddenly from his pages of scrawl & squinting about him, before returning to his weedy overgrowth of text. As his long fingers tapped the table, Padam could see that his nails were all uneven & bitten. Ah, my fine young cannibal! Johannes Sebastian Bach & Giacomo Puccini were no different with their inelegant touches to antique keyboards. Such are the hideous hands of genius. Then the young man would stare outward at the slow fluctuation of waves & stare so intently at the glass that Padam felt those dark eyes were not staring at the movement of black water at all, but in fact at his own reflection. He is looking at me, Maxwell Wittman the Third. Padam sat perfectly still, revelling in this moment. So this was the spark of intensity he had been searching for, this fire in the blood which ignited clay & even threatened to consume any material in the very process of shaping it. That flicker in those dark eyes. Heat? Madness? That spark of potentiality. Looking restless, the young man rose & negotiated a path through a number of tables pulled pell mell together. Padam made a valiant effort not to ogle his firm young buttocks as he glided down the steps that led to the beach. Padam heard the crash of the heavy hotel door. Padam gulped back his pint rapidly, dropping a handful of coins for Grant, before bounding down the stairs in the same direction. The young man was seated on a bench a short distance from the hotel. Padam crossed the street hurriedly & started to creep very quietly towards the bench with the agile steps that had defined some of his greatest roles. The orange streetlamp cast a strange glow over the young man & the book Padam had seen him with in the morning. As Padam walked behind the bench, he peeped over the young man's shoulder & managed to read the title of that corrosive yellow & green cover. *Against Nature.* The object of his interest suddenly rose from the bench & turned around, eyeing Maxwell Wittman the Third with suspicion. He doesn't even know who I am. Padam nodded politely, giving no indication that he had just been skulking about behind a row of trees, & gave a curt wave of acknowledgement. Padam could not blame the young man for his suspicions, & certainly not himself for his own fascination. He had learned over the course of his life about the tension between people who do not know each other & yet have cause to see one another on a daily basis without necessarily having anything in common, other than a shared hour in the same location. There is a peculiar anxiety in such relationships because they are based upon a relationship that does not exist. The first wave of acknowledgement or the first word between two people like these has the poignancy of a musical note that initiates a lengthy sonata. We come to crave the behaviour of a stranger, become attuned to their repetitive movements, as if those traits & social codes were the key to rediscovering some sacred ritual. We anticipate those habits we have come to expect, as anxious to prey upon them for the sake of entrance into the secret world of another living creature, although the conversation at first is merely sustained as the faint cloying & wheedling strokes of a violin. But beneath that intermittent flash of catgut, there are the deep emotive plunkings of piano keys, that hidden part of every individual person who can never truly be known, & that mystery of those elusive fingerings may only be supplied by the imagination. Before we have seized those hands & have examined their uneven fingernails & have studied their arbitrary lines of longevity & fate, we are forced to suspend our judgement, & that is maddening to our minds, to be rendered incapable of judgement. There can be no love without a generous dose of the additive doubt. For this reason, Padam walked away from the young man that evening, letting his fine features burrow into his consciousness, tightening the rainbow scarf around his neck with a subtle flourish that was unique to him, Maxwell Wittman the Third.

About eight. The sun was still heavy with plenitude & a black lab seemed to be smiling across the crosswalk as open hummers sped about the lush columns of brown & green, honking furiously at those arm in arm with their sweethearts. How lovely. Padam had taken the window seat this evening in spite of Grant's warning about a possible draft. He watched the constant stream of visiting bodies on wheels, cycling & rollerblading & perambulating & wheelchairing past the gaze of a very relaxed Padam. There was indeed a light breeze & the water appeared deep & very blue, affected by this cold element. Nevertheless, a mob of children in sopping trunks were wading & then paddling out to the floating wooden platform that supported a grey slide, their yells & laughter drowned out by the rather pompous roar of souped-up motorcycles as they vrroomvroomed by. Sploosh. Padam watched a pair of red trunks disappear. Over the blue slide, a maple leaf flapped in the breeze with lukewarm accord. The flag was obscured by a gaggle of young women, awkwardly walking by in impossibly high heels, leaning on one another's bare shoulders for support. Silly. Go back to the suburbs, my lovelies. But the way they looked together, suspended above the pavement & directly in front of the restless italic surface of the water, set Padam's mind wandering a little ways from his favourite subject: himself. Not all of his friends (or dare we presume, *conquests*) knew that Maxwell Wittman the Third had been married for many years to a little Pavlova of his very own. He had fallen in love with her for the sake of her form & for the placid grace that accompanied all of her crystalline movements, even when she was not dancing. She had adored him for his own years of fame, & even more for his years of notoriety & his ego had been, to say the least, quite tickled by her attentions. He came to prize her, not so much as the talented artist she was to become, once taken under his

173

outstretched wing, but as a living work of art, like an unfinished statuette that he wanted before his eyes at all times. In this way, as an artist only could, he *knew* her the best of anyone, & possessed her in this fashion. It was no surprise that not long after she had *arrived*, & was considered by everyone to be a great dancer, she fell in love with some mere mortal, on the grounds that he was in every way, *a man*. Fortunately for Padam at this time, his idoless had already lost her bloom in his eyes & he could afford to see his image of her break in half & metamorphose into something entirely new. He could not deny that she was far happier now, being truly in love, but for him, she had ceased to possess those qualities he had first admired in her, especially those that made her a subset of his own person & experience. It was only out of habit & for the sake of domestic comfort that he made a half-hearted attempt to reconcile the irreconcilable with her. Yet she pleaded with such quiet courtesy for her attainment of this long-deserved love that Padam felt moved to grudgingly let her go. Through this act of charity, he had gained her eternal friendship, as well as that of her new beau, which had provided him with a secondary ménage for the rest of his life. She had known that he preferred men, naturally. However, some nights he would sit up & wonder whether she truly believed in his admiration & affection for her. What he had felt was a love beyond that of the passing rapture of flesh. He had never missed a single performance of hers, unless he had his own unbreakable engagement to pull him away from his little Pavlova. But the young man was different. In his mind's eyes, Padam had always seen his little Pavlova turning like a figure upon a lathe. She would pirouette about his memory & whenever he watched her, he would try to recapture her movements, to recollect precisely how she had altered from the woman of his imagination. In complete contrast, the young man was a highly strung creature, at times rather taciturn & even surly with regard to his preoccupations. Then, as if from the depths of some orchestra pit, his imaginings would appear about him like the first strains that introduce a cloaked emissary on stage. The young man's face would become flushed with exuberance, & it was evident that he had slipped into the personality of one of his characters without missing a beat. With Pavlova, he had always felt able to retreat into the secure darkness of the audience & to appreciate the distance between them, a sensation so different from their day to day intimacy. But the young man was somehow threatening. Padam suspected that with an unforgiving despotism, the young man wanted to force the world to bear witness to the lavish furnishings of his imaginative talents, to lay out that regal tapestry like a heap of warm linen & wrap every onlooker up within it, slinging them over his shoulder, reducing the much celebrated & discussed value of *life* to a collection of offal in a coarse burlap sack. Suddenly, Padam felt his nostrils quiver.

"We have five senses."

He knew at once without looking that the overpowering waft was trailing behind the slight waddle of Barb, the woman who sat by the window every night, writing. If there were any question of territory among the patrons, she only needed to waltz by the table she desired & before long, the sitters would ask for their damages & disperse into the night. Padam wrinkled up his face. She upset his senses, not for anything she had done, per se. Maxwell Wittman the Third simply had no appetite for her graceless flesh & lack of form. There was nothing that he found more distasteful than having his stroll around the seawall interrupted by the vision of her chugging pistons & huffing & puffing face, powerwalking toward him with only a snort of acknowledgement. Padam would grin & wave back, offering the respect & fraternity that only a common watering hole can fashion between completely different individuals. Hence, Barb took her seat by the window & opened her large notebook & in the fashion of a distracted aristocrat, Padam nodded toward that skunkish scent. He waited until midnight, but the young man did not appear.

The next morning, Padam did not feel much better. He had cancelled his lessons for that week & he stole another hour of sleep for himself. Light began to filter through his closed eyelids, falling at an elevated angle into his bedroom from street level, where the odd pedestrian was sneakering by. The eyes of Maxwell Wittman the Third flickered open to land upon his prizewinning case of St. Benedictine chocolates, his multicoloured Warholesque panels of devout monks, their faces obscured beneath large dark cassocks, faceless yes, but clearly in handsclasped communion with the Lord Almighty, beseeching Him for additional helpings of St. Benedictine. O dear I must do something with that window. He dressed without ablutions (only a splash to face tickling grey moustache). He felt hurried. For what, I wonder? He walked down Giltford Street & briskly onward, close to the shoreline. Mmm … fresh air does wonders. He stopped, realizing he had rushed directly to that spot above the bathhouses where he had previously seen the young man reading. He smiled to himself to find that his heart was still beating rapidly. A spot of arrhythmia? He certainly had not been tossing & turning all night over such a minor experience. Plenty of boys in the ocean. But no one was there. Not wading in the water or walking across the sand or sitting upon one of the symmetrically placed logs. The beach was deserted. The clouds overhead had an ashen look, sick & bloated with greyity. Padam sat on a bench overlooking the bathhouses, suddenly wishing he had a book to read like the young man. That is a plan. Then we might get to chatting & then … ahh, what's the use? No one passed. Out of sheer boredom, Padam began to reflect upon his own youth. Funny how the days went by as if they would never end. I wanted to leave home & see the world so badly. You wait for something, the happy day arrives, & then like everything else, it vanishes. Funny, that. That brother of mine, with a career in salt mining! Given an eternity, I'd never manage. There is that French quote he gave me about Saltzburg, the one that talks about a withered branch that grows into an enormous mountain through the process of saline crystallization. What is it again? Ah yes, the writer says that love is the withered branch that becomes unbearably large through the crystallization of the imagination. Why me? You could tell right off at the arts & crafts fair. That old fishwife was giving out the awards for arts & crafts & produce. Best lettuce, best tomatoes, best peppers (red & green & yellow) & in each category the farmer's boy carries it away! Imagine, the little Russian farmboy! That was all well & good. But when it came to my tea cozy, to the magnificent crochet work I was most proud of, then I really got up her nose. Boy, did she blow a gasket! Reluctantly waving that prize ribbon with her plump fingers & turning redder than my fresh crop of beets, she announced the winner, offering a megaphoned epilogue through clenched teeth that perhaps next year Mrs. Wittman should leave her boy at home, locked in the farmhouse. Mama blushed, but did not hesitate in snatching the ribbon out of her hand, before explaining to me softly.

"She compete in croshay herself, dat bitch."

That day, I became a *man*. Maxwell Wittman the Third reflected pleasantly upon the crocheted tea cozy that now sat upon his coffee table. It was one of his most prized possessions, because the light that fell into his living room & illuminated each stitch repeated that first great lesson to him about the ways of the world. After that day, he had never looked back.

That evening, it was nice & quiet. Padam halted upon entering to prick up his ears, straining to hear the perpetual FEED, the Istoria's laundry cycle of classical showstoppers that more or less spun in a complete loop. Only on occasion would they throw in a ballet piece or one of the Russian composers he adored. Say that dark bit from the *8th String Quartet* of Shostakovich. Tonight, it was one of the more common bits, that placid entr'acte from *Carmen*. Do do do do dum da da da da da. Charming. Maxwell Wittman the Third paused in reflection, thinking of one of those productions where the jilted femme fatale next door had crossed the stage upon a live burro. What a night! He paused, blinking at the dim interior & the tankers scarcely visible upon the horizon, suspended within the VIEW, before focusing to observe the obscure gloom of the woman writing by the window. He could make out a quarto edition of Shakespeare on the table. He looked around. The old woman was muttering to herself. Then she noticed Padam & stopped herself with a watery gleam of recognition in her eyes. Mothers, secretly fretting, always fretting & talking to themselves. The burly man was sitting in front of the other window pane with a characteristically ursine expression on his face, cracking his knuckles & angling out his large knees. Very large, for such a *small* person. It was surely not until Massenet's sublime *Meditation* began its magic that the young man entered the establishment. He sat down in the middle of the parlour while Padam remained poised in a dark corner like a spider, waiting & watching. The young rub rubbed his eyes gently with his knuckles before examining his right pinky for smudges of black ink. How endearing. The young man looked up toward the lingering touches of sunlight that bathed his dark features in a spectral flash of light like the snap second before a photograph is taken. Then the young man laughed out loud, looking directly at the woman by the window.

"KING LEAR," he roared.

"I beg your pardon?"

"I didn't promise you a rose garden."

The woman by the window stared at him directly over her something other than hornrimmed glasses with increasing skepticism. Padam scowled openly, in accordance with his open nature.

"*King Lear*, I mean. That looks like a three loon bargain version in your hands, one dollar given up for each daughter, but by no means the historical version."

"O," she replied, enjoyably annoyed.

"I mean, that's the tragedy."

The young man was in a state of nervous excitability.

"Ol' Shakes changed a pack of lines. Not the same play at all, no no. But maybe the difference is negligible."

He corrected himself with the immediate backwashing of a promising young pedant-to-be.

"O," she countered over those glasses beyond description.

As if the old vamp hadn't drunk him in from the first moment he arrived! Careful, my young friend. She might drink you right up.

Padam watched the sinking sunlight as it outlined the fresh curves of the young man's cheeks. He could not resist throwing his arm over the partition of stained wood between them.

"O, of course, I agree with you entirely. We should talk."

The young man turned towards him, his face full of shaded arrogance, & Maxwell Wittman the Third was entranced. The young man said nothing. His brown eyes seemed to eclipse into themselves. Padam leaned his lithe body against the partition, not unaccustomed to beauty in the slightest, yet bewildered by the beer buzz & the burning edges of those eyes. He felt stung by their glare. He made a number of mechanical gestures in order to free himself from being completely transfixed. He felt very tense & awkward & well, very young! He made a quick flicking gesture & a smooth black card landed on the table beside the young man's pint of raven ale. The woman by the window snorted softly & returned to her three loon copy of *King Lear*. The young man looked down at the black matte finish & the spectrum of muted colours that conspired to impress upon the eyes a bold & tiny [p].

"My card."

Maxwell Wittman the Third, true to his patronym, held up a twin brother to the card he had just dealt out to the young man & tapped it solidly, before caressing it again with increasing affection. The young man nodded politely & Padam scurried off towards the exit, wishing he had said so much more but that was nicely done, indeed. A real pro. He paused on the marble steps, his back to that now treacherous mirror, peering up at the bright & garish glasswork, scolding those knights in brutal colours with lavish crests. Perhaps on their way to that messy affair otherwise known as the Crusades! Another round of mango & gules. Padam let his eyes absorb the patterns of glass, holding his palms over his cheeks. He felt deliriously happy. A little flushed, but happy. Grant noticed him standing like that & came running out of the bar, stopping beside him at the top of the stairs.

179

"Hey Padman, you losin' it or what? This is a twenty. Real green. Tens are purple, remember? How many did you have, anyway?"

Padam looked back at him & laughed melodiously.

"Keep the change."

The man with the red sideburns lumbered up the stairs & stopped abruptly, like a bloodhound stopping to sniff Maxwell Wittman the Third. Padam raised his hand & made a sweeping gesture, a little like the Queen on speed, & waved vigorously.

"Hello Bob!"

While walking up Giltford Street, Padam fell into a blocklong reverie, surprisingly enhanced by the thick accents of the two bench-warmers outside his window, as if they were the sweetest song sparrows.

"You vatch program," the man asked or insisted, pushing a thick finger into her doublesweatered shoulder.

"Yes, I did not like."

Padam smiled at the two of them.

"Evening Maximillian," she offered gruffly.

But who could stay cross with the Supreme Council of Public Works & Benches on a night like this? The air was thick with erotic promise & Maxwell Wittman the Third was reminded of the slow bassoons at the start of Stravinsky's The Rite of Spring & how they twist & contort & culminate into a type of seasonal frustration that can only be remedied by frenetic & savage dances, in other words, by the continuity of that chaotic rite. Padam generously wished the sitters an unlikely romp of their own, according to the passionate devil may care make hay while sun shine mood that had come over him. That night, he tossed & turned & tried to escape those dark eyes which seared his memory & nibbled away at the demidark. Light fell through his window from the orange streetlamp & he could hear mysterious night workers hooking hoses up to hydrants & allowing water to gush along Giltford. So hot. What are they up to? But Padam found some comfort as he listened to this continuous roar of rushing water. That sense of release. But what does tomorrow bring? Something to do about that window, especially if she is going to hold court out there, night after night with her new friend. Maybe a new work, he tossed. Maybe my greatest work, an homage to him, he turned.

Tomasz Geronimo Assu strode into the Istoria in his dark monkish habit. But his black shirt was open, a little risqué for a monk. Hmm, what weather we are having! Maxwell Wittman the Third stirred anxiously in his seat, picking at one or two croutons in his salad in order to be doing something, anything to quell the agitation in his ordinarily rather exceptionally controlled limbs. What was that? From *Thaïs*, isn't it? Now there was a girl who got about. Massenet's *Meditation* had started up once again with its slow dreamy melody of self-discovery, underlining the pompous harrumph of the well-moustached professor & the intense glowering of the redsideburned man with a watery gleam in his eye & the incessant notations of the woman by the window who suddenly had became more immersed in her work than before. Tomasz pulled out a green chair with a gesture of shared formality & peppered Padam with a series of florid phrases. It was all happening so quickly.

"Would you permit me, Sir, to borrow this chair for the interim that the pleasure of your company might allow, since I have on more than one occasion noticed you & to be frank have observed your graceful carriage & have so often longed to speak to this fascinating gentleman before me, namely yourself ... "

Even as it was unfolding before him, Padam had no accurate memory of the young man's grandiloquence. Every time his thoughts returned to the young man's request to join him, his phrases become longer & more intricate in their manner of stark admiration for Maxwell Wittman the Third until a word or two of greeting had become a Petrarchan sonnet upon those almost motionless lips. Behold, this gentle statue that speaks to me! Tonight we dine & drink flaming alabaster! Padam was so startled by the presence of his latest idol that he was uncertain what was spoken between them. He could only recall his ardent Yes. Yes, louder than those cracking knuckles of the ursine chap with the bad investments. Yes. No, I have no idea how many beers ago I arrived nor which karmic act has indubitably led to this prolonged encounter & even the sweet promise of future encounters. But he beamed in such a way that his grey moustache twitched with pleasure. Somewhere in the background, Massenet coughed disapprovingly & Thaïs stopped her writing to glare at his uncontrollable magnetism, catching the watery gleam of a red dragon, but none of this perturbed Max Wizzyman the Fird. His young god had come to the same ancient well to drink & that was renewal for both.

"I've seen you in here before & you look, I must say, wonderful. Your bone structure is lovely & in fact, with permission of course, I would be happy more than happy in fact, to draw you, to sit with you & draw you, night after night … "

The young man looked around nervously as if he were about to bolt. Padam held out his hands defensively, observing that one had turned into a dogwood flower. The other, a handkerchief of clemency. So Padam slurred on, while his new companion listened carefully.

"So you want to draw me," the young man said.

"Because you are so beautiful," added Padam in a tone of passionate self-interest which overcame his usual flippancy.

"I would never dream of disturbing you," he added, switching to the amiable professionalism of a bank manager.

The young man looked down, turning colour, either in blissful surrender to vanity or in some attempt to restrain his fury.

"Of course, nothing you would feel uncomfortable about," he coaxed, now adopting the manner of a concerned guidance counsellor trying to convince a wayward child to go on a camping trip.

"My name is Tom. Well, that is what everyone calls me. Basically, I want to sit here & write, like her."

Tom waved his hand in the general direction of the woman by the window, who like the lead violinist signalled by a barely imperceptible cue from the conductor, began to move her wrist faster, lowering her face towards her book of minute print.

"So how can I write with you sitting right across from me," the young man roared, banging the table to punctuate.

Padam shrunk, lowering his voice.

"Sure, sure, whatever, mmhmm."

He patted the young man's notebook, desperate to change the subject.

"What's that?"

The bearish man relaxed his knuckles. Thaïs lowered her pen & ordered another wine. The man with red sideburns watched her order another wine. The professor went back to his contemporary novel, once again able to consider the ramifications of two compassionate Roman soldiers torn apart by a series of raids by Germanic tribes at the exilic fringes of their centralized urbanity. Playing with his constabular moustache, he wrote down the word *homoerotic* & circled it twice. At least that was part of the story, according to Grant.

" *That* is a dollar store pad, the only kind I like. Thirty-six lines per page. Most notebooks are real shitty—they only have about half of that. If you're ever working on your life story, this baby is what you need."

"But what's inside?"

The young man smiled back, full of mystery.

"A smattering of Chinese, Norse, Greek. Sometimes I write out snatches of Homer for fun. I translate, write, whatever. Nothing special."

Padam nodded, raising two fingers for Grant to see.

"You must know a lot of languages, a lot of things."

The young man shook his head.

"No, I know very little. Almost nothing. & it's getting worse. But whenever I try to talk about it, I can't even wrap my head around the idea. This, for instance, is a Li Po translation I had published, the kind they sell carved into olive pits."

The young man opened the notebook & pointed at some large Chinese characters with English writing underneath.

"See, you can see the wine ladle & the shape of the moon. They are sometimes only sounds & the pictographs are often confused by translators. On the other hand, there is something primitive in every language that I find exciting, the way those characters & letters once altered the mind in so many ways."

Grant glided over.

"Another for you & your buddy, Padman?"

The young man nodded, as Grant perused his open book.

"Hey, Tom, buddy, you learnin' Kanji?"

The young man looked up, scrunching up his face.

"No, it's Li Bai, drinking alone under the moon. I thought it rather apt, somehow."

Grant's mouth became a large semiyawning O as he hurried away to pour two more beers.

"The Greek is not so popular anymore. & Anacreon is not as hot as Sappho. Addicted to liquor & serving boys or was that only the style he adopted, hmm? I was just walking down this street behind a man in beige, or perhaps tan, to do him justice. He had loafers on, a rich reddishbrown colour, the only colour standing out from the rest of him, his slacks, even a cap of the same colour. Yet there was something about him in the sunlight that exuded let us say a shrimpish hue. It would seem preposterous to insist that his weathered complexion & especially huge proboscis were all rather lobsterlike in shade & texture, but there you are! That is what his head looked like as he turned in the light. But what caught my eye most of all was a large book wrapped in an oldfashioned paperbag cover. He held it under, for the sake of argument, one of his creamy pincers, his left to be exact. I walked a few paces behind him & for a couple of blocks, I was unable to pass without attracting attention. He was one of those weavers, you see, one of those pedestrians with a genius for impeding your way, no matter which way you turn. So I tried to slip by him several times & without looking at me once, he floated to the other side of the sidewalk to bar my escape, like one of Dante's creatures that block your escape from your sin of choice. Some moments like this, they ask for your attention, they cry out for it. Like the crinkling veins upon the autumn leaves, the old man's face asked me to understand & even appreciate its lobsterness. At last, I fled into here & there was so much to write about, more than I could capture & certainly more than I can remember at the moment … "

The beers arrived. Grant held a full tray with one hand & pulled out two paper napkins with the other, folding them in half before freeing himself to soundlessly lay down each pint. Then he floated off with winged feet.

"So the Greek is not so popular anymore," agreed Padam quite readily.

He felt unable to follow the young man's diatribe yet also felt increasingly stimulated by his outpouring of words. He listened & watched, thinking of a young friend of his from Bologna & the particular way he whispered the word *stimulare*.

"Watching you now, I see a great work. Watching you now, I cannot think of anything else. It is forming before my eyes."

The young man sneered for a second, which was very unbecoming yet oddly provocative to Maxwell Wittman the Third.

"I've been to your website. Your hypertext agrees with you that you are very accomplished."

Padam went stiff as a thunderbolt freshly honed by the sweaty hands of Hephaestus.

"O," he said.

"You know what your problem is? I mean your art is good art & everything. It demonstrates various principles. But you are too *like this*."

The young man made a tight fist & held it over his beer.

"All that Apollonian shit is soooooo last week."

Padam laughed along with the young man's laughter, happy that he was happy. In fact, Padam laughed & laughed. He had once heard a Liverpudlian describe the row of trees outside as looking just like Irish lyres. At the time, he had thought this was a peculiar thing to say. But now, as he laughed along madly with the young man, who was in a few words denouncing all his nude Apollos riding Roman bulls, Maxwell Wittman the Third thought that he could see them flexing their coarse limbs & bending their knotted elbows & that every motion was a kind of ancient music through a light bluster of leaves. Padam was reminded of an inscription by Theocritus that another friend had written for him. *Where are my bay leaves? Where are my charms? My drugs. I want to bind my man to me, my hard love.* Those lines had meant little to him at the time. The young man sat back in his chair, clasping his hands together, content in his perfection.

"I'm serious. All this talk of a great work! & what would that be?"

Padam did not reply. Instead, he reached for his beer & took a long swig, allowing the fumes & ivy to envelop his already clouded brain. He waited, in fact, until the young man was rapt. Then he swallowed & released a heady breath.

"*The Rape of Ganymede*," he announced at last.

Grant looked in their direction for a second & scratched the back of his smooth neck. The young man narrowed his gaze, nearsightedly fuming. Padam struggled to remain serious, at least in expression, although the young man's fury brought a smile to his lips which was difficult to hide. A certain fury of pride that hardened his soft lines of beauty. He watched the young man in this moment & saw a rough sketch, perhaps even a Dürer.

"O yes."

The lips scoffed with considerable derision.

"Another of your bareassed waterboys in the clutches of some lascivious bird. Granted, I can see in your work that you love your lines & structure of form in the context of beauty. You are intimate

186

with colour schemes, yet limit yourself to an inventory of everything spectral. Forget this high-handed aspiration to greatness! Or why not an American eagle, an endangered symbol of the state? & Ganymede as an Incan sweatshop worker?"

Padam giggled in manly fashion.

"Only, I'm quite settled on *you*."

"What I mean is why choose the same subject manner!? Why reinvent the discus? Where is the violent rupture of fighting forms, the break from harmony? Where is the dissonance in your work?"

Padam smiled & shrugged, as if shaking loose a feeding mosquito. The young man was not finished. "What if the bird were Sidney's or Shelley's, not something so namby-pamby as POESY but in this case a far darker bird that was maybe not even a bird at all but instead an aspect of the mind, maybe the mind of young Ganymede?"

Maxwell Wittman the Third adjusted his glasses & frowned, attempting to focus.

"Then the rape would not be physical at all, but instead a violation of mental processes, performed by what the Vikings call a mind-stealing heron."

The young man raised his pint as a demonstrative model of a Viking mind-stealer.

"Of course, I prefer the phrase *mindcatching kingfisher*, but that is neither here nor there. What I would like to see is a raven, a far darker bird, an emblem of creation. Is this art? Is the obscure bird giving the young Ganymede inspiration or merely sucking all the lifeblood out of him, that ravenous scavenger? No. Out of his moist thoughts. Or no, maybe not. Maybe it means nothing ... "

The young man trailed off, sounding tipsy & uncertain. Padam nodded politely, trying to juggle a number of thoughts, some of which were bouncing across the parlour & landing in the choice poisons of several parties. Why whatever had the young darling said? He watched the lone candle flickering between them & the shadows that it cast across the young man's face. This is art, this very countenance. What was all this talk about a bird?

"Sure, sure," agreed Padam.

Who wouldn't have complied? Such splendid company.

"Wanna go smoke a joint?"

The young man rose.

"Sorry. Some other time."

II

Days passed. A week. Padam had not seen his bran new fancy in that long. Much to his surprise, he had established a new calendar to follow, marked only by the young man's fleeting appearances. I never even got a name. We visit Maxwell Wittman the Third a week after his meeting with the young man, although that is not to say he lacked a certain intelligence about his comings & goings. Grant had dutifully informed him of brief visitations at the eleventh hour. & so it was that Padam pined most for the hour when his pride would least allow him to appear. His years of artistic discipline won out over this rather unscheduled passion that now occupied all of his thoughts. But Grant remained eager to please his buddy Padman in the way that a chef, when insecure about the reception of a Spartan soufflé, may feel inclined to whip up an *arrabbiata* for the next course, one to pique the most jaded of taste buds. Perhaps this unsavoury morsel did not concern the young man. But it was a choice tidbit & Padam was born to sample it, like one of the members of a tribunal (or dare we say one of those roving reporters who whip up hearsay on the matter) who has missed days of key testimony & severely needs to be updated. Something peculiar had happened. The red-haired man had been sitting near Maxwell Wittman the Third one night, a fact he instantly remembered in the telling. Padam had smiled out of courtesy at him, due to the necessity that recognition creates, even when one wishes to keep one's distance. Even if you wish to create difficulties, to piddle where you drink, so to speak, that small flicker of recognition betrays your most ardent desire to be unknown. Only later would the young man repeat a fair speculation by a local writer that perhaps heaven is total anonymity. & what a bitter glass of truth that was to become! For certain types of woolgatherering gossips, that heaven is *their* hell. But we are getting ahead of ourselves. We must hear what happened. The old woman was sitting beside the red-haired man that night, displaying a look of dubious sympathy. There was a pile of Werther's Originals on the table & her eyes were watery with loved ones.

"How's it goin'?"

"Good."

"Good."

"They have that homeless paper downtown & I deliver it yup I do. Mum she says I should only have one beer tho."

The old woman had nodded. Then the burly knucklecracker had entered, quickly acknowledging the existence of the red-haired man, who had given out a gruff hello while fiddling with his sideburns. He had sat in a corner opposite the pushedtogether tables seating a large group of Norwegians. Skoal was the cry & skoal the reply. It was not long after their crashing toast that a distinct smell pervaded the premises. The woman who writes by the window had waltzed into the withdrawing room with her customary notebook under her arm & without so much as a glint of recognition in her perpetually mortified glare, passing right by the agitated nostrils of the red-haired man whose big eyes had followed her & started to bulge like those of a dragon in its sleepy cave, disturbed by the odour of a passing animal.

"I don't like animal imagery."

She had once said this to the young man about Ovid & Ted Hughes, whoever they were. Yet there they were in this Aesopian encounter, the skunk & the dragon. What a subject for a painting! The red-haired man needed only a few quick flourishes of the brush to form the curling flames of his sideburns. He had seemed to be on fire with frustration. His eyes had darted from side to side & then had bulged outward again like those of a man being hanged.

"Skoal!"

His eyes had remained fixed at the edge of their sockets & fixed upon the window that held her prisoner in a reflection of moonlight. It would have been just like the FEED to play *Clair de Lune* at that instant, but neither he nor Grant could remember what had been playing at the time. They were a velvet painting alright. Her darkness & shades of grey in a hospitalgreen window & her release of venomous scent, purely in self-defense. Spinning out her inscrutable scrawl night after night. & the odd moth & the eternal moth fixed upon the wall above one of the washroom stalls & the burly knucklecracker moving his big hands noisily like hammers within the piano trying to crush each of them beneath the power of his particular music.

"Skoal!!!"

So as Grant continued to guide him through the now departed phantoms of memory, losing & gaining realities along the way, Maxwell Wittman the Third's thoughts turned to his father, Maxwell Wittman the Second. When he had died, there had been no question that the thing to do was to draw & sculpt his grief into some honorary work, using the impressions of his father's hands that he had taken. He soon had formed two similar spheres, one with a physical replica of his own hand, his, the hand of Maxwell Wittman, *fils*, & another with only the impression of his father's absent hand. There were still lonely evenings when Padam would hold one sphere in each hand & attempt to weigh the difference between Man & Spirit. Some nights, he would twiddle his moustache & doubt that the handless sphere could weigh as much as the behanded one. He still lacked the means to measure the perimeter of the spirit world. & what did he believe, even with regard to Maxwell Wittman *père*?

"We have five senses."

This is what he repeated to himself. Of course, Padam was very aware of the similarity between his own hand & that of the gruff loyalist Scot. In contrast, he was gentle as a lamb & looked far better in a kilt, even to this day. He could not help but feel that the two spheres were a negotiation between his own hands & his father's hands in the gay old afterlife. There was part of Padam in every work of art he produced, which is a statement that might be attributed to every artist. One of the things that had most drawn him to the young man

191

was the shape of his hands. Their shape bore a great resemblance to his own hands, or so he thought, just as he told himself that the young man was just as he was as a young man. But the length of the young man's fingers was very much part of his own evolution. Padam granted him *that*.

A young man had rapped his fingers up & down on a nearby table. Grant had just informed him that the kitchen was closed.

"Good pizza in one shot, or else you gotta scope out your options."

Padam had nodded agreeably, whether the comment was addressed to him or not. It had been that time of night in a bar when everyone feels hilarious & better looking. Padam had occupied himself by studying the red-haired man, whose tearyeyed listener had long ago gone home. The woman by the window had looked up from time to time, appearing very aware of the red-haired man's intensity with a stern spark in her empty eyes. Then she had returned to her writing. Padam had snorted to himself. She liked to tell people rather loudly that she was a relative of T.S. Eliot. Had that any impact on her minuscule writ & her look of death warmed up? Nonetheless, she had downed her white wine & had hurriedly folded her notebook, holstering it under her arm before slipping down the stairs that faced the beach. The red-haired man had returned from the bathroom to find her missing from the reflection in the window. He only saw himself sniffing the air. His eyes had bulged even wider. He had reached into his vinyl windbreaker & pulled out a bag of sonorous change. He quickly yet methodically sorted out silver from copper. He lumbered back out in the direction of the bathroom, exiting the side or the front of the Istoria, depending on which way you looked at things. Maxwell Wittman had thought he could hear something outside, but what?

"Sure, sure. Of course I remember all that perfectly. But then what happened?"

Grant grinned, once again like a chef receiving inquiries about a secret recipe.

"Ohht, duty calls. Stay tuned, pal."

Even as Grant closed his mouth to monastically contain the conclusion of that peculiar tale, Padam was distracted by the sudden entrance of the young man, who was given only the slightest chance to sit down & read a paragraph or jot down a word or two when a buxom red-haired woman approached his table.

"Excuse me I couldn't help but notice are you a traveller? The moment I saw you taking out your travelbook from your back pocket I said that's me as a traveller. Are you a traveller?"

The young man used his most cosmopolitan voice.

"No. I'm local. Are you a traveller?"

"No. I'm local. I'm afraid the only thing in my back pocket is a book of poetry."

"O. Sorry to disturb you."

She returned to her table in a different corner, leaving the young man rebuffed & perplexed. Tease. Maxwell Wittman the Third could not remain aloof to such mortal suffering. He wanted to run over & comfort the young man with the presence of he, Padam. He also thought of the word TRAVELLER (or TRAVELER) emblazoned upon covers of tourist guides & motorway exits & hostel premises while staring at the idol of his heart staring at the red-haired girl looking out at the beach. The young man had a translucent scar in the middle of his forehead, sometimes skin colour or sometimes flushed with his spells of feverishness. Padam had even seen it take the shape of a deformed question mark, glowing white hot over his eyebrows, as if imagination were lent to its translucence the way the moon lent light to particular stars. Padam had watched it glowing like a neon sign in the night & he wanted to answer it now & always & even felt that he did. With wanderlust in his back pocket. He recalled a time when he had been talking about his first visit to Vancouver & had stopped to ask the young man about the scar.

"This is not Vancouver," the young man had yelled. "This is Enochvilleport."

Padam sipped his pale ale with increasing vigour, wondering if his old friend Father Anselme would have shared in such a celestial vision, a thing that cast its own shadows like those terrible angels too divine to look upon. Nonsense. Everything was there to be seen. The stars were made for gazing. In response, the young man's scar began to pulse more deeply & sweetly & vociferously. Anselme, you would have adored this mark. You would have sketched it in a spare corner of your own *Commedia*. Since he is the misunderstood angel who wandered into our arms. Poet, you are this type of mistaken traveller! The young man caught his eye & appeared to sense his state of celestial reverie. He stood up with an excess of formality. The red-haired woman lifted her eyes cautiously & gave an obligatory farewell, although the rest of her robust features were marked by the disappointment that he was not fresh from Athens or Bologna. The young man turned on his right heel in soldierly fashion & marched out, taking only the least amount of time possible to grant a curt nod to Padam, who smiled back expectantly. Grant returned after refreshing everyone.

"Hey Padman buddy you wann'another?"

"Sure, sure," answered Padam, still in reverie.

Upon returning, Grant instantly proferred the pale ale in order to indicate that he had not held it hostage for the sake of his story.

"So you hear what happened last night, eh?"

If Maxwell Wittman the Third were the kind of chap to answer yes & continue drinking his beer in silence, he might have ended up differently & we might have ended up marginally less satisfied.

"Thought you might have seen something."

Grant made his inference, basking in this sensation only known to the epicurist who eavesdrops or gossips.

"Well, you know that woman who writes by the window ... "

It was a lavish display of discretion on his part not to utter the name that was so familiar to most of the hotel regulars.

"Hmm," murmured Padam.

"Well, last night she was headin' home like usual just up the street & hey you know the guy with the big red sideburns?"

"Maybe you should draw me a picture," tittered Padam.

"Well, last night he followed her out … "

Grant paused for effect, as if gathering his breath, before continuing.

"So he's following her up the street & she don't wanna head home cuz he's behind her all the way so she heads back here to shake the guy first. Man it was some kinda circus."

"So what happened," asked Maxwell Wittman the Third, clearly irritated.

"So all the time he's following her & buggin' her & talking at her sayin' HEY WHY DON'T YOU SAY HELLO WHY DON'T YOU SAY HELLO WHY DON'T YOU SAY HELLO!?"

"Really," laughed Padam, savouring this particular tidbit.

"I had to call the cops."

Padam giggled to himself, thinking of the trollish man staggering along the sidewalk in hunchback fashion, snorting as madly as a cup contender at Belmont & foaming at the mouth like a rabid raccoon he had once seen, growling the same phrase over & over again.

"He's a little not right in the head ya know but he's a nice guy I always thought. & Barb, she felt real bad about it too about the cops & everything."

"I find," began Maxwell Wittman the Third, immediately an expert on the matter, "that he just likes a greeting. Always, I make eye contact like this."

He stared impressively at Grant, who looked away towards other customers.

"I make eye contact like this, so he can see & then wave like so."

Padam waved his hand with the apparent simplicity of a magician & smiled with broad condescension.

"& then he goes right back to what he's doing."

"I felt real bad about it. But I guess it's just another weird night at the circus."

Padam noticed that he had drunk his pint as rapidly as he had drunk in Grant's story. He rose, suddenly wondering where the young man had got to. He smiled at Grant.

"It's like I always say."

"Yeah, I'll buy it, whassthat Padman?"

Maxwell Wittman the Third touched the table like a podium in parliament before delivering the well enunciated keynote of his address.

"If you don't have a problem, then you don't belong in this bar."

The next night gave life to another story. Padam entered to hear the parasitic sublimity of Massenet's *Meditation* & find the young man already engaged in conversation with the old professor with the constabular moustache, excitedly & perhaps rather intoxicatedly waxing on about the primordial nature of Wagnerian opera.

"I wanted to take that course of yours very much."

The translucent scar seemed to darken at the mention of Wagner & Padam empathized with that furrow of sorrow, even as his heart sank. Inside his portfolio, unknown to the young man whose lovely jawline continued to wag, was a sketch completed by Maxwell Wittman the Third over the course of three sittings at the Istoria. This was a sketch for public consumption, unlike the thirty-three nudes of the young man he had drawn for the private enjoyment of Padam. Perhaps tonight he will come to me. Patience. Relax. There is time. Nothing but wonderful time to be had together.

"I prefer *Tristan & Isolde.*"

The professor asserted this fact in a faraway & pained Romantic voice, one that he used readily to work the crowd so well during his mandatory lectures on medieval literature. At least according to the young man, who claimed not to be very fussy on him. The young man had also said something odd about Hamlet killing Polonius out of fear of becoming Polonius. But here they were. The voice droned on, the voice that had chided the impetuousness of Lancelot & had forgiven the transgressions of the Wife of Bath & Padam felt sleepy. He only perked up his ears when the young man once again started to speak.

"How about that Liebestod? It's so fine I mean of course you know that but can you get past the theoretics of Schoepenhauer I mean do you appreciate that sense of transcendence as if the music is carrying those two thwarted souls to the threshold of human existence?"

"Harrumph," snorted the professor in response, punctuated by a sizeable "huhmmn."

Then he smiled in that wry way of his, as if playing a trick on the young man for putting too much stock in his opinion, or his own, or vice versa & on & on all night. Padam yawned politely in the background & the entire bar was appalled. The professor took solace in switching back into lecture mode although he scarcely noticed this by virtue of a certain automatism. So it goes, that the scholar who hardly wished to enter the pub with his hedonistic chums in the first place inevitably ends up the last one there, rounding out the evening with a spectacular lecture concerning some literary or philosophical old chestnut. The next morning, that scholar scratches throbbing head & struggles to mark papers, wondering where eloquence got to on such a loud beautiful day.

"Ahh, so you buy into all that German Romanticism," he stated in his German Romantic voice.

"But the problems of Tristan & Isolde are those of a realist writer. Their experience is even, dare we say, postmodern. In other words, they want to get together ... "

He paused to wink & Padam would later recall without incident that this was truly weird.

"The matter is one of honour to both of the lovers, both that of a knight & that of a woman. You must understand, in those days, the chivalric code was everything. Not like our own tainted times."

He smiled wistfully at the other people in the parlour, who nodded & wept & drank more deeply. Padam frowned.

"Tristan, you see, is acutely aware of a promise he must adhere to, one that puts into question his legitimacy as a foster-son & at the same time his presumed *right* to run away with Isolde. You have birth right as well as marriage right in question. What is left for Tristan but the right, some might say the right, to enact his own death. Isolde is the only woman with any sway over such a man, since she has healed his battle wounds & has brought him back to life, in spite of him murdering her husband. His very mortality remains in her hands. Then she is betrayed & scorned by Tristan, who promises her hand to his foster-guardian. In spite of their apparent feelings of enmity, the only thing standing in the way of their hidden passion is earthly logic. Since this is opera & not life, Wagner supplies a potion. Of course, the potion existed in other versions of the story. One represents love & the other death. But the opera is both a refined form of German Romanticism & an escape from it. The awareness of it within the art form is what matters."

He finished abruptly, as if flubbing the final note of his lecture on purpose in a sorry attempt to imitate his idol Strauss. Padam finished his pint while the other regulars began to sob with intense ecstasy, drifting out of their usual positions & moving towards an enormous feast in the Vanhalla section of the hotel bottom. The professor's dwindling voice then returned from its prescheduled dead space & formed an awkward segue.

"So tell me ... are you still writing?"

"Everyone asks that," said the young man, visibly annoyed.

An admiring Maxwell Wittman the Third drank in that annoyance like some fantastically magical potion of never before tasted delights. He signalled Grant for his damages.

"I guess I keep on keepin' on," answered the young man tartly. "You said yourself sir, that no one writes poetry past the age of twenty-five."

Was the young man past twenty-five? Then he was older than Padam had originally guessed. Time to take it up a notch. The professor reddened at this remark.

"In jest, I might have said something like that in jest."

He seemed less worried about what he had said than about the fact that someone had been listening. Once our own words escape us, we no longer can pretend to possess them. Then someone comes along, scooping them up in a plastic bag & holding them up to our noses in such a way that we scarcely recognize them, if at all. He attempted to backpedal.

"I ... umm ... do some writing. In fact, that's my problem. I just write my books & throw them under the bed."

He smiled feebly underneath his overgrowth of moustache, not unlike a dying Tristan.

"Of course, if you are getting published ... "

"Yes," agreed the young man gloomily, "but is that quite the point?"

"Well, once it's in print, it is *real*," affirmed the professor to himself & the entire bar.

Maxwell Wittman the Third nodded, realizing that the Saskatchewan née British accent was rather similar to his own & therefore infinitely convincing with its experience & wisdom.

"Along with Wagner, I've become a big fan of Marcel Proust, who writes in a lengthy similar style."

"Can't say I've had the pleasure *myself*," came the reply in a Saskatoon Prairie Tune Berry dialect. Home, the voice sang to

Maxwell Wittman the Third, home from whence the little farm boy made good. O don't believe the rumours honey! Home it is. Padam paid his bill & floated off gracefully into the night. How strange to know yet to remember not knowing, being innocent as a babe in stinky swaddlings the way Mrs. Ruteborsch came in to visit Lena (the breath the spirit of the world) & she couldn't take to it or understand it really the way she was telling her I was *different* I was just like Glenn, wasn't I?

"He is just like Glenn, Lena."

Then those nasty Ruteborsch twins, those catty girls who had heard all about it & the way they cornered me in the schoolyard & informed me of their diligence at daily piano sessions & passed along the information that on the contrary, I, Lena's boy, was absolutely nothing at all like Glenn Gould. Of course, they had no inkling that I was to be awarded a grant for dance the same year that Mr. Gould received his for music. Maxwell Wittman the Third had no trouble imagining a pugnacious Leonard Bernstein in adolescence, suavely punching the stuffing out of a crumpled Glenn Gould in the schoolyard & then proceeding to wash his hands of the bloody nose. It was more or less the same thing throughout the history of art, or that of the world. Padam touched his cheeks, feeling tipsy or dizzy or flushed or all of the above. On the bench outside his window, he observed the foreign couple leaning close together & talking quietly. He grinned at them & they didn't notice & the spectacle was grotesque.

It was not until the next evening that Padam saw the young man again. He rushed over to the well-chosen table with poise & elegance in the manner of a powered dandy in the eighteenth century whose physical mechanics keep under control the sudden rush of anticipation to embrace his latest mistress. He stood before the young man, much as he had before the Royal entourage at Covent Garden. The bar was astonished & fell into a soft hush.

"Might I join you," he said with a measure of nonchalance. "I have something to show you."

200

The young man laughed.

"I bet you do. Alright then. Keep it decent."

After such a splendid entrance, the young man could not dare refuse the company of Maxwell Wittman the Third. Padam sat upon a chair with a split seam & began to play with his long grey whiskers. He sat within the penumbra of his own broad smile, or so it looked, according to several accounts after *the incident.* Because if not all of them, most of them were there. Although they had ceased to exist that night for Padam, he could not discount the possibility that all were present. The snorting professor, the ursine knucklecracker, the old dispenser of hard candy, the spiderly scribe by the window. If one were to take roll-call, only the red-haired man could be said to be absent. But tonight, the light refused to shine upon any of these omnipresent images. Their respective stars had dimmed. Padam was centre stage, sensing that the young man was the only one in control of the wandering spotlight. In fact, this magnificent little whelp was kicking the damned thing from side to side. Maxwell Wittman the Third opened his portfolio & sifted out a lone sketch ever so gently, in the manner of a daintilygloved blackmailer drawing out the negative of an incriminating photograph. He placed the sketch upon the table for the young man to peruse with his lovely dark eyes. The young man lifted it protectively out of the way of an approaching beer. Grant glanced at the sketch once before whisking off again, perhaps in order to process this new information.

"This is only a preliminary, you understand. My first attempt at the *Rape* of Ganymede."

Padam sat anxiously, watching the young man's face as he studied the sketch. Would his seed take hold & blossom within the large vanity of the young man, that characteristic he detected & adored & now recognized so vaguely within himself? Not quite. A fire razed the face across from him. He saw an atomic sunset & within those flames, he saw the scar become a cutting lunar crescent. The young man appeared to read each thought of he, Maxwell Wittman the Third, because he pointed to the sketch in the place where his forehead was.

"I like how the bird is eating into my forehead. I like that."

Padam collapsed into his chair & then sprang forward again.

"I made his wings part of your widow's peak & the fall of your hair, which is by the way, absolutely wonderful. What about your background? What did your family do to give you such wonderful hair?"

"I'm something of a Heinz 57 a mutt of fifty-seven varieties. My mother's Native, but also Scottish-French. She was in fact born with fire-red hair, but it darkened as she grew older. On my father's side, they're Irish-Scot-Jewish-Russian-Poles. I cannot say exactly where the darker roots kicked in … "

The young man downed his half-finished beer in one gulp.

"As for my mother's tribe, the anthropological studies say they're heavy drinkers. Rather flamboyant. They love bright colours & excessive theatrics. The Raven is creator, but also trickster & scavenger, immensely clever. The common ravens can open bins with their beaks & pull forth food from the garbage heap of humanity. That's the general idea here. Forget about your Apollos & your watered-down ideals. Come down from your wires, you obsidian nightmares! Come, you bringers of plague & apocalypse! Come to us, you beautiful familiars! The purpose of the universe is not merely to create, but also to re-use. When the Apollos of the world have died, or simply turn out to have lied, what else is left?"

Padam sat back & shook his head with happiness.

"Well, I'm glad you like it."

That night, Maxwell Wittman the Third did not sleep at all. He felt like each of his nerves was splitting in two. Directly after bidding the young charmer *au revoir*, he stopped on his way out to reflect upon the medievalish renderings above the marble steps, as if seeing them for the first time. After all, they were only painted glass & dully so, if a patron such as himself were to comment upon such matters. St. George & the dragon & that sort of hackneyed theme. He turned over his right shoulder & caught sight of his reflection, one to which he would regularly smile & wave with that playful *laissez-faire* attitude he was known for. It was suddenly as if he had never noticed himself before, as if he had never waved farewell to his reflection night after night. There was a wrinkle here. Another there. Then that drooping line over there. He smiled with that customary Cheshire-like charisma, but tonight that did not seem to help matters. Rather, it was like rain in his dry food dish. For the first time in his life, he failed to find solace in smoothing his whiskers dry of ale. He felt like an alley-cat drowning in a sudden flood of increasing years. He stepped out into the night, slowly moving up Giltford Street with that same sense of discomfiture. Even the ageing lovers were outside, leaning against one another. They may have been his age, but he, Padam, was nothing like them! Still, they remained a newfound source of irritation to him.

"No," she stated thickly enough to cut the darkness.

"O da da, come on little chicken … "

Eyes gleaming orange beneath the streetlamp. Padam let the side door to the apartment slam. *Enochvilleport.* He knew Malcolm Lowry had once lived in his building, but no one seemed to know precisely where. The young man had asked, hoping to find a pinch bottle behind one of the kitchen cupboards if not a yellowed manuscript under the floorboards. Such is the life of artists & secret lovers. They leave few marks, perhaps none at all, to insist they ever existed. Where is the great book of life to echo each memory? Who will remember our lives for us when we are gone? Padam sat up for another hour, holding vigil over his rendering of Ganymede as he dipped his left hand into a bowl of raspberries. Were they still in season now? He hated to miss a single evening when they were readily available. He finished the bowl with a small gluttony that he tended for the absence of the young man. Help yourself. He washed his hands scrupulously before turning on his easel table lamp & setting down to work. His eyes grew dim behind the rounded rims of his glasses but his hands began to draw, following the ancient metrics they knew so well. You could draw in your sleep, Maxwell. Yes I could. He felt lines & curves

& flesh returning to him like a nascent fragrance. He paused to appreciate each pleasure as he had enjoyed the raspberries.

"They just slit his tongue, Lena."

Aunt Nadja, where the devil you come from? She had no right to tell my mother no right. To say I needed surgery.

"Boy need tongue slit."

It was a perfectly commonplace speech problem.

"How will he go school Lena if he no have tongue slit?"

But Lena you know why I ran only you understand why I ran & hid behind the barn. I'd better hold my tongue forever! But that did the trick. Behind the barn, I began to scream & yell & rave & yell. I beat my hands against the barn & began to kick away at the assailants who were undoubtedly waiting for just such a moment to carry me off & perform this excruciating operation. To this day, whenever I hear anyone ordering *tongue*, I look around nervously for those Regina butchers. But the words of terror in my head came out like amorphous clouds, in the shapes of fantastic plants & animals & creepycrawlies. But that was not enough & I knew it. Even as a boy, some part of me understood that I would have to mould & shape these sounds until they were like those that came out of my parents, if I were to keep the tongue-slitters at bay. I practised meticulously. The next time Aunt Nadja came by, I was ready. I stopped her at the door.

"Velkom Naadjaaaa."

It sounded to her like *Masterpiece Theatre*. She called off the tongue-slitting & Lena wept & made me a tiny tasty cake. I mastered other words, taking care to master them before repeating them to my parents. I appeared at the dinner table & gave them several perfect enunciations, followed by a respectful bow. So this was how I saved my tongue for Carnaby Street & redoubled the respect & love of my parents for one of my first amazing accomplishments. This was only the beginning of my story. All of this Maxwell Wittman the Third mused over, even while his hands continued their lithe twists & arcs, following the memory of century old masters. His great design was drawing near completion. He sat back like a man waking from a trance & applauded the efforts of his busy hands. This was good to go.

The next day, he arranged to meet with Stephane later that evening. Still groggy, he rubbed the sleep out of his eyes. However, he realized that he felt rejuvenated as he examined his night work on the easel table, especially in the afternoon light. Well done, old chap! He managed a small lupper (*1. Light supper. 2. Combination of lunch & supper.*) of Sushi on Denman Street, adjusting his eyes to the sunlit passersby, before returning to the familiar comfort & various thrills of the Istoria hotel. Stephane was accommodating as usual, always ready for a cold one after work, if not four or five. Stephane was a very able glazier who was very busy overseeing a number of construction projects around town. That did not mean he did not wish to be free of endless squares & skyscrapers & creating something others would acclaim as *bitchin.* Enter Maxwell Wittman the Third. After giving Padam a warm hug, he sat down in a reupholstered chair & pointed toward the window, his face dazed & ruddy with hours of sunlight. Whatever he was pointing at? Stephane scratched his browngrey beard, then coughed up half a lung.

"Hey, Padam, isn't that your writer chick?"

Maxwell Wittman the Third giggled & made a monkish gesture, a desperate prayer for silence.

"Not bad," decided Stephane, his beard pointing west.

The woman by the window continued to write (& one might say even more furiously than usual). "Don't worry. Later, I'll tell you an interesting story about her & another fellow."

Padam winked, as only he could. Then Stephane stopped, agape.

"& there's your poet ... "

Maxwell Wittman the Third turned rapidly toward the rising stairs & discovered with astonishment that Stephane was right.

"You pegged him right off. Whether that is a tribute to his beautiful features or the meticulous artistry of my own hands, I'm not at all sure."

Although of course, Padam *was* sure. However, instead of joining them or forgivably taking a place by himself with his own inscrutable notes, the young man walked right over to the woman by the window & leaned forward, so that the crescentshaped scar was suspended underneath the illumination of the real moon. But not for Padam. He wanted to leap out of his torn chair at that moment & race towards the window & tip Mizz Muffet from her perch & declare that the young man's scar was indeed the real moon. O let us forgo that hideous grey rock that haunts & drags the natural progression of tides! The lowing cow by the window looked up at the scar & offered a flash of crooked teeth to be charitable, like a gleam in the back of a rag & bone shop. They exchanged words, although Maxwell Wittman the Third could not hear them. Then the young man sat down.

"Fresh meat," nearly yelled Stephane.

Padam tried out a smile that soon waned. He drank more than usual, losing track of his signals to Grant, still nibbling at his Waldorf salad & half-listening to Stephane's tales about various jobsites.

"So whatever it is, the guy says no problem with his Ruskie accent I mean these guys are adorable I just wanna take 'em home with me. The way they take to everything. I mean some of this shit is fuckin' heavy! What do they say? No problem. & the way they screw in cabinets! Los gabinetes?!? No matter the weight, no matter how dirty the job, they say the same fuckin' thing. NO PROBLEM! Don't you think that's positively delicious, Padam?"

Maxwell Wittman the Third turned back to Stephane & nodded abstractly, although his eyes crept back to the young man, who was laughing into those dead cow eyes full of moonlight.

"Another study of Narcissus?"

Padam smiled & faced him, offering his complete attention as two more pale ales arrived.

"I have called you here because I want to do a project with you. & his name is Ganymede."

The following evening, Padam looked up from his pint glass & was pleased to discover that the young man desired to join him. He gripped one of the chairs scheduled for reupholstery, nearly tipping it over with a rocking motion, back & forth, back & forth.

"Ganymede, I have some news."

"What is it?"

"You better sit down."

The young man sat opposite him, devoid of gravity. Padam paused for effect.

"One of the servers here has a crush on you."

The young man looked around with annoyance, pointing with a backward thumb.

"Who, Grant?"

Padam hushed him with his hands, urging him to lower the volume of his accusation. His vanity is piqued. How like me he is.

"Well, no. The other fellow."

The young man's annoyance grew visibly into fury & affront.

"O, him. Why? Have you fallen prey to his singular concept of old-world charm, whereby he sits to chitchat with you & neglects all the other guests?"

Padam smiled mischievously.

"He fancies you are the next Dostoyevsky."

"I would rather be Gogol, if it's all the same to you."

"Well, *whoever* you are, he has a small thing for you, a very small thing I might add. He takes you for a turn of the century Russian scribbler, the messy kind he likes. But he doesn't want to ask anything more. He says he wants to preserve your *mystery*. & he told me not to breathe a word to you."

The young man shrugged.

"I suppose you offered to tell him everything you knew about me."

Padam reddened.

"No."

Any spectator would be amused to see such a simpering navvy lumbering about the grace of his automatic stage presence. A mock rival, if there ever was one. But that is not to say that he, Maxwell Wittman the Third, did not feel a touch of sympathy for the sentiment. Did it not honour his adoration to know that he was not entirely alone in his longing? On the other hand, if he had learned anything the hard way at the Royal Ballet School, it was that one needed competition about as much as one needed to be hobbled before a performance. Break a leg, Maxy! He could still see their sinister faces, hopeful for his downfall at the foot of a velvet curtain. But if the young man was a crazed Gogol, then he was one of those mad Russian characters who cannot resist tossing their last rouble into a passing hat for the promise of squandering everything they own in a roll of the dice or in a fantastic toast. This is what he told himself as he counted out his change with care. O dear, the young man was staring at him.

"Why do you call me Ganymede?"

Padam reached across the table & tapped his hand rapidly, one of his soothing gestures that came so readily to him. At bottom, he was known for being a comforting sort of chap. The kind you could count on in a crisis.

"Because you are to me & always shall be, *my* Ganymede."

Padam made a theatrical gesture with his right hand, reaching in the direction of where he imagined his heart to be, as if to underline each word he was uttering.

"Besides, I have more news about Ganymede, but that is a surprise, so you will have to wait, young Ganymede."

The young man listened, demonstrating a pose of desperate *ennui* that embodied the spirit of an autobiographical Byron. Hand cupping chin, the lips began to move again.

"You seem in a strange mood tonight. I feel like I've disturbed you."

Maxwell Wittman the Third smiled with controlled grace.

"Actually, I was just thinking about my time at the Royal Ballet School in London. & no, I don't mean Ontario! We were required to perform small roles with the first & second ballets in the Royal Opera House at Covent Garden. It was what the young people now call a practicum, uhmm, a co-op? We spent a great deal of time in the green room waiting for our next rehearsal or costume fitting, waiting like confined debutantes for our *coming out*. You *are* an opera fan, yes?"

The young man nodded readily, but also with the impatience he displayed for anyone who appeared to have mixed up their facts.

"Well, I was thinking of the time Visconti had arrived in London, intending to launch his own version of Giuseppe Verdi's *Don Carlo*."

The young man grimaced once again, annoyed that Padam was taking his time to drag out every word, refusing simply to say Verdi's *Don Carlo*, as if there were thirty-five globally known opera composers named Verdi.

"Ah, what a time that was! Not to say what an opportunity for us dancers! We were particularly struck by Visconti's elegant assistants. They were a study in fashion with their white collard shirts & silk ties that so stupendously complemented their Dupioni silk suits. In fact, I remember making a solemn vow to myself that one day, I, Maxwell Wittman the Third, would wear duds like those!"

The young man looked across the table curiously at Padam's green jumper.

"What happened?"

Padam grinned & continued his story.

"You know Visconti, surely you know Visconti? Well, what a thrill! He recognized my natural abilities at once, just as in the ancient tales, when one god acknowledges another. He made me one of the most prominent pages in all the court scenes! In fact, I received more time than the principals. The best part was being privy to a veritable feast of sights & sounds, not to mention a few scandals. But the most colourful incident for me, harmless enough, involved the legendary Tito Gobbi."

"O Tito," sighed the young man automatically.

"Well, to be fair, Franco Corelli was surely more dashing. Grey Brownstein offered a very reserved Elizabeth de Valois. Boris Kristof was solid in stature & astonishing in the amount of basso profundo he could provide, as was his wont. But Tito Gobbi turned out to be the one who gave us the most laughs. What I remember most is the period costumes for this production. All the men had to wear bloomer type shorts with an ostentatious codpiece over their unmentionables. The general idea was that this codpiece should be modest in size yet decked out with diamonds & all manner of gems according to royal rank. Incidentally, in Italy, this item was known as a *bragetto*, presumably because the men spent their afternoons drinking excellent cappuccinos while bragging about their encrusted codpieces. & of all the men in the company of artists, Mr. Gobbi was deemed most worthy to wear the longest bragetto. Now, you must bear with me & imagine the most brodingnagian contraption on earth! Quite the equipment! Worse over, it would bounce & wobble whenever he moved across the stage to sing a speech. It finally came to a head, so to speak, when mid-aria, Tito called a halt to rehearsal in the manner of a rebuffed Prima Donna & pointed down at the object that had so brought offense upon the deep resonance of his voice. & to this day I have never heard him sing so well, although he was merely singing in jest. After this lively & moving speech in barbed Italian, he seized the giant costumal protuberance & yanked it free of his elastic suspenders in a single motion. To conclude the long final note of his aria, he made a great spectacle of chucking his codpiece out the window. That satellite shot through the air & out into the daylight with all those artificial gemstones glittering away. But Covent Garden, I don't know if you know Covent Garden, but this was in the fifties. There were few artistic venues about, almost none in fact. One might say there was nothing there, save a large vegetable market, amiably manned by a pair of Cockney lads who were, let us say, more than astonished to witness that glimmering object, that gem-encrusted phallus, sailing into the centre of their barrows full of bananas. I am not certain what qualifies as a miracle, but at that moment they would have made Tito Gobbi a saint. The management, without delay & without another word, in a snap of fingers dispatched a wardrobe underling to collect the wayward article belonging to their costume department. & she, a pretty young thing from Balzac, Alberta, had to endure merciless teasing from the grocery boys in a kind of *English* she had never heard in her life. At last, she managed to leap on her tippy toes & snatch the controversial object from the taller boy's hand, leaving bemused cries of *tuppence* & *tar* & *wocher* behind her. As witnesses to her heroic act, we ballet boys burst into applause. The Italians & British were both out of it & this was one for Canada.

It was later that night when Maxwell Wittman the Third began to feel his mirth dissipating into the darkness. He once more tossed & turned & found himself to be sweating profusely. He could see his steps upon the stage in a number of numbers in movements he knew so well. At the same time, Gobbi's rich tenorial baritone voice filled the empty spaces wherever he had ceased to dance another step. What a voice! What a talent! He might have built all the sets, including the design for the opera house itself, made sculptures of each character in *Don Carlo* with scrupulous detail down to their ears & eyes & noses, & then for an encore, he might have sung all of their parts, just as he might have defended all of their contracts in court. But as Padam sank into the lightest sediment of slumber, the voice became more melancholy than he remembered it. Gobbi had looked fantastic in his monarchial robes as King Philip, decked out with Spanish fervour & colour that accented the torment & guilt of any Inquisition. But he had been betrayed by his wife & the lead singer, nullifying any enjoyment of his power. Hmm, Verdi was starting to get more psychological then. Padam continued to toss & turn toward the edge of his small bed in that charming way of his, permitting the young man's thoughts & opinions on the matter to seamlessly become his own. Fewer barrel organ tunes. More silences. Gobbi, emitting soft utterances from that fantastic instrument of his.

> *Ella giammai m'amò!*
> *No, quel cor chiuse è a me.*
> *Amor per me non ha!*

Then one of the most brilliant jack of all trades & master of many kneeled before the audience & virtually seemed to shrivel up on stage. He physically transformed himself, all of his light bulk included, not to mention the notorious codpiece, into a small figure of beatitude & human minutiae. Then he repeated the low yet full notes that reverberated about Covent Garden & seemed to burn the earlobes of every listener, leaving a lingering chill. She never loved me! No, that heart is closed to me. Love for me she has none! Then his gestures to empty air followed while the ghost of the dead composer seemed to play about the orchestral pit, conducting the stray insistences of the King's pulse with flute or piccolo.

> *Dormirò sol nel manto mio regal*
> *quando la mia giornata*
> *è giunta a sera*

Padam murmured the impossible phrases to himself, suddenly remembering what they meant. *I will sleep alone in my royal cloak when my day has turned to night.* Is that right? All our triumphs earned & our smallest victories won, what is left to do? Gobbi, King Philip, & myself, Maxwell Wittman the Third. What use are our royal robes if we fail to read the hearts of those we adore? But we know nothing of the beloved! Not what they say when we do not see them. Not what they think when they are wrapped in our very own arms. A beautiful smile & a closed book, tossed into our warm laps. Gobbi had sung with the impotence of the King who was powerless to pry open the lock & peruse those hidden pages in agony. Then this aria is the anguish of not knowing. Padam continued to toss & turn, clinging to the edge of the bed & muttering aloud to his handsome cat Chester, who sat in a high corner staring down at his troubled owner & listening intently to the man's gibberish, searching frantically in the dark for one exquisite word.

"Vittles."

III

On occasion, if one is very lucky, Glenn Gould's rendition of Bach's prelude to *The Well-Tempered Clavier* will float out of the FEED, the very cycle of classical pieces we have listened to for the duration of this story thus far. The reader may argue at this point, insisting that during their stay at the Istoria, or even during their years of frequenting the withdrawing room, they have never heard this piece played. Or to settle this argument, they may hunt for the hotel through an intrepid display of literary deduction & laudable *close reading*. In order to save the reader considerable trouble, it is pertinent to point out that at the time of writing, the FEED still exists, but the piece performed by Mr. Gould has been excised for the sake of a number of pulp jazz items that evoke the impression of an eternal loungey Christmas. Meanwhile, the plot-driven souls are shifting in their comfy chairs, nodding yes but asking where is Mr. Wittman the Third & what is going to happen to him next? Already, there have been a few details overlooked for the sake of our friend Padam & his story as he would wish it to be told. Pithy scribe, asks the reader, wherever are you going with this? As I struggle to read my pages of black scrawl stapled together, I begin to wonder myself. A *document in madness* then. The point is, that among the melancholy & reflective pieces that drifted out of the FEED over the period concerning Mr. Wittman the Third, this piece performed by Mr. Gould was unfailing in its ability to lift the spirit of its listeners from their most sad & even macabre reflections. Of course, those are the fantastic hands that complied with Mr. Bach's strict stipulations concerning one of the *Brandenburg Concerti* & their respective launch into space. The classical dilettante (even a number who have come & gone through the back or front doors of the Istoria who remain conspicuously undocumented) might choose this juncture to argue with the hapless author, asking why this piece was chosen among several others from *Das Wohltempierte Klavier*. This sublime piece in C major reeks of virgin sentimentality & what has become of it? How obvious do you want to get? Diluted down to consumer kitsch, utter dreck! Why, the last time I heard it was in a zombie flick! How about one of the other preludes or fugues in E-flat or F-sharp? Why not a sweet Partita in C minor? Well, in terms of intergalactic communication, simplicity is desired. Were we to ascertain the existence of extraterrestrial life, especially the kind to be found in each weekly series filmed upon local streets beneath foreign rain machines, in order to catch their multiplicity of eyes & call attention to a mere microcosm of living organisms cohabiting the same heritage space over a brief temporal measure, for the sake of its simplicity & the allusion to Mr. Gould's splendid work launched into space on *Voyager*, the zombie movie piece might very well suffice for this story. It is without question that such inquisitive otherlings will begin to concern themselves intimately with the legend of Cappelmeister Bach. Was he paid off by his patron Count Kaiserling, the Russian ambassador to the Saxon court, to write some restful pieces to cure his pesky case of insomnia, tailored specifically for the hands of musician-in-service Johann Gottlieb Goldberg? In addition, do the extraterrestrial examiners in question suffer from any symptoms of insomnia & in that case, have they found the thirty-two *Variations* at all soothing to their lobewise protuberances? The point of this authorial harangue is to suggest that the smallest detail might possess interstellar significance, as our protagonist would certainly agree, feeling he had at last received the universal applause & recognition he deserved. Given the magnitude of this tiniest of details that takes up enough narrative space as is, one may ask is anything truly a tangent? Well, yes. It is just such a detail the author may have omitted to mention, in order to satisfy the plot-driven. This is something of a disclaimer then. Close your eyes, dear reader. Clap shut your impressionable ears. Perhaps the smattering of non-details that follows is completely immaterial to the plot. Naturally, there are passing shapes & figures that are neglected in paintings, appearing to be worth no more than a hurried brush stroke, a half-hearted attempt to chance upon their essence in no more than a great blob of oil, a considerable mess in the corner of the work. These are the chimaeras of everyday existence, those readers of daily papers who virtually melt into plush armchairs or creak upon rickety barstools or scrape iron legs against cobblestone. As we cannot prove to our immediate satisfaction that life emerged from the clumsy activity of a single plebian organism, bumbling about everywhere it bubbled, we can no sooner prove that these readers of newspapers exist, aside from their intermittent shuffling of the aforementioned halibutwrap. It is to admit a certain frailty in the author that he can only imagine their resettlement of inky creases in the vaguest of ways. He knows no more about their diurnal existence than he does about that of a clam a few feet under the sand. It may be reasonable to say that they are closed volumes to him, even within a rather open book, & it is his very duty to dream their daily existence as a means of documentation more reliable than the very fishwrap they fold into neat petit-fours. If we were to know all of their secret thoughts & hopes & dreams & intestinal workings, we would surely go mad. Even their daily activity leaves something to be desired. Let us instead be content with the shorthand method, as the observer who admires a gallery painting for a single stroke of charcoal that represents some human entity & finds it more equitable to facial characteristics than the very lines of portraiture that define it. Accept this as another weakness on the author's part, since he tends to take shortcuts that only lengthen the journey. He starts out with a few notes that spew out into several pages. Let us be content then, reader, with only a few lines devoted to the dead space of the Istoria, or the backdrop of souls that was to frame the fantastic spectacle of Maxwell Wittman the Third at the height of his happiness.

There was, to be sure, a series of washed-out couples who appeared irritable but too tired to argue any longer. One member of each pair would make the odd remark out of left field & the other would nod or murmur a resounding uhuh & then they would go back to sipping their drinks in silence. However, they demonstrated a well-established courtesy that had built up over the years. It took the least amount of communication possible to procure their personal favourites with a lime or lemon slice of rhetoric thrown in. A comment upon the weather. A word of homage to the condo that Grant was eternally fixing up. A brief exchange of holiday banter with the other server. An update on the Pacers. A well-watered-down running gag that had long ago run out of steam. There was a sad shortage of the kind of scenes that would have tickled the curiosity of the other *Irregulars* & would have started them from their respective routines, having been given a new item to vociferously rebuke. Aside from *the lovers*, there were a few secondary characters who are worthy of mention. Let us sweep the imaginary camera about the establishment & see who has checked in tonight. There was a teacher or professor type, not by any means to be confused with *our* Professor with the constabular moustache, a pale man with something schoolmarmish about him, an Ichabod Crane type with his grey tweed jacket so ill-matched with his loud vest beneath it, as well as his tight blue jeans that stilted into a thrifty pair of white sneakers. Yet he faded quite readily into the split & faded décor of the Istoria, with grey jacket & grey ponytail & rose-coloured glasses perched about the tip of his long pale nose, fading into a newspaper or occasional text at the end of it. The discordant elements of his wardrobe were enough to prevent him from being completely invisible. But the grey helped him to fade into his newspaper so well that the other *Irregulars*, even from sheer habit, could no longer see him without conscious effort. Then at last, someone would call out his name & he would stare at them inquisitively over his too-red spectacles. Yes, a character by all means. Unfortunately, he is not quite a character in *this* story, so we must bid him *adieu* & let him return to his grey newsprint without further disturbance. As with the woman writing by the window, his silent conjectures & the content of his didactic portfolio shall remain, as in life, unknown to us. At least for now. The author has also failed to produce even a single paragraph concerning the small gaggle of would-be screenwriters, two-bit actors, & *revolutionary* poets that passed through the parlour for two or three or five nightcaps. Aside from the gaunt silhouettes of the washed-out couples & the slim shadows of the intellectual ascetics, there was moreover a certain amount of corpulence that followed around visitors to the Istoria. The hotel, rather than possessing the personality of the owner's daughter, would have best been personified by an ageing playboy with a secret past. The sorrow of the Istoria was like a mild layer of rain pitterpattering upon the burning sensuality of late autumn. There was always time for that last bonfire at the Istoria. Always time for one more. If you had missed your last streetcar, there was always the chance for another chance to darken your greying temples & waggle your eyes at some foreign guest. There was always time for another treatment. It is fair to say that each of these characters had a private aspiration of their own that intermittently blazed within the well-satisfied altar of their flesh. They were free to eat & drink what they liked. They had earned it, hadn't they? Yet night after night at the Istoria, their throats & stomachs were set on fire. The philosophical conundrum that faced our protagonist, Maxwell Wittman the Third, & to be frank, probably affected him the least, was not isolated to his own person. Would the old woman at last convince one of her boys to live in this city? Would the bearish knucklecracker get his chance & at last strike gold in them thar hills? Would the woman by the window one day escape with her spiderly scrawl & move to the Southlands as she so often threatened to do? Would Grant finish his condo? Would the other guy at last earn an eternal holiday? Would the red-haired man ever return from the Downtown Eastside? Even his externalized longing had seemed to seep into the wallpaper & was omnipresent as that moth behind the sickly green door of the washroom. As such, the reader will perhaps expect there to be a character that embodies this figure of an ageing sensualist, not those souls of a certain age with a mode of decorum that lent an unspeakable nobility to their secret passions, but instead a figure more representative of a man in mid-life crisis, only without a particular crisis to trouble him. There was such a figure (a Rabelaisian one at that, who has earned the nickname Gargantua for our purposes) whose proportions of fleshy masculinity seemed to draw & negate that gaggle of effeminate sensualists who orbited his thick fingers full of rings. He was a post-colonialist author's wet dream, a giant Saxon figure who commanded his Canadian friends about like courtiers. But that is not to say he was quite American either. More *International.* Part of the global film race. He lacked the unflinching determinism of Fitzgerald's final tycoon. He had learned how to give the Canadian line, to whine about projects larger than himself & to reflect upon his past *oeuvres* with a tone of justification. According to Margaret Atwood's criteria in *Survival,* as a character, he definitely fell on one side of the 49th Parallel. However, even as a citizen of a colonized victimized country who wanted more than merely rubbing shoulders with the glitterati of Brolleywood on a sunny day (or as they were sometimes to be called, the *pitterpatteratti*) he had a rather robust air that drew the others to palaver about him. There was something grim & unamusing about his manner that undermined his mock-epic-hero status, yet commanded attention. It is most certainly a sign of negligence that the author failed to include the Fisher King of the *Irregulars,* who incidentally bore a remarkable resemblance to a famous portrait of Henry VIII. In spite of his demeanour, he also seemed to exhibit a primal fear of being forgotten, & for this reason, he never failed to douse his entire girth in half a bottle of cologne. While the woman by the window had decided upon a rather skunkish scent, he had chosen a thick cloud of cologne that permeated the other half of the Istoria, so in that sense, territorially, they divided up the Istoria between them. There was no third.

As much as Gargantua deserves this title & our complete attention, it would be remiss not to point out a small irony that tickled the fancy of the author (who is no more than a mere surveillance device in an elevated corner of the room). Gargantua was a cameraman, & his years of panning & obtaining a sufficient shot & rising early with the methodology of a fisherman preparing his lures contrasted sharply with his tyrannical disposition. The author, having little to say on the matter & already hoping to leave the Istoria on both legs, would only postulate that like the pickle salesman or kippermonger, the cameraman felt an overwhelming need to wash away a certain smell from his trade. We have been so preoccupied with Mr. Wittman the Third that we have scarcely noticed the entrance of this cologne factory directly after work. Let us swivel towards him for a moment then. See how he takes his rightful place by the window, looking around expectantly, wanting anything other than the wretched objective eye that has come to define the circumference of his existence. The author ducks, expecting a complimentary bowl of breadsticks to be thrown at him any moment. The fleshy fingers go to work, dialling number after number. It is not long before they appear, a buzz at the time. Buzz buzz. Swiftly, one or two or three satellites arrive, all the while buzzing & seeking that very familiar buzz from the pint in front of them. He offers them topics for conversation like new laws to approve. They nod & smile. Buzz buzz.

Aside from the cameraman, there was the Valkyrie. At this point, the author is tempted to manipulate the details of this story for the sake of adding Wagner's much popularized chunk of *Die Walküre* (a phenomenon that has betrayed the other four hours & has given birth to an often hackneyed image of fat ladies with horns singing themselves toward death) but it was never included in the FEED repertoire of light favourites. A vague member of this twilight family, she appeared younger than the average age & that made her necessarily precocious. Young for the Istoria meant in her thirties, perhaps on the very edge of that decade, but well-preserved to the point of deducting it. The author, rather messily, would like to add here that the young man was only young in terms of being a recent member of the *Irregulars*. He was on the lighter side of twenty-five, which was why he was infinitely concerned about the Professor's jest about poets stopping after twenty-five. The author smiles here, thinking that perhaps the young man still had much to learn from the French poets & authors. In the interest of literature, he still needed to find the right Muse, one who would crush his chimaeras to the point of making them jive with unreality, the kind that paradoxically can only arise from the subtle scars of having loved & having been rebuffed, from feeling the serpent of jealousy nesting about the heart & taking fatal bites, a sting that was to concern Maxwell Wittman the Third most dramatically. Statistically, the young man's best chances of becoming almost completely jaded lay in the form of this woman like a Valkyrie. Although you could never tell. From time to time, she appeared with a group of men & much was made of their gayness, to the point that her entourage gave her entrances a lavish musical quality. On the other hand, she often broadcast her marriage with a flashing of finger or with her sharp nasal voice that seemed a drawback to the shape of her beautiful nose. Even with her entourage of Valkyrie *sisters* encircling her, she possessed a flirtatious quality that surpassed that beard of tittering men. As for the young man, she had noticed him when he first arrived at the Istoria, but not in the multilayered way that Padam did, stripping him down to aesthetic components. She saw him in terms of freshness & functionality. In fact, at the Istoria, there was an expiration date attached to such encounters. She had studied him hungrily in the glass reflection, looking back impatiently for his attention, perhaps merely to pique her touch of vanity. Was he a dark stranger from elsewhere? Where? What tales might he tell? It goes without saying that her delicate cosmetic became an abhorrent toilet for Padam the instant she set eyes upon the young man & he did not look away. The thought of even one four hour encounter in one of the suites upstairs to the tune of *Die Walküre* was too much for him to bear. Such is love, a diamond that slices into the glass of vanity. But this was something in itself, that in the minute illusory world of the Istoria, such vanities could intersect freely. Even the author, who would prefer to remain heartless & unmoved, in yet another dark corner of the establishment, cannot stay that way. It was only Padam who perhaps understood that all of the denizens here, with their triumphs & trivialities, collectively possessed the beauty of a great work of art & went about their lives, creating works of art small & large without realizing their own aesthetic worth. As for the writing process that drew so many of the *Irregulars* in different ways, even so far as to love a single best seller travelogue & talk about it as the other server once did, let alone obsess like the young man or the Professor or the woman by the window or the author of this pittance, it is like all literature, a lost cause, if only because it loses. The author has gone to great pains merely to rub his tired eyes & peep into a handful of lives while suffering over a change in the degree of light or the disappearance of a character or the change in staff or the increase in prices. The faces change, soften or harden. Souls unite & break away. Today, the author walked past our Ichabod near the courthouse just before noon & watched him order lunch expertly & with much familiarity. The author drank in his tweed jacket & blue jeans & white sneakers & rose-coloured glasses & wondered if he was not in fact involved in the legal profession. The Istoria lives on, no more than an intersection of memories, while the author struggles with that indefinable loss, indefinable because the writing has failed to capture it. Already, the painting has altered. The light has shifted once again. The angle is not quite right. Literature is overelaboration then, followed by the cap of a pen. In the long run, these changeling elements & tidbits, why even another story about Mr. Gould himself, have little or nothing to do with the life & times of our hero, Maxwell Wittman the Third, otherwise known to his friends as Padam.

The next morning, after very little sleep, Padam was nonetheless comforted to feel streaks of sunlight warming his moustache, although there was a slight chill in the air. Autumn has come to the coast. He hopped out of bed & decided to take a walk along the beach. & wouldn't a veggie dog be nice after a refreshing sit? The waves stirred, already beckoning that cold blue depth of the approaching season. Soon. Soon. Then he smiled, because a seagull shat upon his log, one of those symmetrically bolted alongside the others, log #73 to be precise, altogether missing his lycrawear in spite of its apparent deliberation. He sat calmly, his mind floating off with the undulating waves & far away from the image of the young man & the mischievous gull. As one comes to recognize, with repetition or training, the first note of *The Well-Tempered Clavier,* as touched by our rather enigmatic Canadian Mr. Gould, although never a West of Denman resident, with time one learns to anticipate the subsequent notes. It was that Nordic breaking of musical ice that would have made Grieg proud. At least that was what Ethan had told him. Padam watched the waves & fell into the warm reverie of those who seriously lack sleep & begin to *dream awake*. It would be so lovely to close my eyes for a moment. Whether the resonance of Mr. Gould's initial finger upon the ocean or of the seagull having shat an emerald omelet, something definitely had fallen out of the empyrean & had struck another key in Padam's memory. Maxwell Wittman the Third was transported then, past his ballet mastery in Darmstadt & the young lady with a coffee cup balanced trepidatiously upon log #88, to the top of a tower in St. Mark's Square. Ahhh, Venice. Below, far more beautiful to see than that miscreant gull, there were thousands of pigeons brunching upon strategically placed scatterings of corn, who by some divine miracle, through the arrangement of their huddled bodies & folded wings, spelled out a single message for the awestruck tourists. C-O-C-A-C-O-L-A. Padam sighed. He had felt sorry for that group of pigeons assigned to feed in the shape of a trademark, since he had a hunch they were underfed, given the whole pecking order of things. But that was only part of the fabulous backdrop. There was also that time with the London Festival Ballet. January! Try getting across St. Mark's in January! We were shopping, yes, me & Tonio & Angelina, who was always late & always sweatypalmed. But they showed me the ropes alright. Believe me, *credami*, these strapping young men will carry you across the square for the minor damage of a hundred lire. In spite of her *expertise*, Angelina nearly tumbled off her fellow's back & out of utter desperation wrapped her arms around the poor chap's face. This struck the studhorseman as hilarious & he began to gallop about as if he had blinders on & had lost his way. Tonio made a remark (this was so Tonio) that it was customary in Venice to *marry* your horse after such an incident. On our way back, after our shopping spree, I was showing my two friends my delightful purchases, wasn't I, when the great beast beneath me reared for a second & I nearly fell off. But that was no way for Maxwell Wittman the Third to end up. I closed my legs about him with such ferocity that he responded with a soft whinny, my freckled brown stallion did, as if I had just dug my spurs into his muscular flanks. As for Angelina, her new hat nearly fell victim to an abrupt gust of wind & in her attempt to retrieve it, she nearly rolled off her own stud's back. For Tonio, riding Italian youths seemed the most natural thing in the world. Yet in all the commotion, I thought of a great painting that depicted the treachery of Nessus for a blushing galpal of Hercules, or that wedding crashing of the Lapiths, as perpetrated by those debauched centaurs, heavy with wine & trotting off into the wood with their gushing bridesmaids on their wooly backs in a state of similar chaos to Angelina & myself, Maxwell Wittman the Third. Long story short, we doubled their fees & received very friendly smiles, crooked smiles of such intimacy & warmth that I do not think I ever shall forget my personal studhorseman. Later that night, while we prepared for the performance, sitting shoulder to shoulder applying our make-up, we shared innumerable tales about those burly Venetian broncos. Sad to think how the Fenice has been gutted three times. But now it is restored, as it was. Maxwell Wittman the Third reached for a very green veggie dog & placed his exact change upon the silver counter of the wheeled cart. & what about us? Shall I rise from the ashes of what consumes me in the same fashion? Shall I reawaken to newfound glory like that infernal phoenix of a theatre? What of my flight, I, Padam?

Later, as evening approached, Maxwell Wittman the Third sat in the Istoria parlour, waiting … The ursine knucklecracker was in a talkative mood, cracking less than usual & letting his fingers dance a light waltz upon the window sill. On occasion, a glint of possibility would balance out his recounted failures to go big & remonstrances for not cashing in on a particular investment or stock trend in time.

"O these computers & anything to do with cellular phones & all that wireless shit. I would have made a bundle in that department on one of those innovations, ahh fuck it … "

He finished with one of his favourite expressions, his voice strangely coaxing in spite of his words. The Hudson's Bay senior saleswoman with a henna coxcomb nodded in ersatz sympathy while sunning herself & shading her eyes. A muscular tourist rose suddenly out of sheer impatience, as Padam admired his black skin in the fading sunlight, & asked with extreme politeness in an American accent for a pint of one of their only four beers, the same ones on the paper list that had existed forever & would continue to do so, so long as the local gods (but not local brewers) feared change. The server looked over at the man left standing & got up with a look of irritation mixed with cordial obligation. Grant was off tonight. It was the other guy, who had been startled out of pseudo-decent conversation by the request. Having received his instructions, he returned to the counter & poured two pints of ale with a sour look for the man & his ladyfriend with dreadlocks. Padam stole glances at the man, who returned to his own conversation with a look of deep regret for having *bothered* the server at all. As if it were the first time for having to *bother* him. Maxwell Wittman the Third returned his attention to the knucklecracker, who was in mid-whine about an entire market of missed chances that had been out there.

"The Jews," he concluded matter-of-factly, a phrase that seemed to punctuate his harangues about as frequently as "ahh fuck it … "

The woman entered, sans window, & seeing that her window seat was taken, she chose an aisle seat in semidarkness. All the better to spin your little web, my dear. But Padam instantly forgot about her as the young man entered, lifting his hand in the manner of a Roman prelate to signal that he required one pint of the usual & one glass of ice water to accompany it. He walked by the woman without a window without a word. He nodded abstractly in Padam's direction before settling down to work without a word to anyone, not even Maxwell Wittman the Third. In less than five minutes, the pint & water appeared as if by the invocation of his imagination & he drank from each figment with vigour. His pen began to fly across the page & everyone felt a chill in the room, except for the woman without a window, who only felt some mild turbulence. Hours passed.

Ganymede & his inky fingers & ritualistic pints stayed the course, writing & drinking & writing & drinking, giving Padam ample time to nibble at his dinner. They say passion is a circle. Maxwell Wittman the Third watched the young man while he lapped at his dessert, like one of the principals who waits & watches the apparition of a native deity from some wildly painted bushes. Since this effigy of Bacchus has been laid upon my doorstep, I must pay him heed. Ahh sweet Ganymede! The woman in the aisle had long ago left without her window. So had the large knucklecracker with his bearsized indigestion. The heavily-moustached professor had made an appearance, but upon spying the young man he had made himself scarce, ducking into a dim corner out of sight. One of his students? Tough luck. But that just leaves more for the rest of us, meaning he alone, the fantassssticallly sumpticiousss leaper across stages, the unparalleled Pppdmmm. He drank his water thirstily, before a surprisingly coherent memory came over to him & cuddled him. It was the young man who had said that thing about train stations in Saskatchewan, something a writer chum had brought up. Only the train station of the imagination. But what about Unity, eh? Was it thirty-eight? No, it must have been nineteeeen thirty-nine, that's right. We were all in our Sunday best. All the men wore three-piece suits & felt hats in those days. They all wanted to give the impression of Bing Crosby & the women were content to merely imitate the arriving Queen herself. As farmers, we had all come out to join the residents of Unity & in total, we were one thousand strong, waiting along the banks of the railroad line in the blistering sunlight with our picnic baskets, waiting for the Royal train to arrive ...

Unbeknownst to us, the train had already stopped twenty miles away in the even smaller town of Scott, Saskatchewan. The Queen Mum was not above traipsing down a dusty dirt road in all her monarchial getup, not even to meet a local girl named Lorna, whose speech impediment prevented her from speaking to the personage she had most excitedly been waiting for. Looorna Dooooone, laughed the dark

& dusty space around Padam, as the Professor looked up at the strange Saskatchewan noise in the front. Lorna led the Queen Mum to her modest home across the road without a word. Meanwhile, we were still waiting for a very special dark blob to appear from the East. I can still see those people with nothing to do, placing pennies on the rails. I imagine they would have felt a great deal of pride in owning a flattened Royal penny. But that was against the law. Fortunately, we had those strapping RCMP officers on horseback who made a great show of brushing them off the track, until a hushed chorus of *here it comes here it comes* began to drown out the sound of their penny sweeping. We were a veritable army of pointing fingers. But we were in the know. Only the last car. Only the caboose would contain the Royal members. At the word *caboose*, the other server looked over curiously in Padam's direction. Dad, you were a young & terribly robust Scot in those days, & when it comes down to it, a stalwart Royalist. He threw Millie up into the air & she landed on his back while I mounted Uncle Jake with a sense of solemnity & reserved delight that was *apropos*. It was just like those serials about train & stagecoach robberies, the way we fell in behind the trains, except this serial would not have a serial cheat, with young Maxwell reaching for a Royal penny with the train bearing down on him & sounding its great horn & locomotiving over him. Then, in the next episode, he would be riding his uncle all over again. Yet in *this* serial, we fell in behind the train & were jogging at quite close quarters. Why, I must have been four. I only remember high-fiving the girls (princesses Margaret Rose & Elizabeth) before the train sped up & I must say, outpaced the superhuman stamina of the Wittman clan. Once the train was out of sight again, the mob dove right into those picnic baskets. & remember when I did that portrait of Queen Elizabeth in grade twelve & the principal kept it? The seagreen walls creaked with envious acquiescence. It wasn't until much later that I saw Margaret again. As our Royal patron, she certainly liked to visit & *observe* the men's ballet class in action. She used to sit at the front, smoking with the help of a long holder studded out with red diamonds. There was a young photographer who appeared at the Royal Ballet School &

then again at the Royal Opera House & there he was again in our green room! We all called him Tony. In fact, everybudddy did. He was just *one of the guys* in the dressing room, snapping this or that, until he was eventually married to Maggie & he became Lord Snowden. But one thing they taught us, the Royals I mean, was that as artists, we were all servants. If not for a monarch, were we serfs toiling away for that feudal lord known as THE UNKNOWN. Padam smiled at his patron, who floated towards him like the Sistine God of Michelangelo, surrounding by lascivious cherub boys who pointed out his strange resemblance to Lord Snowden. It was late. Maxwell Wittman the Third looked up & saw the young man standing in front of him.

"Are you free? I have been asking you for some time."

Padam burst into a broad fumey smile while the rest of him remained entirely invisible in the tangled forest of trampled grapes.

"Wanna smoke a joint?"

He did not inhale at once. Padam snickered at the young man, who shone with flashes of brilliance upon the pages of his notebooks & yet was too inept to grasp the extremely simple principle of the marijuana pincer, which depended upon a gentle hold & not increasing pressure. Ganymede took this jibe well, but he nonetheless resented the need of any mechanical device when fingers had most certainly been invented first.

"You have no physical knowhow," giggled Padam in mild epiphany. "You were born a poet & you've always been a poet & that's what you'll always be!"

Ganymede looked at him sadly.

"I guess."

Padam puffed some more with growing satisfaction in an unconscious imitation of Princess Margaret.

"Ahhhhhhh … "

The author asks that the reader excuse these ellipses (otherwise known as literal eclipses) since his exhalation & fantastical raptures went on for pages.

"Sorry about the bathroom, but if we don't shut the door, Chester will come in & interrupt us & then maybe a neighbour & then maybe another tee hee hee ... "

Ganymede heard a paw at the closed door & a soft miaow.

"Someone's playing Callas," interjected the young man. "Ne andrò lontano."

He inhaled awkwardly before passing back the joint. Padam took a toke & exhaled. "Ms. Lopez always plays opera in the evenings. Especially Callas. Did I ever tell you about the gala night at Covent Garden when we were waiting for the Diva to get ready?"

Ganymede shook his head.

"Well, I had just performed a dance from *The Trojans*, wearing nothing but a gold loincloth & dark bodypaint. Meanwhile, Callas had just performed an exquisite aria from *I Puritani*. It was after the final curtain call when we were all arranged on a festooned rostrum in order to wait for the Queen & her entourage to materialize. All eyes were glued to the pass door, waiting for it to reveal *bona fide* Royalty. Roddy, our resident stage manager, was frantically calling back to the dressing rooms & rushing in to knock rapidly now & again, desperate to ensure all the performers were present before the Queen arrived. His most urgent visit was to the dressing room of *La Divina* Herself. When he returned, he was sweating profusely & looking about wildly. The performers, having nothing to do, feigned swooning & tragic gestures, goading him on to dish about the Diva. It's Madame Callas. Roddy paused to mop his brow. I asked her to hurry along in the most polite manner on account of the Queen & all. The gala cast were murmuring with interest. & you know what she said to me? The performers watched his lips with anticipation. Who is this Queen anyway? All of the performers burst into laughter. As if on cue, a slim female figure appeared, covered from head to toe in black lace. In case you're wondering, that's how she was in her Audrey

Hepburn phase. Roddy heaved a great sigh of relief before starting back into convulsions again, finding himself face to face with the tailbone of the Diva in waiting, through the ultrafine mesh of a very backless dress. Then, as the pass door to the auditorium opened to herald the Royal entrance, everyone of us struggled to stifle our giggles. I could scarcely remember to tell the Queen how I had high-fived her as a girl inside the train passing through Unity, Saskatchewan ... "

The young man answered with a puff of stoogie before dropping it entirely.

"But of course, I *did* remember."

The next night came swiftly upon him. He was taking a distinctly nocturnal turn, just as in his younger artist days. They say old people sleep & eat less. What a crock. Just check out the buffet table. Gran packs it away alright. Why where have all the seconds & thirds gone? It must be a comfort to the young & refreshingly insecure that their elders, the so-called establishment, are daily shrinking & diminishing until nothing is left, before departing for that great smorgasbord in the sky. He had made arrangements to meet Lorn(e), who for biblical or professional reasons had decided to perform a sacred elision upon his name, cutting away the extraneous vowel with God as his witness. However, he had brought it to the attention of Maxwell Wittman the Third that the Romantic poets reinforced this usage as a shortened form of *forlorn* & it was perfect for him, being so passionately *lorn* about some woman or another in these turbulent times & how every-one needed a stage name if you were to split hairs on the issue yada yada. Padam shrugged & accepted. Lorn could be impossible at times. Padam was otherwise thinking about his new project when Lorn bounded up the winding stairs of the Istoria with a nimble lightness. The former lawyer always wore a Trilby with a slight tilt that gave his rosy cherubic face a Mephisthelean air. Over the course of the complete history of literature & sticky postered propaganda, especially from the age of Marlowe to the end of the Second World War (that is, before literature became for the most part, an inverted form of propaganda attempting to rewrite history's wrongs in the hands of faux hip scribes like fashionable Dreyfusards before the First World War) the Jew has been depicted as a caricature, as a gnarled money-lender to creep out of devilish portraits in Nevsky Prospekt, or pawn-brokers to be sacrificed to the ideology of a *greater good* or virtue, a Shylock to cut the credit of frivolous Venetians, a Nosferatu sucking the blood of infants in the crib, a foreign banker with an indecipher-able accent to thwart the industrious virtue of a César Birotteau be-fore the hungry eyes of an admiring Gobseck or Molineux, in short, a vicious parking meter attendant of the free world, smacking citi-zens with usurious service charges right & left. If presented with this opinion, or the usual musings of the bearish knucklecracker about Zionist conspiracies & the newspaper industry, Lorn would no doubt argue successfully that in each case, the character in question had been a bit of a *schlemiel* & was not by definition of the word, a *mensch*. Lorn rarely ever had a conversation without instructing the other party or other respective group of parties (since he often had to ad-dress many gangs of sponsors & often more than one group in one night, which only added to his Mercurial mystique) to be, in all brevity, a *mensch*, as Lorn undoubtedly *was*.

"That," he would gesture, "is the height of Jewish manhood. Forget the whole bar mitzvah thing. One simply strives to be a *mensch*. Men in this world have come & gone without so much as a squeal. Others thunder & lightning their way through the cosmos. Yet how many of these can say without crossing their fingers that in the course of their life, they were a *mensch*? That, my friends, is everything."

With a wave of his hand over the table, like magic, he simplified the entire universe for you. That was Lorn's way, & to be generous, his gift, because as you already understand, he was a real *mensch*.

"Why don't you take your hat off," prodded Padam, flashing his Cheshire Cat grin.

Indeed, if at that moment all the cherubim & seraphim had suddenly transported these two mortals into celestial otherness, all that would have remained in the Istoria to mark their existence upon earth would have been that floating pair of teeth & a Trilby tilting upon an invisible hook, midair.

"Boy, I've had to *schlepp*! I've really *schlepped* a *schlepp*. They use that on the tube all the time. Ever catch that one? I tell ya, Padam, once the ancient lexicon enters the public sphere, you have to emphasize what you're talkin' 'bout to be understood. I mean, this was the genuine article, an authentic while supplies last *schlepp*, a *schlepp* with a capital S!"

"Why don't you sit down," giggled Padam.

Lorn took a seat, extremely well-hatted.

"Now Lorn. To make a long story short, I have had a dream. I have a new project in mind & without question I could use your help."

Lorn furrowed his smooth pink forehead.

"It's for a stained glass," hastened Padam.

"Is this another church deal," his patron asked, starting to rub his beatific hands together. "Cuz I can definitely hustle up some extra special interest. Should I say Roman Catholic or Christ-thing? One of your Russian cathedrals or a few stray Litvaks, what are we talking 'bout here?"

The wheels were already turning, or shall we say the rolodex in Lorn's mind, who for the moment had forgotten his Romantic pretensions. He rattled off the religious differentiations like a card shark & began to organize adeptly as a bookie might, flipping through over a hundred ridiculous names upon a roster of the indebted to make use of at the first opportunity.

"No, not this time, Lorn. This is, shall I say, a *personal* project."

"O," said Lorn, the wheels in his mind screeching to a halt. "What kinda personal project?"

"Well, you see, there's this young man with a striking appearance who most conveniently has formed the habit of frequenting this establishment for a few drinks now & again."

"A hotel guest," offered Lorn abstractly, starting to estimate the nightly revenue for one of the historical rooms.

"No," scolded Padam. "I'm quite sure he's a regular & a local resident. He gave me permission to sketch him. But the thing is, I am planning to do a larger scale project in stained glass. My drawing is only a caricature, but that is really all you need. In fact, a cartoon works far better for glass. Then you only have so many pieces & colours to work with. The cartoon is the map to the essence of a character ... "

Padam trailed off, abruptly aware he was speaking too rapidly or with more passion than usual in his voice.

"So you really like this kid," said Lorn, now a little bored since the conversation had ceased to wholeheartedly concern himself.

"Yes. He gave me the idea in fact. I vowed to undertake it at once. Perhaps we could have a whip round. Even a small contribution would be welcome."

Lorn narrowed his eyes, appearing like one of the angels deciding the fate of Sodom & Gomorrah. Then he cocked his Trilby forward in undeniable affirmation, his seal of approval as *mensch* among men. Padam pressed harder.

"I took the liberty of talking it over with Stephane. A hundred & fifty pieces of glass in total, give or take." Now Lorn bowed his head, matching the angle of his grey Trilby. In this movement of his body, he became a Homeric figure with hoary drenched locks nodding his head in careful assent, with the air of a rather Yiddish Caesar agreeing to the immediate & gruesome dispatch of Pompey or Antony, while also maintaining the aloofness & restraint of Pontius Pilate with a gleam in his eye that said to Maxwell Wittman the Third what business of this is mine my responsibility ends here. On the other hand, if the work of art was a success, as others had been in the past, Lorn would not shy of the credit due. It had, after all, been *his* idea. However, it is unfair to be overtly critical of this *mensch*. Before the next twenty-four hours had ticked by, he would already be schmoozing & waving his arms about with grandeur in order to promote with all his heart this latest project, as midwife to the artistic & poetic genius that had sprung from the metaphorical womb of the illustrious Maxwell Wittman the Third. Already, Padam could envision Lorn seizing the arm of a wealthy former colleague & giving a grand non-stop spiel about its beauty.

"Hey man, this subject of his, when properly framed, would do wonders for your walls. A real beauty! Say, don't you have to buy some more art for your office? This is the cat's miaow my friend! Best to get in on the ground floor with this one!"

Then Lorn turned toward Padam, allowing a black & white cinematic shadow to cross his pink face.

"Of course, I would like to meet this young *find* of yours."

As if on cue, the young man wandered into the withdrawing room, rubbing his eyes before searching for a comfortable seat.

"Tomasz," cooed Padam.

He held up two fingers & waited like a shepherd signalling a herding dog.

"Over here, Tomasz."

The young man flushed & approached the pair, taking a seat as instructed.

"Here Lorn. Here is your chance to *appraise* him."

Lorn was very warm & affectionate by nature & he made the young man feel quite welcome, even to the point that Tomasz forgot he was dealing with an ex-lawyer who had been accused of disembowelling opponents on paper in the past.

"You gotta be a *mensch*."

Lorn stressed this commandment with a two-fingered tap upon the brim of his Trilby.

"Our young Ganymede is an interesting mix. He's Native & Jewish & what was it?"

Lorn eyed the living work of art suspiciously, studying his features in a rather litigious manner.

234

"You go to the Synagogue?"

"Nope," the young man replied with a touch of derision. "I do have a *mezuzah*. That's all I need."

Lorn nodded.

"My brother's a rabbi. When I move, he gets me a new one for nothin'. Nifty deal, eh?"

The young man nodded back.

"Tax-free scrap of Deuteronomy."

At that remark, two points of ice appeared to emerge in Lorn's eyes, just as the roadside mud rifts in Spring freeze over because of a sudden chill, a lingering memory of winter.

"Then technically, you're not Jewish, being unorthodox. He doesn't go to the Synagogue."

He held up his smooth hands helplessly, addressing the entire parlour.

"*If you tickle us, do we not laugh*," countered the young man.

After that, there was a palpable amount of awkwardness. Padam & Lorn talked around the young man, as old friends are wont to do in the presence of a newcomer. It was only after a number of pints that Lorn developed his full rubicund bloom & Padam's smile occupied the wavering expanse of the room. Talk turned to *showtunes*, if we are to debase the great movie works that our predecessors adored with that cliché & thus paint the natural evolution of genius & talent with the same sensitive brush out of sheer lack of understanding. As for the gruff manly love of some fossil of a musicologist for Tchaikovsky or Mozart, it struggles to come to terms with even a Puccini, who like many of the composers of the last century, rewrote the works of his predecessors with the dramatic effect of a theatre in mind. Only he could write such a *showstopper* to end the first act of *Tosca* that Tito Gobbi would later sing to its height, combining a choral *te deum* & the steady toll of Rome with the dark rich tones of a delicious villain, where Mozart would beg our leave to giggle & yawn over a four hour farce with only a few transcendental fragments salient enough for short attention spans. Henceforth, it was to the movie theatre that Tchaikovsky & Saint-Säens were sent, a transposition that preserved the memory of love in the composer's minds for the past & present. It is the dependable short term memory of the public that assumed in a radical manner that Wagner was new & wholly original, just as today we have forgotten that when Nirvana began performing, they sounded almost exactly like the Beatles. A debate here over the raw power & simplicity of the melodic & how the successors of Wagner & Puccini are to be found in the likes of Joy Division & Smashing Pumpkins & uniquely in the work of Art Bergmann, whose best endeavours are beyond some mere dissonant trick. On the contrary, there is more in common in Art's caustic *Guns & Heroin* with the final aria of the hapless Madame Butterfly than we may care to admit or even explore.

"Till the clouds roll by," offered the young man with enthusiasm & Lorn's face became a round *Magnificat*.

"Ahhh yes, Jerome Kern."

Padam pounced upon this lighter moment.

"Yes, Tomasz is a fan of the tenor Mario Lanza."

Lorn was further illuminated beneath his tilting Trilby.

"Mario Lanza! My god, everybody wanted to be him when I was growing up. The Toast of New Orleans. The Desert Song. The Great Caruso! We used to see him on the tube & then go out into the street & sing our hearts out, no matter how terribly. Be my love ... Everyone thought he was some kind of singing truck driver. He only once pulled his father's truck out of the garage, so they say ... "

Padam frowned, feeling the conversation wildly spiralling out of control.

"Tomasz often speaks of *The Student Prince*."

The young man nodded impishly.

"Yes, that's me. Some kind of Native Indian prince. Mario Lanza played the prince who is sent to school in disguise with the other students in Heidelberg. That's where he falls in love with a beautiful barmaid ... "

Lorn smiled.

"Yes, that's a good one. Sigmund Romberg."

Padam leaned across the table & widened his eyes through his glasses, one of his customary occular effects that indicated he had something vital to say.

"Tomasz sang a number from that operetta to a woman one night & she paid for our beers."

The young man grinned.

"*Thoughts will come to me again that are no more. Dear old Heidelberg beside the river shore ...* "

"Yes, & I remember the part about the beers," tittered Padam.

So they spoke on like this about opera, operettas, & even *showtunes* very seriously & in all manner of manly nattering, for it is the author's opinion that men grumble & gossip at least twice as much as women. In addition, even the Istoria provides innumerable examples that the most sober austere level-headed man, once he has imbibed even a glass of beer, can suddenly turn into a bold vociferous titan who continues to drink himself toward beastliness, just as the men of Odysseus turned readily into swine after only a mere sip of Circe's concoction. In this case, with their cockles well warmed, these gentlemen formed a nearly steady triumvirate of affection, what Maxwell Wittman the Third would refer to as an unholy trinity. Lorn had abandoned all of his initial suspicions about the young man. Now they were brothers in all things. He still felt a pang of remorse about being in any way standoffish, which went against his generous nature as, need we say, a *mensch.* Conversation turned back to the young man as Native Jew, as universal prophet & so on & so forth.

"I am Kwakwaka'wakw. Some say Kwakiutl."

Lorn slapped one silken knee.

"Yes, I bought some artifacts of theirs. I, err ... had them in my house & I gave them back. They were originally stolen, as you no doubt know. There was a big ceremony. They gave me an Indian name in their language, something like he who gives … ? The Great Giver, anyway. They gave me this watch."

He turned his wrist towards the young man, revealing the rounded face of a thunderbird in red, with paddles & birds in place of the numbers.

"What time is it," asked the young man, squinting.

"Closing time," replied Grant, who was standing over them. "Anything for last call, *boys*?"

Grant was promptly dispatched. There was still a little time before the red bird on Lorn's wrist. He noticed the young man eyeing his watch.

"You want this … "

His voice trailed off, departing for some strange place where a pound of flesh would still be a nominal deposit.

"Take it. Take it! I can get more. I got plenty!"

The young man stared at him, suddenly imagining a truckload beeping backward, packed with Kwakwaka'wakw watches.

"C'mon. Any friend of Mr. Wittman is a friend of mine. & besides, you're a *mensch*."

After a few more refusals, the young man gave in to Lorn's tenacity & persistence. He fastened the leather watch strap about his left wrist & held it up. They shook on the new arrangement.

"There, a perfect fit. All is well. Now, seriously, we should watch *Carousel* some night. My treat!"

IV

"Have you seen my stained glass?"

"What's that, mistah?"

"O nothing really. I live right up Giltford & I've made a window. Yes, you can walk by & see. Please do."

The woman by the window looked over quickly & then back out of her window.

"O," said Grant. "That must be pretty cool. I'll keep my eye out. Same as usual, Padman?"

Maxwell Wittman the Third nodded, slowly forming a feline smile. The old woman entered & made her rounds, dropping a Werther's Original upon the tables of those she knew, so that no one could refuse candy from a stranger.

"Have you seen my window? Perhaps you would like to take a look at my latest stained glass creation?"

"O, that sounds lovely," she said warmly, taking a seat at an adjacent table.

Her regular beverage arrived & she raised it to her trembling lips absentmindedly, as Padam smiled at her encouragingly.

"My kids, of course, one's an accountant, that's the eldest, he has to travel to Hong Kong all the time. Or Aruba. Or the Bahamas. Well, they sure as heck couldn't stay here. What a noise, if all the boys were here together! O, & they buy all kinds of art. The middle one buys up Aboriginal prints & hangs 'em up & down the corridors where he works. A lawyer, you see. Me, I love all that coastal stuff!"

She clapped her hands together approvingly while her eyes brimmed over. But Padam was not listening. His mind ebbed along with excitement as he watched shapes of late summer clumping together upon the sand. He thought of Paul Klee's numerous studies of harmonies & dissonance. His mind was buzzing as he watched each pigment of the beach brighten & subside along with the glimmer of the rising tide. After downing his pale ale & licking his lips, he felt the scene become more fragmentary, breaking down into colours like those he had chosen for his stained glass caricature. As Grant was wordlessly dispatched to fetch another pint, Padam thought of a study by Klee of a plant preparing for winter. As the dark autumnal colours approached with a threatening darkness, the plant seemed to retreat inward with its polyphonic gradations. Each textured layer was to be preserved in order to survive the cold seasons ahead. Padam felt an organic buzz himself as he imagined the sustenance of his own inner colours that could not necessarily see, yet tendrilled outward in a psychical sense. He knew that such alternate modes of perception created an impetus for Klee & other artists, including Maxwell Wittman the Third. In fact, he was by no means certain how much time had passed or how many pints he had drunk before the young man appeared. His inspiration, nay, his vector of heavenly light, strode into the Istoria with a distinct swagger. Padam leapt up with agility, with a move not unlike one he had used in a modest production of *Salome*, in order to deftly slip past the old woman's sad diatribe & catch the young man by the shoulder before he chose a seat. The young man eyed him suspiciously out of the corner of his slightly dilated vision. Padam slowed down & became cautious.

"I have finished Ganymede," he announced.

"Yes."

"Yes."

He sat down & Padam hopped into the seat beside him.

"Would you like to come & look at the stained glass?"

The young man frowned & his wandering scar seemed to darken, then turn translucent again. Padam watched the sliver of moon & wondered how it would look next to the diamond of blood he had inserted in the stained glass forehead.

"I've been busy," offered the young man, sensing some criticism in the silent face of the dancer. "I have been working on ... for lack of a better word, my libretto."

Maxwell Wittman the Third cocked forward, lifting his right ear. "I thought you said *libretto*."

"Yes, that's right. It has taken six notebooks of nonstop writing. Trying to capture everyday music, even the silences ... I feel that I've run into my Muse, accidentally of course. I didn't mean it. A mess if there ever was one. Something about Rilke. The way the Angel through the visible helps you to see the invisible. Another mystic insists that words are shadows of reality. The work is a metaphor for itself. The music, the silences, the secular rites of an imaginary winter. Unearthly white hands at a morning keyboard. Shadows of reality. I have distilled those six books, have extracted only what I felt were the quintessentials ... "

The young man continued in disjointed phrases like these, waving about a white book he had just printed. Padam watched the talking face happily until the lips stopped moving at one word he would not understand: *Love*. The young man flipped to one of the pages & began to read a number of poems, including the following one:

A cool bath is drawn
for the overheated imagination
& her first breath
is one of appreciation,
descending toward submergence
water up to her lovely
white throat, naked
as a pale caryatid
beneath the fluted cornices
of restful music
amid the resonant clack
of dead Selectrics
& the waft

                    of puffing newspaper
                                    columnists
                                            rolling up shirtsleeves ...

            Water up to the level of
                                    her lovely
                thoughts
                        her eyes
                                turning green
                                            as oxidized copper

The smile of Maxwell Wittman the Third frothed off. His ego slipped
into his beer like the fat monocle of a distracted aristocrat.

"Well, that *is* a poem. That *is* what you write."

The young man sighed.

"Some friends of mine want to get it printed. They really like it.
Something about going deeper. But it is hard to say how I have
suffered, although I feel I have. I have made myself ill with this. This
love. & what do you say about stealing lives for the sake of art? Since
I have felt with all my heart & find that immortality is useless? A great
writer suggests that most of the great queens in literature were
moulded upon barmaids & shopgirls, that the soul was there to be
dreamed & sketched amid the mad laughter of a tavern. But have I
defiled my own idea of love? If so, I am not the first." Padam stroked
his whiskers, falling back on one of his maxims.

"A wise old queen once told me, there is *use* & there is *abuse*. The
trick is to *use* & not *abuse*."

Grant dropped down a fresh pint for each of them.

"On the house, boys. Serious business over here, eh? Lighten up. At
least you have your looks. Hey you guys gonna read all night or
what?"

Grant glided away as Padam considered whether to unlock additional precepts from his memory.

"If you are in fact speaking about Shakespeare & his visits to the local Mermaid for free light & cheap lager, then perhaps the end of my favourite sonnet will help you."

Padam stared intensely through his glasses at the young man & recited the last couplet:

> *All this the world well knows; yet none knows well*
> *To shun the heaven that leads men to this hell.*

After this exposition, he shinnied down from the revolving podium on the ceiling & returned to his beer & the five minute applause of the flapping *Irregulars*. Thank you. Thank you.

"We tend to love the ones we make into our greatest art. How could we resist their charm? But then, they die."

Maxwell Wittman the Third laughed throughout St. Petersburg during prolonged visits to various cathedrals in the snow & at the desk where Dostoyevsky worked to the chagrin of the other server, who had drifted off to sleep with the samovar on.

"She thinks I am insane. Maybe I am."

Padam nodded merrily. He was not completely unsympathetic to the young man. After all, her refuse was shortly to become his spoils. He could afford to listen about those green eyes a moment longer. How like the stained glass the young man was! Grant asked them if they would like anything else with a wary glare.

"Just a glass," said Padam.

"Just one more," said the young man. "I feel potted."

Padam snickered.

"How quickly we recover! Drink up, young Ganymede. Plenty more roe in the sea!"

He paused, thinking suddenly of Hieronymous Bosch & his giant birds feeding little red berries to naked ravers.

"Wanna go smoke a joint?"

Maxwell Wittman the Third was very excited. His hands clenched into tiny claws of unbearable anxiety. Normally, the key turned simply & quietly in the lock. This was a rule, pretty much a stipulation of remaining in the building. But tonight! Tonight! He let the young man in with a short stumble & thought of his father's hand, the shape of which remained in the corridor. Feast your eyes, my young friend. The young man wandered about this time, examining everything with intoxicated confidence.

"I like that," he said at last.

He was pointing to the studio wall. There was a painting from another era in the life of Padam.

"I did that for a Rape Relief benefit. The story was about two men … "

He persisted in that tactless didactic tone of his, as if the listener was half past daft. He held up two fingers to represent the two men he was speaking so slowly about. Every syllable was enunciated beyond the pale of clarity. The author must interject to point out that if we were to represent Padam as he actually spoke, the story would never come to a close.

"They had decided to *rape* this woman."

He inverted the two fingers. The young man waited for the people to come out of the steeple.

"But in the end, they decided against it. Or else, they simply could not go through with it."

He elevated his voice, as if this were the most noble act in centuries. Padam looked into the frameless canvas, trying to recall each stroke of brown or green during that time he had lived within the painting

& nowhere else. Now it felt alien to him. Had he really painted it? & what did his young love see or feel in that framelessness?

"What do you see?"

The young man did not answer. The unadulterated greens & browns began to merge before their four glazed eyes, not including the pair of glasses worn by Maxwell Wittman the Third. The two young men were just beginning to embrace their *victim* in that bucolic field. She was no longer their plaything? She had become their mother? Their caresses threatened to be eternally innocent.

"Quite the ecologue," the young man said at last.

Padam laughed.

"Do you want it?"

"No."

"Do you want it? If you really … "

"No, I couldn't."

"Please take it."

"No, sorry."

"Wanna smoke a joint?"

His old standby, since Carnaby Street.

"Yeah, okay."

Maxwell Wittman the Third seemed even more diminutive than usual as he crept past the dancing bar & mirror & down the narrow corridor toward the smallest room.

"We have to smoke it in here," stated Padam. "The management. We better shut the door, or else Chester will want in, & all over everything."

Padam sat gracefully upon the furry purple toilet seat & pointed to the rim of his bathtub, as if holding court. He produced an instrument like a pair of tweezers that were the wrong way round. Padam enjoyed a long toke before passing off the clinical device to the young man. He grabbed at the silver flash & immediately sent the joint tumbling toward the bathmat.

"No no," Padam squealed. "The key," he instructed with precision, "is to hold it gently, to take it between your fingers like so."

He took another long toke to demonstrate, before risking giving it back. The young man extracted the herbal part of the silver apparatus & took a long puff.

"'Fraid of burning your fingers?"

Padam shook his head.

"Who wants to burn their fingers?"

Pawing at the door.

"Shhh ... Chester."

The young man was still inhaling.

"Aren't you getting anywhere?"

"I'm no good with pot. O there you go. There's something ... hmmmm."

The young man, turning pale as porcelain, read another poem. Padam laughed in what he imagined to be the right places. They were both merrily melting away before the minor thud.

The young man did not get far before he hit hardwood floor, as if flopping his audition, all elbows & knees.

"See sir, how I bleed."

He produced scraped elbows & knees, raw & bleeding. He moved into the bedroom, past the surveillance of Chester & collapsed upon the brown & green coverlet. The cat leapt away at once.

"You can spend the night," said Padam with an unctuous voice.

The young man pushed himself up again & knelt awkwardly upon the floor.

"Must remove my shoes, must untie them. You see how crazy I am. I can collapse like this & still I can't sleep with my shoes on."

"You can leave your hat on," giggled Padam.

Birds twittered. Someone tittered. The young man had no idea how long he had lain there on top of the coverlet. He could feel a pair of eyes watching him in the darkness, as palpable as a touch. Purring ... Something furry. He suddenly flinched.

"Chester," he murmured, eyes agrog. But the observer did not blink or slink back into the dark. It was Maxwell Wittman the Third.

"How long have you been lying there?"

Padam did not answer. He just kept staring through the demigloom. The young man inched back, raising his chin & fluttering his eyelashes to adjust to the lighting, or lack of it. The colours of his own countenance were illuminated by a streetlamp & cast eerily across his face. He was staring at the iridescent caricature of himself. He shivered.

"I'm cold."

Padam unslunk & snapped to attention.

"I have covers."

The young man shook his head, which only disoriented him further.

"No, I need to go home, to go home & write. It's late. I need to go home."

Padam cheshired.

"It's early."

The young man nodded.

"The best time. I need to go home & write."

With that reply, he slipped away from the spectral light & hurriedly knotted his chestnut laces. He threw on his long black coat & reached for the deadbolt. Then he stopped & turned towards an expectant Maxwell Wittman the Third, whose small hands were clenched smaller than the cast of them in the corridor. The young man's lips

247

curled into such a strange smile that his face became a cruel distortion of itself, cruel & mocking to the rays of his own image that moved about the apartment with each alteration of light. Padam's face became an upside-down question mark.

"I hope you're happy. Do you realize you haven't got me down at all? The Rape of Ganymede! I gave you an idea & you merely resorted to your old standbys. Another Apollo in the window. You fucked up, Padam. You wanted to frame me & put me in the window. Already, I have changed. & when you go to bed whose face do you see? Look carefully at your glass cartoon. That is your face. O yes you have slaved. As with all your stories & works, you have yet another costly picture of yourself! Look at the face, Padam! These lips are not mine."

Padam turned anxiously toward the stained glass window, raking his grey whiskers with wizened fingers while the colours began to flood his feline eyes & occlude his usual grin. The door slammed.

"Shhh," said Maxwell Wittman the Third to no one, as Chester continued to lick himself.

It was almost a week before anyone saw the young man again. The narrator is ashamed to profess a complete lack of omniscience. Where did he hang his hat? No one knew. But it was generally understood that if the *Irregulars* did not see one of the others within a week's time, that unfortunate soul was reported to be dead. When the young man ended his sojourn, he showed up at the Istoria with sweaty matted hair & his clothes in disarray. His face was ill-shaven & his odour suspect. Padam did not appear at the hotel that week, but it seemed to him as if he had never been away. Thanks to Grant, he was given a veritable transcript of any *events* that had taken place for the last fortnight. The young man had started early in the evening & had run into the heavily-moustached professor with his usual constabular look. As for the details Grant had left out, Padam was forced to use his imagination, based on opinions & stories the young man would scarcely fail to repeat after a few pints.

"Growing a beard?"

"Why yes, sir. & you?"

The professor straightened up in his chair.

"I'm teaching a course on opera."

"You seem pleased with yourself."

"Yes, well it's something of a retirement present to myself."

"Ah."

"We are doing some Strauss, *Salome* to be exact, & *Don Giovanni*, O & *Tristan & Isolde* of course. You're a fan of that one, no?"

The young man stared back swarthily, scratching his browscar.

"Yes, that I am, *sir*."

It was about this time when the woman who wrote by the window materialized & took her usual perch. The professor followed her with his sagging eyes, as did the bloodshot rims of the young man. He knew without a doubt this would have made a lovely trio for *Le Nozze di Figaro*, not to mention a saucy quartet featuring Maxwell Wittman the Third. A wondrous overlap of voices excited by a multitude of unearthly desires.

"We begin with *Orfeo*. Of course, it goes without saying every opera composer owes a great debt to Monteverdi."

There was a flicker of light in the young man's dark eyes.

"O yes sir, it's practically bankable. I mean, *magnificent*, the part where he sings to the souls in hell to let him across the Styx."

"Naturally," concurred the professor with a slight cough.

"How much do you cover in that class?"

"Brief. Too brief, I fear. A few months. Why, we really need a year to say we have covered any ground whatsoever."

The young man looked around impatiently, searching for something else to say.

"Strauss, eh? You do know Vancouver Opera is doing a Strauss cycle, every other year I think? No? I love that dance in *Salome*. It's so exotic in some way. Hard for me to get into, otherwise. I'm just not *there* yet. Wish my friend was here. Maybe he knew one of the *definitive* dancers from that opera."

"You wish your friend *were* here. Rare case of the subjunctive in English, for those who are keeping an eye on grammar. Now what were you saying? Ah yes, but you must learn to appreciate more than merely the dance. That is the seduction as performed by Strauss. What of the libretto & King Herod & the very disappointed head of John the Baptist? Don't they get even a look in?"

The young man looked around the bar, bemused.

"O. There was that movie with Minnie Driver ... "

"What?!"

Meanwhile, as Grant was relating this dreary turn of events, Padam was filled with regret he had not been there to answer the young man's question. The author pleads an opportunity to interject here, if only to point out what is obvious to an attentive ear. As for these two, the professor & the young man, they live everywhere. They are Hamlet & Polonius. They are Aristotle & Plato. They are mistrustful father & son, the whole of humanity upon either side of an argument about a holy spirit, or for that matter, God. It is not uncommon for neighbours with virtually identical lives to build fences between their properties. The history of mankind is akin to the division & enclosure of public land. Once a free & bountiful gift for all, the earth has become an object to be possessed in its entirety to the point of complete ruination. So it is with the generous liberty that knowledge grants us. As soon as one person knows a fact & another person a different fact, the metaphysical fences are hammered into place between them. Calamity arises from this aspect of humanity. One may speak with universal fraternity in a manner so moving that an audience would be reduced to tears. Nonetheless, that speaker, having stepped away from that magical instance of rhetoric & hyperbole, is capable of inflicting the most limiting actions upon his neighbours, whether it be to spit in someone's path or kick a cat out of the way, not to speak of their distasteful interaction upon a local highway.

However, for some mysterious reason, this germ, this bitter curdle of lactescent limitations, like the transfigured properties of a bottle of milk after a storm, provides the very spoon of gruel to nourish the continual existence of an artist. Knowledge, by virtue of itself, is destined to produce a form of elitism reducible only to its own collection of discoveries. Those that preach universality are far more dangerous, since they prostitute the virtues & industry of humanity for the sake of propaganda, which appears to be the inverse of military drums & horns but is in fact the same thing: propaganda. This is but a slave to Balzac's *Goddess of Public Opinion*. The alternative is to prove that we ever existed through a long process of sacrifice & preservation. If we are to live every moment, is it not precious enough to be recorded for posterity? As far as the mania for photography & digital recording goes, that is only proof to a future civilization that we were always having a birthday, celebrating a religious holiday, getting married, giving birth, or on vacation. As for the most beautiful moments & our most precious reveries, they have departed with our imagination. In other words, with us. To refer back to our friend Glenn Gould, who seemed to serve the world far better in relative isolation than in general friendship, or so the propaganda about his life informs us, since he suggested to himself in an interview that the relationship of artist to public is a 1:0 ratio. If we examine this statement & apply a margin of error for the sake of humanity, we are forced to call Mr. Gould a hypocrite. What he might have said, if we are to split hairs, is that the artist strives for that relationship of 1:0 or imagines it as we imagine sound in a sealed vacuum. Yet is that hypocrisy of being not essential to the work of art being created at all, in other words the industry that gives life to non-being? To return rather lethargically, this sad interplay between young man & professor near retirement is also necessary then, in order to explain why Beethoven troubled himself to crank out a *Pathétique* piano sonata in the first place. With regard to *Don Giovanni*, the young man yielded to the authoritative voice of philosophy.

"Have you read Kierkegaard on Mozart, particularly on *Don Giovanni*? His essay on the nature of the erotic is key. Ha! I bought a pocketsized copy of *Either/Or* in Albion Books a while ago & the bookseller made a remark that it would keep me quite warm this winter. Anyway, he seems to express in words a rough-hewn model of Mozart's opera, at least the lyrical parts."

"Harrumph," responded the professor. "Well, Kierkegaard *would* do that."

"I've also been listening to the 40th," continued the young man with pride.

"40th what?"

"Why, the *40th Symphony in G minor.*"

"Ah yes."

"I am not sure about the start," the young man offered tentatively, deprecating Mozart as any person of talent in the face of established genius impossible to ever rival.

"I mean to say, it's got that more obvious Mozartian sound, that sucrose corrosion of structure. That sweeter than sweet monotony of the concerto bit in *Elvira Madigan*, incidentally to which I love to shave, when in the mood."

The young man cupped his black bristles with his right hand to demonstrate.

"But as I am simply a dilettante with my ear to some cobalt cupola of unreachable sky, I hesitate to stress I far prefer the andante. There is some prophecy of Brahms in that work, his symphonies I mean, that weird universal quotient coming to the surface of an ambivalent universe. By the way, I love that agonizing allegretto of his in the *3rd Symphony*. So casual, so nonchalant, like the last ember or ash of a fleeting passion … "

He paused to look back at the woman by the window, who was pretending not to listen. The young man raised his voice for effect.

"But why can't we enjoy ourselves?! At least Beethoven & Brahms let us, as well as themselves. Why doesn't Mozart? He lacks their clean ebullience. Don't you find him kind of cynical, sir?"

The professor cleared his throat.

"If you were in my class, I would be able to say that was a bunch of hogwash. The college prefers the term *malarky*. You surely know already, those are semantic questions & they lack any formalistic framework. Where are your proofs? Where is your grammar? Your notations? Why, when I was at Oxford, we were tossed a German primer. *Erwächt* the professor would scream. Bloodcurdling stuff. What has happened to the student body these days? We had to learn Anglo-Saxon in a fortnight & then … "

"Indeed sir. & you had to walk miles through the snow to get your Liebestod … "

"Growing up, there was a lot of snow," replied the professor flatly.

The young man pressed on, bolstered by the contents of an empty pint glass.

"But *Don Giovanni* is brilliant really. Personally, I'd like to trim all the talking but I know that would be blasphemous. Forget I said it. Everything, the overture & then its inevitable return at the end, when the dead man demands justice & drags our favourite rake down to the depths of hell. Or that catalogue of conquests in the mouth of Leporello or those marvellous arias of self-abegnation. I guess the style belongs to our age, since there is a hint of arsenic in each of those melodies. No matter how true the note, it echoes false."

"Falsely," corrected the professor, unable to help himself. "So, you've been getting an earful of Mozart, eh? Now what's your take on *Tristan & Isolde*? Or perhaps we've discussed this."

The young man nodded cautiously.

"But I love to hear it this time of year as summer sinks into the waters of autumn. Wonderful to take a few months off & read a few pages of Søren & listen to some Mozart & walk through the coastal mist & hear the foghorns that so remind me of the introductory chords in one of Wagner's masterpieces. It's a guilty pleasure, I know. You would call it semantics perhaps, to see & hear desire everywhere, somehow thwarted, in water & wind & rubicund leaves. After all, it is only a progression of Berlioz, if you want to get technical. No more of that French here's the devil thunk of chords. What about that hint of fog in Wagner? Is it really there? Like that abstract beginning to the opera, the prelude. It seems to vague, so decadent with its pauses & so tentative with its sounds. Have you read Thomas Mann's *Tristan*? That's an excellent short story about a writer in the sanitarium with a woman he starts to admire. She is from a rather musical family, but she has given up her music to marry. One of the oddities is that he imagines a crown about her head from a childhood game, one that establishes her as a kind of contemporary Isolde. The fantastic part is when she sits down at the piano, when all the *patients* are out in the snow, & against doctor's orders plays each vorspiel, all of *Tristan & Isolde*, the prelude & the love motives & at last the Liebestod finale. When she is finished, he kneels on the dusty floor in his long black coat & thanks her silently with his hand over his heart. Very strange. He has written this one mysterious book, you see, & no one knows what to make of it. The insanity is all relative, yet there is almost a musical sympathy between them, & I mean sympathy in its broadest sense, if you believe in that sort of thing. The *psychical*, I mean. Of course, it is to be expected with Mann that the characters are petty & sickly & unworthy of these grand operatic themes. Only no more unworthy than the average person with a touch of something, a certain artistic spark ... "

The professor coughed emphatically.

"If this conversation were in a book, it would neither wash for Carol Shields nor Hemingway."

In answer, the young man's eyes glinted with something *unheimlich*.

Thankfully, Grant had begun his training at the same university in sociology & he possessed an uncanny ability for recalling the most abstruse, albeit scattered array of facts. In any case, no one could say except for the young man, who sometimes burst into inebriated snatches of no longer popular arias, what he had sung, or who at. Grant was uncertain whether he had directed the aria at the woman by the window or the professor. Luckily, Maxwell Wittman the Third was an informed consumer of information. He was aware that one of the young man's favourite pieces was a semi-comical serenade from one of the very operas they were discussing, although he, Padam, had never danced to it personally. Fortunately, he had nothing but time to google this tidbit in its original tongue:

> *Deh vieni alla finestra*
> *O mio tesoro …*

Padam hummed to himself. He could almost hear faint sardonic sounds emerging from the young man's soft white throat, slightly out of tune yet in such beautiful tones that appeared to justify this flaw, this elusive growl that became part of the music, as if it had never been otherwise. The young man had confided in himself, Maxwell Wittman the Third, that he simply adored the baritones in the operas of Verdi & Wagner. Mournful barons in a lonely tower & ill-fated wanderers cast upon those murky waves in C major. It was once again Gobbi who brought to life the buffo aspect of Rigoletto, that pandering hunchback with poisonous intent who wished for nothing more than to slip the body of an insincere duke, his daughter's betrayer, into a sack & dump him into the nearest river. It is this hyperreality of masks & faces that we have abandoned in our contemporary dramas. For Padam's part, he did not understand all of the lovely blitherings of the young man & yet he felt compelled to agree with his own thoughts on the matter, that the world of Petronius & hence Fellini had forever disappeared. It was not that the same events did not transpire in our so-called modern world of debt & monetary credit. However, two crucial elements had been extorted in order to render our world more dishonest than that distant empire. The humour & the horror. Now, we as free citizens were subject to invisible powers beyond our comprehension. The masks were no longer horrific. Not at all. They were perfectly commonplace. Perfectly normal. The lascivious towel flicking & bathhouse exchanges that Plato had struggled so hard to deny in his imaginary republic, even with a warm copy of Aristophanes in his peplos, had now been reduced to a SLIPPERY WHEN WET sign. People less buff & beautiful, having never known an ounce of luxury, were bought & sold every day for a meagre salary or even as embryos over a global network. However, the *word* slavery had disappeared. No more would Padam be able to buy a young stripling in broad daylight with perfumed flesh & a poetic wreath about pink temples. This had been his initial notion for Ganymede. To restore the euphonious practices of Greece & the fast friendship between mentor & protégé. But the young man was right. This attempt was *golder than gold*, as Sappho had said. Gone were Apollo & Hyacinthus of yesteryear. The young man had brought his own brand of chiaroscuro to Padam's colour scheme & it cast an ambiguous half-light upon everything to believe in & made everything appear grotesque. All his talk of firewater brandy & the broken voices of Cádiz, those echoes of Lorca & his plays for *the public* & that terrifying aspect of *duende* in each of his deep songs …

The watering hole he had known for years had become corrupted by this very process of altered perception. The clear smooth tones in his blood had become distorted & toxified. He could no longer parse what Grant had reported to him or the extent of his own imagination to recreate the actual event. He used to say to himself *this is what tomorrow brings & that is that.* Had the young man turned to the woman by the window & had he sung at her? Had she altered her pallid bloated look of microwaved death? Where be Fellini now to express her overturned flask of perfume & memory & the marks of sensuality that made her one of the *Irregulars*? Then the young man. Had he fled in manywhiskered exasperation, off to the Satyricon of another age? An oboe answered the piano insidiously over the FEED. Poulenc. Had the young man abandoned them, for the sake of the red-haired dragon & his fiery sideburns? For his great love, a mere statue in the garden with her smooth back turned? Then the monarchial cameraman had sat back with leonine satisfaction & the old candygiver had withdrawn her extra Werther's like one of

Macbeth's three prognosticators & the professor had returned to his neoclassical musings about Stravinsky, scoffing & saying something flippant to the others & the Valkyrie had recrossed her elegant legs & the woman with the scarlet coxcomb had nervously adjusted her pompadour & the bearish man who had been sleeping on the train when his ships came in cracked his knuckles meaningfully & the instructor or lawyer in his jacket of grey tweed & blue jeans (in Padam's fancy with a pair of dovegrey gloves he had bought himself) had looked down his bespectacled nose at his usual papers & the woman by the window, resolutely & ridiculously sung to in a foreign tongue, had opened her massive notebook & had begun to stitch another spider web of ebony ink magnified through the translucent gold of another glass of Gewürztraminer, which to every patron but Grant was a nameless white entity.

They had let him go! Then they had settled back into those sickly seaside greens, back under the whip of that slavedriver *Habit.* Hospital greens & chairs with split seams. It was another fancy of Padam's that they reupholster each chair with spare material, giving them a harlequin effect one observes in the *Commedia dell'arte.* Maxwell Wittman the Third, in spite of constant awareness of his own greatness, the kind of awareness that St. Francis of Assisi only expended upon a heap of dirty dishes for the sake of meditation, surrendered along with the others to the airborne complacency of the city, the *drag* of even the Queens, as a friend of his liked to say.

> *Otium, Catulle!*
> *Catullus, beware of sloth, the ruin of rich kings & cities!*

Or so the young man was always saying to him, as if he, Padam, needed to be warned of those tempting forces that inhibit industry in artists, as if slowly removing the sting of a jellyfish & leaving it more harmless than you found it. It grows about all our lives like the ivy climbing about the outer walls of the Istoria. Yet every night we creep down to this mausoleum & drink our limit towards destruction. We are the same. We are the dead. We are bouncers, the blackguards at the door. We kick out youth when we can! But he is part of the velvet painting too. Part of the madness, another Harlequin searching for his Columbina in the darkest corners. What stupid thoughts! He is not one of us. & me, hardly among *the dead*. Yet, they had let him go!

Maxwell Wittman the Third was murmuring to his beer like so when a figure appeared in front of his table, half in shadow, & with such a likeness to his stained glass window that he thought it was a dream.

"Hello, Padam. I haven't see you in a while. Have you *Hellenized* this place yet?"

Padam began to laugh in spite of himself, before saying a word.

"The last time I saw you, it was on my bed."

***

Winter. Already, Padam could feel it coming to chill his bones, could feel it even among the small white pages the young man had given him to read. But it was still warm. He drifted off to sleep with his eyelids batting at the small white book upon his nightstand, where a sliver of moonlight was striking the scarcely read pages. Yes. Still quite warm. He could feel the gentle breeze & in fact recognize the dim outline of Vancouver Island with its rich collection of inlets & fjords & smaller islands. In fact, Maxwell Wittman the Third felt as if he were suspended over the heads of an unseen audience like an omniscient god being lowered from the celestial expanse of his bedroom, as Eros sometimes was during baroque operas. He saw the abundance of coastal life, including all things hidden or only briefly visible—slick entanglements of seaweed, sideways scuttling of agitated crabs, escapement beneath the sand by breathing clams, scatterings of sea urchins, pebbly broadcasts of flat abalone, clinging of barnacles, emerging whiskers of sleek-headed seals, clumsy beached lovemaking of sea lions & runnings of pink, chum, coho, sockeye, & chinook. He seemed to intuit whatever he did not know. He saw the depths of land & water in limitless detail. Thick forests of cedar arose before his eyes to fill the primordial darkness about him. They were already more ancient than their beginnings & made unspeakable sounds akin to speech. Then hints of fir, yew & hemlock began to emerge. He found himself earthbound, in a clearing surrounded by ferns, nettles, & very red berries. Suddenly, a large dark shape passed over him. He saw a great beating of wings swooping down at his diminutive body & he wondered where he could run from such a dark horror. But the obsidian bird passed over him without leaving a mark. Only there was a terrifying crash to his right. A massive shell lay broken upon a towering formation of stone. He heard indiscernible cries & bellows & grunts. Then he saw men & women with coarse black hair & brown faces emerging from the blue shards. They were everywhere, all around him, trapping, netting & spearing the wild. He remained there, unobserved & untouched. They were erecting wooden poles & cooking salmon over blazing beach fires. The fish were also being dried & smoked by busy brown hands. The women were gathering shellfish & seaweed & berries & roots, already serious with thoughts of imminent winter. But it still felt like Spring! He could see the olachen at the mouths of many streams, first being netted & then dried. He could see their slippery bodies being threaded through with a wick & then sparked aflame. Mesmerized, he watched the candle-fish burning as night began to fall. He could also make out stone adzes & chisels, working away at pliable bodies of red & yellow cedar wood. Out of nowhere, he watched totems materialize & lift upwards from the beach pebbles. About their base, there was a heap of brightly painted masks within a canoe large enough for at least thirty men. Yes, the cedar was everywhere. He saw several tons of wood being raised effortlessly into a giant crossbeam, while other beams formed posts & walls before the roof planks were carefully laid. He saw it all arise as if by magic. But winter. All action ceased. A time of timeless-ness began. Padam suddenly felt a strange pang of remorse as he thought of the young man's watch. Winter. A small dark figure was dispatched into the woods by his family. Padam observed the lines of his face & body & recognized a distinct resemblance to Tomasz. He had left all his everyday clothes in the village & now wore nothing but a collection of hemlock branches about his body, at least where it most counted. Padam could see a scattering of older men hiding behind trees & bushes & blowing whistles intermittently. Through that same alien knowledge that had suddenly come to him, he sensed that the young man was supposed to stay out in the woods for a few days. However, he saw him sneak into his house at night & leave in the morning before anyone else woke up. Naughty naughty. This young man remained in his hemlock habit & kept shy of the village activity, remaining aloof of their lavish feasts. Padam watched the young man bathe his naked body in a stream of water, shivering all the while, & was reminded suddenly of Hermaphroditus. Were I only Salmacis! However, others from the village came out into the woods & offered him lean scraps of food in accordance with his fast. He would only return to the village for a moment during the day, wrapped in his branches, until he was driven out by the sound of whistles all around him. They are birds, birds of the wood. Then he could hear gas motors being roused, propelling each canoe across the water. The boaters were sporting all of their regalia & singing. They leapt out of their canoes & began to dance. After an enormous ceremony in a great circle involving what looked like a long piece of cedar bark, everyone went inside & continued dancing, undoubtedly in order to call that mysterious young man back into the village. Then Padam saw a great house & inside of it the young man was dancing among his elders. They would howl at him, clearly to stop, & then he would start the dance all over again. Padam did not understand everything that was said but he got the general idea. He figured that the youth had watched & listened for a series of nights until he heard singing emanating from many houses. The boy! They were waiting for the boy! Then night arrived. The young chap in question was kneeling & watching the others through a crack in the wall from the back of the room where he had been practising beforehand. Secretly ensconced

with him, the other elders helped him to climb up onto the roof &
then held his legs as he stuck his upper body through sliding trap-
doors, so that the audience below could glare up at him & wave their
arms about. He was a spirit visiting from above. Time passed. Padam
saw the young lad running wildly about all the assembled guests, after
emerging from the stomach of a rendered creature upon a screen. He
ran at each of them & then tried to evade their grasp. At last, as the
ceremony progressed, they managed to catch him & he seemed to
grow weaker as they pulled the hemlock from his flesh, substituting
it with a large & beautiful covering of cedar. He kneeled & swayed
from side to side as male elders waved smoking staffs over his frail
body. Then without warning, the stripling rose with renewed strength
& bolted from their company, as the young people chastised one
another for their shared mistake of letting him escape, hardly *tamed*.
It must have been the next day that he emerged, & instead of acting
like a wild creature, although he wore a massive bird mask with a long
beak, the young man performed the most meticulous dance steps.
Padam saw in those routines his own formal training & the experiences that were to eventually shape his *roughness*. *A young rough*, as
Whitman says, as the young man had told him. Yet, as he watched
those slim brown feet with soft tufts of dark hair upon them, almost
like animal fur, he sensed the disembodied motions of that giant bird
head & the tremor of its brightly coloured plumage. He wondered at
the faceless strength it took to keep that mask upright & shivered
upon hearing the shrill whistling sounds about his ears that seemed
to initiate the sudden transformation of the bird mask, which opened
into floating pieces like a starfish cut open & revealed another face
that was terrible to behold. An unhealthy white face.

V

There goes the prelapsarian. For Maxwell Wittman the Third, his act of living in the eternal moment had passed as quickly as it came. A season had passed like a movement of complete silence in a long symphony. After such a polite entr'acte all too brief, after such a subdued intermezzo in such a low key, the inevitable had come to pass. To say something of that time, it was best represented by the layers of scaffolding about the outer stonework of the Istoria hotel. There it had remained, obscuring the famous VIEW of the Pacific Ocean for tourist & *Irregular* alike. This was a loss to anyone who desired the perfect view of the pollution that lends beauty to a sunset. A whirr of blender behind the new bar roused him out of reverie. Changes, everywhere. Echoes of the perpetual sound of reconstruction. Have I changed as much? What makes up these hands of mine, these artisan hands of Padam? Now the sun shone across the sea & began to flood the great panes of glass. They had enlargened the windows & had removed the striped awnings that used to cover them. There was a new window on Giltford Street that used to be completely covered by wooden boards & a bit of thatched garden trellis. On the other hand, this change had restored its former window that had originally been part of the hotel a century ago in *the olden days*. So by deleting a decade or so, they had managed to restore the original Istoria, in a manner of speaking. The rays of sunlight intensified through the great pane of glass & seemed to feel heavy upon his grey whiskers. He blinked before sun & water. *Beautiful*, yes. A gawkish family of tourists to the right expressed a similar sentiment & then the rest of that gaggle began to gaggle in turn along the same lines. Beautiful beautiful yes so verrrrry beautiful. The bar & restaurant had been divided more distinctly & yet there was more space in the entire room, for it was a directionless snaking room now

& no longer a parlour. All that was left of the old hotel was a painting in the corridor that no one ever really liked. The painter used to storm into the corridor, terribly envious that what he believed to be a work of genius had fallen into the hands of unappreciative strangers. However, he had never once asked to buy it back. But in the face of the hotel's alterations, this painting had acquired a certain poignancy on account of its mere survival. The autumn leaves seemed richer in their scattered redness. The thick blobs of paint seemed less to paint the outer surface of the Istoria than to paint an establishment one is apt to visit in a dream. How else, but in a sepia-toned photograph or in a painting such as this one, would we be able to appreciate the previous & present incarnations of the hotel exterior? The windows had both shrunk & expanded during its existence & now attested to the strange anomalies of anything with increasing longevity in a process we loosely call *history*. A new painting had been hung over the recent addition of a faux fireplace, a postmodern deformation of the hotel, a Braque or Delaunay ripoff. This painting offered a touch of burlesque to the place, unlike its curmudgeonly predecessor in the corridor. Of course, this was all well & good. Padam had desired new chairs for some time & he approved of the new reupholstery wherever it had occurred during that silent *vorspiel* of the past few months. But since those long hours & days since the *gran rifiuto* of the young man & the resultant schism that had cropped up between them, he had lost his normal appetite for such trifles. He sank into a crinkly creamy armchair & tried to replay in his mind exactly what had happened, as he did every day. It was quiet then, right before the *winter of discontent*, however mild he still admitted it to be, weatherwise.

"Afternoon, sir."

The chirpy voice belonged to a beaming young woman. Padam instantly granted her figure a Rubenesque charm & her rosy greeting a distinct beatitude.

"Ahh," replied Maxwell Wittman the Third.

"Something to drink," she persisted with a hint of crossborder optimism.

"O yes might I have a pint of the pale ale … "

He eyed the hefty new menus under her darkuniformed arm with a smidgen of trepidation.

"Uhh, we only have *sleeves.*"

Padam visibly cringed before offering up a weary *okay*. She walked away primly, leaving him feeling abject, a fallen alien thing in this new artificial paradise. It no longer mattered, not a whit, that he had complained about the sickly green hospital walls or bemoaned the torn stitching night after night. Now these mocha walls & hint of sunlight breaking through grey sky & drab sea felt enough to obliterate him where he sat, like a mosquito that had once fallen into the urinal of the old establishment, caught underneath the scented freshener & slowly cooked to death by light refracted through those quirky old loo windows. Even that possibility seemed out of reach presently, since the trusty old flushables had all been replaced with conservative hands-off touch-free water-conservation models. Padam, a fellow who after the right amount of pints didn't mind getting his gloves dirty, was appalled. The *Irregulars*, those familiar demons whose melancholy & mad laughter he had become so accustomed to, had lost their places in the metaphysical painting of their slow self-destruction. They had reluctantly assumed new positions, so that they seemed a school of devilfish broken up by a few bits of food tossed into their shared tank, dispersing into separate corners & returning to cross paths in zigzag fashion. However, Padam no longer had any idea whether their melancholy had left them or whether this mood had been a psychical force that had belonged exclusively to the establishment & had once possessed them all. The enlarged window panes & the blinding glare off the water had a similar effect to superstore lighting set up over the remains of a corner grocer stripped of its former intimacy. The freshness of new furniture & staff smelled synthetic. The FEED had also been changed by those mysterious powers that be, the invisible gods that managed the course of events & disappointments at the Istoria. The melancholy induced in drinking listeners by sad classical pieces had faded permanently into fresh *crème de la crème* armchairs & calming mocha walls. If the walls reminded one of a hospital before, now the décor was suggestive of a psychiatric clinic. The new music was for the most part beneath description, now a pango-pango mishmash with an instrumental redux of a few *classics* & some diluted soft jazz bits, not to mention some macerated popular & overworn bits. In other words, the kind of muzak one finds in a shopping centre that convinces one to buy this outfit or that, even when the sleeves are too short. Padam was once again appalled. In the old hotel before the FALL, the FEED had provided a classical wash cycle. True. However, in a given instance, a poignant piece might arise out of that predictable loop & no one could understand or appreciate this quirk, being too occupied by their own fleeting joys & lengthy sorrows. But for the astute or overtly sensitive barfly, it created a minute or two of possibility, the time necessary in life to change one's course in a sudden moment of madness & switch onto another track altogether. During that brief interval, anyone might walk into the hotel, even accidentally, & anything might happen to cry havoc with the general monotony of existence. Padam tried to brush his thoughts aside, as the young woman was approaching with his once non-reducible pint, now subject like the musical FEED to the latest & most trendy innovation: *the sleeve.* He took a sip & nearly choked on it, noticing that rather than decreasing, the price of a pint had increased for the blithe reception of a sleeve. Perhaps more than once in his life, he had been taken advantage of, but to his credit, never at both ends at once. Since Maxwell Wittman the Third was distracted by aspects of the renovation, his normally astute judgement of aesthetic values was to an understandable degree impaired at this time, not to mention *demoralized.* Fixated upon the price increase & staring at the sleeve in his right hand, he struggled to make sense of this paradox known as inflation or fiscal belt-tightening or more commonly as *being screwed,* unaware that one of his monk friends had forsaken the day to day world for this very reason in order to concentrate on his art & so that he could paint & sculpt angels without feeling their wings incessantly beating him down into the dust. Therefore, the responsibility falls to the author, who notes that Padam remained that way for some time, shaking his glasses abstractly & rubbing his eyes in disbelief. It is also a matter of opinion & taste that in the freshly hired server, the aesthetic system of Padam allowed for a comparison with one of Giotto's tiny figures. As for the young man, the way he hunched over his work & myopically ordered another from the same type of allegorical entity, whether Charity or Envy on a given afternoon, he was in no position to place her among the masterworks. Ah yes, there was a touch of Giotto. Also a varied collection of demure medieval Madonnas glancing down meekly at the respective wonder of their afterbirth in different alterations of lighting, etc. But what has come to the author's attention, partially due to the enlargement of the panes & the increase of wintry light to suffuse the entire room, is another quality found in not all but one of the frequently *rediscovered* works of Jan Vermeer. It would be one matter to comment upon the subject transfigured by a mere fullness of light. An ordinary girl, no less & certainly no more, save for being a delightful throwback to the fleshy & medium-sized figures of Rubens, for the most part unforgivable by the terms of our own jaded aesthetic that compels women to adopt figures akin to the wanton wastrels of Ancient Rome. In other words, she was the image of vigour & health, an image that writers often ascribe to some manner of *country living*. Her demeanour of being any kind of servitor formed a mockery of the Madonna imagery in the eyes of the surrounding *stable animals*, as in the pre-Renaissance works that offer the first glimmers of techniques involving a light source, while they continued to bray & whinny for another round about her. But what particularly went unnoticed by Maxwell Wittman the Third & the young man (who both preferred pale & sickly poetic types) was the way in which her concentration could be dispelled & completely transformed into an expression of surprise & wonder. The author imagines there is some argument to be made for the celestial illumination found in the paintings of Vermeer. But if the models he studied for his own paintings, such as Van Eyck, were to be brought into consideration, they would undoubtedly be judged to lack the subtlety of a Vermeer. As for the paintings he studied, within their own frames, the maid is always sleeping & neglecting her duties. In fact everyone in the painting is suffering because of the negligent individual. For shame! In the virtually forgotten model for *Het Straje*, all the workers depicted are *virtuous*. Hence, the entire work is a model of virtue. The subtext is do or do not do such & such in relation to sin & virtue, or else look out! Yet in Vermeer's *Little Street*, the characters are faceless, more like the allegorical figures of Giotto, & are perhaps meant to represent some aspect of the same individual. I will not dwell on some tedious theory about the trinity they create. No matter the subtext, it is potentially as secular & enchanting as formations of mere brick. The viewer feels their labour & even the industry of the artist. Nor does this quality deaden any number of spiritual interpretations. In other works of Vermeer, the negligence of the painted figures (if not their industry) becomes a portal opening upon another world suffused in that magical light only he appeared to understand. As far as painting a lesson about "Intemperance" & hanging it in your own public house, as many scholars would have us believe about the man when interpreting his work, the author will leave that logic in the reader's more than capable hands. Undoubtedly, the Dutch wanted to sell less lager & not more. Thankfully, this city has enough bylaws to pack us home just when we are starting to enjoy ourselves, so that our art may flourish without didactic messages about social & self-control, as it no doubt does? That matter aside, there is one painting of Vermeer's that has been called his only *failure* of the lot. It is suggested in rather a facile manner that he painted this one for money, by church commission, as if the other masterpieces had been created completely free of such an object in mind. However, the same allegorical symbols are present within the frame. The same kind of decadent material that the sleeping woman seemed to be neglecting has been used to drape over this strange epiphany. If we finally arrive at Vermeer's *Allegory of the Faith* after passing through innumerable rooms of the Metropolitan, we are startled. Then we cannot help but laugh. Future generations who brush away & blow off the dust will have a countenance to invoke the liveliness of this hardworking young lady at the Istoria. Does it matter? It is perhaps only a matter of vanity on the part of the author that this detail be held up to the light of greater eyes & judged in such an arena of greatness by a mere spectator. How easy for the author to kick about names like Vermeer & Van Eyck! So it is utterly subjective for this observer, who alone noticed that whenever the young lady was surprised or drawn into wild laughter, she exhibited something essential in the study of Vermeer's *Allegory*. The allegorical symbols seem overdone, too overtly displayed for what we know of Vermeer's taste. To be honest, it would be something to titter over in the Mechelen, & increasingly so the more you imbibed. Can the woman be anything but comical to watch? This work had something of the character of that instance in Genesis when God asks rather anthropomorphically why Sarah laughed, just as the author admits to wondering in given instances (despite a reputation for omniscience) why this young lady laughed & why she looked like this painting. Imagine her look of astonishment, even as she appears subject to a beach ball at her feet, rolling about under her long gown. This is no Jeanne d'Arc. Her softness of surface became most paintable by that light of sudden bewilderment. There she was in some brief instance, stepping over the ball of yarn of the world & accidentally crushing the serpent beneath her unshod feet. As for the young man, he belonged in the dim yet illuminated cosmos of Caravaggio, just as Maxwell Wittman the Third was most suitable for a harlequin advert at the hands of Lautrec. The reader may feel, just as Padam might if we were to consult him, that these reflections are neither here nor there & really, what at the end of the day do they have to do with him? Much is made of the artist, such as Maxwell Wittman the Third, who takes a model under his protection & has him strip down to nothing for the sole reason of studying line & form. A wonderful tradition! However, it is through the understanding of light, colour & texture that combine in Vermeer to give the act of a woman pouring milk an unfathomable religious quality. The milkmaid is not a thing of lines. She embodies the nourishment she pours out & she gives it bountifully. As for the literary equivalent, the most fantastic part of *La Cousine Bette* is not in fact the hackneyed maxims about the necessity for industry in artists, but rather the act of Madame Marneffe bringing her sculptor a cup of tea & by proxy seducing him. Balzac waxes poetical about the nature of this act & why it holds such a fascination for artists & perhaps the public in general. He infers that this quality exists in almost all of the great masterpieces we are fortunate enough to encounter. However, would it not be perceived as ridiculous & even offensive if the young man & Padam were to apply their artistic notions to this ordinary woman at our own turn of the century? Yet, to think of her as ordinary & even *contemporary* is hardly fair, since she is entitled to the list of attributes that Balzac & the history of painters & sculptors offers her & deserves their praise & attention no less. It is Honoré, if the author may take such an outlandish liberty in addressing him on familiar terms, who points out that the act of bringing someone a cup of tea (or any drink for that matter) brings into potential play the entire range of feminine emotion, since she can unconsciously or with deliberation concentrate all of her emotion into a single act & create a poetic language that is entirely her own, even without words. She can lend favour within the limits of *her* establishment upon one of her subjects just as a queen might have, or else express disdain & aversion in her manner, offering reluctance or absolute refusal of service, leaving a regal statement in the temperature of the tea or the head of the ale. In these times of mistrust, when the next person you meet may as well be a serial murderer, when communication is at an all-time high & yet almost completely stripped of its former intimacy, what is left but this subtextuality? Naturally, this is not a poetic act foisted upon women alone. Padam could take this opportunity to wax poetical about Jean-Paul, another ageless server who appeared from time to time, whom he considered to be *a good boy*. It is only a matter of taste for the artist, who cannot help becoming obsessive about certain minutiae, say the physiology & aesthetic effects proffered by models they encounter outside of the studio, where the actual art is occurring, frame by frame. This act, this *gift*, this offering of a drink, is perhaps the only vestige of past centuries that can cause us to forget the pecuniary exchange that often underlies it, although we are ultimately mistaken to wander through the great works of the past in awe & remain blind to the poetic beauty that surrounds us on a daily basis. It is perhaps this notion of Balzac's that later influences Proust to write that all the great heroines in literature were based upon some tavern or shop girl. One is led to imagine Gérard de Nerval, perpetually in love with some type of phantom, one of at least three women who accommodated his madness simply by existing until the morning he was found hanging outside a tavern in the frozen cold, his life lost in pursuit of his personal Queen of Sheba. Or Beethoven, who supposedly wrote the *24th Piano Sonata* for Thérèse & then hurriedly penned his famous *Immortal Beloved* letter before dashing the hell away from her. It is a matter of instinctive self-preservation, as a mother running away in order to protect her unborn child. The artist must bare teeth to all attackers who might mar those ideas that are scarcely manifest & yet will be reborn in the minds of readers or the eyes of confused onlookers. Or to paraphrase John Milton in *Areopagitica*, let the author declare a new work first! Let it be born first & judged afterwards.

However, none of these thoughts had arrived to grace the mind of Maxwell Wittman the Third. He sipped tentatively from his sleeve & tried to recall what had happened. It had been about the time of the young man's birthday. It had been a rainy night for sure. The young man had rushed in with his black *habit* soaked through, with raindrops running down his long leather coat. No, that's not right. I arrived late that night. Why so late? I no longer remember. He was sitting with Stephane & they were enjoying one another. Also, he started blithering something about being hugged outside. Already drunk, the little lush. He must have been. I must have been. He was upset about something, the usual falderal, some indecipherable nonsense about his *great love*. & what about mine? The things he said to me. I was very angry that night. Why? How is it possible to recapture the past, a single instance that changes the course of our lives forever? Everything is scattered. In fragments. We had spent such a wonderful evening at the Istoria before this tiff. Yes. The night before. O, but he was off at the gob about his great love! O that great *ineffable* love! & why did he keep on & on about that *libretto* of his? On & on. I had just finished my fantastic memoirs. That I remember. The life of Maxwell Wittman the Third, those stupendous tales I put on the Internet for all to listen to. I told the story of our collaboration on the stained glass project, or more specifically how I, Padam, first saw this delicate young creature, this poet, from the first moment he walked into the parlour of the Istoria & then precisely how I used his Native heritage to produce a coastal motif based upon his likeness. The ungrateful wretch! I have no idea why he should be annoyed in the slightest. He certainly had not taken into consideration, with all his talk of art & eternity, *the price of eggs*. I did not only organize a whip-round to raise the capital to make the first stained glass work. I made another of his poem to hang alongside the other in my own window. I had shed carefully chosen light upon his precious heritage. I had in fact created him from scratch, from the rough-hewn materials that original creation grants any man. It must have been when he declared in a voice not at all soft or lowered that he, Tomasz, did not give a fig *who* I was. No, not I, Maxwell Wittman the Third! Why, that large fair-haired chap from the pictures was right behind us. What if he heard? Imagine what he must have thought of me, with this young upstart calling me down in such a fashion & myself merely sitting there & stomaching every word. I, Padam, nothing? Why, there is a hierarchy, a chain of being for everyone. He had no right to dress me down, no, not me. I felt it was my duty to point out to him that he was being an asshole. I probably should not have laughed. But in the young man's own words, save those lifted from his voracious readings, love is a necessary part of sadism & sometimes the latter cannot exist without a drop of the former. Also, a single act of cruelty is sometimes necessary in order to rejuvenate oneself. Indeed, how young & gay I felt, finally getting a chance to tell him off properly! So Maxwell Wittman the Third mused, leaving the author free to speculate further upon these matters. For Padam had experienced a taste of the fantasy of anyone who loves for a long time, even to the point of obsession, where an act of utter hate may relieve them of the emotions so essential to love. We long for the beloved to love us, until their indifference triggers a darker emotion within us—one of black hatred. Love cannot exist in a state of complete indifference. That is why a series of strong emotions so often lead to love & why love so often leads to a series of strong emotions. The fact that he felt pleasure in such an action was indicative that he felt love to the point of appearing to deny it completely. He was protesting far too much, as a playboy who tries to paint his greatest love with the same brush as his other conquests & slanders them something terrible as he never would a lover he was apathetic to. Padam had laughed as the young man stormed out with only a few words, disappointing anyone in the bar who thought him a fiery poet.

"So now we see the *real* Padam!"

Then he muttered something else about a soul being weighed before rushing to pay his bill & apologize to the server for any *disturbance* caused. Stephane had also laughed, playing with his beard. Maxwell Wittman the Third had watched Tomasz exit with a weak smile on his face & a sour exchange of looks with the cameraman, confident that he would return in a week's time at his mercy, longing to talk with him again. For it is another aspect of love that one lover longs to possess the other & even in situations involving a most flexible compromise, behind the scenes of open affection, that lover is scheming, even unconsciously, to gain some power over the other, to possess the other entirely. If one partner is out with a friend, the phone may ring a dozen times to echo the inevitable question *Where are you?* For this reason, some people are only happy in love when they have complete control or knowledge of their lover's whereabouts, schedules & actions, which is of course only a notion of complete control & an impossible abstraction. Pitiful are the lovers who constantly wish to know what the other is thinking at any minute of the day, or those who stare at a sleeping figure, wanting to know their very dreams, simply because they are unknowable. So even while *trust* remains a promotional aspect & virtue of love, it must also be said that love cannot exist without *doubt*, for love would have no food to eat away the hours of our lives with.

Months had passed. Padam had not seen Tomasz once, even after the renovations. But now, only now, he was starting to appreciate the young man's particular madness. He too remained isolated with his art. He deposited himself in various places about town like a bit of dark bacteria, a bit of mould that through survival of poor conditions became virtually invisible to onlookers. Yet the germ of corruption had been dropped into the soil of shared humanity & had infected Padam most of all. It is a matter of hereditary & atavistic traits, as well as the mystery of shared commonalities between unrelated souls with similar ideas. Is it possible for a bond to form between those who share no blood whatsoever, yet a bond so strong that family & identity are virtually forgotten? This is to be found in the form of any mania that afflicts the artist. Somewhere in the city, there is another artist who is proceeding in an almost identical manner & progressing upon a similar path. Perhaps the two never meet or despise the sight of each other & make derogatory comments under their breath, although both souls would benefit from such a friendship if they could only fathom how to begin it. The author goes on to postulate a theory about these two characters. What if their shared traits & methodologies & ideas were enough to form a psychical bond that was stronger than one of blood or family connection? The author has no doubt that the symptoms of unrequited love are enough to trigger a state of illness & lethargy & send someone to their grave without any need for melodramatics. This idea has a fanciful sound, yet it is no different than the way in which a daytrader's blood pressure may rise & fall in time with fluctuations of the market. In the cases of Padam & the young man, they both shared the same illness & similar symptoms. However, they had each become like a patient who wants to visit with healthy people & not other people who are ill like them. For love has a certain egoism that negates the very thing it seeks. But since this rift with the young man, Padam had lost his sense of well-

273

being & thus lost his immunity & Tomasz's madness had passed to him as if he already had a disposition & hereditary background to receive it. That is why the Istoria, after its renovations, seemed more like a sanitorium than a drinking establishment. The management had as good as bleached the walls & fumigated the place for *Art*.

Just then, the *Allegory of the Faith* returned & thrust her double chin out towards the light. He was admiring her beauty & thinking of Rubens again when a sliver of darkness caught the corner of his eye. The sun had disappeared. He knew then that something was wrong. He felt an oppression in his chest akin to the barometric pressure outside. The grey sky was rolling down on him. Maxwell Wittman the Third was only sure of one thing. The young man was gone for good. He had asked everyone & although the young man still appeared from time to time, it was generally understand that the name & existence of Padam was now *dead* to him. As if to add an exclamation point to all these other changes at the Istoria, the fair-haired leonine chap in pictures had become a Tyrannosaurus of the new establishment. He soon shooed his friends & *hangers-on* away & held fast to one of the new dark wood perches that overlooked the other denizens, just as James I kept to a special chair higher than everyone else for viewing each new masque by Inigo Jones. That robust & recently employed Madonna had caught his wandering eye & this infusion of fresh blood had seemed to affect him dramatically. He was thought to be rather well-to-do. However, in this city, onlookers & passers-by could look up at empty beachfront apartments & never see a light on & never know to the end of their days who occupied a single suite. So then, at least within our vague world of illusory appearances, he was well off. His talk of pseudo-celebrity encounters had been generally accepted & was tolerated by the other *Irregulars* as part of his day-to-day character. However, it was only more recently, since the spectacle of him waggling his innumerable connexions in front of our cheerful & buxom *Allegory* had turned the stomach of more than one customer, that he had become a bit of an embarrassment. By attempting to appear more respectable to this potential paramour who lacked some of his wisdom & years, he had lost some of the respect of the other diners & drinkers who possessed longer memories. Perhaps he belonged to a brighter world that attracted the young woman's attention & rightfully so. But in the eyes of the Istoria, he had lost all distinction. This was quite simply *bad form*. Thankfully, the bucket of cologne was still in practice, now only a sloshing reminder of that sweet old song of yesteryear. In conjunction with his presumably early start, he made his appearance by late afternoon & took his perch, prepared to offer the Madonna a plethora of unimaginable riches.

"Point out the suit, just point it out to me & I will buy it."

Although this man was only comically overbearing before, now he bore invisible emblems in his flesh that seemed to waft upward & smelled, frankly, like a midlife *crisis*. However, if a man wants to do the same thing he wanted to do in adolescence & the same thing he in all probability will want to do in his sixties, if it is at all inconvenient or a source of envy, then it is deemed a midlife crisis. This is indeed a rather petty account of this poor fellow's passion. However, in terms of the general distribution of *bacilli* that had formerly oozed about the far smaller parlour, this turn of events was a great mutation, a distinct outburst of very observable *paramecia*.

"Like what is that music? Did you put this CD on?"

Padam shrugged to himself, surprised that she would so readily discount such an excellent, although lesser known work by Bizet. That duet where the men swear eternal friendship! Ahh ... *The Pearl Fishers*! How sublime. I suppose everyone knows *Carmen*.

"You would think that," shot back the other server, refusing to commit himself, although everyone knew the FEED was still in the mysterious hands of the Management. She turned back to her Henry the Eighth, who was lingering in a cloud of cologne like a supersized god.

"Well, there was this suit I was looking at ... "

At that moment, the young man walked into the hotel corridor, looking around cautiously. He saw Padam & continued to walk toward an opposite corner (in fact the farthest corner from Maxwell Wittman the Third he could get to) without changing his expression. Why, that little ... Not since that minor character in Marcel Proust's chunky masterpiece *In Search of Lost Time*, Monsieur Legrandin, have we known of such a snub recorded in a literary work. Padam stared at the young man with a heady concoction of determination & desperation. Those dark eyes appeared to darken all the more, eclipsing the slightest whisker over Maxwell Wittman the Third's smiling mouth & at the same time looking right through him. Padam looked in his direction imploringly, wishing for even the plainest observation about his own person. For instance, he had grown his hair long for most of his life. Now he had left his hoary grey locks at the apartment of a cute stylist chum, Jerome Swizzel. O how I sit so completely cropped before you! But the young man took his seat & inclined his head towards the window, leaving only the corner of his eye open & inspecting the new world of the Istoria sideways, so that like a stray glint of moonlight upon a curving horizon of black water, his awareness was visible in only the tiniest periphery of his distant glare. Yet there it was, like that inevitable heartbeat in the works of Brahms or that agitated pulse in the operas of Bellini. That minuscule bead or fleck of paint in the corner of his eye said so much. Padam stared for a long time at that *petite danse* of light, a lone Rusalka singing her heart out to the moon from the darkest patches of swamp. Yet to the world, to the plebian watcher, he was being snubbed by this upstart, a poet no less, albeit not too bad looking. To top it all off, while maintaining this watchtower of continual observance in the corner of his eye, the young man whipped out his notebook & began to write. If that were not enough, to be so absorbed in his scribblings & refusing to even acknowledge the unforgettable presence of Maxwell Wittman the Third, after the Madonna asked him if he was alright he scattered his money for the pint (I mean of course, sleeve) & turned on his heels towards the stained glass lintel without a look & went off like a galloping thing. Padam sat in the virtual emptiness of the new Istoria & watched the *Allegory of the Faith* with her dark uniform & bemused expression, as she tidied up the table & took away the full sleeve & gathered up the paper & coins. Somewhat perplexed, she regained her composure in front of the other guy behind the bar, who made a remark.

"Cash *is* cash," she said.

Padam continued to stare at the now empty table. He is not right in the head. Did he really ... ? Why did he do that, because of me? He once said he was only paying for time. Is that what he meant? Money, time, a world full of misunderstandings ... No, he despises me. But it wasn't me not the Padam everyone knows & adores & eventually loves. Why did I call him an asshole? What is the matter with me lately? With him? Maxwell Wittman the Third held up his squirrelly hands, the very hands he had sculpted. Now he examined them by the light breaking through the grey & striking those enormous panes of glass. They seemed far more withered & gnarled than he would like to admit. He held them up & felt his fingers & knuckles tightening, as if by themselves, into objects of anger & scorn under the falling rays of sunlight. Padam flexed each tendril outward & wondered at them, glowing in the bright light like a startled insect. There were knots that had not been there before. He looked out the window sadly. I want this gnarling to stop. Then he thought of the young man again, how smug & arrogant he was & a strange urge overcame him. No. He, Maxwell Wittman the Third, had always advised the young man regarding the perimeters of art: there was *use* & then there was *abuse*. Padam struggled to regain his composure. Only now could he understand the same principle with regard to Tomasz. He had persisted, wanting only to sketch him at first. Then the desire he felt became a thing unto itself. He had thought of the aesthetic he used with such pride, of the life he had lent the young man through his choices of coloured glass & through his irrefutable garnering of expenditure. Cash *is* cash. But why can't I just accept the finest moments in life? They come to you. They trickle down through history & someone is charged with the responsibility of recording them. Yet how they swerve & take strange turns, trying to find some shortcut or out of the way route to the Empyrean. So it is, that artists possess their sources of inspiration in the creation of a work & then are puzzled to comprehend why the same is untrue in life, since life has become only a rough blueprint, a template, a mere negative to their living image. This paradox is seldom understood or reconciled by the artist or their source of inspiration. Padam looked up suddenly & noticed that the Madonna was looking down at him with a worried expression that was less Vermeer than usual. He looked down & realized that he was squeezing his sleeve of beer, hardly touched. His curled hands were trembling & some of the pale ale was spilling out over the table, soaking through the twice folded serviette & running over the edge. The Madonna squinted at him for a second in the sunlight, perhaps out of sheer annoyance, before rushing back to the young man's abandoned table to fetch her white towel. She smoothed & wiped, squinting toward the illuminated window with infinite compassion for his small fault like some nearsighted pièta.

"No worries, sir! S'all good. We'll have that cleaned right up for you."

Padam managed a weak smile, wincing slightly.

"Sure sure."

Maxwell Wittman the Third awoke in the middle of the night, sweating all over. He lifted the covers with a great flap, sending Chester to cold floor with a loud miaow. Always on their feet. He reached for a purple towel with clenched fingers & began to rub & wipe himself down. Then he clawed at the medicine chest, prying it open & searching for his rolled packet of marijuana. Running out. He found his tweezer device, but in thought of the young poet, left it where it was. He shut the medicine cabinet with more than a little anger, even feeling a touch of irritation at Chester's noisy pawing of the closed bathroom door. The medicine cabinet closed, revealing his strange reflection. Who are you? It was the face he had looked at for sixty-odd years. Why not lie, even to yourself? Why should the adorable face of Padam be different, after all these years? He thought

278

of black & white photographs, all of them capturing his glory, his long fair hair & his proud expression, not to mention his customary Cheshire grin, which shone even broader upon the stage. He looked in the mirror presently & tried to reassemble the original arrangement & shape of his features, or at least the way it was during his dancing days when he seldom bothered to find a mirror, except of course, for dancing purposes! Now, they seemed to have wandered off on him, rather abstractly, before crawling back in peculiar acts of supplication for the benefit of his sagging idea of himself. How odd! His features bore the mark of a full life, most certainly. But when the entire life of an individual has been performative & when aesthetic has played such a large part in how one lives, there may be a few incalculable effects upon the psychology of their person in later life, once the footlights have dimmed & the stage has completely cast them off. That artist, having been stripped of their *abridgements*, will no doubt try to preserve the glorious past they continue to occupy. Once the flower of youth has faded, in later years, people begin to take the shape of their personality & habits & vices. Generally, their appearance becomes a function of who they are. The soft-skinned temptress that tormented admirers in her younger years will in her later years become a function of that oft exercised cruelty, a bag of bones & parched flesh. In the same way, the vain actor will become something of a laughable figure in later life, most often a powdered pate & a pair of heavily rouged cheeks. In short, a miserable clown. It is not likely that virtue gives a perennial bloom to beauty. However, the excitation of our darker emotions seems to mysteriously curdle the blood & sometimes grey or dislodge the hair, just as sorrow appears to engrave its lines across a grieving face. A single fixation can polish us off the soonest of all. As for Padam, he had always proclaimed that he was all he wanted to be, a happy old man. & to be fair, he was an excellent specimen among sexagenarians. We are not so jaded in our society not to allow him a lover, a number of years or even decades younger than himself, due to his accomplishments & fitness of frame. We might say he was also prime for a *midlife crisis*. Yet the apparition of the young man, like a purely mathematical textbook problem involving ageism, had warped the very curve of Padam's normally straight rationale while leaving his will intact. Let it be noted that our will often remains entirely intact, even when our mind has become totally skewed. He looked into the mirror & met the asymptotic deformation of his face, staring back like a joke of Dürer's with the mesh points being dragged to & fro, forward & backward, even to the point that he could observe the rise & fall & the ebb & flow of his own drying skin cells. Those faded veils flapped about & hinted at the blotchy corpuscles underneath. He grasped the gilt edges of the medicine cabinet mirror with his growing talons & watched glassy ripples emerge. How rude! Padam felt lost amid each ripple in the now carnival mirror. However, like so many of us at given moments of existence, he began to believe in more than what he saw or knew. He began to find credence in the distortion of those features he had come to appreciate, no, love, after decades together. The face he looked at began to melt & subside, much like the waves he had observed for years beyond the medium-sized panes of glass of the former Istoria hotel. In spite of the reasonable handsomeness he had learned to admire & develop an intimacy with over time, he felt a definite sense of oppression, a dark cloud coming to roost over his facial features, to the point that they seemed, or even felt, prematurely eroded. They were ruined sarcophagi or the lonely cliffs of Dover. Now these sharp creatures & gargoyles & scavengers were expanding in the crags under his eyes & taking flight, leaving their pointed feet all over his face. Cumulus or nimbus, whatever it was, this dark oppressive shape had fallen upon him & had precipitated an entire murder of birds that shat soundly upon his once critically acclaimed beauty on stage. He tried to focus his orbiting eyes & caught another glimpse of his changeling face, suddenly understanding. I am broken. I am dying. I am a dying thing.

VI

Late afternoon. Padam realized that he must have slept in, judging by the angle of light at this time of year. His throat felt much improved. The strains these days. They seemed to last forever. However, he recalled the previous night & reached anxiously for his face. The same. Dry. Good. It took him a while to rise & to approach the mirror, even in order to splash his face & whiskers. So groggy. But Maxwell Wittman the Third knew what would suit him best. However, it took forever to dress, even to throw on a pair of loose slacks & a hooded top. He walked slowly over to Denman. Sushi? Cat got your tongue? A sunnier clime, I think. He decided upon a relatively new establishment with a drab blue front. A few figures sat eating in the corners, well out of sunlight. Padam noted that they looked like malevolent sea-deities waving plastic tritons at him with falafel on the ends, glowering outward from those deep blue walls. They reminded Padam of an absolutely scrumptious Persian boy he had known during his *Middle Period*. He studied the various forms of beauty that surrounded him, trying to decide what struck his fancy. Something spicy. Some type of expectorant, I shouldn't wonder. The beetle-browed woman at the counter smiled at him in rather dazed recognition.

"Falafel it is," announced Padam, desperately trying to remaster his Cheshire grin.

Her son (or hunky nephew) started to race about behind the counter, hunting madly for the correct tinfoil container. He began to count his fingers.

"I will eat here."

Padam raised his voice over the tintillant shimmer of metal, fingering the exact amount of money necessary. He was awarded a plastic triton for his heroic effort. He paid up & sat in another cubby-space, also out of the late afternoon glow. Then his face crinkled up into a smile as he heard & smelt his small dinner being unwrapped from its aluminum casing.

"Watch out. It might be hot."

Padam scrutinized the sleepy hottie.

"*Is* it hot?"

The swarthy hunk shrugged & went back to his graphic novel. Maxwell Wittman the Third ruminated as he chewed & peeked out at the sunlight pervading each undulation of the ocean & each disturbance of sand, now speckled & dappled with people in colour-ful outfits, shifting ever so slightly like pigments in a gallery painting he had wished to study more carefully in the past, although he had been rushed along to a Gauguin by a ruddy sniffling family. He was half-finished his falafel when he noticed a lone figure in the corner of his eye. It was the young man. He knew, even without looking. But of course, he could not help looking. He watched the figure pass & in the doorway crane his head inquisitively toward the inhabitants in afternoon shadow. Then he saw Padam. How could he not? But whether from discipline or out of complete indifference, the young man did not betray even a glint of recognition. As before, he appeared to look directly through the artist in front of him, namely Maxwell Wittman the Third. The sheer nerve! It simply wasn't done. Then he passed, & Padam looked after him with more than a little longing in his face. What is more, he knew where the young man was headed.

There are some moments that occur during our lives, however arbitrarily we come upon them, or however hard they follow upon our own heels, that never return. More likely than not, we want them, because when it is beyond *too late*, we want them like all too familiar things to return to us, to reinvest their potentialities within us, & what is more, the imagined magic of those moments we feel time has robbed us of. Sadly, if such moments result only in sorrow & regret, it is because our memories have saturated them with epithets of perfection. These moments of immaculate perfection have the power to seize our healthy limbs & animate them with nervous anxiety until we atrophy at the mercy of a mere idea of our own creation. We are bound to blame *the thing* that ruined or slayed us. But without a doubt, it was the investment of our trust in these terrible deceivers, *these moments* that ultimately lead to our self-indulgence in the mad emotions of a single moment. Even if one of these moments *were* perfect, we would fail to find contentment there. We want to repeat it, to recreate it, to possess it, until our genuinely pleasant memories suffocate under the pressure of this obsession. Against all advice & good judgement, we have little choice but to desire the perpetual intoxication of that one moment. Padam stood in the blue doorway with the remains of his good sense, like a modest sculpture of Hercules holding his chin & trying to decide which path to take. He had always prided himself on his wisdom & sense of discipline over the years. But is there no reward for our trials, not at any age? Is there not even a single sliver of time just for us, when we can officially *let go* of ourselves & surrender to the immediacy of our senses? By the blue walls, the post-colonial Magi were already clearing away the leavings from his small dinner. He had tried. Failed? Maxwell Wittman the Third released a tiny sigh & detached his elbow from the blue liminal. *Appassionato*, he moved briskly after the young man.

If only Padam had not seen him. He had absolutely no chance of catching him now, although this pang of uncertainty seemed to enhance the quality of his feelings. After all, he only hoped to catch another glimpse of that young frame. This moment was lost. He must have understood that. Yet he followed his instinct. He only longed to recapture that silhouette for the sake of his memory. There, in the distance along the beach. A single inky blot among those other festive pigments. No. Not him. Or … ? Padam stepped tentatively toward the now blinding vacillations of light. The sea appeared white-hot. He half-closed his eyes, covering them with a clenched paw. A great heron flapped its wings mightily over the water, confusing him. Perhaps he shouldn't have ordered a beer with his dinner. Had he? Part of the deal, I suppose. He stared at all the sailboats. One of them was cutting across that particle beam of brightness. He was not certain how to handle this. In sudden terror, Padam took refuge by the nearby double doors of the Istoria, as if wanting to hide from the thunder in his heart. He found a seat in the increasing heat. The girl came, the one he called the *Allegory of the Faith*, & dropped a pale ale into the scatter of light. The gigantic panes of glass seemed to burn any sitters who sat directly in the path of that magnified sunlight. Padam looked out anxiously towards the beach, trying to fathom each shape at play. He watched white & scarlet triangles wave in clusters along the horizon. The candles were prematurely lit. The sun has not gone down yet. No one heard him. A kayak emerged from the light, nimbly negotiating past the sailboats. He recognized the regular movements of passing joggers & the agitated limbs of ferocious power-walkers. He tried to find the young man. At last, he saw a mobile shadow that he suspected to be *him*. Maxwell Wittman the Third fixed his eyes upon the seawall, where streams of jerky people were moving to & fro, as if upon a snaking conveyor of cement. It was among the moving souls that he spotted a particular shade upon the burning sand. He realized that he was dying to see such a thing. Padam coughed. He could feel his side item of obligatory carbohydrates coming up on him. The figure on the beach went out of focus. He struggled to regain his composure as the many-coloured specks began to dance before his eyes like one of those flower ensembles in old pictures. They appeared to be floating upon his own golden sleeve & drifting across a collection of gleaming wine glasses. The post-modern rendition of the hotel jutted out at him with its deep green tones. Padam fancied he could hear its sides rustling, even moaning in anguish, while the painting itself lashed its mauve & emerald tendrils at him. Padam touched his temples & then searched around frantically for the current configuration of his face. Everyone was looking at him, weren't they? Yes. He could see the other gingerly sipping drinkers & cautiously carving diners & even those spinning flecks upon the

beach. They were pointing at him. *Him*! Maxwell Wittman the Third!
He held his face, rubbing his palms over his cheeks. Had he changed,
then? Had he?

That night, he had even more trouble getting to sleep. The stained
glass simulacrum of Ganymede, or, the young man, was propped up
& secured against his bedroom window so that it faced streetward. In
some ways, he wanted to take it down. But then he would have to
explain to the building manager & she absolutely adored it. If she
had her way, Padam would have had to fashion a stained glass window
for every window in the building as the resident Michelangelo for
Urban Queen Apartments. But part of him was afraid. When the sun
was in the right position, just before setting, it would reflect through
his window & strike a mirror in the hallway, reflecting once again to
flood his living room with those stained glass hues he knew so well.
His feelings had changed with regard to the coastal bird rising out of
the young man's dark mane. This bird was now an unwelcome guest.
He could almost feel the lethal touch of its talons, filling blood &
brain with that venomous ink of the artist. Padam averted his eyes
from the scavenger, reaching instead with his fingernails into a brown
bowl of very ripe raspberries as the spectral colours marked his face &
whiskers.

Maxwell Wittman the Third mused, as he rubbed his bleary eyes in
the morning, that after a number of milestones in our life, no matter
how young or old, we come to reflect upon them, even before the
spectre of death presses our startled eyes closed. The most peculiar &
disparate elements may, as it were, crop up. As one of the great writers
indicates in his lengthy masterpiece (it slips my mind which) it is our
hope to find this trigger for the most salient, the most precious
memories of our entire lives, *before we die*. Padam felt a tinge of
sadness in considering this, since he had dedicated the finest or most
passionate moments of his life to his multiple forms of artistic

expression. After his firmest days of physical expression were past, he had felt liberated to return to a new existence more in keeping with his earliest days when he was at leisure to sketch or sew or create to his cardiac content, in other words, when there was no regime, no itinerary for eternity. & the sorrow that the young man felt. What was that? Padam had not thought about it very much, save for the way those emotions lent a means of vague transformation to his external beauty. But now, as the unique pirouettes of his own *Pavlova* had once passed through his mind, he saw the young man writing the way he had observed him on so many other evenings, with his head lowered & his ears raised. Then he sensed that the young man's ears were reddening & burning while he listened & that like a slim & flimsy filter, all of the murmurs that flitted about those ears were pouring some distorted conversation or murky business inwards, & that osmotically, he was sitting in a dark corner & attempting to distill the quintessence of each slippery word. Small madnesses. Sorrows, too. Padam considered this possibility, in fact how the young man might have observed (or heard) the world, & was slightly moved. What was happening to him? He felt a smidgen of empathy for the woman who used to write by the window & now since the *Restoration* made mysterious notes upon her wooden parapet, a two-seater overlooking the rest of the bar. *If you don't have a problem, then you don't belong in this bar.* Padam heard his own maxim upon his lips & felt the faint echo of a giggle in his throat. Ahh, Barb, with her cobwebbed ink & insidious bottle of poisonous flowers! But wasn't it the same with himself, Maxwell Wittman the Third? Hadn't he thrown himself into his art for the duration of his life? & now, what was he doing in his swinging sixties? Lusting after some little piece of totty? Chasing him along the beach? He sank his left paw into the raspberries, searching for the largest ones. He tried not to look up at his latest creation, but the caricature of the young man in stained glass & the large dark bird perched upon his head, a conscious clawing part of him, glared back at Padam through the mirror where so many of his students had watched themselves dance, swallowing fault & triumph alike. Both the cartoon of the young man & the grim bird seemed bolder, more defined. He shuddered, feeling as if the divisions of light & dark glass were protruding out toward him & assuming completely new shapes. Although he had not portrayed the creature from his nightmare in the window, the shadowy bird he *had* fashioned began to claw & tear at the glass in a similar dreamlike manner, which left the impression it was stretching & melting, as if it were only the shell of an egg to this imprisoned thing seeking its freedom. But stronger than his fear were his anger & arrogance in hot pursuit of that anger. Padam held his fists together, squeezing raspberries through his knuckles. He rose & went into the kitchen, the only sanctuary he now had, a private alcove well away from that leering face with a raven emerging from its black nest of hair. He turned on the faucet & let water run over the white bowl smeared with red berries the colour of roe & tried to meditate like his favourite supplicant. What would Saint Francis do? Some dishes. He let the water run warmly over his hands, trying to unthaw the frozen talons they had become. He attempted the trance his guru had taught him. The magic phrase was *gato negro*. Since we are all self-flagellants when it comes down to it. Look how the young man pours all of that poison of choice down scalding throat & into churning stomach, as if performing a sacred rite! Why, that drunken little monk! Drunken little monkey. Yet as the water ran over his unfurling fingers, Maxwell Wittman the Third looked up at the canvas he had presented for a rape relief benefit. Ah, those lovely young men, horrible to look upon! She became like a mother to them, near the end of the play. A mother goddess. They both lay in the meadow with her & all was well. He blinked. The calm shades of green, infused with a thoughtful optimism, were bleeding ambiguous light. A shadow passed over the painting. A pair of wings? The green, formerly thick but innocent & rather devoid of detail, had developed into rampant blades, growing & spreading like the lines in his slowly wizening face. They sharpened obscurely before his eyes. He watched them sway upon the canvas, poised to strike at the first opportunity. No, they wouldn't put me in the way of harm. They are mine? & what were those boys doing in that meadow after dark? He had painted a blatant message of peace & love. Here, before his eyes, he saw the covetousness of a Vermeer. The clothing of the young men & the scarcely older woman had a hint of suggestiveness that he could not recall painting. Even the meadow seemed sinister, with uncontrollable shoots & weeds about their bodies, full of anxiety about their provoked desires, moaning one thing & then meaning another completely. Padam felt the hot water running molten over his clenched fingers, as he felt the helpless heat of the woman & the fierce caresses of the two striplings. The figures lost their shape & blurred into that background of acid green. Padam thought he could even smell the stench of their flesh burning & melting over those emerald blades. Love. Where was love, tonight? Cold. Alone. Eros with his purple mantle & huge prick the cock of the god fallen like manna from heaven. A sign. The mortification of his own broad hues & tones & last minute slap-dashes. Maxwell Wittman the Third stood in that cluttered kitchen alcove, taken aback by a painting he had received much praise for. He thought of the fashionable painters of the past, of the endless portraits in galleries, of varying degrees of accuracy & satire & even ineptitude. Why had *his own* optimistic greens taken this window of time to betray him? These layers of paint, had they no integrity of their own? He tried to look away from the arrangement of tones. But they were positively sulphuric. They were burning & thinning his blood, corpuscle by corpuscle, if it were possible to feel such a thing. What had the young man read him—a line of poetry, from …

What did I drink, as I knelt in the heather, what did I drink?

The next night, Padam arranged to meet with his patron, as he often did whenever he had a favour to ask. & what better place than the brand new Istoria? So he entered, under that liminal of mediocre images tossed together in stained glass, creeping up the marble stairs, & began to hunt for a place by the window. There. Maxwell Wittman the Third sat down & gently sank into one of two crinkly beige chairs. He waited with a synthetic smile on his face, waited as Virgil might have done in a private bathhouse for the lascivious towel-flick of a late Augustus. Another server, also fair in colour yet differently so, materialized. Padam looked up with his trademark grin, albeit a bit wizened, & drank in the prominent curves of her skeletal structure. Her eyes widened with a blasé introductory gleam & shone with a number of shades, as if trying to assume a pleasing tone. He could make out touches of grey & even a subtle blue that lent a rounded oceanic feeling to the dominant green. But they were only hazel eyes after all, as if all the water had suddenly dried up & become suffused with murky practicalities. She opened her mouth & released a rather buoyant affability, yet with a sharpness that seemed poignant enough to move all listeners to contentment, or at least obeisance, as the tone of a Queen to address her favoured hounds. Padam asked politely for his standard, his always by default pale ale, remembering even to ask for a *sleeve*.

"Yessiree."

She glided away in her new black uniform, as Padam ventured that her voice could, in instances of exuberance, quite probably cut glass. At that moment, Lorn winged it up the steps, retaining the theatrical quality of a perfectly executed *stage right*, yet appearing completely unlike himself.

"I didn't recognize you," giggled Padam, wondering in amazement at the bareheaded Lorn. "You can leave your hat on."

Lorn smiled wistfully. He looked around selfconsciously & failing to find anything to refuse to doff, he put his hands in his pants pockets (in the manner of the great Mario Lanza playing Caruso in a stage set Met production of *La Bohème*) & then removed them with a gesture of futility, before taking a soft-spined beige seat opposite Padam.

"You look naked," observed Maxwell Wittman the Third.

Indeed, Lorn had lost his devil-may-care air. On this occasion, he had the appearance of a defrocked (or in this case unhatted) altar boy. Lorn shrugged meekly as he spoke.

"So I'm spieling away with this old lawyer pal, & you um … know how I love to spiel!"

"Yes, you adore spieling," tittered Padam.

"Well, we get to jawing & I'm crowing on about the Native artwork I bought (& mind you returned, from my *own* extensive collection). It's that kid's stuff, your young friend."

Padam blinked, unsmiling.

"Tomasz thinks everything is *his stuff.*"

"So this geezer, he's like tha man. A real *mensch.* Anyway, he's handled a number of these land claim shibangs, all pro bono stuff. Even so, right in the middle of telling him about all the stuff I gave back to the community, right in front of the lobby totem, he turns to me & decides to inform me of the inescapable fact that my hat makes me look more Jewish. Can you imagine? A dressing down if I ever heard of one."

Padam clapped wildly.

"& you've never worn it since!"

Lorn & his balding pate turned scarlet. One of the writers of our day might say *aubergine* for effect. He banged his angelic fist on the table.

"The nerve! That gonif … that cabinet-maker … that pishkeh … "

After his initial stream of Yiddish expletives, Lorn calmed down & straightened his invisible hat. He then went into a long story about this lawyer who found making his own furniture out of wood to be a relaxing occupation & how in fact he had heard from one of his loopier clients that in the Koine Greek, the street lingo of the New Testament, there is no indication that Christ was the son of a carpenter. The word *teknon* was intimately bound up with the word *tekne*, which boils down roughly to skill-set.

"Messiah, Meshiah, son of a dress-maker or tailor? Maybe a cabinet-maker. He was a well to do rabbi, some say, just like my brother-in-law. I just don't make him out to be a sawbuck jones … "

Padam nodded with perfect disbelief. Thankfully, the woman with the sharp voice arrived to *make him a man.*

"A glass, I suppose."

"Okely dokely," she replied, slicing through the air with her peculiar vocables.

"Long story short, cabinet-makers aside, I have no hat. Maybe old Spertz could make me a beautiful box, a wonderful place to hide my hat. You know, all coastal-like."

Lorn smiled, suddenly his old self-satisfied self. Padam leaned forward, happy that Lorn was downing his glass & once again in a good mood.

"I have an *indulgence* to ask of you." Lorn merely looked back at him like a child at his father on the way to the doctor, if not like a dog sheepishly trying to read the word V-E-T upon the lips of his handlers. Maxwell Wittman the Third pulled a crumpled piece of paper out of his matching maroon jumpsuit. "I want to put this poem in stained glass."

Lorn uncrumpled the bird-like folds of paper & examined them with his particular brand of legalistic erudition.

"Ganymede, eh? This is your young felluh, no?"

Padam sat back in his chair, emitting only a creamy crinkly sound of resignation. Or was it deflation?

"I have made a stained-glass creation of his countenance. Now ... Now, I want to put his accompaniment, his poem, into stained glass. However, I must add that we have had a regrettable parting of the ways."

Lorn sat back, unperturbed.

"Yeah, Stephane said something. Well, I liked that kid. He was a huge fan of Sigmund Romberg & you know we were all supposed to get together & watch *Carousel.* But, I guess Mr. Lanza & the *Great Caruso* will have to take a back seat to these plans of yours. Can't be helped, can't be helped."

"Lorn, I want to put this poem in stained glass."

Lorn sipped at his glass & nodded abstractly, only to return to his own preoccupations.

"*Till the Clouds Roll By*. That kid of yours sure loved Jerome Kern. & remember when Tony Martin sang *All the Things You Are*? O we won't see times like those again."

Padam waited a long time to ensure that Lorn was fully finished his nostalgic rant. He wasn't.

"That kid loved Mario Lanza. Who didn't in those days? A time when men wore hats! Everybody thought he was some kinda truck driver, chasing his costars in a jock strap around the set. He is one of the best opera singers of our time. If only he had finished in the great tradition. That's all the kid wanted! & the watch the watch!"

Lorn accelerated his nods to a previously unrecorded tempo. Padam laughed & remembered. It had been his birthday (why a Queen never tells …) & the young man had been very warmly invited. Lorn had made a magnificent mellifluous speech to mark the occasion about the young Kwakiutl not being a Jew, especially in the religious sense of the word. The young man had taken exception to this, referring to both the Old & New Testaments & adding that it was just like the government telling him he wasn't an Indian. Until one day, he *was*. Apparently, they had sent him a card by post. He had also argued back even more defiantly in terms of American operettas, a language that Lorn could fully appreciate. What of the *Student Prince* & his love of a barmaid in Heidelberg? What of that Donizetti sextet in *The Great Caruso*? In spite of the irrelevance of these tangential arguments, Lorn had instantly caved in, overwhelmed by his open passion for Sigmund Romberg & Jerome Kern. Maxwell Wittman the Third even recalled that Lorn had unfastened the strap of his watch & had held it out for the young man, his astonished Ganymede! Lorn declared that it was his watch by right, since it had been given to him by the young man's tribe for the return of artifacts he had once purchased. Oroonoko, watch out! The young man had examined the red animal markings curling around the white circle of the watch face positioned beneath an oval of glass. Lorn turned scarlet & went on to say that he had been given the title *He-who-gives* by the Kwak'wala speakers. It was only later that Padam learned that Lorn had another watch just like it & began to suspect that he had an inexhaustible supply, or at least a truckload of them. After the strap from Lorn's original watch had worn away, he had given the young man his fresh copy in the same manner & with the same amount of pomp & circumstance. Ever since, Padam had taken pleasure in watching the young man in a dark corner, between frantic spells of writing, pulling the red & black watch out of his pants pocket as if it were an old-fashioned fob, & scrunching up his eyes to make out the hour in Indian Time. As Lorn continued to wax on about the fantastic tenor Mario Lanza (formerly Alfredo Arnold Cocozza) who had died before he could make his formal debut upon the operatic stage & as he continued to emphasize the bulk of Lanza (who would both shrink & expand as he passed through a doorway in separately shot movie frames) with excited gestures, Padam watched his smooth white hands & the Kwakiutl watch about his left wrist & tried not to think of the young man, as if this accessory were some private covenant between them, the artifact as it were, that combined Jewish cantors with the background of a tribal beat.

"Hey, remember that play he gave you? It was very good."

Padam sniggered, fingering the finest hairs of his moustache.

"You were furious with him. You couldn't get past the first few pages!"

Lorn turned colour until his balding pate became a sanctimonious sunset.

"Man! Well it was intense. That piece. Don't get me wrong. I've seen things that would curl that young felluh's hair! & I know. Don't tell me. I should schlepp pen to page ... "

Padam laughed.

"I never said *that*."

"My guru at the Cold Mountain Institute, he was also at me. Why don't you write down your witticisms? Why don't you tell the world what goes on in that funky brain of yours?"

Maxwell Wittman the Third frowned.

"The young man," he began, suddenly shifting into his instructive tone, "does not quite approve of that Cold Mountain place. I believe he prefers a place called Black Mountain far more."

Lorn screwed up his face, appearing his old Mephistophelean self for a moment.

"No, you don't know the magic of Cold Mountain! You were not there in that meditative place, not in that realm where I was!"

Padam softened his tone.

"Well, that may be the case. But the young man is under the impression that Cold Mountain is just a pricey getaway for the very wealthy with naïve delusions of grandeur, more along the lines of a spa, or dare I say *brothel*."

Lorn dropped his eloquent hands & fell back into his seat, as if he had just been shot twice. Once the initial spasms of agony were over, he recovered his composure & snorted indignantly.

"The massages & mud packs have nothing to do with it! Gurumaster would quite disagree with such allegations! Without him, I would have no centre-point, no apex of focus. No mantra! He taught me an ancient form of centrifugality. He also helped Rhonda, this hot Shaughnessy mom. & let me tell you, when she arrived, she was very tense. But after just a few visits with master-guru, we were rolling around on the floor making passionate love in the umm … temple."

Padam smiled at this petty profanation.

"Yes, but Captain Tantric, isn't that just your usual form of *meditation*? & what about the guru-master? Didn't he have some reflections about centre-points to add?"

Lorn grinned, rubbing his smooth hands together like dry tinder.

"Beats me. The guru-master was on a brief pilgrimage, picking berries or something. Actually, I think his real name was Lionel. That's what his driver's license said. Ah well, all's well ... That kid should go to Cold Mountain. He's too intense. All that brooding. By the way, alcoholic writing went out a long time ago. How many *Lost Weekends* can you write anyway? Cold Mountain. They'd fix him up real good. Cold Mountain Cold Mountain ... "

Lorn repeated these two words a few times, as if falling into a trance. Under the table, Padam snapped his fingers.

"Cold Mountain yeah, they would straighten out the kinks in that kid. By the way, does he ever have sex or what? His writing is soooo erotic. It's like he's storing it all up like a celibate monk or something. A real waste. The Cold Mountain Institute would sure fix him."

Padam nodded vigorously.

"Yes, an absolute waste!"

Lorn began to wind his tribal watch, whether from anxiety or boredom. Padam watched him, examining the red & black fins & beaks surrounding the thunderbird that stared outward & looked very fierce. He felt mesmerized by those gilt hands ticking round. He looked out through the great pane of glass in front of them. It was that time of evening when the expanse of light & dark blues seemed to be divided into horizontal blue slats in spite of the orange-pink street-lamps burning into his bleary eyes. Then the gradients deepened, & all the while, Padam drank.

"O lorn I am lorn, Lorn I am. The young man, my Ganymede, is grfff ... gone."

He stared off into darkening sky & sea. Lorn tumbled into another casual shrug.

"Hey, the guy was bad news, right?" Padam said nothing. He turned to glance at the servitor with her oceanic eyes & voice that seemed to make the great pane of glass tremble from fear of cracking. But that was not even a fair description. Was that the young man's lot, to try to describe the quality & nature of a voice? At the moment, she was making a face at some flirty remark. Even now, Maxwell Wittman was aware that he could not see her features & skeletal structure as it was, even beneath her artful application of make-up. He was helpless to describe her. She was certainly no *Allegory of the Faith*. Instead, in the tension of her facial muscles in this act of grimacing, he saw a figure painted upon the Northern wall of the Arena Chapel, incidentally the *capella* that Enrico Scrovegni had built in order to atone for the practices of his father, Reginaldo, the usurer who brashly declares his Paduan background & waves his white purse around the seventh circle of Dante's version of Hell. He saw this young woman's face coming to life as the lightning hands of Giotto went to work, first laying down the *intonaco* & then tracing the lines of her face in red ochre. Indeed, as the disparate pigments were put into harmony by his brush, Padam watched the creation of an angel for the *Lamentation*, perhaps the one who instead of swooning, dives in a swooping birdlike fashion, tearing at her long hair from the sides in unspeakable sorrow for the earthly death below, & yet without disrupting the musical balance & order of her angelic counterparts. He was startled as a moth flew out of Scrovegni's purse, attracted by the candle that painted angel of Giotto had lit. He watched for a moment as it fluttered about the rim of his sleeve. A standard, in fact, an *old chestnut* by Portishead, had just started to play through the new & even more arbitrary FEED. Padam listened to the faraway sounds of clunkiness that made him think of a bucket in a well or of his brother's deep explorations for palaces of salt beneath the level of the earth. Even Giotto had climbed down into the ruins of past centuries with only a pail full of inks & dyes to retrace the faint lines of former eras in order to lend them flight. & where is Ganymede? I couldn't capture him either. No more than this moth. All I had for him was a mere *cartone*. & where is he tonight?

Voices increased & intensified. For much of his life, Maxwell Wittman the Third had felt there was an audience all about him, secretly smiling at his finest moments & discreetly averting its eyes from any infrequent *faux pas*. Voices. What is madness? The music, the chief export of my ancestral homeland. That tiny domicile of Dostoyevsky's. There is a certain sorrow that comes to the artist, perhaps less suddenly than it comes to the orderly suburbanite or fluctuating shifter of commodities. There is no scheduled time of quiet, no lull in mood or temperament, no holiday from oneself. But sorrow is often strangely comfortable, a source of inspiration & ultimately a fast friend for the artist. However, a realization that often comes with increasing age is not only that you are alone in the world, but that you are alone within the illusion of your *own* world & ultimately, the public as any kind of beautiful whole will never come to understand your personal magic, nor partake of its fruit. For the noteworthy after death, they will only go through your things, opening the private cupboards & drawers of your life like avaricious heirs in search of a will. The sorrow is for the legacy of your personal phantoms that will only be left to helplessly observe such a ransacking of the soul. Let harm not come to them. If not completely mad, the artist behaves like a mad person whose sudden realization of a mediocre fact may be enough to threaten the integrity of their entire universe. It is the phone call or angry knock at the door or distant foghorn that awakens one from a very pleasant dream. There is the loneliness of the individual, yes. The one that drives people to get together & talk *at* one another rather than *to* one another. But there is also the necessary loneliness required for a work of art that offers the eternal friendship & tempting surrender of blank canvas or page, in fact the most reliable & fulfilling friend that one can have, aside from a handful of choice particulars that are scattered throughout this space. Padam was at the point where his artistic objects which had so reliably provided his imagination with an eclectic series of moveables were starting to move by themselves, even starting to float out of the picture of his life & then back into it again. He had seen madmen on the street, if not lost souls with mechanical failure in only one part of their brain or nervous system. Padam furrowed his brow & thought of the young man hunched over his work with nervous movements & incessant mutterings, followed by intermittent stabs of his pen into page. The *crazy* people wandered up & down commercial boulevards talking to themselves & terrifying each passerby with arms full of parcels. We are a function of what we do, every day. But at some point, life becomes unknown to us or at least the discovery of what that is, a function of something else.

"What?"

Lorn made a gesture toward his new imaginary hat, indicating that Padam had become lost in thought. Then he turned his head. The young man had entered. He slipped into a reupholstered loveseat as far away from the pair as he could sit.

"Hey, there's your Ganymede."

Padam made a downward motion.

"Shhh … not so loud."

He was completely aware that Lorn, hatless or not, wished to make some type of entreaty to the young man, perhaps touching upon their collective failure to rent *Carousel*. Padam stared him down & his look of anguish froze Lorn in his chair. The young man arched protectively over his notebook & clutched the table as if it were to float away any minute. His long dark hair fell over his face in front of his candle & he seemed to be a warlock hastily jotting down preparations for a fantastic & vengeful spell. Lorn cast another glance at the trollish shadow in the corner & then examined the curved bird's head on his Kwakiutl watch.

"Ahh Maxaleh, I gotta run."

Maxwell Wittman the Third raised a palm in protestation.

"Lorn, I said I needed a favour."

"O yeah?"

Padam stared at him meaningfully.

"I want to put the Ganymede poem in stained glass."

Lorn sped down the steps & out the double doors. Padam smiled at the heavy thud of one of the doors that resolutely confirmed his silent assent. So much better than a *yeah, whatever*. The young man downed his sleeve & without his looking up, another raven cream ale arrived to replace the empty one & was clunked down by a faceless server (the other guy, that queen bee, I suppose). The young man then looked up & off into the distance for a few seconds. He closed his eyes & let them flutter in the last reach of sunlight. Meditating. Waiting for inspiration, my young Ganymede? Then he reached for his sleeve & took another large gulp before flying back into action within the small margins of his notebook. I have put this young man in glass. I want to put a few of his words in glass as well. The poem. Only a moment in his life. The blood of Ganymede, the inky trail of his pain, made immortal. Padam thought that was an excellent idea, yes, & then he began to laugh & laugh, reaching for his face, for his whiskers, since they were continually being caught up in the contorted beak of that bird. Glass, not love, no. Glass. Then the beak stretched in length & Padam reached nervously for the twisting cords that would effect the necessary transformation, the one he desperately needed. The young man did not look up from his writing, not even to see the cavorting beak at the end of Padam's nose, drifting off somewhere above his dry mouth. Why, how rude! For I am Jove, my young cold friend. What are you but my young cupbearer? There is no way out of what is decreed. He reached for the dangling cords, but could no longer locate them. Cruel stars! How am I Madam the Thirst to enact my great transfisssssstication? The time had gone. It was dark now. The server from one of Giotto's frescos with oceans for eyes appeared to have already gone home. What! The other guy was still on shift. The queen bee. Buzz buzzzzz. Padam smiled at him, but only as a moray eel might acknowledge a barracuda when gliding in the same territorial waters. They may as well have stumbled into the same party in matching frocks. The other guy leaned forward, casting a number of strange shadows across the withdrawing bird beak of Padam, whose hands shrank back into small gnarled paws. Not time yet. Not yet time to transfigure no no no.

"You've been here for a while. Anything you want to ask me?"

Padam glared at him through his glasses.

"Why? Is there bad news? I only ever ask *you* for bad news."

Maxwell Wittman the Third had forgotten the chap's name, but that was the least of his concerns. The other guy laughed in sharp falsetto tones, but hurried away, except very slowly & in something of a huff. Padam reached for the receipt & then his wallet, taloning out a confabulation of coins & bills. Ye gods. These new prices. The young man had disappeared. The other guy took a seat & stared out at the black water, oblivious of the remaining guests that were itching to signal him by name, but had also forgotten it. For a moment, only a moment, Padam felt a touch of empathy for this sad looking specimen & forgot their usual rivalry to attract the attention of suitable men within the space of the bar. On any given night, the other guy would park his formidable ass & lean over a bevy of semi-interested studs & pump them for the tawdriest details about their travels or even local adventures. In spite of his acclaimed career & clear superiority in every way, Padam was more often than not irked that this buzzing queen bee should hold dominion over such a place, where quite rightly, he, Maxwell Wittman the Third, should hold reign. Wisely & gently too. Instead, these effeminate drones came back again & again to sip honeyed outpouring of nectar from his … Well. Padam headed home, fuming to himself & stroking his elongated beak with a great deal of agitation. What a nerve. He thought of the other guy's sloppy fleshy build & the clumsy display of corpulence that suggested some hidden realm of sensuality about the slack edges of his loosely fastened belt buckle. Why, he was just giving it away. However, by the time he had reached the bench in front of his bedroom window, he had quietened his thoughts, for Maxwell Wittman the Third was many things, but he was by no means *catty*.

He can keep his little sluts. Padam locked his door & looked around nervously. The stained glass.

"Chester?"

He could hear his cat miaowing in response to some unknown terror.

"Puss puss puss … "

They hear & see the invisible, since the land of the Pharoahs. Padam attempted a short glide over to his disc player, suddenly feeling awkward & bereft of nimbleness. His young friend & once fantastic lover Ethan had made him a collection of discs out of sympathy for his failed marriage, including one of his favourite works— Tchaikovsky's *Manfred*. It was only since meeting the young man that he had come to appreciate that stirring music he had only vaguely smiled at before. Padam selected the correct disc & track & pawed [PLAY]. There, the fixed idea, the bassoons of a young man hurled headlong toward the lower strings & the hammerings of inexorable fate. Stark bugles & bells. Then tenderness. The memory of some goddess what's her name but more so the memory of a great love lost & left silent in a very subtle andante. At least that was what Ethan had said in bed. Put out that disgusting cigarette. You want to get fucked. You want to be the boy raped in the mountains by a big black bird then carried off up up higher & higher & harder into the oily clouds. Something about a melancholy B minor. Grief. The grief of *Manfred*.

It is not noon. The sprite of the prismatic waterfall. A musical joke. Scherzo, what a wonderful word. Some threesome. Over *the crag's headlong perpendicular* we go O no. The soft warning of a harp. Inspires. Desire. Then his favourite. The gentle echo of an oboe. Priapus poking through the brambles. Life in the fields. Another Orpheus. Padam wandered into the alcove that was his sorry excuse for a kitchen & began to examine his nude sketches of Ethan. He had focused on his muscular structure, perhaps with only the objectivity a cruel lover can muster. He had created a model of the man's body in its prime. Now that Ethan was warding off death, the disparity between that da Vinci study of perfect health & his now withered limbs was very disturbing. Padam paused to find himself once again among the music of *Manfred*. It is a warmongering march that leads

301

Manfred to hell. He used to say such things in bed & I would reply stupidly, as did he. But I remember the sound of that descent to the underworld & the chaotic steps of the Bacchanalians. Then the sorry so very sorry melody of a lost love. But finally, the end of suffering. Those dying bars of *Dies Irae*. Lorn & the young man might like that! Give me the choice. Give me the chance. Only then will I find my own expiation. I will destroy myself. Yes. I will. But how would the young man go about it? Let me see. How would he *off* one of his greatest characters? A universal problem. Shakespeare with Falstaff & Conan Doyle with Sherlock. How would the young man arrange the final departure of Maxwell Wittman the Third? A grand story, to be sure. But different, as well. An homage. A work of hate as well. Let the heavens open! Let the tapestries beneath my bare feet sink into eternal damnation! Let me race across the flaming sand! Padam listened to the last lingering strains of *Manfred* & wondered about his own life as a fictional character & his own existence as a mere *cartone* of himself.

   It's all about framing.

The young man had said that one evening & Padam had wondered at it & had attempted half-heartedly to uncover the meaning of such a statement. *Manfred*, in those towering Alps, inspired by the learnings of Goethe, & then Tchaikovsky, inspired by musical midwife Mily to pen some of his finest notes. As for his composition, *Manfred* dies upon a redemptive note. & how will Maxwell Wittman the Third meet his maker, I wonder? Smiling, I hope. He reset the disc to the start & found his place upon the bed, where Chester was curled up into a heavy ball of fur, oddly afraid to face his tame master. He pounced down upon cold floor. Padam found this very strange, even as he began to rub his enlargening white beak with increasing agitation. But then he remembered a television commercial he had seen a few days earlier, perhaps while eating some frozen raspberries. The rays of his creation illuminated the room & an idea occurred to him that felt like some type of divine annunciation. He laughed softly to himself. Caw caw racacah. Caw caw. No, *it is not noon* yet. Tomorrow.

VII

The next morning, Maxwell Wittman the Third awoke feeling rather refreshed. He hopped out of bed & landed in a perched yogic stance. What does tomorrow bring? He had thought of that before bed. His appointment of course. He had already got the tiresome preliminaries out of the way. He was one of the first patients to line up before nine outside his favourite drop-in clinic. He was still behind a distraught looking young man with a runny nose who kept rubbing his upper lip & a wide-eyed woman with straw hair who was trying to read a copy of *Time* with trembling hands. A heavyset man with sundarkened skin clawed open the clinic door & looked at the others carefully before selecting a grey seat & starting to scratch furiously under his plaid shirt. Padam turned away. There was a small television in the corner of the room, just high enough so that no one could change the channel except for a very tall woman with blue or green eyes who was still after Padam in the pecking order & was glaring out the window apprehensively, her arms folded. The receptionist kept her eyes glued to the screen. It was a daytime talk show concerned specifically with the latest match-ups &/or break-ups of celebrities. Padam glanced up at a nondescript male face after noticing that the woman with straw hair was as transfixed as the receptionist. Hey, wasn't that whatshisname? He was in that film we saw last week. Was it Tom or Jake? Whoever it was, he was grinning idiotically & declaring his love for some starlet, much to the approval of the madly applauding studio audience. Ryan? Chris? They were screaming questions that only widened his inane grin. He was hardly eager to hear the break-ups part. Wasn't it the cat's miaow that whatshisface had found true love? However, by the time the trembling woman with straw hair had returned to their small & sickly gathering with a mortified look on her face & the receptionist had lowered her eyes for long enough to read a very important word—*Padam*—the owner of that title, was indeed ready to leap up from his grey chair & leave the cheering & jeering studio audience well behind him. He grinned at the green-eyed woman, who scowled back. Other concerns. Very very pale. No wonder. Dr. Mann, a middle-aged man with thinning brown hair & without a crisis to speak of, emerged. Padam noted that the doctor was still very sprightly on his feet for his age (which shall remain unthought) as he led him into a room the size of a water closet & closed the divider. The doctor clasped our hero's hands warmly as if to emphasize his bellicose query.

"HOW ARE YOU?"

Padam bared his teeth & managed a hint of the old Cheshire.

"Still holding together, well enough, heh heh."

The doctor adopted a more formal position, lifting one knee & placing his hand on his hip.

"Well, Padam, what's on your mind?"

"It's rather silly, really, after all, you know. The clock keeps turning & the hours keep turning into years & I would just like to slow down the music a little. I'm talking about cosmetics, of course. I guess I wanted a bit of a check-up before I proceed, or even a pinch of advice."

Dr. Mann nodded sagely, giving Padam a casual once-over & at last shaking his shiny affable dome of a head.

"If that's what you're in the market for, I *do* know a man."

Padam smiled. Then Dr. Mann paused, generating the appearance of a moment of reflection, while Padam waited, as he had waited in the waiting room.

"I have no idea why though. They say beauty begins inside of you. You are in perfect shape for a man in his seventies."

Padam laughed.

"Don't jump the gun. I'm still in the sixties. Free love & all that. Check your chart."

Dr. Mann changed colour & silently looked down at his clipboard. Then he assumed a grave face. "Well, in that case, perhaps some form of treatment is in order, if not a complete overhaul. But when I say that, I'm only kidding, of course."

"About the treatment?"

Dr. Mann shook his round head again.

"No, about the overhaul."

Then, after consulting a binder on the counter, he wrote out a grouping of illegible markings (rather like bird prints as well as their leavings) upon a pink rectangle of paper & handed it to Padam with a look of detachment. Then he assumed his general practitioner cordial face once again & selected from his latest find of amiable diatribe.

"How about that election, eh?"

Padam nodded, not giving any opinion about a matter yet undecided.

"Yes, we are due for one, a real toss-up, I hear."

But now, with the talk show revelations & all of the sniffing & scratching patients behind him, Maxwell Wittman the Third had managed to reach the morning of his appointment with Dr. Saul Xavier Finestretta, who would be best qualified to consult him, Padam, about the particulars of his condition. Admittedly, he had not mentioned anything about his occasional *beaking* episode to Dr. Mann, but surely they would subside after some professional treatment & today was the day. It was time.

Maxwell Wittman the Third felt his shoulders being eased into a comfortable chair almost noiselessly. The doctor rubbed his hands together, pointing to a giant monitor that hung from the bright beige ceiling. Flesh tones. On the screen, the robust men of Kirov leapt into the air over Padam's grey whiskers. He watched the bouncing of their blue tights like a cat checking out tossed balls of blue yarn.

"Ah yes, what have we here? This is right up your lane, Herr Wittman. By the way, you can call me F. My patients find that easier. Of course I prefer to think of them as my *friends*."

Padam smiled. He preferred familiarity as well.

"I used to dance," he offered amiably.

As he said this, his facial muscles began to stretch underneath the intensifying beam of soft focus lighting.

"Well, just sit back & watch the show. I like to acquaint myself with the most intimate details of my new friend's face before making any type of recommendation. Ha. Once again, I suppose I should say *the client's* face. Coco will be after me for that one. But what ever happened to humanity in the medical profession, eh? In my country, when I was a boy, old Rotterdett used to pay calls if I had the slightest sniffle. Today, it's all drop-in clinics & fast food medicine. Is that what's running through your mind, young fellow?"

Padam tried to smile through the man's paddling fingers.

"Hmmnnn Dr. F. I agree absohmmlutely."

F frowned smoothly down at him.

"No no no, this simply won't do, little monkey."

F's fingers picked up excess folds of skin as if they were excess selvage in an old factory & raised them towards the intense lighting. After several more minutes of scrutinizing, F stood back & snapped his fingers, so that the lighting softened once again.

"So what is it Maxy? Trying to catch some frisky tuna with the same old net, eh?"

Padam looked up at the steel rims of the physician, reflecting back into the glasses of Maxwell Wittman the Third on the shelf beside his prone frame that surely felt the limbic memory of former decades. He managed a look of feeble consternation, one of a ballet instructor that he had learned to imitate over the years. In other words, he looked *fierce*. F held up his hands defensively, before smoothing them out in a relaxed gliding motion.

"Here, we like to align ourselves with the direct concerns of our clients. I was only hazarding a guess, my dear Baryshnikov. Anyone can see how spry & dare I say *flexible* you are."

"Um, yes. There is *someone*."
F extended a threatening finger.
"Here. Here. Here. O, & there. You have read about our treatment, of course?"

Padam nodded. He had not. F waggled a very beige brochure in front of Padam's whiskers. Maxwell Wittman the Third was not amiss, although his fingers were taking some small comfort in gripping the flesh-toned armrests.

"Yes. Am I correct in understanding that this procedure will not hurt?"

F burst into laughter & doubled over with the giggles, tickled to the point of nearly falling asleep from exhaustion after he was finished. A distant saxophone horned in on the anaesthetizing muzak & both doctor & dancer were startled out of any lingering trepidation.

"Everything will go smoothly," soothed F. "But I ask you, as a performer, what is life without a generous helping of risk? Without a little pain, can there be pleasure? But I bore you with such philosophy. I laugh because it is like a caterpillar questioning the cocoon that gives him wings … "

He raised both arms in the air, his smooth face illuminating the plasticity of the walls about him.

"Yes! Let's do it! Let's make this happen! It will be our greatest triumph! Why, you'll be the *belle* of the ball, the envy of the middle-agers! & they will come to me! They will weep themselves into slumber in their sleeping bags outside my office until I at last agree to see them. Smile, Maxy! You are to be my sandwich man, my walking advert!"

F held out his hand in dramatic fashion.

"Come with me, Maxy! Let us embark upon this quest together & cease not until we both have drunk ourselves silly. So what if you scrape your knee as you bend over to drink from the fountain of eternal youth! Let's be sensible here. The water of life awaits you."

Padam scarcely noted a slender marquee on the wall behind F that dimly flashed a lengthy disclaimer. Padam shrank pleasantly beneath the aggrandizing shape of F, as he might have for an amorous suitor, for he was stunned into facially paralytic glee, & especially pleased by the association with *middle-agers*. F began to rub his smooth hands together.

"A few injections, at the very least, to please your *paramour*, or should I say your *head over heels enraptured studmuff*. It is but a trifle for such a great reward."

& so F continued to soothe & sweet-talk Padam into his next session for treatment.

Maxwell Wittman the Third entered the Istoria trepidatiously. He felt nervous about tomorrow's appointment. In fact, the question *what does tomorrow bring* was weighing heavily on his nerves at every moment. It was very quiet. Grant had shifted into a pensive chatty mood in order to murder a couple more hours before closing. After depositing a pale ale, he lingered, refusing to betray his servitorial code, yet all the same wanting to talk for a while, provided that a whole party didn't suddenly drop in from who knows where. Why, there are so many wonderful occasions to celebrate!

"Hey Padman, how's it hanging?"

Padam feebled a small gesture in the direction of a grin.

"Still in all the right places, I *expect*. To tell you the truth, I am rather tired. I … the stained glass … Ganymede … is haunting my dreams."

He had not meant to make *that* kind of admission, especially before even taking a single sip of beer. However, it felt good to talk. He projected a sense of whimsy to compensate for his sudden episode of truth telling. Grant stared at him, tight-lipped. Only on occasion did his placid eyes widen like this. As if for effect, his black hair spiked up wildly. A new style, I shouldn't wonder? Padam knew a story was on the way. "A haunting, hey? Like you ... walk home & find stuff all rearranged & stuff like that?"

Grant hesitated & Maxwell Wittman the Third thought he wanted to say *stumble* home instead of *walk* home. But Padam laughed & forgot a few of his anxieties as the pale ale thinned his blood.

"What are you implying?"

Grant paused, looking around for additional customers or empty sleeves before grazing the table surface with his knuckles.

"Hey Padman, you ever hear of the ghost of Floating Gardens?"

Padam shook his head.

"It was a long long time ago. Not long after the turn of the century. This story was passed down for a couple of generations in my family. My mom used to tell it *real nice*. Drove us all squirrelly at night. Down on East Pender, in Chinatown, there was this really sweet nightclub for all tha cats. Before the real jazz got going. But they had a lotta acts over the years. Nothin' sucked like these days. It was all movin' on up. Folk used to frequent those opium dens in the basement & man let me tell you they had stockheaps of artillery down there. That was during the riots ... "

Grant's voice trailed off.

"Was there a ghost?" asked Padam, almost overlooking his almost empty sleeve.

"There's always a ghost. But Padman, this one turned out to be the owner dude! In the thirties, he finally snuffed it & those vultures that had pushed him & drove him crazy don't think they ain't just waitin' to check out that body. But that's just the thing. They never found him. Padman, *they never found him.*"

"I heard you the first time."

Grant waved his hands into the air, then coolly withdrew them & tapped the table with his bony fingers.

"But that's not all. The first week they reopen, word is things are rattling all around in the kitchen. Pots are jumping up & down. Pans are clanging against the pots. Cupboards are banging open & shut. Utensils are flying back & forth … "

Someone in the background dropped a glass & Maxwell Wittman the Third shivered. Grant leapt back toward the bar to fetch a dustpan & raced to the heater to clear away the scattering of glass shards that gleamed beneath the light of the streetlamp outside. Then he did his rounds, talking & joking & refilling & tabulating before returning to Padam with a fresh sleeve of pale ale.

"That one's on the house," he said in a hushed voice. Padam managed a Cheshire grin worthy of his old self.

"Go Grant!"

Then Grant resumed his monologue.

"So all the staff are bitchin' right & left about the knives & forks gettin' lives of their own. I make soup or jook & the heat's not on. Hey man, I know I turned the oven *on*. Some stuff you don't even wanna know. So the new owner, he's givin' everybody shit & eventually the axe. There's no way you can't cook in there coz of a ghost! Get back to your dishes. Everybody here to have a good time! Everything go cold. But nobody wants to work at Floating Gardens no more. & then it gets round to payday & he's there alone, late at night doin' the books. So all the stuff in the kitchen starts rattlin'. The saucers are trembling with the cups & glasses. The entire kitchen is alive, Padman! Maybe the owner would be better off if a dish comes flyin' his way. No. The kitchen to him is just shaking & vibrating all around him & even the stuff he can't see is quivering in the cupboards, just like it's a quake, only there ain't no quake. So he tried to steady his nerves with a dollop of gin & settle back into his books for that no good staff of his. Hell if he's gonna believe in the ghost of anyone, let alone the former owner, that asshole. That's just business. Sonofabitch tells himself it's just a lousy quake. Just a lousy quake,

Padman. It's all behind the guy now. Just business. But you can't legislate a ghost, no way. There ain't no bylaws for ghosts, no way man. So the dude is closin' his ears to all the clatter & desperately trying to focus on the books & say he ain't scared. Then all of a sudden, a real shiver creeps down his spine & he knows he's S.O.L."

"S.O.L.?"

"Shit Outta Luck. So he turns around & sees this white hand curling round the door frame. He sees the knuckles & he wants to cry on the spot coz he knows that hand. He knows the hand & he knows the wedding band on one of the fingers & he is scared shitless. Sammy Wong-Chu has come back from the grave & he is fucked. Pardon my *français*. All the same, he hopes for some kinda rabbit's paw to fall outta tha sky. He gets up & straightens his collar & goes to the doorframe. Hello, hello … Sammy? Sammy, let's have a sit-down & talk about this. But part of him is still thinking some sucker got locked in the kitchen. But that hand, it keeps trembling & tapping on the doorframe where it rests. He walks towards it, closer & closer & closer still, until at last he takes a deep breath & pops his head around the corner. Then he gets it. This is no Jimmy the cook or Angie the waitress. Just a hand, that's all. A white hand floating in the corridor, just like the hand that wouldn't sell him the business outright. Just like the hand that for many years used to reach for his new wife!"

Grant was shouting at this point & Padam was inching back into one of the new chairs with an audible crinkling. Grant then began to jerk his elbows back & forth, strutting up & down briskly in front of Maxwell Wittman the Third, who thought this was an excellent pantomime of a man running for his life.

"So he runs past the floating white hand without a second look, without even locking up. A few blocks away, he finds the police station & he's raving on & on about a ghost. The inspector is nodding & smiling unhappily at the owner in his stiff upper Brit way. At last, a few of them agree to come back with him. Free drinks it is, for the late night trip taken. So the owner gets back & nervously opens the door, the inspector pushing past, along with his officers. So they probe up & down the whole place, but the ghost won't give it up for them. They open all the cupboards & make a big mess, mumbling under their breath all the time. There is sure as hell no ghost. But get this, Padman! Within a week's time, they totally sell out. The Floating Gardens shuts up tight as a drum of whiskey during prohibition. That is, before the bootleggin' gets started, wink wink. Everybody vacates that haunted place. & the last thing the owner hears, after the officers have left, is a faraway laugh all around him, all of this invisible laughter … "

"But what happened to the building in question," pressed Padam.

"O that. Yeah, it was turned into a bank, yeah. But that reminds me of this story about a haunted bed … "

At that moment, a customer came in & Grant never finished. When he at last returned, Maxwell Wittman the Third decided to return the favour & offer a short tale of his own.

"You," he said, emboldened by ale, "make a point of calling me Padman."

He softened his tone.

"Have I ever told you how I got my spirit name? It all began in the sixties. I happened to be in attendance at this incredible party … "

The candygiver lady suddenly let out a little moan from her corner.

"My kids. Where are my kids?"

Grant looked around shiftily.

"Better speed it up, Padman!"

The artist/dancer beamed.

"*Actually*, the name is Padam. Do you know where it derives from? At the party, I met a young chap from India who wanted to learn more than anything how to hoof it. Naturally, I immediately took him under my wing. With my guidance, he was going to be great. I knew this at once, of course. I took him everywhere. Come & live with me. That is what I said to him. He never left my side. You must find your grail castle. That is what I told him. I also gave him a small book that said the same thing. The book is called *He*. Wonderful stuff. You should pick up a copy. It's on the web, in fact. Read it tonight. & at the end of his training, he reached over towards me with tears in his eyes. He held both of my hands like *this*."

Grant shied away from the table he was haunting.

"Then he said, you know who *you* are. You are *Padam*. You are like one of the ancient compositions (*sabhaa gaanam*) in my country, written specifically for dance. Within this dance, the hero & heroine & the close friend gather together to explain, to make mouths of joy & sorrow to do with all matters of love. You are the teacher that leads other men into the unknown. You must understand that Padam is not with the feet. Padam is the slow expression of grace, hand, eyes, face. From this day forth you will be called Padam, for it is your destiny to teach young men your way of being in the world ... so ... too much, almost. Padam. That is your true spirit name."

Maxwell Wittman the Third paused for effect.

"& do you know who that man was? I am writing a tell-all book about my experiences. Later ... " Grant stepped back two paces, with rapid fancy footwork completely uncharacteristic of *The Padam*.

"Sounds great, Padman. Gotta hustle. Allasudden it's all busy. When it rains it cats & dogs my friend."

Time passed. *If you are beautiful outside, you are stunning inside.* That is what Dr. Finestretta had said. Perhaps the Gore-Tex or Teflon treatments would make him unflappable in the face of ageing, not to mention bulletproof to the silent ravages of time. Padam scratched his face. Itchy. Where's the summer come & gone? For maybe the first day in his life, he did not want to ask what tomorrow would bring. He did not even want to think *it*. He had started too early today. How many sleeves had led to this sunset? The months had passed ever so slowly without Tomasz. He had taken the liberty of putting the young man's poem in stained glass, so that it was a constant companion to *Ganymede*, an immortalization of his written work that had only succeeded in vexing him even more. Otherwise, everything was fine. There was a placid sense of happiness without the acute sarcasm & unstable vitriol that accompanied his dark beauty. I am writing your life story, that is what he said to me. In the Vancouver book, something he referred to simply as *the book*. He had changed in the interim, over a number of months that felt like years to Padam. & within less than a year's time, the book had begun to drink him up. The frivolity had faded. The freshness. On the other hand, he accepted that the young man was no longer quite young & that he had loved just as Padam had loved. The most you can accept from another soul of this variety is a kind of psychical sympathy. Here we are, strangers in passage with nothing really to do with one another, except for sharing degrees of failure & necessity & illimitable outpourings of alcohol as the inevitable excuse. Yes, the young man's features had hardened & in some ways become grotesque to behold, even trollish in a certain light, while he, Maxwell Wittman the Third, had in fact become younger. But the inky words had attached themselves to the very bloom of the young man & had stung him like a jellyfish before leeching blood. They were vicious piranha that gnawed bones & heart alike. A diagnosis of *osteopoesis*. That's what he called it. We all gotta go sooner or later. Another year had passed & at this point, Padam felt like passing out. The fireworks had come & gone, applauded by bank managers & abandoned, a huge spectacle of refuse upon grass & sand. Then the Exhibition. *Araby*, he would have said angrily. Wound up in fishwrap & caught between a pair of book ends. Then the chill of autumn had come to the coast. A cold summer. Padam walked leisurely across the street & sat upon a bench, taking a second to nod sympathetically at the three leafless trees, poisoned for the sake of real estate. He watched a few seasonal stragglers wading at the water's edge beneath greying sky, pointing & laughing at someone who had found some fecal matter trailing down their red trunks & furry thighs, now frantically wiping at the sopping smear. He watched the bare feet of boys kicking up the beach. Sand, the accidental discovery of glass in the desert. Burning sand. Sand & salt & limestone. Beautiful windows & stained glass, destroyed at the behest of religion while religion continued to laud them. Choir boys & Theophilus writing of copper & iron & cobalt, alchemic oxides & the colours that graced the face of young Ganymede in his bedroom window. Bedroom eyes. Come & see the *Rape of Ganymede*. Theophilus, that monk of mystery, passing a blowpipe of white glass over red. The flash! & the *calmes* that keep everything calm, everything together. We live in this furnace that burns them together. Pieces of his face, they start to sing an almost whispered *credimus*, cut with the remains of a kimberlite pipe. Then grozed in the half-light, the picture almost complete. Maxwell Wittman the Third scratched passively at his face. It was smooth. He had updated his wardrobe, hardly to Savile Row standards, since in Vancouver the look was always bordering upon an apparition of mountaineering, snow-boarding, skiing, blading, windsurfing, wheeling or scootering, or some related activity, save for the cut of a coat. Padam felt distinctly unwell. Perhaps his raven psychosis had dispersed with his cosmetic surgery but wasn't there some new pandemic about? The availability of chicken was still in question. They destroyed all those birds, didn't they? Not this one, no ma'am. He had gotten rid of his glasses as well. He had decided upon *Zapeyes*, a local outfit robustly recommended by his *friend* F. The recovery had kept him inside for a few days, leading to a spell of cabin fever that overwhelmed him & an old lover who had agreed to tend to him while his vision was correcting itself. Yet, at this moment, he could not even remember the man. Well, someone had taken care of him. The pain had been more than he had expected. But now, he was fit as a fiddle & manly as a mandolin, except for the incessant application of eyedrops at night. He wasn't sleeping anyhow. Aside from that minor setback, he had noticed his night vision had diminished & also that it was starting to get dark. The geometrical patterns in the water were like diamonds, *pure ice* transmogrifying into greying flesh. As he thought of his surgical procedures & how he was himself but also strangely aloof, very unlike himself in fact, he was reminded of a frame of an old film where a woman's eyeball was sliced straight across, to the beautiful tune of *Tristan*. Ah, Buñuel was something else, just wonderful! What was that other wonderful odour? A man had tried to light a cigar, announcing his intention in scarcely decipherable *patois* & was promptly escorted to the patio in rather debatable French, just falling short of being demotic. Yet the smell had managed to waft through the establishment & had occluded the usual waft of warring perfume & cologne. Even outside, Padam was very aware of how the smell had pervaded the atmosphere & how it now seemed to linger about his whiskers, with a light tinge of vermilion to season the grey. He sat back on his bench & contemplated the divisions of grey water. Straining waves. He squinted, trying to see the precise demarcations, the brokenness of the water through the vision of a night that had not quite arrived but would eventually fall wholeheartedly over his eyes. Perhaps it was brighter than he thought. He did think he could make out the young man as he saw him in his window at home at night, exactly the way he wanted to see him, no? There he was, sitting on a log, waiting for his weekly Muse to arrive with her apologetic sympathy or sympathetic apology. As if on cue, a tall woman strode out of the gloom or gloaming, all in black & so very pale. She shimmered before him underneath the orange streetlamp as he looked up at her. Padam expected the young man to fall upon her like night upon untouched silicon, to singe her electrical glow into stained glass, into veritable fragments just as he had been burned by the young man's presence. But I am so sleepy I want to sleep. No.

Anch'io vorrei dormir così ...

He used to sing to me. Such is sorrow of Endymion & the lament of Federico. With everything within reach, to become so horribly desperate that you only want to sleep & sleep & sleep it all off & then when that doesn't work, to want to sleep forever.

"I love Bay Day."

I think that is what she said. A fine Native blanket to wrap yourself in, for the sake of history in the *Istoria*. His eyes dimmed as darkness fell. The longing the deep cold longing for wooden floor & planks &

blocks of cedar. The young man's cure-all for everything. A rock mosaic of rhetoric. A bundle of petristles. The funny things he said. The endless hunt for consumer elegance. Items in arrangements that were the equivalence of *life*. So it is, we mutter like mortar between the bricks, the whisperers. Where be the *calmes* now, to steady our own mad oxidation??? The book is ending I can feel it in my toes. Coming to a close. Contemporary voodoo. The book is being slammed shut by that young man over there. My story. But he could be right in the end. Better to dive in & eat garbage & crap out wisdom before *it is too late*. Maxwell Wittman the Third craned his no longer prunish neck about, feeling like an animal hide stretched over eroding bone, & glanced back at the enormous plate glass windows of the new *Istoria*. It appeared that all the *Irregulars* had arrived just in time & were enjoying a splendid time & staring out with looks of welcome. Go on, fair Padam! The world swallows us all, one way or another, drop by drop, upon moist porcelain or periwinkle tiles. The woodblock slips. The stained glass window is ground under the bare feet of yet another control freaking edict. The sand shifts & is ignited & becomes glass once again, underneath a painted sun of Umbria. Padam was reminded of a much beloved children's book about the hotel & the cat that lived there. As he craned his neck around again, he thought he saw all of them. The *Irregulars* were peeping out. There was the fabulous monarch without his camera to capture Padam & there was the old giver of candy, sad but serene. The bearish knucklecracker seemed to be bidding farewell with a last crackling of fingers & all the buzzing winged sycophants were circling the plates, as joined by the Valkyrie, coming to claim all of the fallen, & the teacher/lawyer in his grey blazer & white sneakers, dear Ichabod, was refolding his newspaper & the red coxcomb was enjoying the conversation about the glamour of Bay merchandise & the professor was fiddling with his toilet brush moustache & the ebbing couples were happily melting & the usual birdlike faces were pecking against the old or new panes & Grant & the other guy & the *good boy* from Québec (Aimé I think) & the *Allegory of the Faith* & the Giottoesque woman with the diamond voice to cut glass—they

were all bowing their heads in solemnity & tearing their hair sideways & the woman by the window was writing & pretending not to
see him dying, merely jotting down whatever the young man had
missed in his absence ... The charcoal cat addressed only as *Mr. Got-
tago* died of fright on the very spot & was expediently replaced by his
tawnier substitute, known affectionately as *Mr. Gottastay*, who quickly
fled down the stairs to the basement for a fine dinner of leftover
kipper. It was the Buddhist penitent with his makeshift cart of atone-
ment, who in the middle of wheeling & chiming his burden down
Mort Street, found Maxwell Wittman the Third seated on a bench,
very still, not far from the three poisoned trees, & staring off into the
grey distance with a fixed look of subtle amusement on his face, as if
at last imbued with the immortal smile of Leonardo.

The next morning, on every streetcorner, hurried passersby were
handed the green & orange details of his death.